Jacqueline Wilson

THINK AGAIN

bantam

TRANSWORLD PUBLISHERS
Penguin Random House, One Embassy Gardens,
8 Viaduct Gardens, London SW11 7BW
www.penguin.co.uk

Transworld is part of the Penguin Random House group of companies
whose addresses can be found at global.penguinrandomhouse.com

First published in Great Britain in 2024 by Bantam
an imprint of Transworld Publishers

A CIP catalogue record for this book
is available from the British Library.

ISBNs
9780857506108 (hb)
9780857506115 (tpb)

Typeset in 11.25/15.75 pt Sabon by Falcon Oast Graphic Art Ltd
Printed and bound in Great Britain by Clays Ltd, Elcograf S.p.A.

The authorized representative in the EEA is Penguin Random House Ireland,
Morrison Chambers, 32 Nassau Street, Dublin D02 YH68.

Penguin Random House is committed to a sustainable
future for our business, our readers and our planet. This book is
made from Forest Stewardship Council® certified paper.

For Trish

1

I wake to find Stella rubbing her head against mine and licking my neck suggestively. That sounds misleading. Sadly I'm not enjoying an exciting sex life. I am currently not having *any* kind of sex life, exciting or not. I might have squeezed a double bed into my tiny flat, but apparently I was being overly optimistic.

'Hello, Stella!' I mumble. 'Have you come to wish me happy birthday?'

She purrs agreeably and I stroke her from the top of her head, down her long silky fur to the tip of her tail. She's absolutely the Queen of Cats, though she came from humble beginnings, like many a fairy princess. I rescued her from Battersea Dogs and Cats Home last year. Lottie says she's my replacement daughter – but my role is more servant than mother to Stella. She gives me orders and likes me to keep to a strict routine. Ideally, she would like to be free at night to roam the streets, but that's not wise on a council estate in London. She feels five a.m. is a suitable time for her first breakfast and seems puzzled when I don't greet her with top-of-the-morning joyfulness. I peer at my watch, prepared to push her away and burrow beneath the covers for another couple of hours. But it's gone seven! Stella's given me a birthday lie-in. Perhaps she senses it's a special birthday. One with an O.

Forty!

Dear God, how did I get so *old*? I slide out of bed, pad over to the mirror on my dressing table and peer at my forehead. Yep, wrinkles – three of them, and two little lines like apostrophes over my nose. I try smoothing them out, but they snap back into place the moment I let them go. I suppose peering over my desk a lot and not always bothering with my glasses is taking its toll. Time for Botox? Magda takes little trips to the Beauty Clinic now and looks great. But then she's always looked great. Nadine's a Botox veteran too. She started in her twenties, which was ridiculous, but I suppose that was because she was modelling then.

I pull a pouty face to try to make my cheeks model-thin. I look stupid. I turn sideways and suck in my stomach. It's the bit of me I still can't bear. I had a mummy tummy long before I had Lottie. I look at the snapshots stuck all round my mirror. There's a Polaroid of Nadine and me in a paddling pool when we were four. Nadine is already willowy and striking a pose, while I'm pulling a face, an infant roly-poly with a belly like a little beach ball.

I peer at Magda's early childhood photo beside it. We didn't meet until secondary school, but I didn't want to leave her out. She's in the bath, shaking her curls and dimpling at the camera, posing even then. She looks like a Raphael cherub.

Nadine and Magda, my two best friends. The two most important women in my life, after my daughter. Lottie's photos have taken over the rest of my frame, starting when she was a baby. I peel off my favourite photo: she is only a few months old, and I'm lifting her up and blowing raspberries on her lovely round tummy, making her giggle. Nearly two decades later, I smile along with her. I thought she might take after me, because her baby hair was fluffy and inclined to curl, and she was delightfully chubby then – but now look

2

at her! I put the old photo back and pick up the one big silver frame that sits on my dressing table and stroke her face fondly. Long straight hair, strong, slim body, huge grin, mad clothes.

'My girl,' I murmur.

The photo was taken just before she went to university. Oh God, I still miss her so much.

Stella miaows imperiously.

'OK, you're my girl too,' I say.

She allows me a quick dash to the bathroom, then we head into the kitchen and I give her a bowl of chopped chicken with a little broth as a special treat. We can pretend it's her birthday as well. I give her fresh water, too, in her special ceramic bowl. She licks and laps daintily, careful not to get her long silvery whiskers wet.

I make myself a coffee and shake a small portion of healthy muesli into my bowl. A few spoonfuls of sawdust isn't exactly birthday breakfast material so I make myself two slices of buttery toast spread with strawberry jam, picking out most of the whole strawberries from the jar. It's my birthday, for God's sake. The diet I'd planned can wait until tomorrow.

Hey, how about Myrtle going on a diet? I wander into the living room, still munching, sit at my desk and put on my glasses. I pick up my ideas book and start sketching her in her own kitchen having breakfast. Big ears, pointy nose, long whiskers – but she's got human arms and legs and is wearing a stripy teeshirt and boyfriend jeans, which have a discreet hole at the back for her long tail to poke through.

She hasn't changed all that much since I started drawing her for a competition when I was a schoolgirl. I've kept the letter Nicola Sharp sent me then. She was my favourite illustrator – still is, in fact. I've tried to keep the letter pristine, but I've read it so many times it's as fragile as tissue paper now.

I can honestly say your Myrtle is outstandingly original. I'd be proud to have invented her myself. You are going to have to be an illustrator when you grow up!

Wonderfully, I *am* an illustrator now. And an art teacher.

I'd never admit it, but I love it when I go to parties and people ask me what I do for a living. I don't usually mention the prosaic teacher bit.

'Oh, I do a little weekly newspaper cartoon strip,' I mumble modestly.

'What, in the local rag?' they might ask.

'It's in the *Guardian*, actually,' I say, though I always blush because it sounds like showing off. Well, it *is* showing off, I suppose, but never mind.

'Come on then, Myrtle,' I murmur. 'Here you are, looking at yourself in the mirror, noticing your jeans are getting much too tight. Then second picture, you're perched on a stool at your kitchen island, frowning at a little packet of low-cal cheese and a carton of fat-free milk. Then picture number three . . .'

But doubt creeps in. My Myrtle comic strip is supposed to be a cute, mousey take on modern life. Do modern women obsess about their figures so much? *I* certainly do. But what about Lottie and her friends? Surely they're all into health and strength and pride in your body, whatever your size or shape? I tap my pencil against my lip, frowning.

I'll ask Lottie when I see her today. I'm meeting her at Victoria. She'll text me when she's on the train. I hope it will be early enough for us to have lunch. We could go to Maison Bertaux and have a private birthday celebration just the two of us. Then we can hang out together, go to a gallery, go shopping, maybe just chill out here at the flat, before we travel down together to Kingtown for the family dinner.

My phone trills. It's Lottie herself! I answer immediately.

'Hi, Lots!'

'*Happy Birthday to you! Happy Birthday to you! Happy BIRTHDAY . . .*'

I wince and hold the phone away from my ear. I love Lottie with all my heart and I'm one of those pathetic mums who can't bear any criticism of her child, but even I know that she sings much too loudly for someone who can't hold a tune.

I rub my ear better and then replace the phone just as she sings the last happy birthday.

'That's so lovely, darling!' I say. 'There, you've started my birthday off splendidly. But how come you're awake so early?'

'I – I've been checking my phone. About my train,' she says.

'I can't wait to see you!' I say eagerly.

I have to make the most of her. We only meet up every couple of months now she's studying at Sussex. I was secretly so upset when she told me she wouldn't be coming home for the summer. I knew she'd want to see friends, maybe go travelling, and I truly wanted that to happen, but I did hope I'd see her *some* of the time. Then she told me that she'd got a job as a summer camp counsellor for international kids for eight weeks. She's fantastic with children, she's full of fun yet responsible too; it's no wonder they picked her. It's just that I miss her so.

Still, it means so much that she's coming home for my birthday weekend. And yet she's paused for several seconds.

'Lottie?' I say tentatively.

'Oh Mum, I'm so sorry, there's some kind of problem on the railway line. I don't know, engineering works, whatever,' she says quickly. 'The trains up to London have all been cancelled.'

'Oh no! What a bore. But surely it'll be fixed?'

'It says all travel on the line is cancelled for the day, Mum. I'm so sorry!'

She sounds really sorry too, but there's something odd about her voice. I nibble at my lip. She's not lying to me, is she?

I take a deep breath.

'All right,' I say, trying to keep my voice steady. 'So, what about the birthday dinner?'

'I'd give anything to be there, but it's just not possible,' she says.

'Oh Lottie,' I wail pathetically, unable to help it.

'You'll still have Grandad, Anna, Ben and Simon at the dinner,' she says.

'Yes, of course.'

'I truly am sorry, Mum. Don't let it spoil your special day.' She sounds really uncomfortable now.

I think she's definitely making excuses. Or perhaps I'm just being paranoid? Maybe this train problem is the gospel truth and Lottie is really sad not to be seeing me on my birthday. And if she's got better things to do than hanging out with her mum, that's totally understandable. She's nineteen, for God's sake. And I'm fucking forty, so I'd better start acting like it.

I fix a smile on my face so that it comes through in my voice. 'Don't worry, love. I've got a lovely day planned. I'll be fine.' Despite my efforts, my voice comes out a bit shaky. I pause and hunt around for a change of subject. 'Lottie, do you and your friends fuss about your figures?'

'What?'

'Sorry. Is it a bit old-fashioned to keep starting diets?'

'Mum, what is this? Do you think *I* should go on a diet?' She sounds baffled, but amused.

'No, it's for Myrtle,' I explain.

'Don't mice want to eat all the time? I don't think they're picky with their food.'

'Yes, but Myrtle's really a girl – well, a woman – in mouse guise,' I explain. 'Oh, never mind. I'm not sure the idea would work. I'll dream up something else,' I say quickly.

'OK. But don't work too much, not on your birthday. Go

6

out and have fun. And don't worry, I just know you're going to have a fabulous time tonight, whether I'm there or not. Lots of love. See you!'

'See you,' I echo, and switch off her call.

I lean on my desk, head in hands. I can feel another worry line forming right this minute. I peer through my fingers at the sketch of Myrtle in the kitchen. I'm really not sure about the theme now. And didn't I have Myrtle on a diet ages ago, anyway? I can't start repeating myself.

I try to think up another idea but I keep hearing Lottie's voice in my head, telling me all that guff about the train. Surely there must be replacement buses? I reach for my phone, then pull back. No, I am *not* going to google her train line to check. What sort of person would that make me? What sort of mother? And even if I see all the trains are running perfectly, it's not a criminal offence to make a travel excuse. It's better than telling me that she simply can't be bothered to come.

I'm going to stop obsessing. Forty-year-old women are strong and secure. They take things in their stride. I'll check my emails, see if the payment for my last batch of Myrtles has gone through to Jude. She often works late on a Friday, clearing her desk for the weekend.

Yes, there's a message from Judith Barnes Agency – apparently, it popped in last night. I open it, and the sight of the payment statement sends a wave of relief through me. That's next month's rent sorted!

Then, below the statement, I see a message. I give it a fleeting glance, then lean in and give it my full attention. My heart starts thudding. I blink hard and read it again, slowly.

Hi Ellie, I'm so sorry to have to pass on some rather sad news. I've had a long phone call with Cassie. It's been decided that your amazing Myrtle Mouse strip is not really chiming with their readership any more. I'm afraid the *Guardian* doesn't want to renew your contract. Still, maybe you'll be able to come up with a new idea for them? Here's hoping!

I slump, blinking back tears. It's real. It's there, in front of me. A chunk of my income, gone. An even bigger part of my identity. And as for a new idea . . . Hope away, Jude. My chime is fading fast. I've lost my touch. I'm not current any more. I'm middle-aged. Past it. Finished.

Myrtle means so much to me. Mum drew pictures of her when I was little, and then I went on to make her Myrtle mine. I was nearly fourteen when I entered the cartoon of her for the Nicola Sharp drawing competition. I went on drawing Myrtle even at art school, having her waving in a corner of most of my works, though you'd have to peer for ages before you found her, like a little rodent *Where's Wally?*

I drew her for Lottie all the time I was finishing my degree as a mature student, getting my PGCE, starting teaching, and doing some magazine illustration for extra cash. Then in a fit of madness I sent a Myrtle cartoon to the *Guardian* and they accepted it. I couldn't believe it. But now they've rejected it. Rejected me.

I give a slight moan and Stella pauses grooming herself and mews. She blinks at me slowly with her great green eyes and then decides to take pity on me. She strolls over, gathers muster, and leaps onto my lap.

'Oh, Stella! This is turning into such a crap birthday,' I say, rubbing my cheek against her soft head.

I want to cry but I can't drip all over Stella. I shut my eyes tight, then blink away the tears, a sudden resolve building within me. You want a new idea, Cassie and Jude? Fine. I'll *get* a new idea. I start doodling in my ideas book. Half-formed creatures bob up here and there in an increasingly frenzied maze of sketches.

Stella gets impatient and climbs off my lap, her sympathy evaporating. Getting nowhere with my doodles, I draw her instead. She looks good as a cartoon. But there are already so many famous fictional cats: Garfield, Tom, Felix, Mog, The Cat in the Hat . . . And why would Stella be any more current than poor, axed Myrtle? I sketch her now, an axe sunk deep into her little mousey head, and print RIP underneath her.

Perhaps I could try turning Stella into a children's picture book? The Story of Stella the Cat. But picture books have changed so much since I was little, since *Lottie* was little.

An adult novel? But I don't seem to be leading a proper adult life now, for all that I'm forty. I draw, I go to school, I read, I message Nadine and Magda . . . much the same life I was leading when I was fourteen, but with WhatsApp instead of whispered conversations on the landline. A wave of nostalgia engulfs me. How I'd love to go back to those simpler times, even just for a day.

I look down at the axe embedded in Myrtle's head. How about a crime novel? Maybe one of the cosy crimes that are so popular now? But crime round here isn't cosy in the slightest, which is why I have a bolt on my front door. And those complicated plots would be a total nightmare too. I'm used to Myrtle's neat layout, a set of little pictures, story told, job done.

What am I going to do without her?

I give myself a shake. Come on, think! What do you *want* to do? Draw. Add words. Then it hits me: a graphic novel! Not superheroes with their underpants over their tights. Not fantasy with pointy-breasted women in skimpy animal skins. Real men, real women. Maybe childhood friends who have grown up together, like me and Magda and Nadine? Or would that be too tame?

Come on, Ellie, I think crossly. I need to try *something*, if

9

nothing else for my finances. I've come to rely on the extra Myrtle money. Now I'll just have my salary.

I still find it hard to believe I've ended up a teacher. I had such big ideas when I started at art school. They were all kicked into touch when I had Lottie so young.

How about a graphic novel about a girl getting pregnant at art school and dithering about whether to choose to have an abortion? Everyone advises it. Even her two best friends, and her parents. Even the tutor she confides in. And especially the baby's father she hardly knows. She's almost persuaded. But she can't do it. Of course she can't, because she knows deep down she wants this baby in spite of everything.

How right I was – and how wrong it would be to write this story, because while I would never judge anyone's choices, I couldn't ever bear for Lottie to know what I was once contemplating.

So what else? I can't just sit here at my desk, agonizing. I've got to seize the day. Yep, carpe diem. Celebrate my birthday. I could still go to Maison Bertaux, a gallery, shopping . . . but it might be a bit lonely by myself, today of all days.

Shall I contact Nadine? Or Magda? Both? I don't see enough of them now we live so far apart. Though I can't help being hurt that *they* haven't been in touch with me. How can they have forgotten my birthday? I suppose we've grown apart over the last few years. Nadine is still busy partying, seeing new guys most weeks. Magda's seemingly settled at last with Chris, her Third Time Lucky partner – plus his two kids.

They probably haven't got time for me now. Oh, stop the self-pity! It's not as if I'm going to be on my own this evening. I'm seeing Dad, Anna, Ben and Simon for a special birthday meal at some posh new restaurant back at home. Old home, I mean. Where I grew up. The Vine? I google it. It looks ridiculously pretentious, not my sort of place at all. Ben and Simon obviously chose it, thinking it will be a huge treat for me. I know how much they love me and it means a lot, but they treat me like a poor old maiden aunt sometimes. I don't *mind* not having much money and living in my little tower block flat right up in the sky. A lot less money now that poor Myrtle's been axed, I remember with a lurch of my stomach, but I'll manage. It's a disadvantage being single because I'll never have the cash to buy a stylish mansion flat like theirs, but I don't really care that much. I'm fine by myself. Really. Whereas they're such an old married couple now they've practically become one person.

I never thought pesky little Eggs would grow up to be such a great guy. No more nicknames. He's not a mouthy brat any more. He's Benedict Allard, the interior designer employed by celebrities to add dazzle to their décor. He looks a bit like a boy band pin-up himself, though he's over thirty now.

Simon is pretty hot too. Both Magda and Nadine had a mini-crush on him, though they both knew he was gay, of course. Maybe *I'd* have had a crush, too, though it would be beyond weird to fancy my brother's boyfriend. Simon earns a lot as a music producer so their flat is out of this world. But it's not *my* world. I'm fine where I am.

Will it be good to see Dad and Anna? I love Anna now, and we get along really well, but she'll never take the place of Mum. I start sketching Mum now, trying to remember every single detail, her wild curls like mine, her beautiful smile, her head on one side, her lovely arms outstretched, ready to give me a hug – but it's getting harder and harder now to remember exactly what she was like.

'Oh Mum,' I whisper. It still hurts after all these years. I don't mind, though. I want to keep missing her. The worst thing ever would be to forget her altogether. If only I could have a birthday dinner with her. But she never got to be forty. Bloody cancer.

I pick Stella up for comfort but I'm holding her too needily and she wriggles away.

I wonder if Dad still misses Mum the way I do. Oh, he does, I'm sure he does, but I don't really know if he was a great husband to her. I used to think he was a great dad too, long ago – but I can't ever forgive him for the things he said when I told him I was pregnant. He was furious with me, horrified that I'd have to leave Saint Martins when so few people were lucky enough to get there. He wanted to pay for me to go to a private clinic for a termination so I wouldn't ruin my life. Did he act like that with any of his former girlfriends? Did he actually want to terminate *me*?

I know he adores Lottie now, but the damage is done. I was so proud when I applied for a council flat as a single mum and managed to get it all arranged. I tried hard to decorate it and make it into a haven for Lottie and me. I hoped Dad would be impressed but he said I was off my head wanting to live in such a dump, and couldn't understand why I wouldn't let him help me find somewhere decent. He even looked down on my teaching job at the failing secondary near my flat, saying he couldn't see the point of trying to imbue a love of art in a lot of rowdy yobbos. He kids himself he's so arty-liberal and then comes out with offensive rubbish like that. Anna said it was because he just wanted the best for me and felt frustrated that I wouldn't let him help me. I'm not convinced.

He was entirely flummoxed when the *Guardian* started running my Myrtle cartoons. Maybe even a bit jealous? I don't relish telling him that they've axed her now. He'll see she's gone missing anyway, because he's an archetypal *Guardian* reader and gets the actual printed version with the magazine.

I could always pretend that it's my decision, that I've got bored with Myrtle, that I'm starting on a brand new project.

Stella leaps up onto my desk, agitating for attention. I stroke her and return her slow blink.

'Maybe I *should* start a graphic novel today? I'll buy a beautiful new sketch book, and begin. No more messing about. Carpe diem, right?'

Stella purrs in agreement.

I've actually got several lovely blank sketch books, all of them untouched. Each time I buy one I think that *this* will be the one. But it isn't. I doodle on the backs of envelopes and receipts, or the standard paper I use for my cartoons, but my Pigma pen wobbles whenever I approach a virgin sketch book.

I pick up one of these pens, fiddling with it idly. I use them because they're permanent, though why I want to preserve my little cartoons I don't really know. I've got several stacks of *Guardian*s in the airing cupboard. Oh God, I won't be adding to those piles any more. They're now as big as they're ever going to be. The thought makes tears prick at my eyes.

I blink hard. I'm going to have an amazing birthday, even though Lottie's gone AWOL and Myrtle's been axed. I really will go shopping and buy a fantastic outfit to wear to the posh dinner tonight. I wish I could buy a fantastic body too. I suppose my boobs are still OK, so something low cut yet not too tight around the rest of me. In a colour I never wear. Red? With a red lipstick to match? Maybe not – I'll look like I'm channelling Magda. Or a black dress, with very dark lipstick and black nail varnish? No, then I'll look like Nadine's small, podgy twin.

Or I could wear my usual go-to dressy outfit, the emerald Indian loose top with silver threads that glint when they catch the light. Plus my best black jeans and black boots. I feel like me in it. So maybe I'll just stick with that for tonight. It's only a family dinner so why am I fussing so? Dad won't even notice what I'm wearing. Anna probably will, but we have entirely different ideas about what looks good. She's a camel kind of woman, camel coat, camel cashmere, camel patent heels. I've never worn camel in my life since I was dressed as a dromedary for a Nativity play in the Infants.

I ferret in my wardrobe for the black jeans. I try them on, just to check. Oh dear, just like Myrtle, I have to wriggle hard to get them over my hips and it's a struggle to zip them up. They still fit, sort of, but I'll have to be careful what I eat tonight. I could buy new jeans but it's such a performance trying them on in changing rooms with other younger, skimpier women all around me. I always imagine they're peering at me, raising their eyebrows, giggling.

'*Shut up!*' I say out loud, startling Stella. She retreats to her cat tower by the window. 'No, come back, Stella! I didn't mean to frighten you. I'm just cross with myself for being so self-conscious.'

I force myself to meet my own eyes in the mirror. I'm a strong, powerful forty-year-old woman. I have a wonderful daughter, a great family, a beautiful cat. I've had a successful artistic career for years. This is my opportunity to branch out in a new direction. A graphic novel. Definitely. And I always have my teaching to tide me over. I'm independent. I certainly don't need a man in my life to make myself whole. When has that ever happened? Not with any of the men in my life so far.

I take my jeans off and breathe out. I look in the mirror and breathe in again. I poke my tummy.

Maybe it's time I got fit. Exercise more. Start classes? No, I absolutely hated PE at school. Jog? I get out of breath in two minutes. I look at the photo of little-girl me at the paddling pool. I've always liked swimming – so why not go again? I search in my drawers for my costume.

2

I wonder what the morning swim session is like? I'm always in a rush on school days and I have a lie-in at the weekend, so I've never tried it before. I imagine a muscly squad splashing up and down the pool, keen to do their fifty lengths before work. It's a bit off-putting. I usually swim during the adults-only early evening spots. They put the lights down low and it's gloriously peaceful, just a few sporty types flashing by in the fast lane and assorted mums having a break from baby care swimming in a little flotilla in the un-laned portion.

When I get into the echoing turquoise world of the pool I can see even without my glasses that the morning swimmers are a different breed altogether. They're mostly much older than me, for a start: ancient men with wizened legs and baggy swimming trunks, and sturdy old ladies with faded costumes and swimming hats pulled down to their eyebrows.

I ease myself into the pool slowly, trying not to scream as the freezing water inches up my body. I bob up and down a bit, too cowardly to get my shoulders wet. I start shivering, take a deep breath, and plunge in properly. It's so *cold*. They've obviously turned the temperature down to save on heating costs. I swim as fast as I can, but I keep getting overtaken. How can all these pensioners be so speedy? They're practically Olympic level compared to me. I'm among truly dedicated swimmers.

I imagine them leaping out of bed, rain, wind or snow, to get their hour's session in. Am I ever going to become one of them? I'm already gasping for breath. But apparently no one here stops after ten or twenty lengths to have a rest or a gossip.

I plough on, counting in my head, and it gradually gets easier. I find the right rhythm, and glide along. All my worries get washed away and I find I'm actually enjoying myself. Mum used to take me swimming when I was small and I learnt quickly. 'You're my little mermaid,' she'd say, and I'd happily imagine my hair growing down to my waist, and my legs turning into a glistening green tail.

I taught Lottie, and she liked being a mermaid too. It's terrifying to think I was just a bit older than she is now when I had her. I gave her very serious talks about birth control before she went to university, while she yawned and fidgeted and looked bored.

'Lottie! It's important. Listen, for God's sake!' I snapped.

'Look, I'm sure they ply you with detailed leaflets the moment you get there. And if you don't mind my saying, you're the last person who should be lecturing me on contraception,' she said.

'Exactly! That's the point! I don't want you to make the same mistakes I made,' I said. 'Though of course you didn't turn out to be a mistake in the slightest,' I added quickly.

'You don't have to keep reassuring me. You've always said I'm the best thing that ever happened to you,' Lottie said complacently.

'Well, you are,' I said.

'Oh Mum!' said Lottie, but she gave me a quick kiss. 'Cheer up!'

I do feel surprisingly cheerful when the whistle goes for the end of the session, just as I'm completing my fiftieth length. I actually bound up the steps out of the pool, grinning all over my face. I've done something significant today. Taken a positive step. The changing rooms are a bit of a nightmare now, with my fellow swimmers chatting behind the curtains and mums trying to stuff kids into their costumes for the family session about to begin. I peer around, hoping to nab the last empty cubicle, but they all seem to be full. Resigned, I grab my stuff from the locker and head into the communal room.

It's still females only, thank God. I join some completely unself-conscious naked older women who are towelling themselves dry as if it's the most natural thing in the world. I suppose it is. Maybe I'll be as matter of fact about my body when I'm their age. There are several younger ones, too: a couple comfortingly size sixteenish, but there's one girl who's got a fantastic figure, supple and sleekly brown. Her damp black curls are like a little cap on her head. She is gorgeous. I sigh inwardly, and although I don't make a sound she looks up; she catches sight of my reflection in the mirror and realizes I'm staring at her.

I feel my cheeks flush crimson. Oh God, she'll think I fancy her! I start towelling my hair frantically so she can't see I'm blushing. I feel such a fool. And now I've got my towel soaking and I haven't even started drying the rest of me. Despite all my attempts to accept my body, the thought of peeling off my tight costume and getting naked in front of everyone else makes me panic.

In one fumbled movement I turn my back, grab my towel and wrap it round me. Then I start trying to get dry bit by bit and clothe each part of me. Another swift glance in the mirror shows that she is wearing tiny knickers now, practically a thong. I'm struggling into an old pair of Bridget Jones big pants. Still at least they cover me up. I wrestle with my jeans, the legs sticking because they're still wet, and then drop my towel and shove on my bra as quickly as I can.

Feeling a bit better now, I shrug on my baggy teeshirt casually, as if communal dressing doesn't faze me at all. Then I sit on a bench spending a long time rethreading my flowery Docs, head down. I hear the door open and close several times and hope she's gone out so I can recover my composure. But when I look up there's only her and me in the room.

She's staring at my teeshirt. I stare at hers. We're *both* wearing Alice in Wonderland teeshirts – the exact same design! She bursts out laughing.

'Hey, are you another Alice?' she asks.

'No, I've just loved the two Alice books since I was little,' I say.

'Did you get your teeshirt from that Alice exhibition at the V&A?' she asks.

'I did!' I say, delighted. 'I went twice!'

'Same. And I loved the exhibition about Beatrix Potter, too,' she says. She pulls up her jean leg to put on her socks. She's got a tattoo on her ankle, like a blue bracelet with a red heart hanging off it. The colours look wonderful against her dark skin. There's a name on the heart. I can just about make it out. Wendy.

'Are you into *Peter Pan* too?' I ask.

'What? Oh, I see. No, Wendy's my girlfriend,' she says.

'Oh! Well, I love the design,' I say. 'It's much more delicate than most tattoos.'

'Yeah, I love it too. I had it done at the Needles Studio. There's a great girl there who specializes in designs for women. Go and have a look,' she says.

'I might just do that,' I say, as if I've been seriously thinking of getting a tattoo for ages. But why shouldn't I? It would certainly be an indelible way of marking my birthday.

She's smiling at me. 'So what name would you have on your heart?' she asks.

I start brushing my hair, thinking about it. *Lottie?* People put their kids' names on their arms – but that's generally when the children are little. I try hard to imagine it, looking at my own arm, and my ankle. It might look a bit weird choosing Lottie's name now she's grown up. *Nadine? Magda?* I'd have to have both or the other one would be hurt. One on each leg would look a bit much.

The only other female in my life is Stella and I'd seem such a sad old maid if I went about with my cat's name round my ankle. I could put Mum I suppose – but that's the sort of tattoo you'd find on the bicep of an old sailor. Mum was called Ros but then people might think I'd bottled out of the whole tattooing process before the girl could add the final *e*.

Then it comes to me, and I snap my damp fingers.

'Myrtle,' I say, talking to myself – but Alice hears.

'Myrtle!' she echoes, sitting on a bench and pulling on her turquoise DMs. 'You have a girlfriend called Myrtle? That's such a cool name.'

'No, she's not a girlfriend, she's a cartoon mouse. You won't have heard of her,' I say, feeling my cheeks going hot. Why didn't I keep my mouth shut? Poor Myrtle's no more, as from now.

But she peers up at me. 'Yes, I have! I love Myrtle!' she cries. 'She's so sweet and funny. I love the way she agonizes over everything. Did you see the one where she was trying to give a dinner party, but her cheese soufflé went all floppy and Myrtle did too?'

I wonder if I'm hallucinating. She's like my perfect imaginary fangirl!

'That was based on real life,' I say ruefully.

'What do you mean? You don't actually know Ellie Allard, do you?' She sounds genuinely impressed. She isn't actually taking the piss.

'I do know her. Well, of course I do. She's me. I mean, I'm her,' I say, blushing again, and I curse the fact that I've already rolled my towel up so I can't hide under it.

'*Really?*'

I hold out my swimming card with Ellie Allard printed on the front underneath a very bad photo of me.

'How amazing!' she says. 'Do you know, I've got some of your cartoons stuck in my diary. You're part of my life!'

'Goodness. I haven't even got them stuck in *my* diary,' I say. I take a deep breath. 'But sadly there aren't going to be any more. They've just axed her. They think my comic strips are dated. They don't chime with the readership nowadays, apparently.' Why am I telling her this? She's a complete stranger. Maybe *because* she's a complete stranger.

'That's ridiculous,' she says, with touching indignation. 'How could they be so stupid? Myrtle Mouse is the highlight of my week. Shall I start a *Save Myrtle Mouse* campaign?'

'That's very kind of you but it won't be any use,' I say. 'She's gone.'

'Then you must definitely have a Myrtle tattoo in her memory,' she says, practically bouncing with enthusiasm. 'Don't have her name in an anklet heart. You must have a special cartoon of her. You draw it yourself and Catarina at Needles will ink an exact copy, I promise. You could have a huge Myrtle all over your back! It would look fantastic when you go swimming.'

'No, Myrtle is tiny. She's a *mouse*. Maybe I could have her inside my wrist?' I suggest, as if I'm really making plans to have it done. Maybe I am . . .

'Yep, that would look really cool. And discreet. Go for it,' she says.

'I will.' I put my boots on and lace them determinedly. But she doesn't look convinced.

'No, you won't,' she says. 'But you really should, Ellie. Tell you what, I'll go with you to give you moral support. The studio won't be open yet so we could have breakfast first. Have you ever been to that little caff near here? They have the most fabulous almond croissants.'

This is so weird. She even likes the same pastry as me. Maybe we're twins separated from birth. Twins with a ten-year age gap – she can't be more than thirty. And she's taller and much slimmer and a different ethnicity. I look up at her properly, her neat short curls, her big brown eyes with long lashes, her high cheekbones, her long neck . . .

'Is that OK?' she asks, suddenly looking anxious. 'I mean, you don't have to. I don't want to bully you into it. And maybe you've got plans for this morning?'

'Not really,' I say. 'Anyway, let's have breakfast, then I'll see if I'm feeling brave enough. Or mad enough. Whatever.'

'Great,' she says, beaming.

Is this really happening? I'm still chilled from the swim but my face is burning. We're walking out of the changing room together as if it's the most ordinary thing in the world. I wonder if she makes a habit of asking complete strangers to have breakfast with her. But she doesn't really feel like a stranger, though I find it hard to look her right in the eyes. I feel so shy with her for some reason.

I've passed this café Alice likes heaps of times but it always looked a bit hot and steamy, with the sort of staff that chat to you. I prefer the anonymity of a Pret.

The woman behind the counter welcomes Alice joyously and wants to know my name and who I am too. I'm right about the staff, then. She's called Rosa. Middle-aged. Well, four or five years older than me. She suits being plump, and her dark eyes are so bright and her cheeks so naturally pink she doesn't need make-up. She's wearing a faded teeshirt and baggy trousers under her white overall and when she brings our coffees and croissants to the table I see she's wearing socks and old-fashioned plimsolls, the sort we used to wear for PE at primary school.

Maybe I'll be like her soon, dressing entirely for comfort. I frown at the thought. I think I *will* get a tattoo, just to have a bit of edge. Nadine's got several after all, had them for years – hummingbirds and daisies and day-of-the-dead images. I teach all the Frida Kahlo stuff to Year Eights, maybe my favourite lessons. I made them fall about laughing this year because I dressed up as Kahlo. I put my hair up, wore a lot of beads and ethnic embroidery, and blacked a monobrow and a moustache on my face. My Kahlo day was a legend in the school. Perhaps I'll try it again the last day of term – though that might be pushing the joke too far.

Sometimes I think my whole life is on repeat. I seem to be doing the same things again and again, seeing the same few people. Yet here I am, with an interesting new friend, sitting in a different cosy café. Even these almond croissants are an entirely new experience, golden brown twirls sprinkled with icing sugar, crisp to bite into but the almond paste is thick and soft as it coats my tongue with sweetness. My little birthday cake. I don't have any candles to hand, naturally enough, but on a whim I take a wrapped strip of brown sugar from the bowl on our table and stick it in the squidgy almond paste of my croissant. I twist the end so it stands up like a little flame.

Alice looks at me quizzically.

'It's my birthday,' I explain.

'Really? Oh, happy birthday, Ellie!' She puts her head on one side. 'So how old are you?'

I can't quite say the figure.

'Don't say you've forgotten!' Alice says.

'I'd like to forget, actually,' I say, snatching my makeshift candle out of the croissant and laying it at the side of my plate. I take another big bite. 'You are so right, these are great.'

'You're surely not bashful about your age!' she says, raising her eyebrows.

'You wait till you get to my significant age, then,' I retort.

'Which is what? Three score years and ten?' she says, teasing again. She takes a deep breath, tucks a paper napkin at her neck so it looks like a vicar's collar and intones: 'The days of our years are threescore years and ten; and if by reason of strength they be fourscore years, yet is their strength labour and sorrow; for it is soon cut off and we fly away.'

She rattles it off with old-fashioned, holy intonation. I gawp at her.

'You're not a vicar, are you?' I ask.

She takes a sip of her cappuccino as I speak and laughs so much she snorts some up her nose. She has to mop herself with the napkin collar.

'Of course not, you nutcase. Do I look like one?'

I shrug. 'Well, I'm not well up on lady vicars, so how should I know? You're not quite as cheery as the one with the novelty teapots who used to be on *Gogglebox*, but I've heard the Church is trying hard to attract cool female celebrants,' I say.

'Oh, I love her – Kate Bottley. She's often on the radio now,' she says. 'I have a thing about the Reverend Richard Coles too; he's a sweetheart. But *I'm* not a vicar. Although my dad is. Hence the biblical knowledge. I was bored out of my mind most Sundays in church so I used to learn bits of the Bible by heart. Some women my age know the words to every Taylor Swift song. I'm word perfect on most of the Psalms. You've winkled out my hidden talent already. So it's only fair you tell me how old you are, ancient lady.'

'Oh, don't call me that!' I protest, stirring my coffee. 'That's what my daughter says when she wants to tease me.'

'You've got a daughter!' she says. 'How old is *she*, then?'

'Nineteen,' I reply, trying to sound nonchalant.

'*Really?* Were you a teenage bride?'

'Well, I was never a bride, but I had her pretty young. OK, I'm forty.' I actually stammer over the *f*. It sounds so odd saying it. She looks strangely impressed.

'Forty, eh? That's nothing. Though I thought you were younger. More my age,' she says.

'Which is?'

'Thirty-two.'

'Well, actually, I thought *you* were younger,' I say truthfully.

We smile at each other. This is weird. We're saying all this daft stuff as if we're flirting, looking into each other's eyes, heads on one side – yet she's got her Wendy and I'm straight. I did once get a bit carried away with Nadine when we were teenagers and very drunk, but it didn't really do anything for me. We never mentioned it afterwards, both of us a bit embarrassed.

'I feel bad now, practically kidnapping you, when it's your fortieth birthday and you must have a hundred and one things you want to do,' she says.

'No, I woke up with this burning ambition to get a tattoo to celebrate,' I say, deadpan.

'OK, no going back now!' She picks up her coffee cup and clinks it against mine.

We pay and leave the warm café. I hunch into the neck of my teeshirt and rub my arms, giving a slight shiver.

'You don't have to go through with it, Ellie!' she says, misunderstanding.

'I'm not trembling; I'm shivering, that's all,' I say, but I'm wondering now if I've really got cold feet. Do I actually want a tattoo? They suit someone like Nadine, they certainly suit Alice, but won't it just look a bit sad on a woman like me? Especially a little mouse with a kink in her tail. And if anyone recognizes Myrtle it will look as if I'm showing off. Plus, it will be painful!

Nadine said it wasn't painful at all, she rather enjoyed the whole sensation – but then Nadine's always been a bit like that. The little she's told me about her sex life sounds very dramatic. Perhaps she's a total masochist and even gets turned on at the dentist.

I can be stoical about ordinary oven burns or accidental Stella scratches, but I'm hopeless with real pain. I screamed so loudly when I was having Lottie that a bossy Sister came and ticked me off, saying I was frightening all the other mothers.

I'd planned one of those water births, where I'd lie back serenely and gently pant my way through the whole process, like a Naiad in a waterlily pool. The only thing floating in my pool certainly wasn't a fragrant flower. I had to be hoicked out of there anyway because they thought Lottie was getting stressed inside me.

She didn't have a beautiful peaceful birth at all; she was yanked out violently, with me still screaming my head off – but as soon as she was in my arms it was so wonderful I'd have laboured willingly for weeks just for that moment.

My arms always feel empty since I left her in that bleak student room, with its single bed and single bookshelf and single reading lamp.

'Ellie?' Alice says, not reassured by my expression. I jump and force a smile back on my face.

'Sorry! I was just pondering.'

I still have a few qualms, especially when we get to the Needles Studio. The window graphics are very Heavy Metal and brutal.

'It's OK, ignore all that tat. That's just to draw in the weedy guys who fancy themselves as hard men. Catarina's work is on a different level altogether,' says Alice. 'Come and see.' She takes my hand and pulls me into the studio. There's loud music playing and in the background there's a man lying face down on a long couch, another crouched over him with a machine. It's like a vision from hell. My feet clench in my boots, ready to make a run for it.

Alice waves to a hairy man hung with several kilos of silver jewellery, and points to the ceiling. He nods and signals for us to go upstairs. I follow Alice, even though I really am trembling now. We can still hear the music but it's muted, and the atmosphere is much lighter. The artwork on the white walls is beautiful, delicate and ornate, and Catarina is too. She's petite and elfin, with big Bambi eyes, wearing a pinafore dress over a vintage lace blouse, and cream boots patterned with pink and lilac flowers.

She smiles when she sees Alice. 'Hey there,' she says. She's even got a little-girl voice.

'Hi, Catarina. This is my friend Ellie,' says Alice.

She's called me her friend! It's like being back in Reception, when you make friends instantaneously in the sandpit, like Nadine and I did.

'Do you think you could squeeze her in just now, before you get busy?' Alice wheedles.

Catarina wrinkles her nose. 'I'd love to, but I'm really pushed for time today. I've got a client booked in at half past and—'

'Well, there's still plenty of time then, isn't there? Ellie knows exactly what she wants. And it's just a little wrist job, you could do it in minutes. Go on, Cat, be an angel, before she changes her mind,' Alice begs.

'Look, it's OK, it's not as if it's urgent,' I say, embarrassed.

'See, she's changing her mind already!' cries Alice. 'She's a really important client, you know. She's Ellie Allard, who does the Myrtle Mouse cartoons. You know!'

I'm not sure that Catarina has a clue who I am but she smiles and folds her arms, peering at me with renewed interest.

'What design do you want?' she asks.

'Well, I'd really like Myrtle Mouse,' I say. At her blank expression, I say, 'I'll draw her for you.'

'Perfect!' says Alice. 'Bung her some paper then, Cat.'

My hand steadies as I draw. I breathe slowly, feel my whole body relax. I never have any difficulty with Myrtle. I just go into my own Myrtleworld. I don't have to direct the pen. I just imagine her and she appears on the paper, with her daisy stud in her ear, one arm raised and her tiny fingers clenched in a power wave. I make her skinny legs knock-kneed to show she's anxious. Her tail has its usual kink, but it's at a perky angle.

'Wow!' says Alice. 'Here she is, as if by magic!'

'Will you be able to copy her?' I ask Catarina.

'Don't worry,' she says. 'I just put your design into the machine and it'll transfer it onto thermal paper. So, if I'm going to do it, I need you to show your ID so I can check your age.'

'Are you joking?' I say incredulously.

'Well, you might be a very mature sixteen-year-old,' Catarina pipes in her infant voice. But then she laughs. 'But I do need you to pay first. You seem ever so nice, and you're Alice's friend, but even so – people have been known to try to scarper before coughing up.'

I flash my credit card against the machine, forking out £100. I suddenly feel daft spending so much money on something I'm not even sure I want. But a sexy frock might have cost more, I suppose. And it would go out of fashion and eventually fall to bits. A tattoo should last for ever. I have a sudden image of me double my age, my skin all wrinkled so my tattoo looks ridiculous. My mouth is suddenly desert-dry, and I feel my pulse beating in my head. My hand circles my wrist protectively. What am I doing?

Oh sod it, it's time to live dangerously. Why shouldn't an old lady have a fun tattoo? And I'll be able to hide it with one of those alarm wristbands for senior citizens, when the time comes.

'OK, sit in the chair, Ellie,' says Catarina. She turns her head. 'Are you hanging around, Alice?'

'Of course I am!' says Alice, coming to stand right beside me. 'Don't you worry, Ellie, I'll hold your hand if it gets really painful.'

'Thanks,' I say uncertainly. I rub my palms on my jeans, hoping they're not too sweaty.

'So where do you want your little mouse?' Catarina asks.

'Here,' I say, pointing to the inside of my left wrist, where the little blue veins are standing out prominently. The skin is so delicate there. Will the needles go right into them? I'm shivering just at the thought, though I've obviously got to keep as still as I can. What if I get some kind of infection?

'Don't worry, you'll see we always use new needles,' Catarina says, as if she's reading my mind. 'Everything's new. Even the razors.' She takes a disposable one from its packet.

'I want it on my wrist, not under my arm!' I say, panicking.

'I'm just making sure there's no fine hairs that'll get in the way, that's all,' says Catarina, rubbing at my wrist with alcohol.

Then she makes the stencil from my sketch and shows me the image on the thermal paper. She uses a bit of soap to moisten my wrist and places the transfer on carefully. When she peels it off, I peer at the little likeness.

'OK?' she asks.

'Could she be coloured in a bit?' I ask on impulse.

'Sure. Purple dress. White daisy. Tiny trace of red on her lips and pink nose?' Catarina suggests.

'Perfect,' I say.

She rubs ointment on the design to make the needle slide easily. And now is the big moment. I take a deep breath and hold it.

'No, breathe slowly, girl!' says Alice, and she holds my right hand unselfconsciously. 'It'll feel a bit weird at first – OK, bloody painful – but you'll get used to it, I promise.'

'Now you tell me!' I protest. It *is* bloody painful, and I nearly shriek at Catarina to stop. I'm in danger of having a one-dot tattoo like Phoebe in *Friends* but I grit my teeth, breathing slowly in and out of my nose, hoping it doesn't start dribbling snottily. After several minutes, though, I really do get used to it. I can't say I'm enjoying the process, but I'm starting to feel excited, especially when Catarina switches to different needles and starts colouring little Myrtle.

I bite my lip, wondering if she really knows what she's doing. I daren't look. No, I've got to. I'll have to stop her if it's too garish. I move my head and peek. Oh thank God, she's good at it, the purple dress is gorgeous and she's given her ruby slippers! I've never coloured Myrtle myself and it's great to peer at her in glorious technicolour, a little Oz version of herself.

'Here she is. Finished! Like her?' Catarina asks.

'I do! In fact, she's great! Thank you so much!' I say.

'She's amazing!' says Alice, squeezing my hand. 'I love her in colour. You'll have to start Myrtle merchandising now! A Myrtle mug, Myrtle pen, Myrtle phone case, Myrtle teeshirt, Myrtle pyjamas, Myrtle knickers – they'll be so in demand the *Guardian* will be desperate to lure you back!'

'You're crazy,' I say, laughing.

'I have to put some ointment on you now,' says Catarina. 'Then a bandage. I'll tape it up for you.'

'Let me take a photo first!' says Alice. 'Oh, I do love her.'

'So do I,' I say. And I truly do.

3

'What are you planning for the rest of your birthday?' Alice asks, as we walk into the sunshine.

'Oh, seeing friends, different stuff, you know,' I say vaguely, keen that she doesn't think I'm pathetic, spending most of my birthday on my own.

'Well, I hope you have a good time. It's been great meeting you!' She gives me a hug. I give a little shiver. 'Oh no, did I touch your arm? I'm so sorry if I hurt you!'

'No, you didn't!' I reassure her. The hug just took me by surprise. We've known each other less than a morning, after all. And I've been secretly hoping we might hang out, go for a stroll together, grab a sandwich at lunchtime. We seem to get on so well together. Why am I too stupidly shy to suggest it?

She's obviously got plans – maybe she's going somewhere with this Wendy?

'Oh well, I'd better be going. Thanks for being so supportive,' I say, rubbing my arm awkwardly. Pain tingles all the way along it and I turn round so she doesn't see my screwed-up face, and start walking.

'Hey, Ellie! Hang on! Give me your number! Let's keep in touch,' she says.

'Sure,' I say, trying to sound super-cool, but my heart's beating fast. So she really wants to be friends! It's hard to stop grinning. I recite my number quickly and she taps it into her phone. 'Thanks. I'll give you mine. It's a new number and I keep forgetting it. Hang on, I've probably got a card some-where.' She ferrets in her bag and brings out a crumpled card.

I fish my specs out of my bag a little self-consciously and glance at it. It's a smart cream one, with a logo made up of initials in such an intricate design that I can't immediately de-cipher it. But her name is printed plainly enough.

Dr Alice Forward.

Doctor? She doesn't seem remotely like a doctor, though what exactly should a doctor look like? Why am I thinking of some stereotypical middle-aged man in a suit? Why shouldn't a doctor be a cute young woman with an ankle tattoo?

'Well, I'll know who to come to if my tattoo gets infected,' I say.

'What? Oh, the doctor bit. I'm not a *doctor* doctor. I teach here,' she says matter-of-factly, tapping the logo.

It's the local university where Lottie could have gone and still lived at home, but of course she chose one a good hun-dred miles away.

'What do you teach?'

'Animal behaviour.'

'Oh, brilliant! Can you teach me how to stop my cat jump-ing on me at five a.m. for her breakfast?' I ask.

'I wish! No, I'm more into observing wild animals. I had a wonderful year camping in southern Kenya observing wild elephants several years ago.'

'Wow,' I say inadequately. I feel I'm being adventurous camping in Wales with Lottie and think twice before walking through a field containing cows.

I wave and walk home, hoping we really will stay in touch. I keep peering at my arm, lifting the edge of the bandage to see if I can get a glimpse of my new tattoo again, but it's impossible.

I don't want to take the bandage off altogether in case I can't get it on again properly one-handed. It's good I'm planning to wear the green Indian top tonight, because the sleeves are long and loose. I know Anna's going to be horrified when she finds out. She's always thought tattoos very downmarket. Dear Anna. She must find me a terrible trial at times: her single-mother stepdaughter who lives on a council estate. She's always so sweet to me, though, and makes far more of an effort with me than Dad ever does.

I feel a stab of dread at the thought of tonight's family dinner. I wish I wasn't going. I always love seeing Ben and Simon, though, because they're such fun. We can chat for hours, and tease and gossip and drink too much – and yet if they sense I'm down about something they're always so sympathetic and make a fuss of me. They don't ever act like they're *worrying* about me.

But Dad and Anna always end up getting serious and asking me questions. They want to know what I'm doing, have I met anyone, how's my work going, am I *happy*? I know it's because they love me but it's such an effort reassuring them that I'm absolutely fine. Well, I was, until today. Maybe life's going to go rapidly downhill now I'm forty.

Plus, I'll feel like the odd one out. Dad has Anna. Ben has Simon. And I've always had Lottie, but obviously not now. If only she was coming too. I feel another pang. Shall I try phoning Nadine and Magda to see if they can come instead? Lifelong best friends are family too. Although I'd thought they might have messaged by now to wish me happy birthday. Forty's quite a big deal, after all. If I'm honest, I feel a bit hurt that they didn't suggest getting together to celebrate.

Still, we didn't do that when *they* turned forty. Nadine went to a glitzy London club with some rich guy she hardly knew and then had a night of passion in his warehouse flat. I heard

her telling Magda some of the details. They think I'm pathetically vanilla and don't always share as much with me. It's just
as well. From the little I caught, it sounded very *Fifty Shades*.

Magda had a private celebration for her fortieth, but of a
very different sort. Chris took her for champagne cocktails at
the St Pancras Renaissance Hotel, presented her with a big
bottle of Chanel No. 5 and then took her to Paris on Eurostar.
A total older man cliché, but very romantic all the same.

They're both leading such different lives from me now. But
they're still my best friends. I find my hand reaching for my phone
and I try Nadine. Her phone rings a long time and then goes to
answerphone. I sigh and sit on a wall while I leave a message.

'Hey, Nadine, it's me. Just wanted to say hi,' I say lamely,
and cut off the call.

I'm about to try Magda, but my phone rings.

'Ellie?' Nadine's voice is husky with sleep. 'Was that you
just now?'

'Yes, sorry. I've woken you up, haven't I?'

'Yeah, but never mind.' I hear a deep voice mumbling something in the background. 'Hang on.'

I hear the creak of her bed as she gets out of it, and then
the pad of her feet as she walks somewhere else. Maybe the
kitchen. Yes, I hear the gush of a tap and then gulping noises
as she drinks a glass of water. It was obviously another big
night out last night.

'Nadine? Sorry. You've got someone there, haven't you?' I
ask, embarrassed.

'It's OK. No one important,' she mutters.

I bite my lip. Why is my beautiful creative friend sleeping
with some random guy she doesn't care about? Still, it's her
life, not mine.

'Anyway, I was just phoning because . . .' I hesitate. It suddenly seems so silly.

'Because it's your birthday. Happy birthday, happy birthday, happy birthday and another thirty-seven times,' says Nadine.

I feel a wave of relief that she's remembered, even though she's obviously half asleep and hungover.

'I love you, Naddie,' I say.

'And I love you too, Ellie-Bellie,' she says softly.

'Anyway, I know you're otherwise engaged at the moment but might you be free this afternoon, do you think? We could maybe go to a film? I've got to go to Kingtown for a family dinner tonight, but there should just about be time.' And I can surprise her with my tattoo!

There's a little silence.

'Sorry, sorry. Stupid of me. I expect you've got something else arranged?'

I can hear Nadine swallowing. 'Well, sort of,' she says eventually. 'It's a bit awkward. Maybe we could meet up for a quick coffee somewhere – but I'll have to come back and get changed because . . .' She lets her voice tail away.

'No, it's fine. *I'm* fine. Well, see you soon,' I say as breezily as I can. Maybe I'm trying to convince myself as well as Nadine.

'Really soon. Lots of love.' Nadine rings off hurriedly.

I stay sitting on the wall, wondering whether to go home or to get the tube into central London for a solo birthday celebration. Maybe buy a new outfit after all. I'm not that keen on clothes shopping on my own, though. Magda loves shopping. She'd love steering me here and there and giving me advice. Maybe she'd jump at the chance to go with me.

I stare at my phone, wondering whether to ring her or not. She might be having a bit of a lie-in with Chris, unless his children have already been delivered and she's bouncing around like a kids' TV presenter, trying to keep them amused.

An old lady wheels her shopping bag around me, and nods at my phone.

'Go on, love, give him a ring, you know you want to!' She cackles at her own joke and toddles off. I shake my head and tut at her back, but ring Magda's number.

She answers almost immediately.

'Hello, it's Magda here,' she says, in her poshest voice.

'It's me, Mags,' I say.

'Oh Ellie! Happy birthday, babe!' she says.

'Thanks! I was wondering if you were free for lunch, then maybe a bit of shopping? I've got to buy an outfit and I need your help.'

'Oh! Well, normally I'd love to, but Chris's kids will be arriving any minute,' she says apologetically.

'Can't you slip out for a bit and let them have special Daddy-time?'

'I really need to make a big effort with them, Ellie. I want them to get to like me more. I'm so sorry. I don't want to let you down.'

Yes, but you are, aren't you? Nadine too! Where are my two best friends in all the world when I really need them?

I don't say it, of course. I'm probably overreacting. I don't want to sound needy. Of course they've got their own lives to lead.

'No probs,' I say. 'Well, we'll fix a date to meet up soon? It's been ages.'

'I know. I'd love that too. I really miss you, Ellie. Have a good day. Bye, sweetheart.'

I stand up, resolving to see both of them soon – maybe at the Hare and Moon, our favourite pub – and we'll have a lovely long catch-up. It's weeks since we got together. Maybe months, even.

I can't wait to see their faces when I show them my tattoo. I could have Myrtle herself pondering a tattoo and – oh God, how could I have forgotten? I lay the soft pad of my finger on top of the bandage as if I'm giving her a stroke. My head aches as if I've been axed myself. I truly feel as if a piece of me is missing. I'm no longer Ellie Allard, successful cartoonist for the *Guardian*. I'm just Ellie Allard, a pretty rubbish art teacher who struggles to keep control. And will struggle to pay the rent too.

No, stop it! Get a grip! I'm not going to whine and whimper any more. I'll make the most of my birthday, even if no one wants to spend it with me. I start marching to the tube. Soho, here I come!

Maison Bertaux is a perfect place to eat alone. There are several tables crowded with friends, but lots of other people on their own, reading, scrolling, emailing, with cream round their mouths and pastry crumbs down their fronts. The raspberry cream tart I order slips down so easily I manage a coffee éclair too. And I don't feel the slightest bit guilty either – though perhaps this isn't quite the day to go clothes shopping after all.

I walk to the big Waterstones at Piccadilly and spend half an hour in the Graphic Novel section. My fellow browsers are either giggly teenage girls or hairy men with fantasy teeshirts and elaborate tattoos that make my little Myrtle seem totally insignificant.

Most of the graphic novels seem to be Superheroes or Manga. I flick through them, unmoved by the chiselled men or the cutsie-pie women. I toy with the idea of Stella the Supercat, but feel I'd be betraying Myrtle Mouse, and I find other cat graphic novels anyway. I need to think up another animal.

I used to doodle countless Nellie the elephant cartoons on my workbooks when I was at school, based on the much-loved blue toy I cuddled in bed right up to my teens. Mum gave her to me when I was very little and she meant the world to me.

I loved drawing Nellie. She had similar adventures to me,

like Myrtle Mouse. I drew her with her trunk waving in the air and one leg kicking sideways. But then Russell, my long-time boyfriend, copied her practically line for line for an art competition. It felt like such a betrayal at the time.

But perhaps now I could resurrect Nellie in some way? My heart beats harder at the prospect. I always reckoned she'd be around my age – so she'd be forty, too. Still, elephants can live long lives in the wild. And they're very good mothers. A perfect matriarchal storyline. Female elephants stay in the tribe with their mothers for life. Oh, if only!

Mum gave me this little woolly elephant when I was a baby. I madly threw her away, then bitterly regretted it. When Lottie was born I found the same knitting pattern and made a Nellie elephant for her.

I read somewhere that real elephants remember their dead, touch them very gently with their trunks, and visit their grave-yards. My eyes fill just thinking about it. I want to take this seriously. I'm not going to draw Nellie as a cute cartoon. I'll draw her and her relations true to life. And now, I don't need to tell their story in sets of four pictures – I can do it how-ever I want! I can devote an entire double spread to just one illustration of the whole tribe. I can feel myself tingling with excitement. I'll have to find out much more about elephants. Not in zoos, in the wild. Then I remember: *Alice!* She said she's been to Africa, she's studied them. She's so friendly and relaxed, I'm sure she wouldn't mind telling me stuff. And it'll give me a good excuse to get in touch with her again.

I waltz out of Waterstones, grinning at my reflection in the shop windows. I'm so excited to have a brand new idea, some-thing that might actually work. I walk along Piccadilly, then wander up little streets of stylish shops and galleries. I picture Nellie leading her tribe, plodding along purposefully, one care-ful foot in front of the other – then she stops dead. I've stopped too. I blink at the large pastel work displayed in the window. It's a Paula Rego!

I see the stocky, dark-haired woman slumped in despair on the canvas. She looks unbearably sad. It's as if she's mourning for her own wonderful creator. I've never seen this portrait before, though I've pored over my big Paula Rego book at home. I think back to the first time I heard of her, in Mr Windsor's art lessons at school. He showed us pictures of this same model as a ballet dancer, an evil mermaid, even as a dog.

Magda and Nadine had giggled at her, thinking her ugly. I thought she was beautiful in her own way. Powerful, even when she was depressed or humiliated. I think that was the message Mr Windsor was trying to get across to us. To me.

We all wanted to be his favourite. I secretly hoped he liked me best, because I was the artistic one. It's weird remembering how much he meant to me then, when I was thirteen, fourteen. I think I even wrote in my diary that I loved him. I wonder what's happened to him? I'd probably not even recognize him now.

I psych myself up to go into the gallery. I know anyone can look around private galleries, in theory, but I find them so intimidating. I peer down at my teeshirt and jeans, and my bandaged arm. I run my fingers through my hair, which is in a terrible frizz after swimming. I certainly don't look like a serious art collector. No, I look like a forty-year-old woman who admires Paula Rego.

A girl with long blonde hair in a gorgeous loose white shirt and a gold choker looks up from her desk and smiles at me, and I give a nervous smile back. I wander round the gallery, self-conscious at first, but Paula Rego's art works its magic and I'm absorbed in her world. I sigh with pleasure, though some of her pictures are disconcertingly savage, even the nursery rhyme illustrations.

I'm the only person there apart from the blonde girl, who's absorbed in her phone. I walk around slowly, twice, staring hard, trying to remember every detail.

Who on earth just wanders into the gallery and buys one on a whim? If only I had that sort of money! Could I ever afford a tiny etching? I've hardly any cash in my ordinary account, but I still have savings for emergencies. This is hardly an emergency of course, but you only have one fortieth birthday in your entire life.

I walk over to the reception desk as casually as I can.

'I wonder, do you have a price list?' I ask.

'Certainly,' she says, and hands me a piece of paper, still scrolling.

I start a third round of the artwork, consulting the prices on the paper. I can feel my eyes widening. They are *enormously* expensive. Rightly so – but *way* out of my league. Still, I pretend to be interested and take my time. When I'm finished I smile regretfully as if it's been a hard decision, and shake my head.

'Thank you so much,' I say, giving her back the price list, and head for the door. If I start saving now, maybe in another forty years I might be able to afford a Paula Rego for myself.

I get the tube home, my head still bursting with elephants. I could be as fierce as Paula in the way I draw them, showing the truth of their lives in the wild. I make a few notes on my phone – and when I'm walking to the estate I try calling Lottie one more time, just in case she's coming after all. An automated voice tells me that she's unavailable.

'Oh Lottie,' I whisper, but I am *not* going to despair. I walk past the general store and the betting shop and the chicken and kebab outlets and the nail bars, a different world from Mayfair galleries. The lift is working but I climb all the way up to the top floor to prove I'm still fit at forty. I'm breathless when I get in the front door and flop down on the rug. Stella stalks over to me, mewing in feline, 'Where on earth have you been? Feed me immediately!'

I stroke her until I can breathe without gasping and then give her a bowl of wet food, even though I know she will slurp up the jelly and spit out most of the meat in an imperiously picky fashion.

Then I hang up my damp swimming stuff and strip my clothes off. I rootle in the cupboard for an old plastic bag for life, wrap it round my tattoo bandage, and hold it right out of the water when I shower. I'm left with one hand to soap myself and wash my hair, which is far harder than I'd thought. Still, I manage, I towel myself dry, then patter into the bedroom to get ready, Stella on my heels.

I dry my hair, and for once the frizz is tamed, though it's really awkward brushing and drying at the same time. Make-up's easy enough, though it's difficult pulling my eyelid smooth when I'm drawing Kohl outlines. If I overdo it, I know Dad will ask why I want to make myself look like a panda, as he's been doing for the last twenty-five years. I've grown up and he's grown old, but some things never change.

I get dressed in my best Simone Pérèle underwear. God knows why. I'm hardly likely to attract some gorgeous hot man having dinner with my dad and Anna and Ben and Simon. But it makes me feel special.

Then on with the best black jeans, black socks, black patent boots, and the green top that covers the bandage completely, thank goodness. I wear the green stone pendant that Ben and Simon brought me back as a present from their honeymoon in New Zealand and poke several little silver rings on my fingers. They make tiny clinking sounds as I move around.

'Do I look OK, Stella?'

She considers, then gives a small mew, as if to say, 'OK-ish.'

I fill my tote bag with pyjamas, clean stuff for tomorrow, washing things and an old copy of *Mrs Dalloway*. My Penguin paperback has yellowed pages but it's not too ruffled at the edges. I love Virginia Woolf but it's rare that I actually read her. I have the briefest flick of the pages and find it comforting that Clarissa Dalloway is eleven years older than me. Perhaps I'll concentrate on books about older women in future so that I feel young by comparison.

I leave Stella enough food, drink and treats for six cats, and then set off, journeying back to Kingtown by tube and then train from Waterloo. I read *Mrs Dalloway* on the journey. When I look up to check stations I see I'm the only person who is reading a book. Everyone else is squinting at their mobiles, thumbs working hard. I glance quickly at my own just in case there are any messages.

There are a few happy birthday messages – and one from Alice Forward!

Hope Myrtle's not hurting too much! x

How sweet of her! I find I'm grinning like a fool. I try to think of something short and funny in reply. I'm still pondering when it's nearly my stop.

She's dancing a little jig on my arm but if she's happy so am I! x

4

I open the doors of the Vine and peer around. It's bizarrely dark, with real vines in planters against the walls. The wallpaper itself is forest green, with a midnight blue sky, and strange feral animals are lurking, scarcely visible except for their amber eyes.

There are several couples perching on green velvet stools at the bar, but no sign of my family. Irritation gnaws at me. It's dead on seven. Why can't people be on time?

I linger uncomfortably, wondering if I should ask the guy behind the bar for a drink or wait until everyone arrives. He's seen me now and smiles.

'Are you looking for the Benedict Allard party?' he asks.

'I suppose I am,' I say, my irritation growing. Surely it's *my* party? Though four people and me is hardly a *party* party.

The barman smiles at me somehow significantly. My heart starts beating fast. What's going on?

'Follow me,' he says, beckoning. The strangers on the stools are smiling at me.

Oh God, I hope this isn't what I think it is. I follow the bar guy reluctantly, wondering whether I could simply make a bolt for it out the door. No, I'm being ridiculous, imagining all sorts of nightmare nonsense. They'll simply be sitting in the restaurant waiting for me. Ben probably told everyone to come ten minutes early, so they'll have a bottle of champagne on ice, ready and waiting. It'll only be mildly embarrassing, and no one in the restaurant will even notice.

But the barman leads me straight past the restaurant.

'Where are we going?' I ask.

He peers over his shoulder, and he's smiling too.

'You're in the Sparkling Suite,' he says.

The *Sparkling* Suite? He raps twice on a door and then flings it open.

'*Surprise!*'

I cringe, desperate to run away – but I'm grinning idiotically, practically exposing my back fillings. I don't know if it's lovely or awful. And it's not even a small, select surprise party of ten or twelve. There seem to be people sparkling shoulder to shoulder in this dazzling, huge room, which is all silvery walls and big chandeliers and rainbow fairy lights. Twenty, thirty, thirty-five. Oh wait, I get it. There are exactly forty people here, one per year of my life that we're celebrating. They're all trying hard to keep still, as if posing for a photograph. Then they laugh and raise their glasses to me, and throw streamers in the air.

I don't recognize half of them! Well, I know Ben and Simon, who are standing right at the front, looking ultra cool in gorgeous shirts, tight jeans and the latest designer trainers. And Dad's got his arms round their shoulders, trying his hardest to look cool, too, in a black shirt that barely does up, jeans that are tight in entirely the wrong way, and leather brogues showing his pale hairy ankles instead of socks. Anna is immaculate as always, in a sleeveless silk shift dress showing off her gym-trim arms, the only woman I know who wears pointy heels as if they're comfy bedroom slippers.

Nadine and Magda are side by side, singing 'Happy Birthday'! They totally hoodwinked me! Nadine's in slinky black with huge silver bangles, all gothic glamour, but Magda's in an unusually girly flowing floral affair that looks pretty, I suppose, but not very Magda. She usually wears short, tight, sexy things with high heels – not these pink ballet slippers. Why the change of style? Who's the girl next to Nadine, with those long blonde curls and gold fringing on her white dress, and five-inch heels? She's the exact opposite of Nadine and yet she looks a bit like her. Is it her little sister Natasha? What on earth is she doing here?

And oh God, why didn't I spot her first – here's Lottie, my darling Lottie, jumping up and down, rushing to give me a hug. She's wearing a tiny satin minidress like a slip (*is* it a petticoat?) with clompy silver boots.

'Hey, Mum! Surprise, surprise, surprise!' she says, like a little kid. 'It was all my idea, I thought it would be so fantastic! You didn't guess, did you?'

'No, I didn't,' I say. 'You little minx, telling me all that rubbish about trains being cancelled!'

'I know, I felt so bad too – I hadn't really thought through the fact that you'd then be alone all day. I had to get here ever so early to liaise with Ben and Simon and get it all organized and make sure everyone was coming. You weren't too upset, were you?' she asks anxiously, peering at me closely.

'Of course not, silly,' I say. I'm as good at fibbing as she is. 'But how on earth did you get in touch with all these people?'

'It was easy – last time I came home I pinched your phone out of your bag while you were working on a Myrtle, and copied anyone who seemed likely. And then Ben and Si and I acted like detectives for the rest. It was such fun!' She moves closer so I can smell her sandalwood perfume and whispers in my ear. 'But forty is a huge amount, so we had to include a few makeweights. Eyes right!'

Dear God, it's Aunty Freda. She looks older and meaner than

ever, in one of the bizarre woollen suits she makes herself, this one in an unpleasant shade of ochre. She used to knit me terrible jumpers that never fitted properly and made me itch. She always sighed at me when I was a little girl – 'Such a shame when a girl has to wear glasses – and can't she do something with that wild hair?' Then of course when I became pregnant so young she treated me like a junior Whore of Babylon. It's a wonder she didn't make me a scarlet sweater.

My cousin Nigel is standing beside her. We've never got on either. He was always very peculiar as a little boy and insisted on sleeping in their cupboard under the stairs, like a poor man's Harry Potter. He's got a good job now in a building society and I'm sure all the members think the world of him – but he still seems pretty weird to me. The knitted tie doesn't help.

Still, there's Cath and Pete, teachers from school, my special mates – how nice of them to come all the way here. They must have known all about the party when I was treating everyone to birthday doughnuts in the staff room yesterday, and yet they never let on. Is that another teacher with them? No, she's much older. Who on earth is it? She has the unmistakeable air of a PE teacher . . . I gasp. It's Mrs Henderson, *my* old PE teacher, the bane of my life. I haven't seen her since I left school. Her number certainly isn't in my phone! She's laughing at the shock on my face. She actually looks a jolly old girl now, and she still seems pretty fit in her smart trouser suit.

'Here, Mum,' says Lottie, grabbing two glasses of champagne from the waiter's tray. She clinks hers against mine. 'Happy birthday! Don't worry, I'm not going to start singing it all over again. Isn't this a lovely surprise?' she says, grinning at me.

I take a sip – actually large gulp – of champagne and beam back at her.

'It's fantastic, darling. I suppose I should start circulating, chatting to everyone?' I grimace.

'Take your time, Mum. Wait till you're on your second glass, it'll be easier. Ben and Simon are busy working the room so that people will mingle. Just have a good look around and check you remember everyone first. I'm here to help you out if necessary. I've been busy swotting up on them all,' says Lottie proudly.

I give her another hug. My lovely, grown-up daughter, party hostess, in her element. I wave at a balding guy with a little beard, Andy, the art editor of the magazine where I used to work freelance. I must have a proper chat with him – I might need to do more work for him without the *Guardian* money. He's talking to a woman with a pixie haircut a few years older than me – Carol! She had her baby the day that Lottie was born and we used to hang out together when they were little and still meet up every December to exchange Christmas presents – so that girl with the heart-shaped face and big blue eyes must be Katy, her daughter. She was such a pretty baby and she still looks stunning.

Then I look at the guy in the well-cut suit that can't quite hide his stomach, smiling at me smugly.

I nudge Lottie.

'Who on earth's that pompous twat?' I whisper.

Her grin falters. 'Ah. I wasn't sure about including him. It was Ben's idea. He tracked him down. It's Russell,' says Lottie.

I'm drinking as she says it, and splutter helplessly. Russell, my first serious boyfriend, barely recognizable now! I went out with him for four whole years, and thought he was wonderful. I feel like Titania when she realizes she's fallen in love with a donkey. He's standing with his arm round a scarily immaculate woman in an expensive black cocktail dress. She's got glossy dark curls, newly coiffed, probably tamed for a fortune at Toni & Guy. His wife? Probably the girl he dumped me for long ago. Oh well, good luck to her. They match perfectly.

'Why on earth did Ben suggest inviting *him*?' I hiss at Lottie.

'He said he wanted to show you off to Russell, let him know about the *Guardian* stuff, make it clear to him that he's a total pillock for walking out on you,' says Lottie.

'Oh. Well – that's sweet of him,' I say, because he's not to know that Myrtle is history.

Is this going to be a nightmare journey through my past? Who else have Ben and Lottie discovered? They've clearly had to work really hard to dredge up a full forty guests. I look round warily for a goofy guy in an anorak and a bobble hat, weird Dan from way back, but mercifully he's not here.

There's my agent Jude, and Cassie, the editor from the *Guardian* – *really?* – and it can't be, it *is*, Nicola Sharp, who used to write the fairy books I loved as a child, the author who wrote to me when I entered a drawing of Myrtle into the art competition in Year Nine. The first person to praise Myrtle Mouse.

She'll want to talk about Myrtle and what a success she's been, because she's been thoughtful enough to message me from time to time – and it'll be right in front of Jude and bloody Cassie, and it'll be so awkward.

'Mum? Are you all right?' Lottie asks anxiously.

I realize I'm screwing my face up, blinking hard to stop bursting into tears in front of all of them. Then Ben's beside me too, his own face creased with concern.

'Ellie? What's the matter? Are you hating this whole idea? I know you're not really a party girl but I couldn't resist giving it a go when Lottie suggested it. You're not mad at me, are you?' he shouts above the hubbub.

'I'm not mad – I think you're the best brother, best daughter, in the whole world,' I say, hugging them both. 'It's just a bit . . . overwhelming. And it's so grand here! It must be costing you a fortune!'

Ben waves my worries aside. 'Don't worry, Dad chose the venue and paid. We just did all the arranging. And that was a job and a half. Didn't we do well!'

'Scarily so! Lottie lied her head off to me and I just thought she didn't want to come,' I let out.

'Oh Mum!' says Lottie. 'As if I'd ever miss your special birthday party! I'm staying over at Grandpa and Anna's, and then I'm going with you to London in the morning and don't have to get the train back to the campsite till tomorrow evening. My friends are all covering for me because this is so important. You're looking so great too. No one else I know has such a young, cool mother,' she says.

No wonder I love her so!

'Present time, now!' she says, producing a tiny tissue-wrapped package from her silver clutch bag. I feel it carefully, then undo the blue ribbon and slide the tissue apart. It's a beautiful bracelet, made of deep bluey-purple crystals.

'It's indigo iolite. It means wisdom and long life. I think you're very wise and I want you to live for ever,' Lottie says solemnly.

I do burst into tears then.

'Oh *Mum*, you're hopeless,' says Lottie. 'Come on, put your bracelet on. Give us your wrist and I'll help you put it on.' She reaches for my left wrist but I snatch it away. I want her to see Myrtle, but not here in front of everyone.

'I think I'll wear it on the right,' I say quickly.

'OK, fine.' She puts it on and I admire it delightedly.

'It does look great, doesn't it?' Lottie says happily. She looks round the room. 'They were supposed to be starting the canapés now. I'd better go and chase them up. I'll just be two minutes.'

Nadine and Magda are waving at me. I'm dying to rush over to them – but I suppose I have to see Dad and Anna first.

Why did Dad pay for all this? It's fantastically generous, and yet it kind of annoys me too. Did he really have to make such a flamboyant gesture? He could have hired any old room in a pub for a surprise party and it would have been just as good, wouldn't it? Why does he always have to be so controlling?

Now I've got to act so grateful for something I didn't ask for. Or am I just being the world's most ungrateful daughter? I see him staring over at me. He gives me a little thumbs-up sign, his head on one side. He's looking a bit uncertain, and I soften. Oh Dad, I do love you really. I hurry up to him, raise my glass and clink it against his.

'Thank you so much for this, Dad!' I kiss his cheek. It's very red and blotchy. He smells like he's been drinking long before the champagne came out. Maybe he was nervous. I feel a swell of love for him.

'I've only got one daughter, haven't I?' he says. 'I can't believe you've got to forty already. You're looking great, sweetheart.' He pauses. He looks a little watery-eyed. 'Your mother would be so proud of you.'

'Oh, Dad,' I say, overwhelmed.

'You've achieved so much,' he says. He scratches his head. 'Yet I don't know, you've seemed a bit down this last year or so.'

I stare at him, amazed. Dad's always seemed so wrapped up in himself, especially since he retired. I'd been so careful to act upbeat when I went back home. I had no idea he was tuning into my moods. I tuck my hand in his arm, nestling up to him the way I did when I was a little kid.

'I suppose I've been missing Lottie,' I admit. 'It's a bit pathetic of me.'

'Not at all! I missed you terribly when you went off to art college. I was even more of a grumpy old sod than usual,' he says.

'You, Dad?' I say, teasing him.

'Yes, me. Ellie, tell me, are you really lonely?' he asks anxiously.

'Dad, I'm crammed in a room with forty people!'

'I don't mean right this minute. But most of the time? *I* felt lonely when you left home, and yet I had Anna and Ben. But there was also this great big Ellie space,' says Dad.

'You don't have to emphasize the big part,' I say. 'Remember you once called me Ellietubby?' I say it teasingly, though it still stings.

'I didn't, did I?' Dad puts his hand to his mouth, looking stricken. 'It was just a play on those weird Teletubby creatures. But a crass thing to say. Oh, it wasn't why you went on that mad diet when you were thirteen, was it?'

'No, absolutely not. Promise. I was just going through a sad phase then.'

'And you're happy nowadays?' he persists.

'Yes!' I say. Then, in a rare burst of honesty I add, 'Well, most of the time.'

'I'm going to say something even crasser now, but I can't help it. Don't you feel lonely without a man in your life?' Dad says.

'Hey, that really *is* crass!' I say. 'This is the twenty-first century, Dad. You can't say that sort of thing to an independent professional woman. I'm fine.'

'You've never thought of going on Match.com?'

'Dad! No, I haven't!' (Of course I have.)

'I know that swiping thing is a bit icky. But there's another dating site that's for single professionals – that might be more your sort of thing,' Dad says.

'Have *you* been trying them out?' I ask, horrified.

'No! I've got Anna and I love her very much. And there wouldn't be much point my meeting up with anyone now, anyway,' Dad says. 'An old fart like me?'

He clearly wants me to contradict him, but I'm not playing that game.

'Dad, stop it,' I say. 'And please don't worry about me. I don't want anyone else in my life, thank you! I don't buy into the myth that we've all got a soulmate somewhere.'

I'm not a kid any more. I remember dreamily writing Russell's name in my workbook at school and surrounding it with hearts and stars. Would I like to be the wife hanging on his arm right now? Absolutely *not*!

'Anyway, I'd better go and circulate,' I say, keen for the conversation to be over.

'I do love you, Ellie,' he says, catching hold of my wrist as I move away. Pain shoots up my arm and makes me screw up my face. 'What is it? Did I hurt you?' Dad asks, alarmed.

'It's nothing. My wrist is a bit sore, that's all,' I say, trying to pull away.

He hangs on to me, pushes up my sleeve – and sees the bandage.

'Oh God,' he says. 'What have you done? You haven't started cutting yourself, have you?'

'No!' I say. I get close to his ear to whisper, '*It's a tattoo!*'

'What?' he says, blinking. 'How amazing! What have you got?'

'It's just a tiny cartoon,' I say.

'Like . . . Popeye?'

I snatch my arm back. 'Not bloody Popeye! It's Myrtle, my mouse.'

'Oh, brilliant! Great idea! Let me have a look!' Dad asks eagerly.

'No, I've got to keep the bandage on today,' I insist.

'Did you know I've got a tattoo?' Dad asks. 'I had it done ages ago when I was at art school.'

'Really?'

'Yes, I've got a sun shining just above my bum hole!'

'Oh *Dad*! Well, I don't ever want to see it, thank you very much,' I say, wondering what Anna's reaction was when she first saw it.

I ask her when I go to thank her. I imagine she'd have been horrified, but not a bit of it.

'I burst out laughing,' she says.

'Oh well, good for you,' I say, surprised.

'How come you were chatting about your dad's tattoo?' she asks.

I hope she doesn't kick off. No, I'm forty years old, for God's sake, I can have forty fucking tattoos if I fancy, like a true illustrated mum.

'I've just had one myself, only I can't show it to you because it's still covered up in a bandage,' I say.

'On *your* behind?' Anna asks.

'No! Wrist,' I say. 'Don't worry, it's only small. It's of Myrtle, my cartoon mouse.'

'Perfect choice,' Anna says, smiling, wonderfully relaxed about the whole thing.

I take a deep breath to tell her that Myrtle is no more, but it's not really the time or place.

'I hear Dad paid for the party,' I say instead. 'It's incredibly kind of him.'

'You mean so much to him, Ellie. To both of us. I'm sorry to inflict the party on you, though – I have a feeling it's not your sort of scene at all. I wanted to ask you how *you'd* like to celebrate your fortieth, but Lottie and Ben and Simon were so set on it being an amazing surprise. They have gone to immense trouble, though, so try to grin and bear it for a few hours, darling.'

'It's actually fun, in a weird sort of way,' I say, 'now I've got over the shock.' I really do feel touched that they've gone to such great lengths to bring everyone together like this.

Ben and Simon are bouncing around introducing people to each other – and there are my best friends, beaming at me! I rush up to them. 'Oh Nadine, Magda, it's so great that you've come! Why didn't you *tell* me when I phoned?'

'Well, it wouldn't have been a surprise then, would it?' says Magda.

'But aren't you staying with Chris and his kids?' I ask.

'I wouldn't miss your party for the world!' says Magda. 'And it's such a relief to be free of those bloody kids! No, no, they're sweet really. They just don't seem to take to me. But I suppose it's natural to hate your stepmum anyway.'

'Stepmum?' says Nadine.

We peer at her left hand. No ring. But Magda's stroking that finger.

'Maybe someday,' she says wistfully. 'Actually, we're talking about getting engaged.'

Nadine and I blink at her.

'But you've only known him a few weeks,' I say.

'It's five months, actually. And I *married* Dave after three months,' says Magda.

'And look what happened there,' murmurs Nadine.

Magda is the only one of us who's been married. Not just once. *Twice.* The Dave thing was a whirlwind romance that only lasted a year, when Magda found out he was still sleeping with his ex-girlfriend. She was slightly more cautious after her divorce, but about ten years ago she married her personal trainer Mario and she was determined to make that last. But they fell out a lot, partly because she really wanted a baby and he wasn't as keen. Magda wasn't able to conceive, and after drifting on a year or so they parted company and that was divorce number two. Nadine and I wondered if the reason she was so keen on Chris was because he already had children, but apparently not.

'Didn't Ben invite Chris too?' I ask.

'Yeah, he said bring any boyfriend, partner, whatever – but I felt it would be a bit over the top if we brought his kids too, and he's always lumbered with them at the weekends. Well, he *wants* to have them, he loves them to bits, and he didn't think they'd like a grown-up party, so he's at home with them. I'm sure they wouldn't have wanted to come anyway. I don't think they'd behave. They're eight and six and yet they often act like toddlers. I told you, they don't like me very much. They probably cheered when they discovered I'm not around this weekend.' Magda sighs.

'Oh, Mags, you'll be a wonderful stepmum, if that's what you want. It just takes time. I positively hated Anna at first, but now I think she's great,' I say.

'Well, in actual fact, I'm going to be having a baby of my own!' says Magda, and she puts her hand down on her stomach, pulling her dress tight.

It's unmistakeable: a bump!

'Oh my God, you are!' says Nadine.

'How wonderful!' I gush.

'Isn't it!' says Magda, her face glowing.

'So what does Chris think about it?' Nadine asks.

'He's thrilled too,' Magda says firmly. 'I didn't tell him at first because I was so scared that it would somehow jinx the baby. He's only recently found out. And I didn't tell you two either, just in case,' says Magda, clasping her hands and holding her little bump as if she were rocking it. 'It's better to keep quiet until you've passed the first trimester. It's so much safer beyond the twelfth week.'

'You're talking like a baby manual already!' says Nadine.

'And we're your best friends!' I say. 'Remember, I told you when I was twelve *days* late and going out of my mind wondering what I was going to do. But I forgive you. Have you started morning sickness yet?'

'I feel a little bit sick when I get up, but I'm so happy I don't care. It's certainly nothing to make a fuss about. I think it's mind over matter,' says Magda serenely.

'That's absolute bollocks!' I scoff. 'I was sick as a dog every single day. The moment I went into art school and smelt the oil paint I threw up. It was terribly embarrassing. And I had to carry a sick bag around with me on the bus going home. God help the poor person sitting next to me.'

'Yes, but you were very young and scared,' says Magda.

'No I wasn't. Well, I *was*, and I didn't know how I was ever going to finish my course, and I knew I wasn't going to get any help from that guy at the party, but I was still happy about having a baby. That's why I wouldn't listen when everyone said I should have an abortion,' I insist.

'Shh!' says Magda, as if I've said a terrible word.

Nadine raises her eyebrows at me. What's happened to our Magda?

'Surely Chris must be a bit thick if he couldn't see what was happening to your body?' she says bluntly. 'Your boobs have got bigger too, as well as your tummy.'

'Well, I've always had big breasts,' Magda says, a little smugly. 'He loves it that they're getting even bigger now. But then one day when he was kissing my navel, ready to go down on me—'

'Stop it!' I cry. 'If you haven't had sex for years then you don't want to hear other people showing off about their love lives.'

'You haven't had sex for *years*?' Nadine echoes, appalled.

Cupboard Nigel is standing nearby and turns to look at me. '*Shut up!*' I hiss.

'Anyway, Chris was saying how curvy I'd become, and then at last the penny dropped,' says Magda. 'He was just a little bit taken aback at first. In fact, it put him right off his stride and we didn't have sex at all, we just discussed it for hours, which was a bit of a waste because it was a week night and no kids around and we can be really abandoned . . . But I'm not saying he didn't want our baby, he was thrilled, just a little bit worried about how Nat and Corrie will feel.'

'Is Nat short for Natasha?' Nadine asks.

'Nathaniel and Coriander,' Magda says, with exaggerated enunciation. Nadine and I snort. 'I know! But I'm certain Chris didn't choose their names. His ex-wife sounds very showy,' says Magda, who's always been the showiest one of us three. It's a struggle to keep my face straight.

'Don't you get terribly frustrated, Ellie?' Nadine persists. 'I mean, you can have fun on your own, but it's not quite the same, is it?'

'Please shut up!' I beg her, conscious of all the friends and relatives (and ex-work colleagues and former neighbours and practical strangers) milling round us, some coming closer to wish me happy birthday.

'Don't you miss it?' Nadine continues relentlessly.

'Not particularly,' I lie. It's not just the sex, though of course I do miss that. It's the cuddling afterwards, and curling up together and feeling a warm body beside you every time you turn over. It's waking in the morning and hearing someone whistling in the shower. Then they bring you coffee and you chat and play silly games. *What's your favourite bit of me?* and *If I were an animal what would I be?* and *Who can stare longest without blinking?* Then you make love again and have scrambled eggs together and then you even shower together and get dressed and go out to a street market and wander around hand in hand until it's time to have a pub lunch. You might even share titbits from each other's plate. Then you go to a cinema and hold hands in the dark and if it's a sad film you cry and he gently wipes your eyes when the lights go up and then you decide to walk all the way home by the river simply because it's more romantic.

I can't help sighing.

'You *do* miss it!' says Nadine.

'I miss romance,' I admit.

'You sweet old-fashioned girl,' says Nadine, but there's something a little wistful about her tone, as if she might occasionally hanker after romance too rather than wild adventures. 'Here, babes, happy birthday.'

She hands me a black satin package tied with silver ribbon.

'Ben told us to put our presents on that table over there, but you'll never get round to opening them all tonight. I want you to see mine now!'

I undo the ribbon carefully and see a glimpse of black material inside – it looks like a teeshirt. I spy part of a design on the front. I hope it's not one of the bands Nadine loves. There was this guy Neville she hung out with once, the lead singer of some indie band considered ultra cool. He was very charismatic in a dark gothic kind of way, and quite famous. I suppose I was a little impressed then, but he was into drugs in a serious way, and I'm pretty sure Nadine started experimenting, though she swore to us she didn't. I was so worried about her, especially when it all got very heavy and he hit her several times. He kept trying to make it up to her afterwards – but thank God she started to see how crazy it all was and broke off with him.

She's never really settled since, but I don't think she's got any regrets. Neville has carried on seeming ultra cool to the un-initiated, and has quite a big following, but Nadine just thinks him pathetic now. At least, I hope she does.

I pull the teeshirt from the package. It's nothing to do with bands, thankfully. It's everything to do with me! It's a perfect reproduction of a recent Myrtle comic strip, where she has a mouse mid-life crisis. I thought it was one of my best.

I feel my tummy clench. This is so bloody painful. I hoped my readers would love it – but clearly it didn't *chime* with them, according to Cassie. Still, here it is, beautifully embroidered, not just stuck-on plastic appliqué.

'It's incredible!' I whisper. 'You must have got it done specially.'

'Harry tipped me off about this great design place. He got all his staff uniform teeshirts there. He's just opened this really cool wine bar. Typical!' Nadine smiles. She's been seeing this Harry on and off for years, but he's got a wife and kids.

'Aren't you and Harry ever going to get it together?' Magda asks.

'We're happy as we are. He's too settled and I'm not ready to settle at all,' says Nadine breezily.

We're not sure she really means it, but we keep up the pretence.

'The teeshirt will look great with my tattoo,' I say quickly, breaking the silence.

'You haven't got a tattoo?' says Nadine.

'I had it done this very morning! A little birthday present to myself,' I say.

'Show us!' Magda demands.

'I can't – it's still bandaged. But it's Myrtle, so now I have the teeshirt to match. Perfect!' I say.

'Give us a little peep,' Nadine insists, pulling at the edge of my bandage, exposing a couple of inches of tiny mouse.

They both peer as best they can and exclaim enthusiastically.

'Are you going to get one now, Magda?' Nadine asks.

'Not now, just in case of infection,' Magda says, patting her tummy. 'Here, open my present, Ellie. I'm afraid it's a bit ordinary,' she adds, producing a tiny, pale turquoise package from her (pre-used, but much loved) Chanel tote handbag.

'It's Tiffany,' Magda says, in case I didn't realize.

Nadine and I make brief eye contact. Magda is a true Holly Golightly girl. She would have Breakfast, Lunch and Dinner at Tiffany's if she could. If her baby is a girl, it's a sure bet she'll name her Tiffany. I open the elegantly packaged present. It's a little bracelet with an infinity sign, very pretty.

'I chose it because our friendship is infinite,' says Magda, which is a very sweet thought.

I hug her too. In fact, we have a joint hugging session, already sightly tipsy after only two glasses of champagne.

'Oh, you girls! You haven't changed a bit!' A familiar voice from the past. We peer round. Mrs Henderson! We break apart guiltily as if we're back in Year Nine and in disgrace. She laughs at us.

'Oh my lord, have I still got the Power?' she says. 'You girls were never *scared* of me, were you?'

'You terrified us but we kind of liked you too, Mrs Henderson,' I say.

'It's Jean. No need to be formal now. It's so fascinating seeing you all grown up. Happy fortieth birthday, Ellie. Goodness, I was only your age when I was your form mistress!'

'But you seemed ancient to us then, Mrs Henderson – I mean, Jean,' says Magda, not very tactfully.

'I felt old having to deal with you three girls. You really were a handful. Totally lazy and conniving when it came to PE. You were always claiming you had a period, begging to be let off, remember?' she says.

'You never *did* let us off. But you were a good sport too,' I say.

'If we were really upset about something you always listened, even if we didn't take your advice,' says Nadine.

'And you were never a girl to do that, Nadine! You're still looking very striking. What are you – a singer in a band?' Jean guesses.

'Well, I *lived* with a singer in a band once,' says Nadine. 'But I've got a voice like a frog. I'm a producer at Gem radio – it's a little indie set-up, I don't think you'll have heard of it.'

'I shall see if my ancient Roberts Radio can find it,' Jean says. 'And what about you, Magda?'

'I'm the marketing manager for Jewel Cosmetics,' says Magda. 'But I'm going on maternity leave in a few months.'

'Congratulations!' she says. 'Perhaps you'll supply me with a few samples so I can try to look as glamorous as you?'

'I'll send you a whole boxful,' says Magda, grinning.

'And I don't need to ask about you, Ellie,' Jean says, turning to me. 'Guy says you have a very popular comic strip in the *Guardian*.' She smiles significantly.

'Well, I wouldn't say it's very popular nowadays,' I mumble. I can't bring myself to say it's so unpopular it's been jettisoned. I imagine Myrtle drooping underneath her bandage.

'Who's Guy?' Magda asks.

'My goodness! Have you forgotten all about him? You three thought he was the bee's knees at one time,' says Jean, but our faces remain blank. 'Your art teacher?'

'Mr Windsor!' we cry together.

'THAT Guy!' says Magda.

That Guy indeed! Oh God, if Ben has somehow contacted Mrs Henderson, has he got in touch with Mr Windsor as well? Is he right here in this room, about to wish me a happy birthday?

I look round hopefully. That would be wonderful. But Mrs Henderson is shaking her head, looking amused.

'I don't think he's been invited,' Jean says.

'I think we'd have noticed if he'd been here!' says Magda, who also had a huge crush on him.

'Is he still gorgeous?' Nadine asks.

'Reasonably so,' Jean says, laughing at us. 'We go for a drink every now and then and enjoy ranting about today's educational system.'

'Going for a drink isn't a euphemism, is it, Jean?' Magda asks outrageously.

'That's the remark worthy of a cheeky schoolgirl – not a successful marketing manager,' she replies, looking severe. Magda looks mortified.

Jean laughs. 'This is wonderful! You still mind if I tell you off! And of course it's not a euphemism. I'm almost old enough to be Guy's mother!'

I count on my fingers, trying to work out how old Mr Windsor is now. Oh my lord, is he fifty? It seems so old! But actually it's only ten years older than me.

'What does he look like now, Jean?' Magda asks, saving me having to ask.

'Not too bad,' says Jean. She smiles wryly. 'He's kept all his lovely hair.'

'Does he still teach?' I ask.

'In a boys' school now,' she says. 'It used to be a grammar and it's still very academic.'

'I teach in a challenging comprehensive, but the kids are actually great,' I say. 'So, Mr Windsor – Guy – he's seen my Myrtle Mouse cartoons?' I try hard to act like I don't really care either way, but I don't think I'm fooling any of them.

'He thinks they're great. He said he used to tell you off for drawing little cartoon creatures, thinking you were wasting your talent – and yet you've proved him a total fool. When I told him I'd been invited to your fortieth, he asked me to give you his huge congratulations,' says Jean.

I gape at her. Mr Windsor knows what I've been doing. I don't think she'd say it if it wasn't true. But it still seems amazing. Magda and Nadine look seriously impressed.

'Did Mr Windsor stay with that gorgeous model?' Magda asks.

'No, they split up long ago. I believe he's had rather a chequered love life. He might even have got married once, but that didn't last,' says Jean.

'But who is he with now?' Nadine asks.

'Mm. I don't think he's with anyone at the moment, not seriously, anyway,' says Jean.

'There you are, Ellie! Get in touch!' says Nadine.

'Shut *up*!' I groan.

'*I* will, if you're not quick off the mark!' says Magda. I know she's not serious – she's besotted with Chris, and she's pregnant into the bargain – but there's still a spark in her eyes.

'You girls! You haven't changed a bit,' says Jean, smiling fondly.

'Mrs Henderson – Jean – if you don't mind my asking, how did Ben get in touch with you?' Nadine asks.

'It was Simon, actually. We both go to the same badminton club. He's such a lovely boy, we always have a chat and a smoothie afterwards, there's a little crowd of us, and Simon was telling us about this surprise party he and his partner were helping organize for a fortieth birthday. Then he said it was for Ben's sister, Ellie – and I put two and two together because Allard's a relatively unusual name. I told him I used to teach you long ago and he was delighted, and insisted I had to come.'

'Well, I'm very glad he did,' I say, and we smile at each other. My colleagues Pete and Cath wave at me, and I wave back. 'I'd better go and say hello to them, and generally work the room,' I say with a grimace.

They wish me luck and I take a deep breath, then stride back into the fray.

5

I smile and wave at people, but the sparkling room is so dazzling that it's hard focusing – and I'm still not sure who everyone is. Some are obviously familiar but for some reason (two glasses of champagne in quick succession?) I can't think of their names! It's very hot in here too. I catch a glimpse of myself in one of the many mirrors and I'm bright red in the face. Ben fetches me another glass of champagne (is that wise?) and comes round the room with me, cleverly reminding me who people are when he senses I'm floundering.

'I'm feeling bad now,' he murmurs to me. 'I wanted to make the party a lovely surprise for you, but I can see it's a bit of an ordeal. Are you absolutely hating it?'

'No, I'm having a fantastic time,' I say determinedly. I look at his earnest face and although I can see he's this successful, sophisticated man, I also see that little kid Eggs who'd plague me to death all day and yet always gave me a huge hug when he said goodnight. 'It's so sweet of you, Simon and Lottie to go to so much trouble. And it's such fun meeting up with all these faces from the past.' Most of them, anyway . . .

I'm dying to catch up with Lottie but I keep getting waylaid trying to reach her right at the other side of the room. I chat to more teacher friends and we bitch about school stuff, and they tell me how lucky I am to have my Myrtle sideline. I can feel my jaw tensing as I keep smiling. Blurting out the truth would hardly help the party atmosphere.

I have to have a proper chat to dear old Mr Roberts, who owns the local bookshop in Kingtown and still works there on a Saturday, even though he's ancient. I used to be a Saturday girl there, and he jokes that now he's a Saturday boy as Claudia and Ibrahim run the shop. They call me over and they're talking to Nicola Sharp, and even though I'm forty years old I feel myself reverting to the little girl who declared herself her Number One Fan.

I go up to them and see they've been joined by Jude and Cassie, the very last people I want to see right now. I find I'm gripping my left wrist protectively, my champagne glass wobbling, in danger of spilling.

Jude smiles at me ruefully and gives my shoulder a little pat. Cassie is much more flamboyant. She rushes to put her arms round me and says how sorry she is about the Myrtle decision, and if she had her way she'd keep her going for ever, and please please please will I come up with another idea.

I smile magnanimously at her and begin a conversation with Nicola, but Claudia and Ibrahim interrupt, asking if she could see her way to doing a signing event with them and I don't like to butt in again. I peer around, keen to make sure I've spoken to everyone I should – and, with a sinking feeling, spot Russell and his wife.

I start another glass of champagne and then resolutely approach them.

'It's lovely to meet you,' says his wife, who he introduces as Elinor.

'Oh, snap!' I say.

'But I'm spelt differently, the unusual way,' she says, as if that makes it superior. 'Fancy you inviting us to your fortieth!'

'Yes, it was quite a surprise,' says Russell.

'I daresay we were just making up the numbers,' says Elinor.

I smile sweetly. 'I think Ben was trying to gather all kinds of people from my present and my past.'

'And is there a man in your present life?' Russell asks. 'Or indeed a woman?' He gives a little smirk to show how modern he is.

He's made an effort with his clothes too, wearing a white teeshirt with his suit, and white trainers. Elinor is wearing a tight dress that clings to her curves. Her dark hair is salon smooth and glossy, but little fronds are already trying to be curly. She doesn't wear glasses, but as she turns her head I can detect a sliver over her iris. She's wearing contacts, so she's got poor eyesight too. We're bizarrely alike, though she's the smartened-up version. We've even got practically the same name. She's a replica me! I bite the inside of my cheeks to stop myself laughing.

Does Russell realize? I wonder if she's artistic too – but no, it turns out she's a dentist.

'At the Gentle Touch Dental Practice,' she says, flashing her own white teeth.

'Elinor's also a bit of a writer,' Russell says proudly. 'She's working on a series of children's books. Our two absolutely love them.'

'Really? I'll look out for them,' I say, attempting politeness.

'Well, they're not actually published yet. In fact, we were wondering – perhaps you'd introduce us to your friend Nicola Sharp? She might be able to give us a few tips about publication, whether we need an agent or whatever,' says Russell.

He keeps using plurals. It suddenly dawns on me.

'Are you illustrating them, Russell?' I ask.

'Well, yes, I am. I'm finding it great fun. Remember when we used to do sketches of each other, Ellie?' His face has softened and I catch a glimpse of the old Russell.

But Elinor flinches, and I gasp at his lack of tact.

'Perhaps I'll just go and talk to Nicola Sharp and let you two have a proper catch-up,' she says.

It's his cue to stop her and go off to harass poor Nicola, too, but he stays right where he is, staring at me. Ben will be thrilled if he's watching. I'm not. I can't imagine being attracted to Russell now, and I don't want him to try to tempt me down Memory Lane.

'And I'd better carry on mingling,' I say quickly.

'Hang on a minute, Ellie,' says Russell. He lowers his voice. 'There's something I have to ask you.'

Oh God, what's he going to come out with now? He leans forward, very near me now. I can smell his expensive aftershave, and a little whiff of sweat. I remember how I used to respond to his proximity long ago, and wonder at my teenage tastes.

'It's about Lottie,' he whispers.

'Lottie?' I repeat, wrong-footed. I turn and look at her. She's telling my art school buddies some joke and they're cracking up laughing. My heart swells. My own special Lottie.

'Is she in the middle of A-levels now?' he asks.

'No! She's just finished her first year at university,' I say.

'Really? What's she studying?'

'English Literature.' What else? She's loved books ever since I read her *Where the Wild Things Are* when she was two and we roared our terrible roars together.

Russell isn't looking impressed, though. 'Surely that's a bit of a waste of time, nowadays. Couldn't she have done a STEM subject? It would be much more to her advantage jobwise,' he says.

I bristle. 'It's her passion, Russell,' I say shortly.

'But she can't live on passion,' he says. 'You know how much I loved art, but how many art students can support themselves adequately later on?'

'I do,' I say, stung.

'Yes, I know you do your cartoon thingies, but your dad said you have to teach too. That can't be easy nowadays when kids run riot in secondary schools,' he says.

I want to punch him in the face. *Cartoon thingies!* And the kids I teach can be a bit lippy at times, but they're mostly fantastic. He sees my chin go up and looks wary.

'I'm just thinking of Lottie's future, that's all,' he says.

'Lottie's nothing to do with you,' I say haughtily.

'Well, that's the point. *Is* she?' he asks.

'What do you mean?'

There's a loaded pause. 'Is she my daughter?' he whispers finally, going bright red.

I stare at him. 'Are you crazy? Of course she isn't!'

'But are you sure? I can't help thinking she looks a bit like me,' he says.

'She looks nothing like you! And for God's sake, you're a banker. Can't you count? There's no possible way Lottie could be yours, unless your sperm were Olympic-level swimmers who treaded water for a very long time!' I say, forgetting to keep my own voice down.

Only then do I realize that I'm near Aunty Freda and Cupboard Nigel. Aunty Freda looks outraged, but Nigel squares his shoulders and comes over to us.

'Are you all right, Ellie?' he asks, staring belligerently at Russell.

I suppress a smile at Nigel's attempt to be the knight in shining armour, but appreciate the gesture.

'I'm fine, Nigel, but thanks,' I say. I give him a grateful peck on the cheek, and then force my way over to Lottie, wanting to protect her if Russell lumbers along and starts claiming paternity.

Ben and Simon are making an announcement, pretending

to be jostling with each other to get to the mike, like a glamorous Ant and Dec.

'I hope you're all enjoying yourselves – but maybe getting a bit peckish?' Ben says.

'Dinner is about to be served,' says Simon, and they both draw open the heavy silver sequin curtains at the end of the room. But it's not the end of the room at all, there's a fabulous dining area, five round tables with little glass vases of roses and place cards by each plate.

'Anyway, my darlings, our beautiful birthday girl is going to swap tables every now and then,' Ben announces. 'We will bask in her company for the starter, two tables will have their chance to chat with her during the main course, another table for the pudding, and the remaining table will sip coffee and nibble petits fours with her. She will return to us for the grand birthday cake ceremony,' says Simon.

'Don't worry, Ellie, we're slipping a packet of Rennies into your handbag,' says Ben, managing to charm everyone into compliance.

Ben and Simon might well have gone over the top choosing my birthday meal, but Lottie's clearly given them advice. She knows I like very simple food. We have a heritage tomato and beetroot salad, pan-roast fillets of Dover sole with baby potatoes and green beans, vanilla ice cream with blackcurrant sorbet, and tiny macarons with the coffee. They keep an eye on me and carry my plate and cutlery and glass for me whenever it's time to move.

Wine is flowing and it's surprisingly easy to make happy conversation with everyone (though a struggle with Russell and the Replicant, and Aunty Freda and Cupboard Nigel). It's a delight when I move tables to sit next to Nicola Sharp, though I'm still a bit shy with her. She tells me she's a big fan of Myrtle Mouse.

I take a deep breath. OK. It's time. I have to tell her. She'll understand. She might even give me some advice.

'Actually, I've just heard that they're dropping the Myrtle strip,' I say.

'Really? How stupid! Don't let it get you down, Ellie. Maybe it's time you branched out and wrote a book?' she suggests.

'Well, actually, I was wondering about having a go at something like that,' I say.

'Oh, perfect! About Myrtle?' she asks, sounding really interested.

'Well, I love Myrtle, but perhaps she's had her day. I thought about trying something completely different.' I hesitate, not wanting to say it outright in case she looks doubtful. I'm not sure a literary treasure like Nicola would approve of graphic novels.

'Give me a clue!' she says, reading my mind.

'Well . . . I wondered about . . . a graphic novel,' I mumble.

'Fantastic!' Nicola says, to my amazement. 'Perhaps you could send me a few pages when they're ready? I'd love to see how you're doing it. I'm not supposed to tell anyone yet, but I'm turning one of my early fairy books into a kind of graphic novel myself. My publishers think it will give them a new lease of life.'

'*Really?*'

'Apparently they're all the rage now. You go for it, Ellie!' she says. 'You'll be brilliant at it.'

'Oh Nicola!' I say, beaming at her. 'Do you really think so?'

'I *know* so! I knew you were really talented right from when you were a child,' she says. 'I used to have thousands of children send me their drawings, but yours really stood out.'

'I bet you still get heaps of fan mail,' I say.

She fiddles with her long amber necklace, and pulls a wry face. 'I don't get that much nowadays. My fairies and I have sadly gone out of fashion.'

Carol's daughter Katy overhears and tells her she still treasures her fairy book collection. Then various guests queue beside her to get her to sign her name and draw their favourite fairy on their place cards. Nicola chats to everyone, her face lit up. She's got grey hair now, and an elegant walking stick is leaning against her chair, but she doesn't seem to have aged much at all. All my art school buddies are fans and want little pictures too.

They are all envious of my Myrtle cartoon strip. Bloody Russell is right. None of them are doing a job remotely to do with art now. They work in offices, a toy shop, make artisanal bread – and my favourite friend Jacob is a gardener. I quickly change the subject by asking if any of them are still in touch with Mick. Mad Mick, My Mick, a guy I'd adored when I started at art school. Perhaps he's ended up with an unlikely career like a sanitary inspector or a traffic warden.

'Last I heard he'd gone to live on some remote Scottish island,' says Jacob.

'By himself?'

'No, with a whole harem of girls, like he's the leader of some sinister cult,' he says.

'Yep, that's Mick for you,' says Rhona, who was also once in love with him.

'I always wondered, Ellie. Is your lovely Lottie Mick's daughter?'

'No! Absolutely not!' I insist.

'Though she looks a little like him,' she says wistfully, staring over at Lottie. She's sitting between her uncles now, who are both gazing at her adoringly.

Dear God, Lottie looks like *herself*, not Mick – and certainly not Russell! I can feel my skin prickling. I'm getting fed up with all this speculation.

'So who *is* her dad?' Rhona persists. She peers at the guys in our group suspiciously. I fidget uncomfortably.

'It was so long ago I can hardly remember,' I lie ridiculously.

Of course I remember that awful party. Maybe all the gang were there, maybe not. I don't know what *I* was doing there. I was just lonely and unhappy and wishing I was still with Mick, and this boy started drunkenly kissing me, and then we were on a pile of coats and somehow we were having sex, and he didn't force me, I just went along with it because it was starting to feel good, well, not that good actually, but at least I didn't feel so lonely.

I didn't even know his last name. He was just Steve someone. I never thought we'd have to see each other again – until I realized that I was pregnant. I spotted him in the student café and thought he seemed vaguely familiar. I wasn't sure until I saw him looking at me warily. He was with a whole crowd, but even so I went up to him.

'Hey, can I have a word?' I asked, trying to sound casual.

He came with me to another table. He looked reluctant, but I think he was worried I might make a scene in front of his mates.

'I'm Ellie. You remember me, don't you?' I said.

'Maybe,' he replied cagily.

'We got together at that party, right, the one in Stoke Newington?'

'If you say so,' he mumbled.

'I know so. And now, unfortunately, I'm pregnant,' I said.

He winced at the word. Then, predictably, he came out with 'But how do you know it's mine?'

'Because I haven't slept with anyone else for months. It's definitely yours,' I said.

'So what do you want from me? Money? Because I haven't got any,' he said.

'I don't want your fucking money,' I spat. 'I just thought I should let you know you're going to be a father.'

'Well, I'm not interested,' he said. 'And you can't prove it, anyway.'

I didn't want to prove it. I'd have been happy if it *wasn't* him, he was such a tosser. I didn't want my baby to be stuck with a father like him. But even so, when he'd cleared off I went and asked one of the girls who'd been sitting with him what his last name was. She told me, Steve Fedden. If Lottie ever feels the need to find her father, I can help her track him down.

I asked her if she'd like to trace him when she turned eighteen.

'Why would I?' she said. 'I've got lovely men in my life. Ben and Simon and Grandad and all my mates at school. Why on earth would I want to go looking for someone who walked out on us?'

She's got so much sense. She won't make the mistakes I've made. She'll find someone really special and fall in love. I join her as my birthday cake is brought in, shining with forty candles. She helps me blow them all out.

'Don't forget to make a wish, Mum!' says Lottie.

'I'm a bit old for wishes,' I say.

But then a wish pops into my head, taking me completely by surprise.

I wish I could find someone special to love.

6

We all have a slice of birthday cake. It's a wonderfully light sponge with three layers of cream and elderflower jam and lemon icing. Simon made it himself and takes a bow, grinning.

When we go back into Sparkleworld we find it's all set up for dancing, with a DJ playing a great selection of music. Dad asks me to dance first, which is quite sweet of him – but then he dances with nearly all the women in the room, making a particular fool of himself with Natasha. Anna manages to stay composed and smiling. I dance with Ben and Simon, then with Lottie, though she leaps up and down a lot and it's hard to keep up with her. Then I dance in a threesome with Nadine and Magda and it's just like we're back at school again. We know each other's moves, we do the old routines we'd once perfected in the playground, and sing along to all the old tunes we still know by heart.

Practically everyone gets on their feet at the end to dance to 'I Gotta Feeling' by the Black Eyed Peas. Lottie even persuades Nigel to attempt an awkward shuffle, though Aunty Freda is a totally lost cause, refusing to even wave her arms around. The DJ plays it again because we'd all enjoyed it so – and then the lights come on, and the party's over.

People start to leave and I stand at the door hugging everyone, thanking them for coming. Jude tells me to keep my spirits up and Cassie says she's truly looking forward to seeing what I do next. Nicola Sharp makes me promise to email her my new book when I have my first draft ready. Mr Roberts overhears, and says he'll give it an entire window and organize a big signing when it comes out (as if!). Aunty Freda even says she's enjoyed herself, though she wishes the music hadn't been so loud. Natasha gives me a big hug and invites me to her wedding, which comes as a surprise.

Ben, Simon and Anna are busy collecting up all my presents and packing them carefully in big carrier bags, then Nadine and Magda come back to Dad and Anna's with us. When the eight of us are home we enjoy several leftover bottles of champagne and more birthday cake like kids at a midnight feast.

I start unpacking all my presents. Magda's stayed responsibly sober so she keeps a careful record of each one so I can send polite thank-yous. There's an envelope from Anna and Dad, so I assume it's just a card, as they've very generously paid for the party. There's a cheque tucked inside, for a great deal of money.

'Dad!' I say, taken aback. 'I can't possibly accept this. It's way too much!'

'Darling, I want you to have it now, while I'm still here,' he says, blowing me a kiss. When he's drunk nowadays he tends to get maudlin. 'I'd like you to use it as a down-payment on a flat in a nicer area. Maybe a mansion flat like Ben's? Or somewhere new and modern? Anywhere! I just worry about you still renting on that awful council estate.'

He's doing it again. He's trying to change my life. He's always hated my trying to be independent. He cares about me, he's being incredibly generous, but I don't *want* his money, his patronizing concern. I hate having to be cravenly grateful. I feel my throat tightening. No, I'm not going to cry! I fight to gain control.

'I like it where I am, Dad,' I say as calmly as I can. 'And I'll never get another view as fabulous.'

'Are you sure, Mum? We could find another top floor flat somewhere!' Lottie suggests, raising her eyebrows when she sees the number of noughts on the cheque. 'Or you could buy a flash car or go travelling or do anything you really want to do?' These are the things that Lottie wants to do, bless her.

'Pop the cheque back inside the card and we'll talk about it in the morning when we're not all so tired,' says Anna, ever the peacemaker.

'It's very kind and generous of Grandad,' says Lottie, and she gives him a fond kiss on the top of his head, where he's bald. I'm glad *they* have such a simple, loving relationship.

She's grinning at Ben and Simon now.

'Wait till you see what else you're getting, Mum!' she says. Ben and Simon hand me a present beautifully wrapped in shiny silver paper tied with red ribbon. 'Can you guess what it is?' Lottie demands.

'Lottie says you've got the mankiest old phone ever. So Si and I bought you this!' says Ben, as I unwrap a box that reveals a sleek black iPhone.

'Oh boys, it's wonderful – but they cost a fortune!' I say, overwhelmed all over again. 'You really shouldn't have.' Somehow, I'm thrilled that they've been so thoughtful and generous, yet I can't force myself to be grateful to Dad. I can't help it, though I know I'm maybe being unfair.

'I'll have it if it makes you uncomfortable, Mum,' says Lottie. 'Come on, open some of the other presents. Let's all see if we can guess what they are.'

It's mostly easy enough: expensive candles and various Jo Malone gift sets, which I donate to Anna and Magda, and Nadine and Lottie are happy with big gift boxes from Hotel Chocolat and champagne truffles.

Aunty Freda has given me a box of assorted chocolates without its cellophane wrapper, and when I look I discover all the caramels are missing. It strikes us as so funny we all laugh hysterically. Nigel has donated a bottle of sherry, of all unlikely alcohols.

'I suppose it must be Aunty Freda's special tipple.' I laugh, though I'm a touch offended. 'Still, at least he hasn't already opened the bottle.'

There's one flat rectangular package which is obviously an old-fashioned DVD.

'What do we think? *How to Cope with a Mid-Life Crisis*?' I suggest, sending myself up.

'*Tantric Sex*?' says Ben.

'*Fifty Shades of Grey*?' Simon offers.

'Boys, boys, behave!' says Anna, but I love it that she's sniggering too.

We all laugh more when we see it's from Mrs Henderson: *101 Ways to Keep Fit!*

I feel warm and fuzzy with love for them all, even poor old Dad, who's now sprawling on the sofa, head back, eyes closed, mouth open, completely out of it.

There are several more exciting bottles of champagne – I'm having them! The last present is huge and heavy and I really hope it might be an art book. And it is, a big glossy volume on female artists from Roberts Bookshop.

'Oh, how wonderful!' I say, carefully leafing through the pages.

'When I got in touch inviting Mr Roberts to your party he asked if there was any book I thought you might particularly like,' says Lottie. 'I thought this would be right up your street, Mum. Did I choose right?'

'You chose wonderfully,' I say. 'And look, there's a whole section on Artemisia Gentileschi!'

I revere her art and admire her as a woman. Imagine being

tortured with thumbscrews to show she was telling the truth about the man who raped her! And then she went on to out-paint all the men of her century and beyond. The summer before art school I Interrailed to Italy and gloried in the Artemisia paintings in Florence and Rome.

'She's your favourite, isn't she, Mum,' says Lottie, putting her arm round me and peering at the book too.

'Absolutely!' I say. Or possibly 'Absherlootly!' It's not an easy word to say when you've had too much champagne. 'In fact, I very nearly called *you* Artemisia.'

'Thank God you didn't, Mum! The kids at school would have made my life a misery.'

'I was thinking of calling you Frida too, because I've always loved her paintings,' I say, so enjoying wandering down Memory Lane with my girl.

'People might have thought you were calling her after Aunty Freda!' says Ben, screwing up his face.

'Frida Kahlo wouldn't have been a good namesake for me, though, as I'd have to pluck like fuck to stop developing a monobrow,' Lottie jokes.

'Lottie!' Anna remonstrates fondly.

'I think you should have called her Nadine,' says Nadine, drinking out of a bottle because she can't find her champagne glass.

'No, no, no. *Magda!*' says Magda. She's holding her tummy, her eyes dreamy, obviously pondering names for her own baby, male or female.

'So how come you ended up calling me Lottie?' she asks. 'Are there any famous women artists called Charlotte?'

'Oh, it was a book I liked when I was young. It was about a girl who wrote a Victorian project on a little maid called Lottie. I've still got that book in a trunk somewhere at home, if you're interested.'

Lottie makes the vague *mm* noise she uses when she doesn't want to be too cutting in her refusal. Magda gives a great yawn, stretching like a cat. I look at my watch.

'Don't you and Nadine have to head home soon?' I ask.

'No,' she says sleepily.

'That's your final surprise,' explains Nadine. 'We're staying here for the night.'

'Brilliant!' I cry. 'We'll have a sleepover like we did in the old days.'

Anna wakes Dad, and I have the grace to thank him for the party *and* the cheque – though I've already resolved never to use it. Dad gives me a hug, swaying alarmingly, and stumbles to their bedroom, Anna steering him. Ben and Simon go to Ben's old room, Lottie insists on curling up on the living room sofa with a spare pillow and duvet, and Nadine, Magda and I squeeze into my old bedroom.

It's always so weird coming back to it. Anna has kept it totally unchanged so that I can feel instantly at home here. It's like travelling back to the past. It's deep purple – I thought this a highly sophisticated colour choice when I was a teen-ager. Anna's even kept the same posters on the wall: Frida Kahlo herself with her pet monkey, Van Gogh's *Sunflowers*, Leonardo DiCaprio and Clare Danes in the movie of *Romeo and Juliet*, and Maurice Sendak's *Wild Things*. There's also a drawing of my own Wild Things, and various photobooth snaps of Nadine, Magda and me clowning around and stick-ing out our tongues.

We're clowning around now, flipping through rumpled copies of *Sugar* and *Just Seventeen*, and discovering Spice Girls cas-settes and remnants of Rimmel make-up in drawers, as well as an old bottle of Aqua Manda that still smells slightly orangey.

I've always had the luxury of a double bed, so it's just about possible for the three of us to squeeze in together. Nadine wears a black satin slip and looks like Morticia Addams. Magda is in a girly white broderie anglaise nightie that hides her little bump, though the low neck shows off her impressive new cleavage. They tease me when they see I still wear the same kind of stripy pyjamas I used to wear as a teenager.

Magda gets to lie in the middle, because we can't have her falling out of bed when she's pregnant. Nadine stretches out one side of her and I huddle at the other edge.

'This is the time when we used to talk about boys, remember?' says Nadine.

'Yeah, remember when Ellie told us all sorts of stuff about her boyfriend Dan and then it turned out he was just some goofy kid she met on holiday,' says Magda, ruffling my hair. 'You were such a good liar, Ellie.'

'Well, I wanted to keep up with you two. Shall I invent a new boyfriend for myself now?' I ask. 'Not that I want one.'

'Honestly?'

'Truly,' I say. I'm sure I mean it. Scrub that birthday wish. That was just a moment of madness.

'I think you've just never met the right man. You too, Nadine,' says Magda.

'What? I think she meets way too many men already,' I say, reaching out over Magda and holding Nadine's hand.

'*Girls just wanna have fun!*' Nadine sings, channelling her inner Cyndi Lauper.

'That used to be my motto,' says Magda, 'but the moment I met Chris I just knew he was The One.'

We're kind enough not to remind her that she said the same about husbands one and two, and multiple boyfriends as well.

'You were a total shocker once, Mags.' I laugh. 'Remember when you stalked Mr Windsor? You actually turned up at his flat!'

'Good God, so I did. And I was disappointed when he

79

behaved like a perfect gentleman!' says Magda, unabashed. 'Oh well. I've changed considerably since then.'

'We all have,' I say – and yet here we are, gossiping like those giggly girls of long ago, though we're getting very drowsy now. I'm nearly asleep when Magda clutches her tummy, her whole body suddenly tense.

'Magda? What is it?' I ask.

Nadine gasps. 'Is it the baby?'

'It *is* the baby – but it's all right, it's wonderful, feel! Put your hands on my tummy!' Magda lies flat on her back and Nadine and I put our hands out tentatively on her little bulge. Nothing happens – but then suddenly her tummy moves in the weirdest of ways.

'Can you feel it? It's the baby, moving!' Magda says. 'It is, isn't it, Ellie? You're the mum. Does it feel like this?'

'It does! It's kicking its tiny feet!' I say. My own tummy clenches, remembering the unborn Lottie tumbling about inside me. It felt so incredible that she was a real little person and that I'd actually made her. 'Do you know what you're having yet, Magda?'

'I'm going for a scan next week. Chris is coming with me. We don't really mind what sex we're having, we just want to know it's all right,' says Magda. 'And you *are* all right, aren't you, little darling?' she whispers down towards her tummy.

'Yes, Mum,' Nadine and I say in unison, and then dissolve into drunken giggles.

'Sorry, sorry,' I say. 'We'll take the greatest care not to get drunk in front of him/her when they're out in the world.'

'We'll be the most lovely token aunties,' says Nadine.

'We will, we will, we will,' I say, so happy to be with my two best friends, knowing that my daughter is just twenty steps away in the living room, my brother and his husband next door, and Dad and Anna along the corridor. I wonder if the shade of my mum is somewhere too, hovering over me, wishing me a happy birthday. She's touching her lips with her fingers and blowing me a kiss, the way she always did when she put me to bed.

'I love you, Mum,' I mutter, slightly slurring the words, and the girls seem to understand, their hands finding their way to mine in the darkness and squeezing tight.

'Night, Magda. Night, Nadine. Thanks so much for making my birthday so special,' I whisper. Then I fall instantly asleep.

I wake with a splitting headache and a sawdust throat, but a hangover doesn't stop me smiling at the new middle-aged me in my childish pyjamas reflected in the mirror. I even start singing in the bathroom, though I'm feeling too delicate at breakfast to manage more than a glass of orange juice and a slice of buttered toast. We all squeeze together round the kitchen island. Magda looks fresh as a daisy, but the rest of us are pale and hollow-eyed. Dad hasn't even managed to get up yet, though Anna is bustling around in a crisp white shirt and jeans, making a fuss of us.

I want to stay here, but I need to get home to make sure Stella's all right. She'll have words to say about being left on her own.

'I have to get back to Chris's house to make sure he's coping OK,' Magda fusses too.

'And I have to go back to my vampiric coffin to sleep the rest of this bright day away,' Nadine mutters through her curtains of black hair.

'I guess Si and I had better get back to relieve our neighbours from dog-sitting duties,' says Ben. They have two dachshunds called Hockney and Freud, the most spoilt dogs in Britain.

'Well, I don't have to go anywhere just yet, so I'll go back to yours, Mum,' says Lottie. 'And you'll need help carting back all your presents.'

It turns out there's too much for both of us to manage, so I just take the family presents, the art book and one bottle of champagne, because Lottie and I are both feeling weak and sickly.

As we say goodbye to everyone, Dad gets up to wave us off. He looks particularly under the weather, his face grey-white and sweaty.

'Grandad, you look so ill!' says Lottie.

'I *am* ill,' Dad says dramatically. 'In fact, I'm bloody dying!'

'Stop that!' says Anna. 'The only reason you feel like death is because you drank far too much last night. You can't take it at your age.' She's joking, but she looks concerned.

'I can't do anything at my age, apparently. I might as well be dead already,' Dad mutters.

We kiss him goodbye and leave him slumped in a chair in his dressing gown. Anna comes to the door with us.

I look at her. 'Shall we stay a bit?'

'No, he'll be fine. I'm going to put him back to bed with a massive glass of water and he'll feel much better when he wakes up.'

'He just seems so wretched,' I say.

'He's depressed. He hates being old. Well, he's not *that* old, but he feels it. He doesn't know what to do with himself now he's retired. I've tried to get him involved in my firm, asking him to do some designs, but he's scathing about, quote, "woolly jumpers for nitwits".'

I tut. Why does Dad have to be nasty to Anna, when she's so good to him?

'Doesn't he paint any more?' Lottie asks.

'He does – but they're very bleak, dark paintings, kind of sub-Francis Bacon,' says Anna. 'I suppose it's a way of expressing himself.' She sighs.

'It can't be much fun for you,' I say, giving her a hug.

'It's the downside of marrying an exciting older man,' Anna says. 'They end up much less exciting and so much older. Oh dear, I shouldn't have said that. And it's silly – he was the life and soul of the party last night, having a great time. Stop looking so anxious, girls. I'm just a bit hungover too.'

We trek to the station, feeling downcast.

'Don't you dare get old and ill, Mum,' says Lottie. 'I've only got one parent so I need you to stay spry and bouncy well into your nineties, OK?'

'I'll do my best,' I promise.

I wait until we're on the train, and then I say, 'Lottie, about this one parent thing. I mean, obviously, you *have* got a father. Maybe it's time you made contact with him?'

'Oh, not this *again*. People were whispering about it at the party last night, weren't they?' She pauses. 'Was he *at* the party?'

'No, of course not!'

'I'm not so sure.' She looks at me sideways. 'Please tell me he's not Nigel!'

'Stop it, you bad girl. You're just teasing me, aren't you?'

'Sort of. Though I did have a good peer at all your art school buddies. I wouldn't mind if it's one of them. I especially liked Jacob. I'd quite like it to be him,' she says. I look at her, not sure whether she's teasing or not now.

'I'd like it to be Jacob, too, but he's got a husband who works in a museum,' I say.

'Well, all the better. I love having two uncles. Two dads would be a spectacular bonus,' says Lottie.

'Lottie, I swear to you, your father was not at the party. Oh God, I should have told you all about him ages ago, right from when you asked why you didn't have a daddy when you were little. Remember, I fobbed you off by saying something vague about him having gone away, and you just seemed happy to

83

accept it. Though you did start asking if he'd gone to Australia once, remember?'

'Oh, that was because someone's father at school was in Australia and she went to visit him every year and came back with a really cute koala bear toy every time,' Lottie says cheerfully. 'I wanted one too – but I wasn't bothered about a father.'

'Not even when you were older?'

'I assumed he was probably just a quick fling and you were too embarrassed to tell me.' She shrugs.

'Well, you're absolutely right! And of course I'm embarrassed. In actual fact, I barely knew him. I was drunk at a party. I'm so sorry, Lottie,' I say. 'I feel so ashamed.'

'Don't be so daft, Mum.' She pats my hand reassuringly. 'It happens.'

'Not to you, I hope!'

'Not to me, promise,' says Lottie.

'However, if you want to get to know him then I'll help you all I can,' I say earnestly.

'No, thanks. Mum – was it your first time?'

My cheeks heat up. We're on a crowded train and Lottie has a loud voice.

'Shall we talk about this later?' I suggest pointedly.

We get to Waterloo, negotiate the tube, and then start walking to the flat.

'Is this later?' Lottie asks.

'I suppose,' I say grudgingly.

'So, tell me all about the torrid night of my conception.' She grins wickedly.

I grimace. 'It feels so weird talking about it. I'd much sooner not.'

'Look, I've heard you nattering away about all sorts to Nadine and Magda.'

'Yes, but they're my best friends, not my daughter!'

'I'll tell you about my first time if you'll tell about yours,' Lottie bargains.

'Oh Lottie, you *are* taking precautions if you're having sex, aren't you?'

'Yes! Though I'm not sure I could possibly have got pregnant anyway, because it was all over before it had barely begun,' says Lottie.

'Oh dear. Well, it can be like that at first,' I say. 'Not much fun for you, though.'

'I didn't really mind. We had a bit of a laugh about it and then phoned for a Deliveroo,' Lottie says brightly. 'So, come on, Mum. Tell me about your first time.'

'It wasn't with your father. It was with . . . Russell,' I admit reluctantly.

'*What?* That total berk in the gleaming white teeshirt? With the wife?'

'I started going out with him when we were both at school. I was really nuts about him at first,' I say, though it doesn't seem real any more. 'We went out together for ages. But then he went to Manchester and I went to Saint Martins and we grew apart.'

'Thank goodness! I can't imagine you two together! So what was the sex like?' Lottie asks directly.

I'm glad I brought her up to be a modern young woman with no inhibitions, but I'm an old-fashioned middle-aged woman now and I don't want to talk about my sex life with my own child.

'It was OK,' I say. It was actually more than OK for a while, because Russell carefully studied a book about sexual technique. He knew what he was doing and made sure it was good for me, and yet I got the feeling he was murmuring his way through the paragraphs of the manual, diligently applying vigorous attention to this bit and then that, rather than being carried away by grand passion.

'So was my father at art school with you, then?'

'Yes, but I didn't really know him that well. I went round with a different crowd. I was involved with this guy called Mick. *Not* your father. He was the exact opposite of Russell. Great looking in a dissolute sort of way. Wild. Untrustworthy. Talented. Total cliché. And I fell for him,' I say.

'Ah!' says Lottie. 'That hasn't happened to me yet.'

'Well, don't let it. Avoid the Micks of this world like the plague. Anyway, it didn't last. And then – then I went to this party and—'

'Met my father,' Lottie finishes for me. 'So did your eyes meet across a crowded room?'

'Something like that,' I mumble, because I can't bear to tell her how sad and sordid the whole encounter was.

Thank goodness we've reached the Artists' Estate now. We live right at the top of Constable. The bleak seventies concrete doesn't look remotely like Salisbury Cathedral, though, and there are no haywains in the grounds – just an abandoned car without wheels, a broken pushchair and a stolen Boris bike.

But it's home, even so, and thankfully the lift is working, and when we get out on the fourteenth floor my neighbour Andreea is coming out of her door with a knapsack on her back and a carton of milk in her hand.

'Ah, Ellie. I am away for a week. You want this milk for your cat?' she asks.

'Oh, that's so sweet of you,' I say, deciding not to mention that actually you should never give cats cow's milk. 'I hope Stella hasn't been yowling too much. She's probably been feeling lonely.'

'I yowl when I get lonely,' says Andreea, handing me the carton.

'Actually, me too,' I say.

When Lottie and I are indoors and I am down on my knees, trying to tempt my way back into Stella's favour by bribing her with Dreamies, Lottie sorts through the considerable pile of post by the door.

'Do you, Mum?' she asks.

'What, yowl?'

'No. Get lonely.'

'Of course not.' I gesture at the post, some obviously birthday cards. 'Look at all the friends I've got.'

'Really? I mean apart from Nadine and Magda?'

'Yes!' I say, stung. 'Actually I made a new friend only yesterday. Alice. I met her at swimming.'

'Yes, but heaps of people chat when you go swimming,' says Lottie.

'They don't go to breakfast with me afterwards and hold my hand when I'm getting a tattoo,' I say.

'Really? Well, that was nice of her. Though if you'd only have told me, *I'd* have loved to go with you to a tattoo studio. I could have got one too!' says Lottie. 'Can I have a proper look at yours?'

I'm still not sure I should take the bandage off, but it looks pretty healthy when I peep, no bleeding or swelling, so I gingerly peel it off.

'Oh, Myrtle! She looks so cool. I'm so proud of you, Mum, for working for the *Guardian*,' Lottie says.

I must be pulling an agonized face.

'What?' Lottie asks.

'I'm not going to be drawing her any more,' I admit. 'They've got sick of her.'

'Seriously? Stupid bastards! They must be mad.'

'Thanks, lovely. I'm OK about it, I promise.'

Stella glares at me, so I give her a couple of Dreamies and she gives me a very small lick of forgiveness.

'I wonder what the ingredient is that makes cats so dotty about them?' I muse, keen to change the subject.

'Maybe we should try one,' Lottie says, sifting through the post. 'I don't think I'm ever going to touch alcohol again. Bubble tea for me in future.'

'Any interesting cards?' I ask. I rather hope there's one from Alice – until I realize she doesn't know my address. I suppose I've been overstating our so-called friendship. Still, it would be fantastic if she could help me find out about elephants.

'Do you fancy a trip to London Zoo to see the elephants, Lots?' I ask – but when I google I find out they don't keep elephants there any more. Which is good, because elephants need to be able to roam wherever they want, not to be contained for crowds to gawp at.

'So where shall we go then?' I google again. 'Aha! Spitalfields.'

'Oh great, I love that market,' says Lottie.

'Apparently, there are now twenty-one life-size bronze elephants there,' I say happily.

'So you're really into elephants now, Mum?' Lottie wonders, amused.

Shall I tell her? But what if she thinks it a totally mad idea? She'd probably bluff and be enthusiastic – but I'll know she's just being kind. And even if she thinks it's a really great idea it's maybe like tempting fate. I want to hug the idea to myself for a while. I didn't even tell Nicola.

'I've just got interested in them, that's all,' I say.

'Well, I like elephants too. Maybe it's because of Nellie. OK, Spitalfields it is.'

We have great fun finding all the elephants and I do a few sketches. Someone peers over my shoulder and offers me a tenner if I sell it to them. Lottie snorts with laughter. I'm flattered, but decline. I want to keep it for myself. Then we walk round the market. I buy Lottie a little vintage dress and she insists on buying me a small ebony elephant from a junk stall. We have a bowl of pasta each and freshly squeezed orange juice, and realize we haven't got hangovers any more.

We wander with linked arms, slowly making our way home. Horribly soon we have to go out again for Lottie to catch her train back to this camp of hers. I can feel my stomach churning already. I hate the time when we've had our hugs and she's on the train looking out the window and I'm on the platform looking back at her, and the train stays stationary so that we're looking and looking and looking. Even though I love Lottie with all my heart it's hard to stare intently at anyone like that, so she starts goofing around and I pretend I'm peering round at something until at last the train starts up and then we wave wildly – and she's gone.

I trudge back home and now one of my boots is rubbing the front of my foot and my back's started twinging and my headache's returned. There's a gang of teenagers hanging out at the kids' playground, laughing and vaping and scrolling on their phones. I know most of them because I've taught them at school and they yell out friendly banter – *Have you been out on a hot date, Miss?* – and they all explode with laughter because it seems such a bizarre idea to them, a forty-year-old woman having any kind of love life. Maybe it is, I think gloomily.

But I banter back, making out I've just got back from an amazing weekend with Harry Styles, and this makes them laugh even more. It's fond laughter; they're basically good kids, just a bit lippy.

'You like them young, Miss? Fancy me, do you?' the oldest says, puffing himself up.

Careful now, I tell myself. *It's getting too much. Shut it down.*

'In your dreams,' I say lightly, and walk off to the lift as casually as I can.

The lift seems to have got stuck now – some randy kids

jamming it deliberately so they can have quick loveless sex? –
and so I stomp up fourteen flights of steps, and fall into my flat,
gasping, and flop on the sofa. Stella yowls at me indignantly.

'Don't give me grief, Stella, please,' I beg her.

She jumps on my chest, which doesn't help my breathing
but is soothing all the same. The flat feels very silent now. I lie
stroking her, missing Lottie. No, come on, stop the self-pity,
I've had a great weekend, everyone's made such a fuss of me,
I'm *fine*.

I gently ease Stella off me, feed her, ponder opening the champagne and decide on a sensible coffee instead. My thoughts
roam to my elephants. I shut my eyes and see them trudging
along, a long line of them. Then I try picturing the leading elephant close up.

A familiar feeling settles over me like a comfort blanket: the
irresistible urge to draw. I select one of the virgin sketch books.
I sit at my desk, pencil in hand, and start. It's Nellie, not as she
used to be, a cutsie-pie cartoon. A real Nellie, her skin loose
on her huge bones, her face wrinkled and wizened, her eyes
tiny, as if a small creature is peering out of her vast head. Her
trunk is reaching out curiously. I find I'm swaying from side to
side as I draw her, imagining what it would feel like to be this
glorious creature, the queen of a matriarchal tribe.

I hesitate every so often, not sure how long her trunk should
be or what her feet are really like. Do elephants have toenails?
I've got so much to check and learn, but she's becoming real
for me, my Nellie. Although Nellie is starting to sound wrong,
now she's a life-like elephant. I'll have to find the right name
for her, and for all the others in her tribe. Her daughters, her
sisters, her cousins. There will be infant males, lively little boys,
but no joshing adolescents. Male elephants go off adventuring when the hormones kick in. Maybe elephants have got life
worked out better than us.

I break off for a quick snack supper – raw carrots, a wodge of cheese, an apple, another slice of birthday cake and a Diet Coke (though I look long and hard at the bottle of champagne) – and then I carry on sketching, experimenting with a night-time scene now. How do elephants sleep? Do they manage it standing up or do they sink to their knees and lie down on the dusty plain? Do they huddle together in a circle, little ones protected? Do the mothers stroke the babies with their trunks?

I know who could answer all my questions. I could message her right this minute. I flex my fingers, pick up my phone, trying to compose a casual short message inside my head, but for some reason I can't get the tone right, either too formal or too familiar. I put the phone down, pick up my pen again. It's Sunday, she'll be with her girlfriend – she won't want me badgering her. Tomorrow.

7

When I get back from school on Monday, I decide to tackle my thank-you letters before doing anything else. Well, thank-you texts, though I don't just compose one to send to everyone. I add little details, commenting on the presents, adding personal notes here and there. Plus there are a few that need proper cards, like Aunty Freda, along with a note to Nigel. Ben and Simon get a very special card, and I order a huge bunch of flowers for them. I order more flowers for Dad and Anna too, and take a deep breath before writing in their card how very grateful I am for the cheque. Maybe I'll bank it after all, keeping the money to help Lottie in the future.

I'm exhausted by the time I've got in touch with everyone. I stretch wide-armed, wanting to take a break. It would only take a couple of minutes to write a quick message to Alice too. I draft one, but it still doesn't feel right, and I delete it. I'll have another go tomorrow. I browse elephants on the internet for a while but it's all very general information. I'm sure Alice could tell me all kinds of unusual details. She won't mind. Yet I feel somehow weird about it. I can't quite work out why. She was the one who gave me her details, after all. We got on so well. I'd really like her as a friend.

My thoughts drift to her girlfriend. What's she like? Wendy. It's such a soft, sweet name. I can't help thinking of the Wendy in

Peter Pan. J. M. Barrie made up the name because some lisping little girl said she wanted to be his 'Fwendy'. Could Alice's Wendy be soft and sweet and a bit sickly, turning their flat (presumably they live together?) into their own cosy Wendy House, all plump cushions and pretty ornaments and slightly twee pictures?

No, it seems highly unlikely that someone as cool as Alice would be attracted to that sort of woman. Perhaps Wendy is another academic? An actress? A lawyer? I wonder how long they've been together. Alice must be pretty sure it's true love to risk a permanent tattoo with her name on it.

Why on earth does it matter anyway? I do a couple of neck-rolls to ease the tension across my shoulders and then look down at my newly revealed tattoo. Myrtle looks incredible, so bright, so perky, skinny arm raised, fist clenched.

'Good for you, little Myrtle,' I mutter, and I blow her a kiss. I'm not going to replace her with any old cartoon strip. She's my one and only, and always will be. But I'll still give the graphic novel a go. I'm not going to care if it never gets published. I'm going to do it anyway.

I go back through my initial sketches. The matriarch looks back at me. I google Swahili female names. I like Mosi, and it means first born. It used to be reserved for boys, but now it can be used for both sexes. And little toy Nellie *is* my first born.

I go to Lottie's room – something I generally avoid because it makes me miss her too much. It's heartbreakingly neat. Nellie's sitting on a shelf, next to a battered copy of *Babar*. She's very worn now, her blue faded to the exact shade of Farrow & Ball Elephant's Breath. Her trunk dangles, and her legs sag so she can no longer stand up – she's morphed into the original Nellie now, given to me by my own mum. I kiss Nellie on her limp trunk and then prop her back on Lottie's shelf to doze away her retirement days. I don't send a message to Alice, though I compose three or four more in my head.

I search online for books about elephants and purchase several. I do a few more sketches but none are quite right.

I can't seem to settle to anything the next few days, when I'm so used to thinking up new Myrtle ideas every week. I'm not even that busy at school, because all the GCSEs and A-levels are over, and I can ease up and get away with doing art projects that aren't even on the curriculum.

I ask some of the older years what they'd like to paint or draw or model, and one bright spark immediately responds with 'Nudes, Miss! Preferably with a real model!' Could he be one of the lads who were joshing me on Sunday evening? There are so many boys with the same sort of arrogant charm, with their cocky little grins and their swagger.

Thank goodness they daren't go too far in a school setting. I warn them off nudes – not that I really object, but I think the Head might have reservations. I suggest they might care to illustrate some favourite book or film – or better still, come up with their own ideas.

They do some good painting, as I hoped, but most of them conform to stereotype: the boys paint violent war or crime, using up pots of scarlet paint, while the girls paint fantasy ladies with slender figures and ultra-long hair, swooning in the arms of rugged men with jutting chins and swollen biceps. I'm amused to find one boy painting butch leather men who make Tom of Finland look girly (he must have been indulging in some very old-fashioned porn) and a girl depicting a herd of unicorns in what's clearly their rutting season. Who knows what *she's* been reading recently.

Still, it keeps them quiet and gives me a chance to do more elephant sketching. I try to do it discreetly, but someone sees, and then they all cluster round. They're surprisingly enthusiastic, along the lines of 'Bloody hell, Miss, you're a genius!', which is embarrassing but quite pleasing.

The more I draw and think about elephants, the more questions I have about them. How long does it take for a female to give birth? Do the others gather round, giving encouragement? How soon can a baby stand up? When do the females stop giving their calves milk? Do they actively protect them from danger? Is there always a close bond between relatives?

Message Alice, you fool! I tell myself, but I don't. I decide to wait until Saturday, when I can see her in person. On Friday night I set my alarm early so that I can bump into her casually at swimming.

I get to the pool extra early and then hang around the communal dressing room for ages without seeing her. I check the pool in case she's somehow snuck past me, but there's no brown girl in a white costume flashing up and down. I sigh, feeling ridiculously disappointed. I have my own swim, craning my neck every now and then to see if I spot her in another lane, but she's definitely not there. She said she came regularly to the early Saturday session, but perhaps she's avoiding me for some reason? No, of course she's not – why am I always so paranoid? What's the matter with me? There are a hundred and one reasons why she might not be here.

I go to the café afterwards and have an almond croissant, but Alice isn't here either.

'Have you seen Alice around?' I ask Rosa.

She just shrugs and shakes her head.

I wander up and down the road afterwards, looking into all the cafés and restaurants, peering through the windows of the nail bars and betting shops and mini-marts, and then get on a bus to the proper shops. On the off-chance I look for books about elephants in WHSmith, then walk all the way to Waterstones, but have no luck there either.

I carry on mooching about pointlessly, do some food shopping in Marks for a treat, including six cans of beer so I won't be tempted to drink the champagne, and then I clank them all the way home.

It's lunchtime by the time I get back to Constable block. My hair has dried frizzier than ever and my swimming things are a sodden ball in my tote bag. The lift is working again, thank God, though it creaks and jerks once or twice, making my heart beat fast. I've never heard of anyone plummeting to their death on our estate, and I've only been stuck in the lift once all the time I've lived here. It happened when Lottie was little so I had to pretend not to be scared to reassure her, and it ended up as a bit of an adventure being winched out. Not one I ever want to repeat, though. Perhaps I really will spend that cheque as a whacking great deposit on a private flat, preferably ground floor . . .

Still, I'd hate to give up the fantastic view over thousands of London rooftops, with iconic silhouettes way in the distance. I peer at it as I walk along the balcony – and then I'm brought up short on my own doorstep, where a bunch of flowers is lying in wait for me.

I bend down and pick them up. Red roses. Not an elaborate florist's bouquet, artfully arranged with baby breath and tied with a matching ribbon. These are just ordinary fresh garden roses fastened together with a paper towel and an elastic band.

When I get indoors, I lay them carefully on the kitchen table. I check for any kind of note, wondering if it's been tucked inside the paper towel. Nothing there. Curiouser and curiouser. I put water in a pottery vase Lottie once made me at school and arrange the roses carefully. They smell beautiful, just the way they should. Could they be a belated birthday present from Andreea? No, she said she was going away. Besides, we're friendly enough, but not really on flower-giving terms – well, not red roses, anyway. They're not just any old flowers. They signify love and passion . . .

I rack my brains. I'm reasonably matey with Jason, the smiley guy on the other side of my flat, who I highly suspect is a dealer from all the comings and goings there. He's nice, though, and we get on, but judging by the girls I sometimes see him with, I'm definitely not his type. So who on earth could it be? I think of those young lads from the estate teasing me. Is it their way of saying sorry? They don't have gardens, but they could easily have nicked them from someone else's. No, I've taught these boys, I know them well. They can be surprisingly sweet to me at times, but they're never sentimental.

Could it be someone playing a joke on me? That would be so mean, though. Why would anyone want me to think someone's secretly in love with me? It all feels a bit creepy somehow. I give a little shiver and wrap my arms round myself. This is daft. Does it really matter where they came from? Perhaps they've simply been left outside the wrong door.

It occurs to me to check my phone to see if there's an explanatory message. There are quite a few texts and emails replying to my thank-yous. I scratch my head, exhausted at the thought of all the responses now required, me thanking them, them thanking me in an endless circle. Then an email from Mrs Henderson wipes all thoughts of the roses from my mind.

Hi Ellie

I was so happy to meet up with you and Nadine and Magda! I'm glad you're doing so well. I emailed Guy to tell him all about your fabulous party. As I said, he's thrilled that you're such a success. I'm attaching his email address in case you want to make his day and tell him it's all due to his incredibly inspirational teaching!

Jean x

A kiss from Mrs Henderson of all people! I read her message twice, trying to take it all in, though it's simple enough. Mr Windsor's thrilled that I'm a success. Guy? Wait till I tell Nadine and Magda.

So now I've got two challenging communications to deal with. I concentrate on writing to Mr Windsor first. I fiddle with my hair, murmuring little phrases, wondering what on earth to say. Am I writing to him as if he's still my teacher, or as one adult to another? I briefly contemplate asking Nadine and Magda for their advice but decide against it. I'm a grown woman – I should be able to write an email, for heaven's sake.

> Hi Mr Windsor (I can't make myself type Guy)
> I hope you're well. Jean says you've been saying sweet things about my Myrtle Mouse cartoons. It's so kind of you. Thank you for all those inspirational art lessons. You were always so lovely to me, Nadine and Magda. We all remember you fondly.

Now what? I can't say *Love, Ellie*. *Best wishes* is a bit boring. I hate abbreviating it to *Best. Warmest wishes?* Meh, a bit formal. *Ellie* with a kiss? It's somehow OK for Jean and me to send kisses, but it's a bit odd typing kisses to the teacher who was once young and hot and fancied by half our class. I end it simply with my name and send it before I get cold feet.

Now Alice. Time to stop dithering. I pick up my phone and open WhatsApp.

> Hi, it's me – Myrtle Mouse girl!

Oh, for God's sake. I'm forty fucking years old, hardly a girl. I highlight it all and press 'delete'.

Hi, thanks again for being so supportive when I got my Myrtle Mouse tattoo. No regrets whatsoever, I love it. Anyway, I wondered if you could possibly help me with some information about elephants? I'm really keen to learn more about them for a special project, as there's so much I don't know. I can pay you for your time – and/or treat you to multiple almond croissants. Let me know! x

I realize I've added a kiss instinctively, but that's just what girls do, isn't it? *Women!* I send it before I can change my mind. Then I make myself a coffee and start drawing a whole line of elephants, with Mosi at the front. Elephants have it so right. When the females get older they are valued for their wisdom and experience. And by her side there's another full-grown elephant, but smaller, somehow perkier, swaying from side to side as if she's about to start dancing.

I look up Swahili girls' names again. Binti! It means daughter. My Mosi will have other daughters, sons too, but Binti will be *her* first born, and forever the most special. She will have a son next, a naughty little calf who will take a lot of looking after, but Binti will help her mother, guarding him when he's tiny, nudging him with her trunk when he is being mischievous, scooping him out of the lake when he's splashing too wildly.

I go to my computer again to look up Swahili boys' names this time, but pause when I hear my phone ping. Alice, replying already? There's no need for my heart to be beating a bit faster. It will just be some newsflash or an arts supply advert or a Waterstones book of the month notification. I reach for my phone.

It's not Alice. It's an email from Mr Windsor!

Hi Ellie
It's great you got in touch. How are you? Well, I know how you are – ultra successful and looking great, according to Jean.

I don't suppose you remember, but I once banged on about Paula Rego in your art lessons. There's an exhibition of her work in a Mayfair gallery (see attachment). I expect you're tied up but I'm planning to see it this afternoon, 3 ish. How about coming along too?

Guy Windsor

Oh my God! I seize Stella and lift her up so we're face to face. 'Mr Windsor wants to meet me this afternoon!' I tell her.

She doesn't seem at all impressed. I put her down, give her a bowl of her proper food. Shall I ring Nadine and Magda? No time! I'd better get cracking!

Am I really going to go? If so, what am I going to wear? Should I dress up? I don't look too bad for once. I look down at my big black silky shirt, blue jeans matching my bracelet from Lottie, and silver sneakers. I run my fingers through my hair despairingly but I can't fuss with it now.

I slap a little make-up on, trying hard not to smudge my eyeliner. Stella jumps up onto my dressing table and stares at me as though to say, *Seriously?*

'Come on, Stella. I don't look too bad, do I?' I ask.

She gives me one more long look and then jumps down onto the rug. She delicately scratches at it, though I've told her a hundred times that it's Persian and cost a fortune, and then stalks off. She is not a sisterly cat.

I touch the photo of Lottie on the dressing table, wishing she were here to give me a bit of moral support. But I'd feel a fool getting in such an obvious state if she were. She'd probably laugh at me – but in a fond way.

Then I realize I haven't replied to his email yet. I'm about to mention that I've already been, but hesitate. If I do that, won't it sound like I'm going along just to see him, not the art? Which might make me look a bit too keen? So instead I just tap *Great idea! I'll be there. E.* and send it to Mr Windsor – Guy, Guy, Guy. Get used to it.

As I leave the flat, I check the notifications. Still no reply from Alice.

The older lads have disappeared, but some little kids are squatting in a corner stabbing at the patchy grass with sticks doing 'gardening'. Three teenage girls perch on the swings, in earnest conversation. How come they can all do their eyeliner perfectly? They suddenly shriek with laughter, hands going up to their mouths. Oh, I remember that helpless giggling! I smile, thinking about how Nadine and Magda and I would crease up laughing, sometimes in class. Often in Mr Windsor's class.

No matter how nonchalant I try to be, it does seem seriously weird to be seeing him. I catch a glimpse of myself in a shop window and wonder what thirteen-year-old Ellie, Magda and Nadine would make of it all now.

I try to lose myself in *Mrs Dalloway* on the tube but it's not the easiest of reads and I end up scrolling through my phone, just like everyone else.

I exit at Piccadilly Circus and walk briskly up a side road. Not *too* briskly, because I don't want to arrive damp and sweaty. Will we shake hands formally? Embrace? A father/daughter awkward hug?

Oh God, will he actually look like Dad now, with a balding patch and a belly and clothes that are trying too hard to look cool? And what is he going to think when he spots me? He knows I'm small and dumpy, but maybe he's fantasizing that the ugly Ellie duckling has somehow grown three inches, shed three stone and turned into a sophisticated swan?

As I near the gallery, I see someone standing outside. It's him, definitely him – Mr Windsor, Guy, whatever! And thank you God, he's hardly changed a bit! In fact, he's better looking, now he's older. Still slim, Paul Smith shirt and tight jeans showing off his flat stomach, and he's got every lock of his dark blond hair. He looks up, sees me. And smiles.

8

'Hey, Ellie,' he says, as if we only just met last week.

'Hey – hm! What should I call you?' Stupid, stupid! I want to look so cool, so casual – and here I am, gibbering like an idiot.

'Guy! You're not seriously going to call me Mr Windsor?' he says.

I'd forgotten the way he smiles. It's a slow smile, and he's looking straight at me. I'd forgotten he's got lovely eyes too. Jesus, I'm sounding like a romantic novel. Is *this* going to be a romance? Stop it, you idiot, calm down!

I manage to smile back at him. 'Well, it would be a bit odd – but then this *is* odd, isn't it?'

'Does it feel odd?'

I shake my head, but then add 'Sort of.'

'It's not as if you're still a schoolgirl!' he says quickly.

'Hardly.'

'On which subject, happy birthday for last week. So, why did you invite Jean and not me?'

'I didn't do any of the inviting – it was a surprise party,' I explain. 'It was Ben, my brother. His husband knows her from badminton. My daughter Lottie nicked my phone for a couple of hours and got all my contacts – a very random bunch. But you weren't on there.'

'Though you knew where I lived once. Well, Magda did,' he says, raising his eyebrows. 'Did she tell you she came round to my old flat long ago?'

I grin at him. 'Yes, she did. I don't know how she dared.'

'She was a very forward girl, your pal. And Nadine too, come to that. Jean was fascinated to see you're all still great friends,' he says.

'Of course we are!'

'Though you've gone down very different paths,' says Guy. 'But all still single?'

'Magda's been married twice, and now she's head over heels in love with this divorced guy, Chris. He's got two children, who sound a handful. Still, Magda's going to have her own baby now and we're so happy for her. She's been longing for children for ages.'

We're still standing outside the gallery, but he shows no sign of wanting to go in. 'Have you got any children, Guy?' I ask.

'No, sadly not. As yet,' he says.

'And you broke up with the beautiful model?'

'Yes, that didn't last. And from what Jean told me, your big romance with Russell didn't last either?' he says.

'No, it didn't,' I say. I raise my eyebrows too. 'Thank God!'

'And you've got a lovely daughter?'

'My Lottie. She really is lovely. But definitely not Russell's.'

'Are you still in touch with her father?'

'Nope. Very happy not to be,' I say.

'Well, it must have been hard for you, Ellie, being a single mum so young. Good for you, though,' he says.

We pause. Shall I tell him more about Lottie and me? No, it's not the time or place for life histories. The pause is lasting too long. I open my mouth but can't quite think what to say next.

'And Nadine?' he enquires. 'Jean says she's still very striking.'

'She is indeed. She's had various interesting boyfriends of

course, but she's just enjoying her freedom and concentrating on having a good time at the moment,' I say. No need to go into details!

'That's great,' says Guy. He pauses again. 'And you're having a good time, too, Ellie?'

I blush. 'Mm. Not quite as exotically. I just hunker down at home most of the time and work.'

'And create fantastic cartoons on a weekly basis. They're brilliant, Ellie!' he says. It sounds as if he really means it. I wither at the thought of telling him I'm an ex-cartoonist now.

'I'm an art teacher too,' I say.

'Yes, Jean told me. Are you enjoying teaching?' he asks, head on one side.

'W-e-l-l,' I say. 'You know how it is. Sometimes it's fun, and sometimes it's fucking awful.' Oh my God, I'm swearing in front of Mr Windsor. I feel my blush deepen. He'd have probably given me detention when I was at school – but he just laughs now.

'It certainly is,' he says. 'Still, nearly the holidays. Are you going anywhere special?'

That's a laugh. I haven't got any plans at all, now Lottie isn't going to be around. I struggle to think up somewhere interesting, but my mind's a blank. I give a little shrug.

'I'm rather a last-minute, spur-of-the-moment girl,' I say. *Woman!* And what a stupid thing to say when I'm the exact opposite – I can't go anywhere without a detailed itinerary. Relax, Ellie, relax! You don't have to try to impress him. He's just your old teacher. Even though he looks like a movie star.

Luckily, we are interrupted by a couple coming out of the exhibition.

'Shall we go in?' says Guy and I nod, relieved.

The same blonde girl is lounging gracefully at the reception desk, fiddling with a lock of her long hair. I worry for a moment that she'll recognize me – but she gives me the same blank face and professional smile as last time.

'Oh, this looks wonderful,' I say, gazing round. I'm not lying: Paula's work seems even more impressive the second time. He steers me round, telling me things I actually know already.

'I'm so grateful to you for introducing me to her work,' I say, hoping it doesn't sound too cheesy.

His whole face lights up, and he gives me a little pat on my shoulder.

'It meant a lot to me that one of my pupils responded to her work,' he says.

'It meant a lot to me too. I was going through a difficult patch just then.' I wince slightly, remembering that semi-anorexic phase, when I tried my hardest to stop eating. 'You knew, didn't you?'

'Well, a lot of the staff were worried about you. You were getting very skinny,' he says.

'But I've recovered now, obviously,' I say brightly.

'You look great, Ellie,' he says – though of course he's obliged to say that.

Unsure what to do with the compliment, I concentrate on the artwork, and Guy does too.

'Let's go round again,' he says, when we come to the end. This time he can't resist giving some background history as well as interpretations, and it starts to feel a bit strange. I'm not in Year Nine any more – why is he going all 'teacher' on me? Besides, Paula Rego is one of my passions. I know all this stuff. The assumption that I don't begins to chafe. Why do even the nicest men want to mansplain? And why am I nodding and smiling as if it's all new to me? But I suppose it's rather endearing that he's showing off to me, wanting to make a good impression.

We've come to the end of the show again. I glance at my

watch surreptitiously. We nod at the blonde girl, go out the door and stand looking at each other.

'Well, thanks for telling me about the exhibition. It's wonderful,' I say. There's a little pause while we look at each other, look away, back again. 'I'd better get going,' I say quickly.

'Oh, so soon?' he says. 'Do you have to be anywhere?'

'Well, not really,' I say.

'Then shall we sit down somewhere and have a proper catch-up?' He says it very quickly and casually, but slightly trips up over the end. Maybe he's not as sure of himself as he seems.

'Sure,' I say, keeping it light too.

'Great. Let's wander until we find somewhere quiet.'

He takes hold of my elbow gently and steers us back to Piccadilly. I smile at our reflection in Hatchards' window, just like Mrs Dalloway, and then Guy takes us to a café that's trying to be traditional and elegant, and chooses a table near the window. We sit down opposite each other, glancing up, looking down, suddenly at a loss.

'Is this all right?' he says, gesturing at our surroundings. He's got lovely hands: well-kept nails, no hairy knuckles, no rings. He sees me studying them and I look away quickly, peering at the cakes in the window.

'Which one would you like?' he asks.

'No, I'm fine, I'll just have a coffee,' I say.

'Oh go on! What about the chocolate éclair – or that amazing strawberry tart?'

While I want to protest that I said I didn't want anything, in actual fact, he's picked the two that I like the look of best.

'All right then. I'll have the éclair – no, maybe the tart,' I dither.

'Let's order both and have half of each,' says Guy.

I nod approvingly. It's the sort of thing I do with Lottie or Nadine or Magda. He smiles, knowing he's pleased me.

'So, how long is it since we last saw each other?' he asks.

I shrug, though I've worked it out exactly.

'I think you were in Year Nine when I first started teaching,' he says. He's sounding vague, but I'm pretty sure he remembers.

'Yes. We were all thrilled when we saw you. We'd had an old lady before with dyed black hair who always wore a knitted suit covered in cat fur,' I say. I suddenly brush at my knees, hoping that Stella hasn't left cat hairs all over me. I love brushing her while she closes her eyes dreamily and purrs and purrs with pleasure.

Why am I thinking of Stella? Is it because I have a sudden mental image of being naked with Guy and getting stroked all over? I seem to remember imagining something like it when I was in Year Nine and just discovering how to pleasure myself. Oh God, I can feel myself blushing.

'So I made a bit of an impact, did I?' Guy says, looking delighted.

'Well, what do you expect, the only male under sixty in a girls' school like a nunnery?' I say, not wanting the flattery to go to his head.

'I was quaking my first few lessons,' he says. 'You all seemed so grown up. And very cheeky. But I quite liked that.'

'I quake sometimes before a lesson, though I hope it doesn't show. Especially when it's Year Nine. They're so determinedly trying to be laid back that they flop about, barely able to pick up a pencil. Or they're fizzing over like cans of Red Bull, out to get me,' I say.

'I think your students are very lucky to have a girl like you teaching them,' he says.

I frown slightly at the word girl, though I've used it myself. Is it a compliment? Is it patronizing? I decide not to mind.

'Do they know about your Myrtle Mouse strip?' he asks.

I snort. 'Guy, my kids wouldn't read the *Sun*, let alone the

Guardian. A newspaper is a weird relic of the past to them, like a landline phone or a video recorder,' I say.

'Still, they might be impressed by your tattoo of her,' he says, taking hold of my wrist.

He's spotted it, he's seen what it is, he's *holding my wrist*, turning it to look at Myrtle properly. It's the lightest touch but somehow it feels incredibly intimate. I have to hold myself very still so I don't shiver.

'It's a very recent tattoo. I got it done on my birthday. A friend talked me into it,' I say. 'Alice,' I add unnecessarily.

At that exact moment my phone vibrates in my bag. Have I somehow summoned her up? But why is she phoning rather than messaging?

'Excuse me,' I say. 'I'd better take this.'

I fish the phone out of my bag in a fluster, and it isn't Alice at all. It's Nadine. I take a deep breath, tap the green button and before she can say anything, I say, 'Hi, Naddie, can I call you later? I'm out.'

There's a long pause, then: 'Ellie Allard, you're on a date, aren't you? I can tell from your voice. Who is it?'

'It's not a date! It's – I'm – it's Guy – Mr Windsor. We're—'

'Oh my God!' she shrieks. 'You're kidding? You're on a date with Mr Windsor? Are you going to fuck *Mr Windsor*? What are you—'

'Ring you later,' I say, and switch the phone off. My face is on fire. Did he hear? I dare a glance at him. He's keeping a straight face but his eyes are gleaming.

'A friend,' I murmur.

'Which one? The tattoo girl? Magda? Nadine?' he asks. He's smirking like anything. I think he did hear. Now she's said it, though, I can't get the idea out of my mind. I'm tingling all over. And immediately I start wondering about my underwear and worrying that I haven't bothered waxing and what about contraception? I haven't bothered for ages because there hasn't seemed any point. It's bad enough getting pregnant at twenty but I can't risk it at forty years old, for God's sake.

What is the *matter* with me? *Calm down*, I tell myself, *stop getting all het up, you are a mature sophisticated woman now, so act like it.*

'Yep, Nadine,' I say breezily. 'I think she's only just got out of bed.'

'Presumably you've told her and Magda about our little gallery trip?' he asks, his voice innocent.

He obviously heard. My face fires up again.

'We still tend to overshare with each other,' I say sheepishly.

'I hoped you'd all three stay in touch,' he says.

'Well, I think it's lovely that you and Mrs Henderson – Jean – are good friends too. So were you really matey right from when we were at school?'

'Staff room buddies,' he says. 'We often discussed you three, especially when Jean was your form teacher. You drove her demented at times and yet you were also her favourite girls because you were so much fun.'

'Really?' I say. 'Did you think we were fun too?'

'What do you think? I thought you were great.' Then he looks anxious. 'But not in an inappropriate sort of way, of course. You were just kids. It's all so complicated being a teacher now. I have to be extremely careful not to single anyone out, and if someone wants to talk to me about something private I have to make sure we're not alone in the art room, which defeats the whole purpose. You know what it's like. I mean, I see the point of all the new rules, but teaching is such a minefield now. I keep thinking about quitting, actually.'

'To do what?' I ask.

'God knows. I'd like to paint, but that's not going to pay off my mortgage, is it?'

'My dad said he'd spend his days painting when he retired, but in actual fact he's hardly touched a paintbrush since,' I say.

'That's meant to be encouraging, Ellie?' Guy says wryly. 'I know I'm a lot older than you, but surely I'm not your dad's age?'

'Of course not,' I say, horrified that I've offended him. 'You're not a bit like my poor old dad.'

He rubs his neck. 'Look, maybe I shouldn't have tried to get in touch.' He looks at me directly. 'It *is* a bit weird, isn't it? If we had never known each other back in the past, it would be fine. If we'd met on some niche arty dating app, I'd think myself incredibly lucky to be sitting here with you and hopefully you wouldn't mind too much either.'

My pulse races. So this *is* a date?

He's waving politely at the waiter to pay. 'But as it is – look, you don't have to hang around. I think you're just being kind to me because you're a sweet girl. Still, it's been great meeting up, even if it was probably a mistake.'

No, it isn't! I want to shout. *You're just as I remembered. Better! I still can't believe we're here together. I want it to be a date!* I take a deep breath.

'What if I don't want to go?' I say.

We look at each other. I hold my breath.

'Then I suggest we go for a proper drink in a quiet pub somewhere and pretend we've only just met. No history. OK?' he says.

'More than OK,' I say, and I dare to reach out and lightly touch his hand. It's meant to be a reassuring pat, but he clasps my own hand, and another secret shiver happens. Oh God, it's madness, but I really do fancy him. And I know it's probably crazy, and maybe it's because I haven't been on a proper date for ages and I hate being forty – but I don't care. I want this.

He pays for the coffee and cakes. I try to pay my share but he won't hear of it. We go to a pub down a side road in Piccadilly, which is wonderfully dark inside, and he orders a bottle of wine. It's nowhere near six o'clock drinking time, but who cares? We drink and we play a game that we've only just met, and I tell him about my sad affair at art school and then my drunken fling and then the long years of bringing up Lottie. I even tell him about the one or two disastrous boyfriends while she was growing up. I talk about Myrtle and how thrilled I was when I got my first acceptance, but now I've just heard that they're dropping the strip because it doesn't bloody chime with the readership any more.

'She chimes with me,' he says, and he strokes my tattoo. Then his hand slides down and strokes the palm of my hand. He tells me about the girlfriend he was keenest on, who went off with his best friend, a humiliating story that makes me feel so tender towards him simply because he's admitting it to me. I edge up closer, and he puts his arm round me. I rest against him, and I struggle not to lean in and touch my lips to his. What's happening to me? I don't do this sort of thing. We only met up a couple of hours ago. And yet, when he himself leans in, I kiss him regardless. Very tentatively at first, scarcely brushing his lips – but after a few agonizing moments, we shift and it blooms into a proper kiss. It is amazing. Absolutely bloody amazing, better than any fantasy. We're kissing each other, his hand behind my neck, and I want him so much and I know he wants me too.

When we break apart at last, we look at each other blurrily.

'I can't believe this is happening,' he whispers. 'What shall we do now? I could order another bottle and we could get very drunk. We could go for a walk in the park holding hands and then go and find somewhere quiet and romantic to have dinner. Or . . . or we could go back to my house and I'll cook you something.'

'Perhaps . . . your house?' I suggest hesitantly.

'My house,' he agrees, his voice husky.

It's an easy journey to Earlsfield, where he lives – three stops on the tube, then three on the train from Waterloo – but he calls for an Uber instead.

We sit together in the back, and we don't kiss. Guy talks to the driver, making pleasant, bland conversation, but all the while he holds my hand, his fingers stroking it sensuously. It feels as if he's stroking me somewhere else entirely, and I feel myself melting.

It's a long journey because the traffic's so bad, but I want it to go on for ever. I'm longing to be at Guy's, and yet I've started to worry again. What if it's really awkward when we get there? Maybe the sex won't work at all and it will be horribly embarrassing, maybe it's way too soon anyway. I'm generally an old-fashioned girl who waits for the third date, or even longer, before I jump into bed. I don't want him to think I do this with everyone. But I've never passionately kissed an ex-teacher before. It's somehow both liberating and inhibiting at the same time. My stomach clenches with nerves.

The car starts slowing down at last and Guy directs it the last hundred yards down a quiet road of smallish, well-kept houses. There's a huge palm taking up one front garden; an ironic circle of gnomes; a rainbow striped door; a knocker in the shape of a man with a Magritte bowler hat. Guy's house is simple but stylish, not trying so hard. Neat grass, shiny blue door and simple curtains that manage not to be reproduction William Morris.

'Come in,' he says. Thank God. I once went home with a man who said, 'Welcome to my humble abode.' And then there was another guy who blurted out, 'Right, let's fuck' – which was clear, I suppose, but not exactly romantic.

He doesn't lunge at me as soon as we're inside the door,

thankfully, or back me up against a wall and expect me to leapfrog up onto him while simultaneously whipping off my knickers. He sits me down on the dark green Chesterfield in his living room and I have time to peer round. His bookshelves are an interesting mix of old orange Penguins, a few modern hardbacks, several white-spined modern classics, big fat art books, and touchingly some relics from his childhood, Richard Scarry and Thomas the Tank Engine, a set of Narnia, and a *Beano* annual.

I'm looking at a Bash Street Kids comic strip when he comes back from the kitchen with a tray holding two gin and tonics in crystal tumblers, ice cubes, slices of lemon, and a bowl of nuts. What a relief we didn't go back to my place. We'd have had to make do with the champagne, which would have seemed over the top, and an already opened bag of stale crisps. And Stella would probably have used her litter tray, whereas Guy's house smells faintly and pleasantly of his own lemony aftershave.

'Are you a fellow fan of *Beano*?' he asks, sitting beside me and handing me my gin and tonic.

'My dad was stupidly sniffy about kids' comics. I wasn't allowed them. I'm just looking at the layout to see how it works.' I pause. I'm more shy of confiding my plans than I am of taking off my clothes, it seems. If I tell him about my elephants, he might come up with all sorts of unwanted suggestions and teacherly encouragement.

'Ah!' he says. 'Great idea!' But he jumps to the wrong conclusion and takes hold of my wrist, looking at the tattoo. 'She'd like her own full-length script.' He puts his head on one side and peers at Myrtle quizzically. 'A big fat comic book about Myrtle's adventures?' he says. His voice is huskier than it used to be – did he used to smoke? – or is it more the consequence of yelling at unruly kids for a good thirty years? It sounds very sexy, whatever the cause.

He clinks his glass against mine. 'To Myrtle, in a new format!' he says, and I don't correct him.

We both take three sips, looking at each other, waiting. I'm not quite sure what to do now. Do we just wriggle sideways on the Chesterfield? It's lovely, but the leather is rather slippery. If we're too energetic, we might well scoot off onto the floorboards, beautifully polished but very hard.

He puts his gin down, budges up closer, and kisses me again, gently at first, but then much more urgently, and I melt against him.

'Shall we?' he says, when we break away at last. He's looking up at the ceiling. For a mad second I focus on the modern chandelier, but then realize he's simply asking if I want to go up to his bedroom.

'Yes, let's,' I say.

This is it. I take a deep breath as we go up his stairs, brushing together a little awkwardly as we're holding hands. He opens his bedroom door. The walls are midnight blue, with a large Lucian Freud framed poster above the bed: the beautiful portrait of elfin Lady Caroline Blackwood leaning up on one elbow in bed. I love that painting, but I wish he'd chosen the wife before her, Kitty Epstein, because she's a little plumper and has hair very similar to mine.

'Do you want to . . .?' He's tactfully indicating the ensuite bathroom.

Yes, I do, what with nerves, two coffees and half a bottle of wine. The bathroom is dark green, with a painting of Hylas and the Nymphs above the clawfoot bath. They are all very slim and small-breasted, with long, straight hair. These tiny women are a bit inhibiting. Is this his ideal woman – or is he just choosing interesting paintings of a bed and water to match the functions of the rooms? I peer at myself in the mirror framed with green deckled glass. My face looks back at me, obstinately plump and rosy, and in spite of my determined styling my hair's become madly frizzy. I bare my teeth to make sure I haven't got any remnants of nuts stuck in a crevice, and check that I don't smell sweaty. I'm clenching my fists and the image in the mirror is nibbling at her lip.

Will he have any condoms? Or are they considered pathetically old-fashioned nowadays? Is he expecting me to have some sort of contraption, to save him the bother? Does he think I'm in here inserting it right now?

The me in the mirror sags. I feel unsophisticated and ashamed, my former sexy confidence whizzling rapidly away. Perhaps he is feeling the same – and his whizzling away will be even more embarrassing for him. *Well*, I tell myself, *time to go and find out*. I have a quick wee and wash here and there too, and dry myself on the hem of his towelling dressing gown hanging on a hook.

It occurs to me that it'll be easier if I undress in here in privacy. I whip all my clothes off quickly, standing on tiptoe to peer at myself. Oh Joe Wicks, why don't I do what you say and bloody exercise?

I can't dither in here for ever. I wrap myself in his dressing gown, holding it over my nose like a cuddle blanket for a moment, and then I go into the bedroom. He's dimmed the lights so that there's just a warm glow from the bedside lamps. He's lounging casually on the bed in black trunks, looking good. Very good.

'Hi,' he says and holds out his hands to me.

'Hi,' I say, and climb up beside him. 'Listen, Guy, can I get the awkward bit out the way right now?'

He looks at me carefully. 'Second thoughts?' he asks.

'Not at all!' I reassure him. 'But I'm not actually on the pill or anything right at the moment – so I was wondering, would you possibly have any condoms?'

'Yep,' he says, as if it's no big deal at all, and gets a packet out of his bedside drawer. A pristine pack of three, and I smile at him, relieved.

'Come here, gorgeous woman,' he whispers.

He kisses me again, properly, wonderfully, and all the desire comes flooding back as he pushes the bathrobe down from my shoulders.

'You've got the most beautiful breasts,' he murmurs. No one's ever told me that before.

I try to think of an appropriate body part that I can compliment back. There's the obvious one, now nudging at my thighs, but I'm not quite sure how to word it, so I think better of it. Silence is sometimes the best option. I concentrate on his chest and flat stomach, admiring it considerably, and he murmurs something bizarre about my gorgeous womanly curves while caressing my hips.

Then his hand moves downwards, and for a moment the commentator inside my head is stunned into silence, until Mrs Dalloway's famous remark 'What a lark! What a plunge!' echoes in my mind. *No, not the time. Don't think. Feel.*

When he enters me, it's so good and so easy that I don't have to fantasize to make myself come. *This* is my fantasy, and it's better than I'd imagined, and then I'm there, crying out, and after several seconds he does too. Then we lie, dazed and gasping, until both his arms go round me and he squeezes me tight.

'Well, Mr Windsor!' I say, looking up at him.

'Well, Miss Allard!' he replies, grinning, and his confident façade breaks. 'Oh, thank God, I was so worried I'd make a mess of things. It was OK for you, wasn't it?'

'I'm not that good an actress,' I say. 'If I were giving you a mark, it would have to be ten out of ten.'

He's like a teenage boy now, practically crowing, leaning up on his elbow. I ruffle his lovely hair and he runs his fingers through my own curls and then traces the contours of my face tenderly. Then he pulls me close and I nestle against his neck. I feel his heart and it's beating as fast as mine.

Maybe my birthday wish wasn't so ridiculous after all.

9

He makes me a beautiful herby cheese omelette with a perfectly tossed green salad. We sit at his kitchen island to eat. It's like a romantic fantasy: delicious food, stylish house, fantastic man admiring me.

It would have been a great Myrtle cartoon: I'd have her sitting eating bananas/coconut/fish at a kitchen island on a real desert island, as a dashing pirate rat twirls his whiskers at her. But never mind. It doesn't hurt so much when I'm here, naked, with Guy's dressing gown around my shoulders, and my 'gorgeous womanly curves' on show.

'Can I sketch you like that?' he asks.

'If you want, sure,' I say, immensely flattered.

I sit up straighter, trying to adopt the most fetching pose, while he draws in a little black book, occasionally helping himself to his supper at the same time.

I can't keep an idiotic smile off my face.

'What are you thinking?' Guy says.

'I'm thinking how good this all feels. Almost too good, like I'm making it up,' I say. 'What about you?'

'That's what I'm thinking too. And that old Kylie song is bouncing about in my head – *I should be so lucky*.'

'Feel free to dance to it,' I say.

'I'm not a dad but I'm sure I dance like one,' he says, shaking his head.

'Do you wish you had children?'

'Not really. Especially when I go round to my brother's house and the two eldest are yelling at each other and the toddler's screaming and kicking on the floor. But I suppose sometimes I think of some cherubic little Guy and he's drawing me a picture with his felt tips, or we're going round a gallery hand in hand or we're building a sandcastle on the beach,' he says.

'I did all those things with Lottie,' I say.

'You must be a fabulous mum, Ellie. How old is she?'

'Nineteen. Just a year younger than I was when I got pregnant.'

'Good lord. That must have been tough for you,' he says.

'Sometimes. But most of it was fine,' I insist.

'So, is she still at home?'

'No, she's at university – and she's got a holiday job at an international kids' summer camp. She'll be brilliant,' I say. 'Especially demonstrating the zipwire! Mrs Henderson would adore her – she's very sporty, unlike me.'

'So you don't have to go home tonight?' he says hopefully.

My heart starts beating fast. He wants me to stay! He's acting like he really cares about me. He reaches out and holds my free hand.

'Please stay,' he says.

I look at him and he looks back at me and my heart lurches. Yes, I'll stay, and we'll go back to bed and have sex again and then curl up round each other and share breakfast in the morning and live out the romantic couple fantasy and I can't believe it.

I nod happily and then go to the bathroom again, wondering how I'm going to manage without my own toothbrush. Is it too intimate to borrow his? I decide he won't mind. We're already so close now. The sex was really good. I shiver, remembering, my body responding. I brush away. I've never felt like this with anyone before. I hope he hasn't either. It's the way it's supposed to be, the way I've always dreamt it could be.

I shrug his dressing gown off so I can have a proper wash. Something white falls out of the pocket. Just a tissue. I pick it up – and see the crimson imprint of a mouth. Someone's blotted their lipstick on it.

I stand very still, staring at it. Guy seems highly unlikely to be nonbinary or trans, although I have a little flash image of him in full make-up. He would probably look quite sexy even then. Yes, I'm trying to turn it into a little joke, but it's not funny. I've started to tremble. It's ninety-nine per cent certain that a woman pressed her lips on that tissue. A woman wearing Guy's dressing gown.

It's lying on the floor, navy towelling, immaculately clean – but I kick it all the same. I feel like casting myself down on the shiny tiles and howling. It was all so beautiful and perfect and I was so happy and felt so special – and yet now I see there's someone else. Maybe several. He's a good-looking, charming guy who doesn't look his age. Of course he sees other women.

I look up and scowl at myself in the mirror. What is the matter with me? Do I seriously expect him to be living like a monk? OK, he said he was single – didn't he? – but that simply means he's not in a serious relationship.

I open the cupboard below his sink. Loo rolls, cleaners, spare soap – and a packet of Tampax. Oh God. Does this mean he's living with another woman? He might keep a packet of contraceptives in his bedside drawer on the off-chance he brings someone back to his place; he's practised with his gin and tonics and his sweet talk and his beautiful love making and all the little tender asides, but he surely wouldn't keep a pack of emergency tampons for some poor hook-up who starts her period at precisely the wrong time?

No, this is a serious girlfriend, who wears his dressing gown, carelessly leaves her used tissues lying around, and keeps her sanitary products at his place. I look in the bathroom cabinet too. Ah! There's another toothbrush, well used. A woman's hairbrush, with several fair hairs still stuck on the bristles. Mum deodorant – although my vision of this girlfriend isn't at all mumsy. I see her as a femme fatale, a cartoon sexy woman – and yet if she's a regular girlfriend then *I'm* the usurper, stealing her boyfriend's attentions.

No, what era am I in? We're in the twenty-first century, for God's sake. We're free and independent and there are no ties and everyone sleeps around casually, so why are my eyes stinging, my throat aching? I wipe my eyes, appalled. Grow up, Ellie! Nadine would be laughing her head off at you. Magda would be too, pre-Chris, pre-baby. And Ben, who had a seriously busy love life before he met Simon.

I can't say I have, but I've had several encounters myself, mostly disastrous. There was that one day when I thought Lottie was going to hang out at her best friend's house all evening and I got it together with that guy I met at a book launch, and Lottie came home and let herself in just as . . . no, no, I can't bear to think about it.

I'm no saint. So why would I expect Guy to be? Just because we've had surprisingly great sex it doesn't mean we're falling in love.

I slap cold water on my face, trying hard to sober up and be sensible.

'Ellie?' Guy is knocking on the door. 'Ellie, are you OK in there?'

'Yeah, sure!' I say, in a madly jolly voice. I force myself to put his dressing gown back on, though my body shrinks inside it, thinking of all the women who could have worn it before me.

'We've got ice cream for pudding. Salted caramel. Come on, it's melting,' he says.

'Yum yum,' I say ridiculously, and I have another dab of my eyes with a cold flannel and then prance out as if I haven't got a care in the world.

Salted caramel is my favourite, and he's made black coffee too. I sit beside him and chat away, pretending I'm fine.

'I'd so love to stay,' I say, cuddling up to him. It's true, but it's somehow all spoiled now. 'But I have this cat, Stella. I can't really leave her on her own all night, she'd go a bit crazy.'

No, she wouldn't, she's perfectly capable of looking after herself, and she rather enjoys giving me a hard time when I eventually creep home in the morning – but she's the only excuse I've got.

He's frowning at me, looking puzzled, a little hurt.

'Ellie? What's the matter?' he asks softly.

'Nothing! Nothing at all!' I say wildly. I have to get away. I can't let him realize I've been thinking this is practically a true romance, the sort you dream of as a teenager. It would be too humiliating.

'You need to get back for your cat?' Guy says. 'Seriously?'

I nod, aware that it's a ridiculous excuse, that he sees right through it – but he has the grace not to question me further.

After that, everything changes. He's polite, tender – and yet he's not at ease. We eat our ice cream, drink our coffee, making awkward conversation. It's strange to think that we were having the best sex ever an hour or so ago. I feel suddenly uncomfortable half naked and scurry to get dressed properly, but he won't let me leave for the simple train and tube journey, though it's not even late. He insists on phoning for another Uber to take me all the way home. It's going to cost him a fortune, but I can't talk him out of it.

Then he kisses me – and almost immediately the magic is back, I'm melting, he can have hundreds of girlfriends, I don't even care. No one has ever made me feel so sexy, so sensual. I want him even more this time – how could I possibly have been such a fool to insist on going home? But the Uber is outside and even though he asks me if I want to change my mind about staying – Yes! Yes! – I kiss him one more time and then go.

'See you very soon,' he says, though I don't know if I believe him.

I hunch up in the car, feeling sad and humiliated, because it looks as if I've been sent on my way like a good-time girl. Of course he didn't treat me like that. He was lovely to me, he wanted me to stay. Why did I have to discover that wretched crumpled tissue? It's such a cliché.

I feel as crumpled as the tissue. I force myself to make desultory conversation with the driver, trying to act like someone who's just had a lovely time, thank you very much. I haul myself up the stairs, let myself in the flat and call for Stella. She's curled in her cat tower like a Cumberland sausage, so relaxed and comfortable she only gives the faintest purr as I stroke her back. She has a mound of kibble in her bowl, and a full water bowl too. Her litter tray is unsullied. I could have stayed all night and she wouldn't have cared in the slightest.

I make myself a mug of black coffee and sit sipping it by myself. The smell of red roses in the vase beside me is initially beautiful, but then it becomes more and more intense, almost sickening. I open a cupboard door and shut them inside, but the smell still leaks out. I go to bed and lie there sleepless, feeling a total fool. I've overreacted big time. I wonder about sending Guy a text and try typing it out, but I'm not sure how to word it and can't get the tone right. I don't send anything – don't want to make an even bigger fool of myself.

I get hardly any sleep, going over and over it in my mind,

and then dreaming it, waking up hot and aching. If only I could turn back time, rewind to the moment in Guy's bathroom. I don't throw his dressing gown so the tissue falls out of the pocket. Or I do, I see it, and I don't give a damn. It could be a remnant from someone he saw months ago. And anyway, it doesn't matter. He's not married. He's perfectly entitled to see a different woman every day of the week. From all accounts, Nadine's seeing plenty of different guys. It's the dating game, for God's sake.

But I don't like the dating game very much. I don't want Guy just to be a happy fuck. I want him to be The One, the man I've been waiting for, the one who won't let me down.

There's a little ping on my phone, and my pulse leaps. Is that him? I peer at my messages, my eyes blurry without my glasses. Oh please God, let him be suggesting another date, telling me how much the evening meant to him. But it's not Guy. It's not Alice either – she's obviously not going to bother with me. It's not Nadine. It's Magda.

Just spoke to Nadine – WTF?!?! Mr Windsor??? What happened??? Come on, TELL! Did you kiss? More?? I can't believe you actually had a date with him! Phone me – I'm down in the kitchen, shoving mucky sheets in the washing machine. Corrie has got some God-awful stomach bug. She's whimpering that it's my cooking, would you believe. Motherhood has its drawbacks! Magda xxx

I don't feel up to a whispered phone conversation now. Besides, Magda clearly has problems of her own, so I don't want to burden her with mine. I worry about her. I hate thinking of her humbly clearing up after ungrateful kids. What's happened to my glamorous friend? I worry about Nadine too. I'm not sure her easy hook-ups are really making her happy.

I worry about me, too. I'm supposed to be the so-called success story, with my comic strip in a national newspaper. It meant so much. I don't feel a valid, interesting person any more. Part of me is missing now, and all I am is a teacher who can't keep the kids under control. I'm still a mum of course, but I can't pretend Lottie needs me the way she used to. She's moved on. It's time *I* moved on. I thought I was doing just that today – but now I've just fucked up royally. I lie on my front and put the pillow over my head, as if hiding from hostile strangers pointing at me, judging me, laughing at me.

I try to distract myself by doing that meditation exercise where you concentrate on each part of your body in turn, consciously relaxing them. My feet are obedient, not the slightest toe wriggle. My ankles, my calves, my knees, my thighs. Every muscle still and sleeping. All the way up my legs, between my legs, and – well, that's wide awake and clamouring for attention.

When it's eventually morning, I'm in need of another big mug of black coffee. I'm still thirsty so I swig orange juice from a carton a little past its sell-by date, and decide to settle my stomach with some toast. I peer in the fridge and find I've forgotten to buy a fresh pack of butter, so have to settle for dry toast. It's time I outgrew this slobby studenty way of living. I don't seem to bother to eat healthily now that Lottie's not around.

I should rush out to Tesco's and do a quick shop. I should go swimming again. I should google everything I can find on elephants. I should think up a replacement strip for Myrtle, much as it pains me to consider. I should read more of *Mrs Dalloway*.

I don't feel like doing any of those things, though. I google, but not about elephants. I type *What should you do if you find a man you've started dating is seeing someone else?*

You could very well enjoy that person's company, and they may decide they want to be exclusive with you down the line.

Good God. Is this really what dating is like nowadays? I'm not sure I can get my head round it. I text Nadine. I wait ten minutes. And then I actually ring her, and just before it switches to voicemail she answers.

'What?' she murmurs groggily.

'I'm sorry, I've woken you up, haven't I? It's me, Ellie. I was just getting a bit worried, I thought you'd be on the phone to me demanding to know what happened with me and Mr Windsor,' I say.

'You and—?' she mumbles.

'Sorry, you're in bed with someone, aren't you?'

'No! I'm just . . . not very well,' she says.

'What sort of not very well?' I ask.

'Oh, some bug,' she murmurs.

'Stomach bug? Magda's future stepchild is throwing up all over the place, poor her.'

'No, it's more—'

'Sore throat? Cough? Temperature?'

'I'm just – I don't know – achey.'

'Have you taken your temperature?'

'I haven't got a thermometer. Do stop nagging me, Ellie. My head hurts,' she moans.

'OK. Sorry, babes. Go back to sleep,' I say.

I'm worried now, nibbling at my lip. She must be feeling really ill if she doesn't want to know about Guy and me. This bug or whatever has come on really quickly. Nadine lives alone, like me. Should I phone her mother, Natasha? Definitely not. It's Ellie to the rescue.

I get washed and dressed quickly, find my own thermometer, grab my wallet and my tote, put down more kibble for

Stella, and charge off to Tesco's after all. I buy orange juice, mineral water, green tea bags, paracetamol, tissues, grapes, crackers, shove them all in my bag, and then go to the tube. Nadine lives in a much nicer area than me, but pays a very low rent because married-guy Harry is technically her landlord and claims a few benefits.

Is Nadine really happy with this semi-relationship? Does she really prefer having lots of exciting encounters with different men?

She has the garden flat in a street of big smart Edwardian houses. I go down the steps and ring the doorbell. Then again. And again. She's obviously gone back to sleep. Or maybe the bell's not working? I knock instead, but the door stays shut. I open her letter box.

'Nadine?' I shout. 'It's me, Ellie! Come on, wake up!'

I'm making enough noise to waken the whole street, but she still doesn't come to let me in. Horrible images flood my head: Nadine draped in various terrible positions, dead for ever. A tiny passageway leads to the back of the house. It's full of wheely bins and a ladder, but I thread myself through them, round to the garden.

I go to her French windows and push my nose up against the glass. She's not in her living room but I press my ear to the pane and think I hear something from the next room across – her bedroom. Her curtains are shut, but faintly I detect a wardrobe door opening, and the fumbling sounds of someone hastily dressing. Thank God, she's all right.

'Nadine, don't bother getting dressed. It's only me. Ellie!'

'I know you're bloody Ellie!' Nadine says, coming to the French windows. Her head is bent so that I can't see her face for her tumble of hair. She's pulled a polo neck on, though it's a really hot day. She undoes the bolt, the locks, and then opens the doors.

128

'*Bloody* Ellie?' I say indignantly. 'Who's trekked all this way to nurse you better like Florence fucking Nightingale?'

'Sorry, sorry. I'm feeling lousy but it's just a hangover. I don't need nursing. It's very nice of you, but really, I just want to be left alone to sleep it off,' she says.

She's not quite looking me in the eye. Her face is even paler than usual. Her eyes are bloodshot and her nose looks swollen.

'Well, let me make you some green tea, now I'm here. You sit down. You do look a bit rough,' I say.

She sighs weakly. 'OK. It's very sweet of you.'

She sits at her kitchen table, head bowed, while I make tea.

'Just nipping to the loo,' I say. I do need to go – but when I come out, I open her closed bedroom door as silently as I can. The bed looks chaotic, duvet thrown off, pillows too, her underwear and clothes strewn all over the place. There's an empty bottle by the bed, and another bottle has pooled its contents onto the carpet. I stand the latter upright, and try mopping it with a towel. It looks as if Nadine and some stranger have had a heavy night of it.

My heart thuds. Oh Nadine, why on earth do you get yourself in these scary situations? It looks so sad, so sordid. But who am I to act shocked? I had sex last night with a *comparative* stranger, although our own encounter was much less wild. I creep out and close the bedroom door silently, but Nadine looks at me suspiciously when I get back.

'You've been snooping,' she says flatly.

'It's OK.' I assume a comic accent to try to lighten things up. 'Whatever floats your boat, darling.'

Nadine bends further forward and makes a little sound. It might be a sob.

'Oh Naddie!' I go to her and put my hand on her shoulder. I feel her wince. 'What is it? Have you hurt yourself?'

'No! I'm fine,' Nadine insists pointlessly, when she's clearly anything but.

'Come on, tell me. I promise I won't come over all prudish. And do take that jumper off, you must be roasting.' I suddenly remember long ago, when we were at school, and Nadine arrived with a big purple mark on her neck after a boyfriend got carried away. Surely she's not fussing about love bites?

I pull down the neck of the polo jumper before she can stop me – and gasp. Her neck has unmistakeable livid fingerprints marking it – a thumbprint one side and four fingers the other.

'Oh my God!' I squeak. 'Someone's tried to strangle you!'

'No! No, not like that,' she mumbles. 'It was just a bit of choking.'

'A *bit*? Did you phone the police or call an ambulance?'

'Of course I didn't. It was consensual – well, it was supposed to be. He just got a bit carried away, that's all. I knew you'd make a fuss. You're so . . . suburban, Ellie,' she says.

'Well, thank goodness for that, if it's suburban not to want to be strangled. We're *both* suburban girls, remember, and as a matter of fact I live a much edgier life on my London estate than you do in this posh neck of the woods. And what do you mean, consensual? You *wanted* to be strangled?'

She glares at me. 'Choked. It's a perfectly ordinary way of enhancing sexual pleasure.'

'*His* pleasure, surely – because he's sick and wants to dominate women?'

'Mine too. But anyway, he kept on pressing and wouldn't stop and I got a bit frightened then.' She sips her drink, frowning. 'I kept protesting so then he hit me and made my nose bleed.'

'So what did you do then?' I demand.

'I had to knee him in the balls,' she murmurs.

'Well, good for you!'

'And then I think I passed out, just for a bit, and he must have got frightened then, because I came to with him splashing wine all over me, trying to bring me round, and he was crying, scared that he'd killed me. We were both very drunk. I know it might sound maudlin and ugly to you, but it was all fine until he got carried away. He kept saying how sorry he was.' I stare at her, appalled. 'Stop looking like that, Ellie, he's not a mad serial killer, he's just an inexperienced guy who's watched too much porn. I'm not ever going to see him again.'

'What if he comes back?' I ask anxiously.

'He won't. He'll never want to see me again in a million years. He was so scared he couldn't get out of here fast enough, and so drunk he could barely call for an Uber.'

I thought of all those polite Uber drivers delivering drunken people home after brief sexual encounters. What must they think of us?

'But why do you risk everything with all these guys you meet online?' I ask.

'They're mostly perfectly ordinary guys – just a bit boring or so full of themselves they never ask me a single question. And it doesn't always end in sex – in fact, sometimes we just have a quick coffee date and go our separate ways.' She strokes her throat ruefully. 'It's still a bit sore. I don't want to talk too much, OK?'

'Then don't say another word, hon. Drink your tea. Have a few grapes. And I'll tell you about my own sexual encounter,' I say.

A little colour comes into Nadine's face, and her puffy eyes widen. 'You really did it with Mr Windsor?' she says, her voice much stronger now.

'Well, I'm not one to kiss and tell, but . . .'

Nadine looks at me carefully. I struggle to keep my face impassive.

'Then why aren't you over the moon? Didn't it work? Oh no, is he hopeless at it?' she demands.

'He is brilliant,' I say. 'Ten out of ten. Though obviously I'm not very experienced.'

'Is that a dig at me?' Nadine asks indignantly.

'No, absolutely not! I'm sending myself up. I've lived like a nun these last few years, you know I have. I mean, I couldn't bring guys back to my tiny flat with Lottie there, it would have been weird – but now she's at uni and it hasn't made any difference whatsoever. Until now,' I say.

'And it really was OK, even though it was your first time together?' Nadine asks, her head on one side.

'Do you want me to go into graphic detail?' I ask. Stupidly.

'Of course!'

'Look, it's enough to say a good time was had by all.'

'You included?'

'I think that's the implication of *all*.'

'Well, whoop-di-doo for you,' says Nadine. 'And it didn't feel the slightest bit strange doing it with Mr Windsor, of all people?'

'Initially, maybe,' I admit.

'It possibly added a bit of spice to the experience?' Nadine prompts.

'Sort of,' I say, shrugging uncomfortably.

'I bet *he* was getting off on it,' says Nadine.

'Are you implying he was remembering me as a drippy schoolgirl hanging on his every word?' I say, horrified at the idea.

'Mm. Like, a power thing?'

'Nadine. Stop it. You're the one who's just had the most terrible experience with a crazy guy on a power trip – please don't project that on to me,' I say. 'OK, Guy mansplained all Paula Rego's work when we went to the gallery, but he made love very tenderly – he didn't beat me up and try to strangle me. What must that guy think of you to treat you like that?'

Nadine blinks at me and then two fat tears roll down her cheeks.

'Oh Naddie, I wish I hadn't said that. It was mean. I'm so sorry!' I put my arms round her and she sobs on my shoulder. I stroke her back very gently, trying to soothe her.

'It's OK. I was mean too. I suppose I just feel . . . jealous,' she whispers.

'Of me? I'm the fool who got herself pregnant at art school, the saddo who's never really one hundred per cent fallen in love with anyone – well, apart from Lottie and maybe Stella, though I don't think she gives a stuff about me,' I say, sighing.

'Stella?' says Nadine, twisting round and taking notice. Then she droops. 'Oh, Stella your *cat*! I was wondering if you had a girlfriend on the quiet. I sometimes wondered if you might be a little bit gay.'

I try to remember our one long-ago encounter. We were still practically kids and just messing around anyway, wondering what it was like to kiss a girl. Did I make the first move? I stop stroking Nadine's back.

'I'm not the slightest bit gay,' I insist. 'But I've made a new gay friend. She's called Alice. I met her at swimming.'

'Are you sure you're not trying to act out all the fantasies? You've fucked the teacher and now you're thinking of trying a girl,' says Nadine, her tone snarky again.

'Shut up! Don't be so simplistic and insulting!' I say, furious with her now. I feel like shaking her, even in her sad, forlorn state.

'OK, OK, I told you, I'm just jealous. We all had a big crush on Mr Windsor, remember? You were always going to be the one he'd choose, though. He made a huge fuss of you,' says Nadine.

'That was years ago. It's a completely different dynamic

between us now. Two very adult adults. And he asked me heaps about you and Magda yesterday, acting really interested,' I tell her.

'Maybe he fancies a foursome!' says Nadine.

We both burst out laughing, though Nadine has to clutch her throat. 'It's bloody painful still,' she admits.

'I think we should go to A&E,' I say.

'And wait six hours to be told I'm a silly girl and I mustn't take risks like that again,' says Nadine. 'Look, I *know* I've been stupid.'

'You won't ever go along with that sort of stuff again?' I beg her.

'I won't, don't worry. In fact, I'm sore in other places too, if you must know, and I don't fancy having sex any time soon,' says Nadine.

'Whereas I feel I want much more,' I admit. 'I didn't know just how good it could be. He was so loving . . .'

'Like – he said he *loved* you?' Nadine asks incredulously.

'No! Of course not! It was all so intense, though. It does make me start wondering whether eventually . . .' I tail off, too embarrassed to finish.

Nadine shakes her head at me, her expression one of mingled fondness and exasperation. 'Ellie, you are so mad. You belong in a romantic novel.'

'Maybe I do. Oh Nad, I think I really *am* mad. It was all going so well, and I was so happy, and then I went to his bathroom and – and found—'

'And found *what*? Kinky sex toys?'

'A tissue in his dressing gown pocket. With lipstick stains.'

Nadine is looking at me blankly. 'And?' she prompts.

'And I looked in his cupboard and found a box of Tampax. So he's obviously seeing some other woman, isn't he?'

'Probably. Oh Ellie! You might live like a nun but you didn't expect him to be living like a monk all these years, waiting to meet up with his little schoolgirl?' she says.

'Will you stop all the schoolgirl stuff, it's so unfair! That's not what he wants at all. He – he talked about my gorgeous womanly curves,' I say. Oh God, why did I have to tell her that? I bite my lip, as if I could somehow swallow my words.

Nadine splutters with laughter, and then holds her throat, wincing. How dare she laugh! Yet I feel my own face twitching and before I can stop I'm laughing too.

'All right, it does sound a bit much, but he was kissing me at the time, *appreciating* them,' I explain.

'So I don't see what he's doing that's put you off. He's seeing other women. As long as he hasn't got a wife and two kids shut up in a cupboard somewhere, he's not doing anything *wrong*. You can't expect him to want an exclusive relationship *yet*,' Nadine says.

'That's what some bossy agony aunt put on Google,' I say. 'I suppose I was a bit daft just walking out on him, then?'

'You walked out?' She looks amazed.

'I didn't make a scene, or even mention it. I just said I had to get back home because of Stella,' I say. 'But he didn't make a firm date to see me again. He just said he'd see me soon.'

'Well, he probably will,' Nadine says.

'What about all the men you go out with?' I ask. 'Is that the sort of thing they say?'

'I wish you wouldn't keep on as if I'm entertaining an entire football team every day,' says Nadine, exasperated. 'I do date, you know. I go out and have a dinner, see a movie, have a picnic, all that stuff. It's usually me who gets fed up first. Because they either go on and on about some ex, or they whinge about not seeing their kids enough, or they boast about their job or their car or their safari holiday – that's when they flick through five thousand photos on their iPhone.'

'Of elephants?' I say, distracted.

'What? No, mangy lions mostly, faraway on the horizon. And those poor wildebeesty creatures that always get eaten,' says Nadine. 'You don't want to go on a safari, do you, Ellie?'

'No, I'm just interested in elephants,' I say.

'Elephants?' Nadine wrinkles her nose and rubs it ruefully, because it's still swollen and sore. Then she looks at my wrist. 'Are you thinking of a new cartoon? Ellie the Elephant Girl? To replace Myrtle?'

'No one can ever replace Myrtle,' I say, stroking her on my wrist.

'That's where you're so lucky. You've had a job you really loved. Something creative. My job's OK, I suppose, but I can't really get worked up about it. I'd give anything to create something special,' she says wistfully.

'What sort of something special?' I can't resist it. 'Kinky sex toys?'

'Well, it's not a bad idea actually. They're usually so tacky-looking. I'd go really upmarket.'

'A designer noose made of Italian leather?' I say. Nadine's usually up for dark teasing, but she winces now, and ducks her head. I've gone much too far.

'Sorry, sorry, sorry!'

'It's OK. I'll let you get away with it,' she says. 'You've been a pal – even though you nag a lot.'

'Well, no wonder! Don't you think you'll ever meet The One?'

'What, like Magda? What she sees in Chris, I can't understand. And his children sound awful. I'm not the slightest bit envious. This new maternal look is just weird on her,' says Nadine.

'Do you think Guy could be *my* One?' I ask.

'If he's what you want,' she says. 'Though will he still feel like The One when the buzz of fucking your teenage crush is over and you're living with a guy who snores, and scratches, and sniffs yesterday's socks to scc if he can wear them again?'

'Stop being so brutal!' I say. But maybe she has a point.

10

I stay with Nadine most of Sunday. She's feeling much better by the afternoon, thankfully. We eat the crackers and grapes, but they don't make much of a lunch.

'Hey, you know I said that stuff about having a picnic?' Nadine says. 'Shall we go shopping for some food now? I'm thinking cold chicken, salad, cheese, ciabatta, nectarines – and a bottle of rosé?'

'Perfect!' I say.

It's too hot for her to wear the polo jumper out, but she ties a long silk scarf around her bruised neck and wears it with a black ruffled top and tight black jeans. Her nose still looks a little puffy but she wiggles it gingerly and promises me she doesn't think it's broken. Her eyes are still slightly bloodshot, but she always wears dark glasses outside anyway. She looks stunning, swollen nose or not.

She lives in an upmarket area so we get our provisions from Waitrose, and then she calls an Uber to take us to Hampstead Heath. We find a good picnic spot near Kenwood House. We eat all the food and manage to get through the rosé too, even though Nadine had vowed not to drink any more.

'Oh, well, hair of the dog,' she says. 'No more tomorrow.'

'And no more creeps who want to strangle you?'

'Absolutely not. Celibacy, here I come!' says Nadine, though she's eyeing two much younger guys who are sprawled near us.

'Nadine! They're much too young. Stop it!' I hiss.

'I'm not doing anything. They're the ones who keep peering in our direction,' says Nadine.

It turns out they're looking at two girls directly behind us, both wearing crop tops and very short shorts. They give the guys coy little waves, and within minutes they're a foursome, clinking cans together. I don't think any of them even registered the two middle-aged women with their Waitrose bags.

Nadine has the grace to laugh.

'It's just as well I've embraced celibacy because it looks like it's my only option. I *am* truly sick to death of online hook-ups,' she says, draining her glass in a meaningful way. 'So, Ellie, what am I going to do with the rest of my life?'

'Cram it with culture,' I say, brushing crumbs off my jeans. 'Can we go to see the art in Kenwood House? They've got a fabulous Vermeer in there.'

Nadine groans but agrees. We wander round together. Nadine looks at her fellow gallery-goers. I look at the paintings. *The Guitar Player* is as wonderful as I'd hoped. I wish I'd been able to get tickets for that Vermeer exhibition in Amsterdam. I imagine Guy went to it. I wonder if he's been here recently? Perhaps I could email casually, say I was here with Nadine and would he like to see it too? It could be the perfect way of getting in touch without looking too eager. In touch . . . oh, those touches last night . . .

'You're wondering about coming here with Mr Windsor, aren't you?' asks Nadine uncannily.

'How did you know?' I ask, startled. Nadine's always looked as if she's got witchy powers – can she actually mind-read?

'We've been best friends since we were four! I always know *exactly* what you're thinking, Ellie Allard,' she says, laughing. 'Maybe you two are really soul mates, so into art. You should go for it. What does it matter if he's seeing someone else? He'll come to realize you're the only girl for him.'

'Do you really think so?'

'For God's sake! You have great sex, you like doing the same things, you're both teachers, you're made for each other,' she says. 'You'll be getting married this time next year and if you think I'm going to be a Matron of Honour, you're crazy. It's enough that I have to play the role for my bloody sister this December.'

'Yes, she asked me to the wedding, but she was flirting with every straight man at my party!'

'That's Nat for you. It's going to be a winter wedding, with red velvet dresses for me and the bridesmaids, and white fur at the neck, sleeves and hem. We'll all look like Father Christmas!'

I stifle a laugh. 'Why does she want to get married in December?'

'Oh, she's into a Winter Wonderland theme. There'll be fake snowflakes at the church, baubles and fairy lights, Christ knows what. Santa's probably going to turn up with his reindeer to give his blessing to the happy couple,' says Nadine. 'Hey, wait a minute, you can't cop off with Mr Windsor after all. I was counting on you being my Plus One. None of the men I know are suitable partners for such a bizarre wedding. Oh, the humiliation of being the older single sister!'

'Do you ever want to get married, Nad?'

'Absolutely not,' says Nadine, but her face is hidden by her long hair as she bends over a display case of miniatures. 'Hey, I like this one, where it's just a picture of an eye! Remember I used to have a Great Frog ring with an artificial eye in a silver setting? I'll have to start wearing it again.'

She's artfully changed the subject. She might be able to peer into my head with her own eyes and see into my mind, but I can't always work out what Nadine's thinking. But I feel so fond of her now, standing looking so thin and pale and vulnerable with her silk scarf tied round her neck.

I put my arm round her. 'I do love you, Naddie,' I say, and she hugs me back.

We wander round the heath after we've had our art fix. I look about, trying to get my bearings. I wish I had a better sense of direction. In my life too, not just literally.

'There's a ladies' pond somewhere,' I say. 'I've always fancied having a swim there. How about coming with me some time?'

'I hate swimming – especially in a muddy outdoor pond with ducks pecking at me!' says Nadine.

I wonder if Alice likes outdoor swimming? It would be fun to go with her. But she clearly isn't bothered about me. And Wendy might start wondering what I'm up to, contacting her girlfriend.

I glance quickly at my phone to see if she's replied, but of course she hasn't. Nadine sees me looking.

'Aha! You're checking to see if Guy's messaged!' she says.

'I was looking to see if my new friend Alice had got in touch, actually. See, you can't always read me like a book,' I say – though to be fair, I did look for a message from him too.

When I get back to my flat later there's a brown carrier bag on the doorstep, the handles tied with a red ribbon. I peer at it nervously. Is it another present? I untie the ribbon and peep inside. There's an oblong cellophaned box with another red ribbon round it. My throat dries.

I wait until I'm indoors, and I've stroked Stella and fed her too, before nerving myself to open the box. I scrabble with the cellophane and discover it contains chocolates – old-fashioned plain ones, each one decorated with a crystallized rose petal.

I pick one out of its crinkly paper cup and wonder if it could be contaminated in some way. But the box is pristine, and was wrapped in cellophane. I have a very tiny nibble. It's delicious. So who on earth is this secret admirer leaving me gifts with a rose theme?

It's intriguing, flattering I suppose – but kind of creepy too. I go back outside and peer up and down the walkway, leaning against the balcony rail to steady myself. How do they know when I'm out? Are they keeping watch on me? I imagine a disembodied eye, like the one in Nadine's miniature, tracking my every move.

Yet another idea for Myrtle: A secret admirer is leaving her gifts of cheese and a miniature bottle of wine in a silver thimble. She keeps watch and is amazed to discover it's . . . I don't know. And it doesn't matter, because Myrtle's no longer chiming.

I head back inside, giving my left wrist a little stroke, and determinedly sit down at my desk to sketch elephants while I snack on chocolates. I've eaten half the box by supper time, and feel sick. Perhaps I'll give the rest to Andreea if she's back home. I pocket my keys, pop next door and offer them to her.

'They're from my secret admirer. Goodness knows who he is. But the chocolates are fine, I promise. I've just eaten too many. So please, you have the rest,' I say.

'Well, that's very kind. These chocolates are very expensive! Come in and have a drink with me. My aunt gave me a bottle of cherry brandy, home-made!'

Andreea's flat has the same layout as mine but it's very different in atmosphere – lots of swirly carpet and a Dralon sofa and tapestry cushions with religious scenes. I edge away from a picture of Christ being crucified, looking very agonized.

'I didn't know you were religious,' I say.

'I'm not, but these were the ones they had in the Oxfam shop,' she says, laughing. 'They remind me of my grandma. She kept all kinds of religious artefacts in her flat, defying the Regime.'

She pours us a generous glass of cherry brandy each – perhaps too generous, because it's very fiery, and I've already had half a bottle of wine at the picnic, though that was a while ago.

I feel an urge to tell her all my problems, but I'm aware they're very minor compared with hers. She has a degree and speaks four languages, but she can only find manual jobs. She does a day shift in an old people's home and then works as a waitress in a restaurant three evenings a week too. She never seems sorry for herself, though.

She says she's fond of old people and likes to hear their stories, and she's in love with the Italian owner of the restaurant so it's good to be in his company, even though she knows it's hopeless because he has a wife and three children he adores. She's only about twenty-five but seems much more grown up than I am.

'How is Cat?' she asks politely.

'She's fine. And thank you very much for the milk,' I say, even though it went down my own throat.

'And how are you, Ellie? You seem a bit . . .' She turns the corners of her mouth down, looking rather like Mary Magdalene mourning Jesus at the foot of his cross.

'I'm fine too, more or less,' I say, swigging down my brandy.

And I am fine too, finer than fine, because when I'm back in my own flat and check my mobile yet again I find I have a message and a voicemail.

The text is from Alice.

Hi, I've been laid low with food poisoning. Never ever eat prawn gumbo! But bit better today, and sorting through elephant books. If you're free next Sat morning shall we go swimming, have coffee at caff, then go to my place so you can see which would be helpful?

The voicemail is from Guy.

Hi, Ellie! So good to see you yesterday. How about another gallery next Saturday and then you come back to mine again? Yes?

Yes, definitely! He sounds really keen. He certainly acted keen back at his place. I close my eyes, sinking into the memories.

I feel too shy to phone him back – which is mad, when we've lain naked together only yesterday. And I'm a bit worried my voice might sound slurred. That cherry brandy was lethal. I send him a text instead, and decide to keep it simple.

Hi Guy, I'd love to see you on Sat. Stella the cat has given me special permission to enjoy a sleepover this time. xx

Now Alice.

You poor thing, food poisoning is awful. Did Wendy get it too? I'd love to go back to yours on Saturday. See you then. x

I send one more message.

Darling Nads, Loved our picnic. Hope you're in your nun's cell, saying the rosary like a good girl. xxx

Thank goodness I get a reply from her straight away.

Dearest Mother Superior, You've been a sweetheart today. Don't tell Mags! Humble hugs and xxxx

I don't tell Mags, though she phones my mobile during morning break at school the next day.

'OK, El, at last I've got a moment to myself,' she says. 'So tell all. In detail. Especially the sexy bits.'

'Aren't you at work?'

'It's a working-from-home day, darling.'

'Well, lucky you. I'm in the middle of a crowded staff room. I'm not going to blurt out details of my sex life, Magda!' I tell her. I thought I was whispering, but the staff near me make mock groans and lewd remarks, especially the older men, all repellent in the extreme in their check shirts and knitted ties and scuffed suede shoes. Thankfully Guy isn't remotely like them, even if he's around their age.

'Go in the Ladies' loo, for heaven's sake!' Magda hisses.

'How about waiting till I get home?' I suggest. 'The children are with their mum now, aren't they?'

'Thank God! But Chris sometimes gets off early. He's so sweet, he insists on cooking supper now and is forever telling me to put my feet up and take it easy. He's the most thoughtful man in the world, Ellie. Talk about third time lucky!'

'Yes, yes,' I say, wishing Magda wasn't quite so besotted. Sometimes I wonder if she's trying to convince herself as well as me. She's so determined to make this work, even if she has to turn herself inside out and become a whole different person to fit in with Chris.

'Please, darling, go in the Ladies' loo so you can talk freely!' Magda begs.

It's impossible to talk freely because there are four cubicles, and female staff barge in and out all the time. I keep my voice down, especially when I hear Cath's clompy boots, but manage to tell her some of what happened on Saturday night.

'You promise this isn't an elaborate wind-up?' says Magda. 'You swear you actually had sex with Mr Windsor?'

There's an incredulous note to her voice. I frown at the cubicle door as if it's Magda's face. She doesn't have to act so surprised.

'He left me a voicemail last night too. He wants to see me again on Saturday,' I say.

'And the sex was really good? He can still get it up OK?' she asks.

I'm really glaring now. Guy is only fifty, not eighty! Why should she ask such a stupid thing? Could *Chris* possibly have difficulties in that department from time to time?

'It was the best sex I've ever had,' I say truthfully.

'He's really good at it? Lots of foreplay and sexy talk and taking his time?'

'Yes. And yes. And yes. And we came almost simultaneously, and he cuddled me close afterwards and said lovely things,' I say.

'Oh.' Magda is silenced. She sounds so subdued that I feel the need to reassure her that it isn't quite perfect.

'I think he's seeing someone else,' I admit.

'Well, only to be expected, I suppose,' says Magda. 'But he hasn't been married before?'

'I'm not sure.'

'But he hasn't got any children?'

'No.'

'You lucky girl,' says Magda wistfully. 'Oh Ellie, what am I going to do? I've tried so hard with Nat and Corrie and yet they still seem to hate me. And Chris always takes their side, even when they're being positively vile. You've had Lottie, you teach, you understand children so much more than me. Could you come round this weekend and tell me what I'm doing wrong?'

The bell goes for the end of break.

'I've got to go, Mags. Lesson time. And I can't come round Saturday. I'm seeing Guy then.'

'Well, Sunday then,' says Magda. 'Even better! In the afternoon? Chris is playing in some incredibly boring golf match, leaving me in charge. Ellie, I'm desperate. I'm sure it's bad for the baby to be getting in such a state. It's swimming about like a little piranha fish at the moment.'

'Sunday afternoon, OK. Got to go. Lots of love.'

I have a Year Nine class next. They're goodish kids, but Year Nines are always a bit scary until you suss them out. The boys still look boyish, but a few of the girls seem like grown women, with their exaggerated eyebrows and thick foundation and their perfected posing. Even these girls seem childish today, though, and their hitched-up skirts make them look vulnerable and coltish, not sexy in the least – though maybe they fantasize about all sorts of things like we did? And still do, for that matter.

I wander round the art room, giving advice, praising, having little chats. I'm boring old Miss Allard in her white shirt and smart black trousers, every inch a teacher. But in my head I am stark naked on the bed with Guy with my legs spread.

How am I going to get through the rest of the day, and then Tuesday, Wednesday, Thursday and Friday before seeing him again? I could be bold and suggest meeting up one evening – but maybe that's when he sees Lipstick Girl? Or Girls, plural . . .

I go home after school, walking along the balcony a little warily, but there's no secret admirer crouching there, no flowers or chocolates by the door, which is a relief. I have a shower, then pull on a grey baggy teeshirt and ancient trackie bottoms. If my life was a rom-com, there would be a ring at my door any minute and Guy would be there, overcome with lust, not at all put off by my appearance. He'd take me in his arms and kiss me so passionately that my glasses go flying, and we'd make love right there in the hall with Stella hissing at us indignantly.

I give myself a mental shake. *Stop thinking about bloody Guy! Get to work on your elephants.* I feed Stella, sit down at my desk with a cup of coffee and flex my arms. I shut my eyes for a moment, imagining Mosi and her tribe. They're walking at dawn, dark silhouettes against a brilliant orange sun. I get out my watercolours and paint it as vividly as I can, using a whole page. The shapes aren't quite right yet, the position of the trunks, the movement of their legs, but it's still a dramatic picture. Maybe a good cover design?

I start on another page, a close-up of Mosi and her latest calf. Do elephants and their young really twine trunks like in *Dumbo*? I watched it over and over when I was little, sitting on Mum's lap, and when Mrs Jumbo and Dumbo were separated we both cried.

Then Mum and I were separated too. I cried every night for months and months. I've grown up talking to her inside my head but I'm not sure I've got her tone of voice right. I wish she had a grave. I'd love to visit her and buy her flowers and lie down on the grass beside her.

Dad had her cremated, and he didn't even keep the ashes. He sprinkled them by the sea and didn't take me because he said it would be too upsetting. For a long time I couldn't ever go to the seaside without staring into the waves, wondering if little specks of Mum were still bobbing backwards and forwards with the tide.

I tried to talk to him about her but he couldn't bear it and did his best to shut me up. Then he took up with Anna, and I was landed with a young stepmother. I hated her at first, simply because she wasn't Mum. Perhaps she secretly hated me too, but she was mostly kind and patient and rarely lost her temper. I goaded her repeatedly, trying to get some reaction from her. 'Now, Ellie, calm down,' she'd say in her clipped little voice, when all I wanted her to do was scream back at me.

I am clearly the perfect friend and advisor for Magda. I can tell her honestly that after a while I grew to depend on Anna. Not as a mum. She's more like a big sister to me now. I love her dearly, maybe more than Dad. No, not more. Just . . . differently.

I do love him, of course, but we've never really been close. I couldn't stand him when I was an awkward teenager. He was forever trying to tell me what to do, always furious if I came home late, and yet *he* often stayed out till midnight or beyond.

My mobile rings, making me jump, so half of Mosi's head receives a brushful of black paint, and I curse under my breath. I reach for my phone, hoping it's Guy – but no, it's Anna! Weird, when I've just been thinking about her. She rarely rings, rarely even messages. I frown as I tap the green button, wondering what's up.

'Hi, Anna,' I say, holding the phone with my left hand and dabbing at the black splodge with a tissue. 'Is anything wrong?'

'No, no. Well, not really,' she says.

'Has something happened?' I put my brush down, waiting.

'Well, your dad's been a bit depressed recently,' says Anna. She's lowered her voice now. I think she's in the kitchen, and Dad must be in the living room watching the news.

'In what way?' I ask.

'He's just . . . *flat*. Bored. Fed up with life. I've tried so hard to get him involved in the firm, but he's not interested. He's acting like he hasn't got a purpose in life any more.'

'Oh, for goodness' sake!' I cry, exasperated.

'Anyway, as he had such a good time on your fortieth, I was wondering about having another little celebration, just immediate family. You and Lottie, hopefully, if she can get away from the camp. And Ben and Simon, of course. OK?'

'Lovely,' I say, and then ask warily, 'When?'

'This Saturday. You could maybe have a good chat with him, see how things are going with him. He'll probably tell you more than he'll tell me. And then we could have a slap-up meal in the evening. It'll really cheer him up, especially if he feels he's the centre of attention.'

Saturday!

'Anna, could we fix it for later on some time? It's a lovely idea, but I'm afraid Saturday's booked up already – I'm seeing people morning, afternoon, evening. It's all writ in stone. I'm so sorry, but I can't really rearrange stuff.'

I suppose I *could* – but if I'm honest, I really don't want to. I feel sorrier for Anna than I do for him. It must be tough for her, having to cope.

'Then how about Sunday? Perhaps you could come in the morning and go for a walk with your dad, and then we could have a big roast lunch?' Anna asks.

But I want to stay over at Guy's this time and have a proper Sunday morning with him. And I've promised Magda I'll go round to hers in the afternoon. A day with Dad in the doldrums isn't a tempting change of plans.

'I wish I could, Anna, but it's just not possible.' I run my free hand through my hair, feeling a heel already. Especially when Dad forked out a fortune for my party, *and* gave me the cheque. But I didn't *ask* him to.

'Shall we make it another weekend? When I can make sure I'm free?' I say quickly.

'Yes. Yes, of course. I realize it's ridiculously short notice, and you've got your own life all planned. Sorry, darling. Don't worry. Everything will be fine. I think I'm just a bit down myself, over-anxious. Well, I'm sure you have things to do. Love you. Bye bye,' Anna gabbles, and hangs up before I can get another word in.

I feel truly dreadful. I quickly phone Ben.

'Hey, Ben, you and Si couldn't possibly go to Dad and Anna's this Saturday, could you?' I say hastily. 'Anna's just invited me and I've actually got a hot date and don't want to cancel.'

'Oh wow, big sis! A hot date! Tell us! Can I put you on speakerphone so that Si can hear too?' he says.

'No, you can't! I don't want to tempt fate. I'll tell you all about it later on. But can you go there on Saturday and make a fuss of Dad? Anna sounds a bit desperate.'

'I wish, but we're going out with Dean and Michael, trendy restaurant booked,' he says.

'Right. Well, soon, let's all go together on a mission to cheer up the ageing parent,' I suggest, and ring off.

I don't call Lottie, though I do text. I can't possibly ask her to travel all the way back to see him, but I ask if she'd send Grandad a few photos of her with the kids at summer camp, along with a loving message.

Poor Anna will simply have to cope by herself. I can't go cancelling all my plans just because Dad feels a bit down.

And yet I keep waking up in the night, my conscience heavy.

11

I work hard all week, teaching each day, sketching elephant ideas most of the evening, trying to distract myself. On Friday I wonder about catching the train to Dad and Anna's straight after school and taking them out for a meal, then getting a late train back again. I know it would please Anna. It might even cheer Dad up temporarily.

But what would we talk about? I'd love to see Anna's new knitwear designs for the winter, particularly her annual up-market Christmas jumper, but Dad always goes a bit droopy when Anna talks shop. He's a hopelessly old-fashioned husband, always resenting her success, especially now he's retired. Dad himself certainly won't have any news because he doesn't *do* anything, just sits at home mouldering.

I've certainly got news, but I don't want to talk about Guy. I'm sure Dad would disapprove, though it's none of his business who I get involved with now. Maybe Anna might be a bit uncomfortable about it too.

In the end, I don't follow through with the Friday night meal plan. I fidget around at my flat instead, having a little personal grooming session, peering in my wardrobe to see if it has somehow hatched the perfect cool, ultra-flattering outfit for tomorrow all by itself, and jot down as many sensible-sounding questions about elephants as I can think up.

I consult one of my new elephant books crammed on top of my huge art book collection. I smile at the two identical volumes on the Pre-Raphaelites. One was a Christmas present from little Nick Rivers, my favourite pupil. He's a sweet boy of sixteen who could easily pass for twelve. He's got the faintest down above his upper lip but otherwise puberty has passed him by. He's very bright academically but not much cop at art, actually. He's chosen it as an additional GCSE – 'Because I love your lessons so, Miss Allard,' he told me earnestly.

I much prefer it that he calls me Miss Allard, instead of the irritating abbreviated Miss that all the others hiss at me. He blushed painfully when he thrust the book at me at the end of last term. I already have a copy at home, but I thanked him profusely for his thoughtfulness.

I clap my hand over my mouth. I've told the kids all about Rossetti because some of them live in Rossetti block. I gave them a mini-lecture about the incidence of roses in his paintings. Could little Nick Rivers be leaving the rose-themed tributes on my doorstep? It seems highly unlikely that he'd dare go that far – but not impossible. What a relief if it's him, though a bit of a disappointment it's not someone more exciting.

I shall have to tackle him about it on Monday, as tactfully as possible. He's a hopeless blusher. I'll just have to murmur the word 'doorstep' and if he's the culprit he'll go as red as the roses.

I dally with *Mrs D* for a while and then curl up in bed with Stella lolling next to my feet. She's soon breathing steadily, even giving the softest of little snores, but I stay relentlessly awake for a very long time.

Then the alarm goes off and it's Saturday at last. I leap up, shower, shove a piece of toast in my mouth, swallow scalding coffee, give Stella a scattering of biscuits, then rush off with my tote bag bulging with towels, shampoo and body lotion.

I dare to get changed in the communal dressing room because I've put my costume on under my teeshirt and jeans – but Alice isn't there again. It was all arranged too. I'm surprised how disappointed I feel. I'd really love to find out more about elephants.

I hang around for ten minutes or so, while energetic women dash in and out, but start to feel self-conscious, scared they might think I'm spying on them. Then I wonder if perhaps she's in the water already, and go to the edge of the pool to look. I'm hopelessly short-sighted without my glasses – and give a little scream when a hand suddenly thrusts itself out of the water and seizes me by the ankle.

I burst out laughing when I make out Alice grinning up at me.

'Sorry! I didn't mean to startle you!' she says.

I beam down at her. The turquoise water is suddenly dazzling, the municipal tiles as white as marble.

'Jump in, then!' Alice calls.

I usually creep slowly down the steps adjusting to the freezing water, but this time I do as I'm told. It's a shame we're not at the deep end as I'm quite a neat diver, but I make do with as graceful a leap as I can manage. She gets splashed but doesn't seem to mind.

'So, how are you?' I ask.

'So much better, thanks. Starving hungry all the time now,' she says. 'Looking forward to my almond croissant. You can still come back to mine after, can't you?'

I like it that she says mine instead of ours. Though why on earth it should matter, I don't know.

'I'd love to,' I say.

She reaches out and takes hold of me by the wrist this time. It's suddenly hard to catch my breath. She's looking at Myrtle.

'She looks great,' she says. 'How's it been? Not too sore?'

'Not at all. And I really like her,' I say.

'Maybe I've started you off down the slippery slope and you'll end up with a tattoo addiction. I read a book as a kid about two sisters whose mum gets heaps of tattoos and then she paints herself all over to cover them up,' says Alice.

'I read that book too!' I say, delighted. 'Don't worry, I won't go that far.'

Another swimmer comes thumping up between us, turns and kicks off again, splashing a bit more than necessary to show he doesn't approve of us hanging about chatting.

'Not very subtle, eh?' says Alice, raising an eyebrow. 'Still, I suppose we'd better get going.'

She leads the way, darting forward through the water like a fish. I swim full out but I can't quite catch her. In fact, when the hour is up she's actually managed to lap me twice, which is pretty impressive seeing as she's been ill. She waits for me, grinning triumphantly.

When we dress we stand with our backs to one other. I still struggle under a towel, but Alice doesn't bother.

'Hey, you've really lost weight,' I say without thinking, then want to bite my tongue off because she'll know I've been staring at her.

'I know,' she says, groaning as if it's a bad thing. Which maybe it is for her because she was pretty slim to start with. 'I shall have to publicize my miracle new diet: just make a gumbo with a packet of seriously dodgy prawns, and there you go!'

'You must have been so ill! Did Wendy bring you Lucozade and dry toast while you were convalescing?' I ask.

'Did she fuck,' says Alice. 'She insists it's not food poisoning at all. She says it's Norovirus and that I probably caught it from one of my students.'

Alice sounds quite fed up about it – and I don't blame her. Wendy doesn't sound a very sympathetic partner at all. 'Well,

155

if she ate the gumbo too and didn't get ill, maybe she could be right,' I say vaguely.

'But the thing is, she *didn't* eat it. She made it because it was her turn to cook, but then she decided the little pink prawns were making her feel sad, and that she thought she was ready to go full vegan now. So I ate it all, and the little pink prawns made me feel *way* worse than sad,' says Alice.

'Oh dear,' I say, for lack of any other suitable comment.

'Sorry. Nothing's more boring than other people's domestic squabbles,' says Alice. 'Come on, let's go and have our croissants.'

It's raining when we come out of the leisure centre, but we've got wet hair anyway and it doesn't really matter. My careful taming of my frizz has been a complete waste of time. Alice's short hair looks as cute as always. She's wearing a tight black teeshirt, skinny black jeans with a belt and big black boots today. I wish I could squeeze into jeans that skinny. And I love her statement Docs. Lottie's got that exact style. I remember when I used to paint her little boots with all the things she liked: Disney characters, unicorns, mermaids. She called them her magic boots and loved showing them off.

'You OK, Ellie?' Alice asks.

'Yes, fine,' I say quickly. I must have been looking a bit wistful. 'I was just thinking about my daughter, actually. I miss her sometimes.' *All* the time.

'It must be great to have a child, especially now she's grown up,' says Alice. 'Wendy and I used to talk about having babies when we first got together.'

'But you didn't go through with it?'

'It was always going to be in the future, next year, or the year after. And it's the year after that now, and it probably isn't going to happen,' says Alice. She says it very matter-of-factly, so I can't work out whether she minds or not.

'Oh well,' I say inadequately. 'It might have been . . . complicated.'

'Not really,' she says. 'We're friends with these two great guys who'd have been happy to be the fathers. There for their child whenever – four parents for the price of two.'

'Ah. Well, Lottie's father was never there for her. But we were fine just the two of us. We didn't need him,' I say.

'She's met him?' Alice asks.

'No. We don't even know where he is,' I say. 'And she doesn't want to, anyway. She's got my brother and his husband, and my dad, and heaps of other lovely men in her life. In fact, I've just met someone I really like, so if we become a real thing then obviously she'll meet him. And it'll be great, he's lovely, she's lovely, they'll get on splendidly – I hope.'

'That's good,' says Alice. She pauses, looking at me. 'So what's so special about this new guy? How did you meet him?'

'Oh, sort of a friend of a friend. Actually, I used to know him ages ago, when I was just a teenager, and now we've met up again.' For some reason, I'm not sure I want to say he used to be my teacher. 'He's a bit older than me, but that's OK. Men my age seem to want girls in their twenties. Or even younger.' I pause. 'Is it the same for elephants?'

Alice bursts out laughing. 'Female elephants have it more sussed out. They're tribal animals, and the older females do their best to protect the young females from getting pregnant too early. The males aren't very subtle. They get quite aggressive and fan their ears a lot so that their scent wafts about.'

'Like young men with Lynx!' I say. 'Do female elephants ever have relationships with each other?'

'Yep. They sometimes groom and wind their trunks round each other and are really affectionate. It's adorable.'

'So they really do twine trunks! And the daughters stay with their mothers all their lives?' I check.

Alice regards me thoughtfully. 'Do you wish you were an elephant, Ellie?'

I laugh. 'I do! But they don't have hands so they can't draw.'

'They can, actually. Some Asian elephants have been given special paintbrushes so they can grip them with their trunks and they stand at big easels and paint lovely pictures.'

'You're joking!'

'No, truly,' she insists. 'They're abstracts of course, but very decorative all the same.'

We're at the café now, and Rosa greets us both warmly.

'Coffee and almond croissants?' she asks.

'Would you think me an awful pig if I have two?' says Alice.

'Go for it! I'm not sure I should have any,' I say, patting my middle.

'Are you crazy?' she asks. 'You haven't got an eating thing, have you?' Then she pulls a face, embarrassed. 'Sorry, that was a bit direct.'

'It's OK. Well, I did once have a thing about food, not full-blown anorexia, but pretty nearly. I still get a bit obsessed, if I'm honest. And there's this new relationship. It's rather unnerving taking your clothes off at first,' I say. Oh God, why am I telling her all this when I still hardly know her? Though it feels so easy, so comfortable, like a conversation with Nadine or Magda.

'Oh, it's always awkward the first time,' says Alice, surprising me. She seems so easy and confident. I thought she'd strip off without turning a hair.

'When was your first time?' I find myself asking. Now *I'm* being too direct. But she doesn't seem to mind.

'Oh, when I was about fifteen, with a friend from school. We didn't really know what we were doing,' she says. 'And you?'

'I was a year or so older. It was a bit fumbly and embarrassing, but I suppose it was OK. After a few times it got a lot better.' I pull a face. 'I saw him again the other day actually. He wouldn't be my cup of tea nowadays.'

'But now you've met this special someone?' she asks.

I shrug. 'Well, he might be.' I take a deep breath. Could I possibly ask her when her relationship with Wendy became 'exclusive'? But no, I can't say that, she might think I'm asking if her relationship is an open one, and think I was coming on to her. Which of course I'm not.

Luckily the coffee and a big plate of pastries arrive, almond croissants and plain ones too, and pain aux raisins and an apricot Danish.

'Take your pick!' says Rosa.

Alice grins, and we both dig in. The almond croissants go first. And then she tucks into a pain aux raisins and I can't hold off any longer and eat the apricot Danish. Alice eats the pain aux raisins by nibbling round and round the spiral, saving the gooey bit in the middle till last.

'That's exactly how Lottie eats them!' I say.

'Is there any other way, "says Alice"?' she says.

'I recognize that! *They're changing guard at Buckingham Palace!*'

'*Christopher Robin went down with Alice*,' she adds, grinning that I get the reference. 'My mum used to read it to me, and I'd add "says Alice" at the end of each verse. She read the Winnie-the-Pooh stories too. In fact, my nickname was Piglet.'

'My mum read them to me, too. And I read them to Lottie,' I say.

'Is your mum still around?' she asks softly, picking up on the twinge of sadness in my tone.

'No, she died when I was little,' I say. 'But it's OK, I get on wonderfully well with my stepmum, Anna. Better than I do with my dad actually. He's a bit sorry for himself at the moment.

He taught at an art college for ages and now he's been forced to retire he's kind of at a loose end, you know?'

'I know,' says Alice. 'I'm going to take early retirement if I'm ever offered it, and then I'll still be young enough to go off adventuring for a while. Perhaps even back to Africa.'

'What does Wendy think about that?' I ask.

'Oh. I can't really see Wendy in Africa somehow,' says Alice.

'Why? "Lions and tigers and bears, oh my"?'

'"I've got a feeling we're not in Kansas any more,"' Alice says without hesitation.

'I can't believe we speak the same language,' I say. 'How many times have you watched *The Wizard of Oz*?'

'Well, it's always repeated on the telly at Christmas, and I've got a special gift version DVD anyway, so I guess it must be thirty times,' says Alice. 'I bet I can chant it all the way through. And I do cracking Munchkin voices. Shall I demonstrate?'

I peer around at the rapidly filling café. 'Maybe not here . . .'

'Maybe not,' she says. 'I was teasing.'

We smile at each other. It's as if we've known each other all our lives. Yet it's not all samey and comforting and taken for granted, the way it is with Nadine and Magda. It's new and exciting and makes me feel so alive.

I try to tempt her to eat a third pastry just to see if she could manage it, but she's wise enough to say no. Then we settle up and hesitate when we get outside.

'Is it really all right for me to come back to yours?' I ask.

'Of course. We can take a bus, or it's about a twenty-minute walk. What do you think?'

'Walk? And then we can kid ourselves that we're working off all those thousands of calories,' I say.

'Ellie! Stop that calorie nonsense,' she says.

I'd bristle if Nadine or Magda said anything similar, but for some reason I don't mind being lectured by Alice. Besides, she's not really serious. I can't believe how quickly we've got to this stage. It's usually so much harder making adult friends.

Nadine and I were best friends after our first day in Reception just because we'd made each other necklaces. It took a little longer with Magda when we met her at secondary school, but we were doing the same lessons five days a week, all three of us feeling very new and uncertain though we were doing our best to look cool. Then after our first PE lesson we all had a good moan about Mrs Henderson and the awfulness of communal showers and became best friends.

I've made other friends obviously, my art college buddies and the teachers at school, but we haven't ever got to the stage of confiding practically everything immediately. Perhaps it's just that Alice is so friendly – and not just to me. On the way to her house, four different people wave to her or say hi, and one old lady stops her and chats at length about her new grandchild, proudly showing her photos. It looks the most ordinary of babies to me, but Alice is immensely enthusiastic, and the old lady goes away with a spring in her step. Oh God, perhaps *I'm* one of Alice's old ladies, and she's just feigning an interest in me because she's so kind! No, that's rubbish. She likes me, I'm sure she does. Well, I *hope* she does.

We take a shortcut through a park where people are walking their dogs, and Alice seems to know most of them too. They all come running up, a huge German Shepherd, a wildly barking terrier, a puffball Pomeranian. Alice makes a big fuss of each one and has treats for them in one of her pockets.

'I'd give anything to have my own dog,' she confides. 'But it wouldn't be fair. I'm out teaching all day and Wendy doesn't get up till the afternoon.'

I blink. Does she do shift work? A nurse? A policewoman?

'Does she work at night then?' I ask.

'Yeah,' Alice says vaguely, and then gets distracted by a

golden teddy bear of a dog off its lead who jumps right up into her arms and licks her lovingly.

I like dogs myself but I'm not sure I'd like dog slurp all over my face. Alice doesn't seem to mind in the slightest. She's cuddling the dog, tickling it under the chin, encouraging it. The teddy bear's owner is a no-nonsense-looking woman with very short hair who greets Alice enthusiastically, looking as if she'd rather like to lick her face too.

I realize I'm just the latest member of the well-subscribed Alice fan club. I feel a twinge of annoyance. I wanted to feel special, not one of a crowd. What's the matter with me? Perhaps I want exclusive friendships as well as relationships. I think about Guy and Lipstick Girl. Does he see her often, two or three times a week, or is she just a once-a-month encounter? Are there others too? I picture a line of gorgeous women queuing up outside Guy's house, waiting for their turn to grace his bed, all younger than me and elfin skinny. It's a depressing thought.

I sigh and suddenly remember that I'd meant to get in touch with Dad. I mutter an apology to Alice, and send a quick message.

Hey there, dearest Dad. How are you doing? Thank you again for coughing up for the most fantastic party of my life. See you very soon, lots of love xxx

Hopefully he'll show the text to Anna and she won't think so badly of me.

Alice is looking at me. I can't quite read her expression. Is she annoyed? Concerned? Amused?

'Texting the new man?' she asks.

'No, texting the very old man. My dad. As I said, he's feeling a bit down at the moment,' I say apologetically.

162

'Oh, that's lovely of you,' says Alice.

No, I'm not lovely at all – a measly text is hardly consolation for not going to see him – but I let her think the best of me.

'It's great to be on good terms with dads. And mums,' says Alice. She's pulling a face, though I don't think she realizes it.

'I gather you're not?' I ask gently.

'No. They've got big problems about my being gay. They hope I'm just going through a "phase",' she says, sighing.

'In this day and age?'

'Yep.'

'That must be tough.'

She gives me a grateful smile and we walk for a couple of minutes in comfortable silence. I've never felt this relaxed with someone in so short a time.

'Well, this is my street.'

I look round eagerly. It's two rows of terraced houses without proper front gardens. Some are plain brick, others painted white, and one a pretty shade of blue. One person full of Pride has painted a huge rainbow on the front of their house, but the arc is a little off-centre and indigo and violet have been blended together. A few houses have pots of flowers either side of the front door, and one has a bizarre waist-high model of a sheep.

Alice's house isn't the rainbow one, or the sheep home; it's an ordinary white one, with a plant being trained up the wall on a trellis. It's being wilful, hanging loose and failing to thrive.

'It's wisteria, but it's clearly dying,' she says. 'Are you any good at gardening, Ellie?'

'Simon is – my brother's husband. I'll ask him if he's got any tips, if you like.'

'That would be great,' she says. 'I had this picture in my head, graceful purple flowers hanging against the white wall – but it hasn't happened yet.'

'I take it Wendy isn't a gardener either?' I ask.

Alice looks at me sideways, as if this is a mad suggestion. She fishes for her keys, opens the door and beckons me in.

'Should we whisper?' I murmur.

'No, she can sleep through anything,' says Alice. She looks up the narrow stairs. 'And the bedroom door's shut.'

There are large-framed photographs up the stairs – all of elephants! Amazing ones of mothers and babies twining trunks, a study of a huge wrinkled head with tiny wise eyes, a massive bull elephant with great ears spread, a shot of an entire tribe silhouetted against the orange sky exactly as I'd imagined.

'They're wonderful!'

Alice looks really pleased.

'Could I maybe take photos of *your* photos?' I ask. 'So I can get their stance just right? These are so much better than anything I've found online.'

'Sure,' she says, switching on the stair light.

I snap away on my mobile and then follow her into the living room, gaping as I look around. I hoped there might be more elephant photographs, but the walls are covered with shelves. There are a few books but they're mostly full of old LPs, all obsessively neatly arranged, and there's a massive music deck, looking very technical and intimidating.

'So you're obviously into music in a big way,' I say, glancing at the covers. It's mostly people I've never even heard of.

'Not really,' she says. I think she's being funny and smile. 'No, I mean it. These are all Wendy's.'

I shake my head, and Alice sees my surprise.

'Didn't I tell you? She's a DJ at Catz.' She sees I look blank. 'It's a nightclub, very popular, open till four in the morning. It's where we met. It's not my sort of place, but a couple of girls I know like to go there on gay nights and dragged me along. And I saw her dancing about, doing her stuff, and thought she was brilliant. Well, she still is.'

I can't think of a single thing to say in response. Old Wendy crawls away, New Wendy bounces in. Brilliantly.

I perch on the edge of a small sofa, feeling distinctly out of place. This isn't really a living room. It's Wendy's studio. I wonder if Alice minds.

'My room with all my research and stuff is upstairs,' she explains, as though reading my mind. 'I'll make us some coffee and then take you up there.'

I look at the bookshelves. They're arranged in alphabetical order, but they're in jangling juxtaposition: music books, celebrity autobiographies, mindfulness manuals, cheek by jowl with nature and animal tomes and paperbacks – Maya Angelou and Toni Morrison and Bernadine Evaristo and Zadie Smith. It's easy to guess whose books are whose. I'd hate to have them all mingling like that, though. I've always had to have separate shelving, even keeping Lottie's books separate from mine. My books are part of me, a physical manifestation of my personality.

Alice comes in with two coffee mugs.

'I keep all my elephant books upstairs,' she says. 'Coming?'

I follow her up the stairs, admiring the elephant photographs even more as I pass. I see the closed bedroom door, the bathroom – and another door to a smaller bedroom. Only it isn't a bedroom at all, it's Alice's study, with more elephant photography, a large desk and computer and various files and paperwork, and home-made DVDs and various books. She's also got her own tribe of wooden elephants marching across the window sill, carefully arranged, with a large matriarch leading them, followed by various sister elephants, and all the young calves carefully protected by the older ones.

'Is this how they really march?' I ask.

'Absolutely,' says Alice.

'Can I take a photo of them too?'

'You can take any photos you like. And have free access to any of my research. I'll treat you like one of my students,' she says, grinning. 'I hope you hand in your work on time, Miss Allard.'

'I'll do my best,' I say.

'So what else do you want to know? Shall I give you a potted version of my introductory lecture to first year students?' she asks.

'Please!'

She starts talking rapidly, while I take hasty notes. She's hamming it up, trying hard not to be too scientific, telling me all sorts of anecdotes. I start to get more and more ideas on how to develop my own story and give it more depth.

'There's just one problem though,' I say. 'Well, heaps of problems, but the main one is writing the speech bubbles. I'm going to have lots of linking prose, but obviously graphic means illustrations. I'm calling my elephants Swahili names because it sounds so much better than giving them English names – but I obviously can't write their speech in Swahili too. Yet it will sound dreadful using Disneyfied talk: "Hey, Ma, stand still and gimme some milk." I was wondering whether to use a type of archaic language, like the animals in *The Jungle Book*. What do you think? Be honest, please!'

'I think you've cracked it,' she says, just as I'd hoped.

She tells me how females listen to all the males who want to mate and select the ones who make the most noise. This makes sense if you're just concerned about having a big healthy calf – but not if you want a companion.

'They just want the males for mating,' says Alice. 'Then they're sent on their way. It's as if elephants live in one of those feminist utopias.'

'Maybe they've got more sense than we have,' I say.

She laughs.

'Alice?' someone calls, and then the door opens. A young woman is standing there, scratching her head and yawning. She's beautiful, with fantastic braids hanging over her shoulders. And she's stark naked.

Wendy.

12

'Wendy, for God's sake!' Alice says sharply.

'I *thought* I heard you yattering away,' says Wendy. She makes no attempt to cover herself up. She smiles at me. 'I'm Wendy,' she tells me unnecessarily. 'Who are you?'

'I'm Ellie,' I say, my cheeks flaming. 'Alice is showing me her elephant research.'

Why do I feel so flustered and guilty?

'Is she indeed?' says Wendy, raising her eyebrows.

She turns on her heel and saunters back to the bedroom.

'Is she going back to bed?' I whisper.

Alice shrugs uncomfortably. 'Maybe.'

But she's back almost immediately, wearing a silky kimono. Now I can look at her properly I see she's got a distinctive tattoo on her ankle, a daisy bracelet with a heart. She and Alice probably had them done together, when they became a couple.

'So you're into elephants too?' she says to me, looking amused. 'Are you a mature student?'

'No, she's not!' says Alice. 'Wendy, this is Ellie Allard. She's a famous cartoonist. Myrtle Mouse. You know.'

Wendy clearly doesn't know and doesn't care either.

'Any coffee on the go?' she asks Alice. 'I might as well stay up, seeing as you've woken me. Let's go downstairs, eh? It's too cramped in here.'

'You go downstairs. I'm just finding some photos and notes for Ellie. She's going to be doing a graphic novel about elephants,' says Alice.

'Cool,' says Wendy indifferently. 'You should be called Nellie, Ellie. Trump trump trump!'

I bare my teeth in a tired smile. So many kids at school come out with that hilarious display of wit.

Wendy patters downstairs. Alice and I try to get back to where we were, but it's not the same. It's as if Wendy is still in the room, yawning at us. Then after five minutes we hear music. 'Nellie the Elephant'.

'How on earth does she have that old record?' I ask.

'She's maybe streaming it. Though she has some very old children's tunes too – she mixes them up with something current. She can be very funny. They all think she's wonderful at Catz,' says Alice. It doesn't sound as if she necessarily still thinks Wendy wonderful herself.

Could it be that she's going off her?

Then the music changes. It's that old 'Alice' song, turned up even louder. I can remember dancing to it at school discos, when we all thought we were so bold yelling, '*Who the fuck is Alice?*'

Alice sighs. 'I think we'd better go down and have coffee with her. She's just going to keep on like this. She's like a kid who can't bear to be ignored.'

'I think I ought to be going anyway,' I say awkwardly. 'I've taken up too much of your time already.'

'It's been great,' says Alice, and I think she really means it. 'It's lovely to find someone to talk to. Not just about elephants.'

'It's been great for me too,' I say.

We look at each other, smiling shyly.

The music is turned up even louder. Alice grabs some folders and a couple of books and we go downstairs. Wendy is waiting for us at the bottom of the stairs and waggles her fingers at me, looking pleased that I'm going. Alice hesitates, then gives me a quick hug.

'See you at swimming next week? And have fun with your new guy meanwhile,' she says.

'Thanks,' I say uncomfortably.

Then I'm out the door and on my way, with Alice's elephant stuff in a borrowed tote bag bumping against my hip one side and my swimming gear thudding damply on the other. I wonder what it would be like to live with Alice – well, someone like her – and share a little terraced house together. Would we start the day having coffee together, chatting, planning our day? When we came home from work would we relax with a glass of wine, take turns cooking supper, watch a box set together, and then . . .

I get back to the estate. The lift is working, thank God. I walk along the balcony. My heart's thudding as I peer towards the door, but there's nothing there and I feel my shoulders relax. I go into my flat, call for Stella, and make myself another cup of coffee, glad to be drinking it here and not with Wendy. There's no denying it: I did not like her. And maybe Alice isn't quite so enamoured of her now, and no longer thinks she's brilliant.

'You're *my* brilliant girl, after Lottie,' I tell Stella as I stroke her. She arches her back complacently.

I sip my coffee and leaf through a couple of Alice's folders. They're a bit dry and scientific, but every now and then I catch a tone of her voice, her way of phrasing things. When I get past the first few pages I really get into it. I take further notes and then have a quick look through the books and start sketching a couple of the photographs. I'm surprised by their differing tusks, and the way some have much more ragged ears than others. I sketch a few calves just for the joy of it, and experiment with ways they might play together. I decide a new baby will arrive towards the end of the novel, and maybe struggle to thrive, or get in some kind of trouble . . . be ambushed by lions? But then Mosi and her older daughters – and the male calf who's been quite belligerent with the baby so far – will try to protect her.

The storyline is almost writing itself. Perhaps we'll start with the death of Mosi's mother, and the mourning period, and then she'll take over as matriarch. She'll already have a daughter, Binti, who's her most loyal companion – plus several sons who have left the tribe. One might only recently have left and be wandering around with another young male. They could be especially affectionate, an elephant Ben and Simon couple.

We'll have a drought, and things get desperate, but then there'll be lovely scenes when they manage to reach a beautiful lake. They can all drink their fill and play games and splash each other. I draw and draw, just rough sketches, not in any order, but it's getting there, my whole story, with spaces to insert further ideas when they occur to me.

I'm so absorbed I just nibble a sandwich and sip coffee as a working lunch. Guy phones as I'm experimenting with a tricky sketch of the elephants from behind, Mosi's splendid, saggy bottom in the forefront, with the youngest calf tucked underneath.

'Guy? What's up? Can't you make it this afternoon?' I ask.

'I was just checking you know which way to go when you get to Russell Square,' he says. He's already messaged to suggest going to the Foundling Museum and told me which tube to catch from Waterloo. 'I could meet you at the tube station if it's easier?' he offers.

'That's sweet of you, but I know that area quite well. I often go to the Curzon in the shopping precinct,' I say. I'm about to add that I've been to the Foundling Museum with Lottie, but he's too busy telling me all about it, as if it's the most amazing secret.

'I know you'll find it fascinating, Ellie – and there's a fantastic surprise for you there!' he says happily, as if he's arranged it personally.

It won't be a surprise because I know exactly what he's referring to: the magnificently grim painting by Paula Rego called *Oratorio*. It's like an altarpiece, with eight paintings and eight wooden figures depicting mothers and babies. I've stood in front of it for a full half hour, taking in every detail. But it seems such a put-down if I interrupt him now he's in full flow, giving me a little lecture about Thomas Coram being so concerned about abandoned babies that he raised money for a foundling hospital where they could be fed, sheltered and educated.

Lottie and I were both tearful, looking at the cabinets of tokens left by mothers forced to give up their babies. Some are pitifully humble: a small coin, a thimble, a bottle top.

Stomach cramps interrupt my train of thought, and I rub my belly. Perhaps I gobbled my sandwich too quickly. Or maybe I'm just irritated by Guy treating me like a kid.

Why on earth don't I shut him up and tell him? I suppose I don't want to hurt his feelings, or make things awkward. I tell myself there's no harm in going along with things if it pleases him. He wants to please *me*, after all.

I breathe a sigh of relief when he's finished at last, and we say goodbye. I go back to my elephant bottoms, but I've lost my concentration now and can't get their proportions right. I end up scribbling over that page in childish frustration.

Stella jumps up on my lap. Perhaps she wants to console me. I give her a guilty kiss between her ears.

'I'm afraid you'll be on your own tonight, darling. Now don't look so reproachful. I'll leave you extra treats. And when I get home, tomorrow morning, lunchtime at the latest, I'll cook you fresh fish even though it stinks the flat out, and

maybe I'll throw in some prawns too. Would you like that?'
I ask her.

I cuddle her for a long time, though I know I have to get
ready soon. I don't want to be late. I remember Guy getting
quite tetchy if we weren't in the art room on time. I shake my
head at myself. Why do I keep forgetting we're both adults
now? He's hardly going to consult his watch and say 'Eleanor
Allard, please get to your desk at once, you're holding up my
lesson.' It seems I still can't get my head around the fact that
I'm dating Mr Windsor.

I have another quick shower because I probably got a bit
sweaty with the shock of Wendy appearing stark naked. I do
my best to tame my hair. Then I dither over what to wear, in
the end plumping for a deep red dress that is a little bit too
tight, so plump is the operative word. The womanly curves are
on show in all their glory, but he did seem to admire them, so
what the hell.

I wear Lottie's indigo crystal bracelet on one wrist and
Magda's Tiffany eternity bracelet on the other, and have another
go at eyeliner. I peer in my mirror, trying to get the right angle,
screwing up the other eye so I look like a gargoyle. I try the
other eye, but now they're uneven, and I give up and wipe
them both clean. Why am I making such a ridiculous effort
for him? I wonder if he's doing the same for me, rearranging
his hair to look casually stylish, slapping on his aftershave,
trying on a polo shirt (too golf course) then a patterned poplin
shirt (borderline comical), and craning round at his bum in the
mirror, checking his jeans aren't too tight for an older man.
Probably not.

I glance at my watch, alarmed at how late I am. But I hate
stopping drawing with a failure. I attempt one very quick
sketch of a great bull elephant in full musth, ears spread wide,
desperate to mate.

I wish I felt sexier today. I can't imagine wriggling out of the red dress and lying on Guy's bed and hearing him grunt in my ear. If I were a female elephant I wouldn't bother listening to all the roaring. I'd just feed my baby, tend my other children and chat to my sisters, perfectly content. Was it just the slightly wicked novelty of dating an ex-teacher that turned me on so much last week? Is he just an ordinary older bloke, still quite good-looking but just a little bit dull? Am I trying to think this to comfort myself in case it all goes wrong?

Stella gives me a pitying look. *You're over-thinking things again, Ellie*, she says. *Live in the moment. Seize the day.*

So I seize it and rush off towards the tube station. I'm really late now. I try to run, pounding along as if I'm doing a parkrun, but my dress is hobbling my knees and now my ankle twists in one of my suede heels and I nearly fall over. People are staring and I feel a fool. I carry on with my head held high, trying to pretend that I'm absolutely fine, but when I'm on the tube I give my ankle a tentative rub, hoping to God I've not sprained it. I've had the presence of mind to bring an elephant book in my bag, so I can distract myself on the tube, though I get so engrossed I very nearly forget to change at Waterloo.

I'm fifteen minutes late when I emerge at Russell Square. I check my phone and see Guy's sent a text.

I'm on the steps outside the museum.

It's a bit curt, and I grimace.

Sorry bit late, just coming x

I shuffle along as quickly as I can on my sore ankle. There he is, peering around with a frown, exactly the way he used to look long ago. My stomach lurches. He's not going to make a scene, is he? I clench my fists, feeling anxious and angry simultaneously, exactly the way I used to feel when a schoolgirl.

But when he spots me he relaxes and as I get closer he walks towards me to give me a hug.

'Ellie, at last! And you look fantastic!' He looks me up and down, obviously appreciating the red dress. 'I was starting to worry you weren't going to turn up. Why didn't you text me before to say you were running late?'

'I couldn't, not on the tube. And there was some massive hold-up somewhere, it was so frustrating,' I lie smoothly. 'So sorry. What am I, fifteen minutes late?'

'Nearly half an hour,' he says, which isn't totally true either. 'Never mind, come on, darling.'

Darling! What sort of darling? It's hard to tell from the way he says it. Is it a serious endearment or is he just using it casually, like Nadine, Magda and I do? But didn't Lottie tell me recently that most young people feel patronized if anyone calls them darling? Do I feel patronized or flattered? I just don't know.

I wish we could go somewhere for a coffee or a beer first, so we can relax a bit and feel comfortable, but we plunge into the museum immediately and it isn't quite the lark I'd hoped for. I love this place but not quite at this pace, going round so slowly and seriously. Guy wants to look at every single item, commenting on everything, even giving me a potted biography of all the pompous-looking portraits. It's exactly like a school trip. It's on the tip of my tongue to say it, but I know he'd be offended, so I keep quiet, nodding and murmuring, and occasionally making a hopefully witty comment that pleases him.

Well done, Ellie. Nine out of ten.

What's the matter with me? He's simply trying to make it interesting for me. He wouldn't be doing it if I'd told him I'd been here already. Why do I have to be so hard on him?

175

He puts his hand under my elbow, and steers me gently towards the Paula painting. His eyes are bright in anticipation. He's trying so hard.

'Isn't it powerful?' he murmurs, as we get to the huge artwork. He's still holding my arm – and I can feel he's trembling slightly. Maybe he's not as self-assured as he seems.

I suddenly melt, really touched, and it's easy to feign surprise and delight. I *am* surprised to be here with him, I *am* delighted that we had such a wonderful time in bed last week, and in a few hours we'll be naked together again, and he'll be kissing me all over . . .

I feel a shiver of sexual excitement – thank the lord! I take his hand impulsively. He squeezes mine back and we stand close together, looking up at the stark painting. It's sad and savage and marvellously powerful. He's silent now, savouring the moment, and then we look at each other, our easy, intimate dynamic from last week finally restored.

We go for that drink afterwards, sitting in a corner of another dark pub, sharing a bottle of wine again, red to match my dress. I had such a scrappy lunch I feel it going to my head, and his own eyes are slightly glazed. By the time we've finished the bottle, we're squeezed up close together, looking in each other's eyes again, practically groping in public. He kisses me on the lips without even looking round to see if anyone's watching.

'We could go for a walk round Coram's Fields and see where the old Foundling Hospital used to be,' he suggests. 'Or we could go to Skoob, a good second-hand bookshop only five minutes away. Or we could stroll down the Charing Cross Road, and go in the Portrait Gallery. I've researched all sorts of things we could do, like a good teacher,' he says. I laugh. He's actually sending himself up – I just love that he can do that.

'They all sound great ideas,' I say. 'Or we could just go straight back to yours?'

He grins. 'That's the best idea of all.'

We hold hands in the Uber all the way back. We hurry along his road, and there's his house, and we're in the door, kissing properly now. His hands are all over my red dress, he's pulling it right up, pressing me against the wall. But we're neither of us gymnasts, and it's simpler just to go to his bedroom.

I slip to his bathroom while he's undressing, still not quite ready to yank my dress over my head in front of him in spite of the fact that I'm so turned on my knickers are damp. When I peel them off, I see why and give a groan of despair. More red. Blood. I've started my period. What the hell shall I do now? Will he mind? Some men don't. Mick at art school seemed totally fine with it. But Russell was horrified the one time we attempted sex in the middle of my period, fussing terribly about the slight mess, and scrubbing himself frantically afterwards.

I think of Guy's pristine sheets. We could use a big towel, but they're all snowy white and fluffy. I can feel the slight pulse of the blood dripping out of me. I mop myself as best I can with loo paper, fill the hand basin with water and do my best to wash myself properly.

I put Guy's dressing gown on and feel in the pocket. The lipstick tissue has gone but when I look in the bathroom cupboard the box of Tampax is still there. I help myself, grateful to the unknown woman. Then I wash my hands thoroughly, hoping that I just smell of lime and basil soap.

I walk back into the bedroom, my heart thumping. Guy's sitting up in bed, looking bemused.

'What were you doing in there all this time?' he asks.

I take a deep breath. Come on, we're adults. Surely this can't be the first time this has happened to him.

'Guy, I'm terribly sorry but—'

He looks stricken. 'Oh God, have you changed your mind?'

'No, no, but I've started my period,' I say. I can feel myself blushing like a fool.

'Oh Ellie, is that all?' he says wonderfully, and he gets out of bed and puts his arms round me. 'It'll be fine.'

'No, it won't,' I say miserably. 'I couldn't bear it if I bled all over your sheets. And what if it goes right through to your mattress?'

'We'll use a towel,' he says.

'Yes, but it might get rucked up,' I protest.

'Then we'll use two towels, sweetheart. Don't worry so. I don't mind in the slightest.' He's doing his best to reassure me. But *I* mind. I've never been one of those earth-mother women who embrace menstruating and praise Mother Nature. I've tried hard, but I feel our grandmothers calling it The Curse were dead accurate. I'm grateful to be fertile because I wouldn't have Lottie otherwise, but it's a total bore carrying on and on being fertile. It will be good to be shot of the whole process, although that means going through the menopause and that's clearly no picnic.

I fidget in hot embarrassment as Guy covers his beautiful sheet with a couple of towels that'll need soaking in salt water for ages if they can ever be used again. He's trying to act as if it's all perfectly fine and takes a long time trying to turn me on. Yet when I finally feel ready, have nipped to the bathroom, and we tentatively start to have sex, he's the one taking a while to get excited. I feel so self-conscious that it's hard to let go and eventually I fake it just to get it over with.

I can't even snuggle up afterwards. I have to sort myself out in the bathroom yet again, using another one of Lipstick's Tampax. When I come out at last I murmur, 'I hope it's all right, but I've had to use tampons from the packet in the bathroom.'

'Yes, sure,' says Guy. He's already removed the towels and

so I have no idea if there was a terrible mess or not. 'Would you like a glass of wine, darling – or a cup of tea?'

He doesn't seem to realize the significance of what I've said.

'Obviously they're not yours,' I say.

'Oh, they're probably Kim's,' he says. He doesn't look the slightest bit ruffled.

'And Kim is . . .?' I say, trying to sound just idly curious.

'Oh, she's a friend of mine. You know, a friend with benefits,' he says. 'She hangs out here occasionally. But we're not seriously involved, if that's what you're worried about.'

'Oh, that's fine,' I say, but I know I don't sound convincing.

'We're just mates, Ellie,' he says patiently. 'She's one of the teachers at my school.'

I think of Pete from my school – or indeed Cath. We're definitely mates, but it's almost impossible to imagine having sex with either of them. 'What does she teach?'

'PE,' he says. 'Wine, then?'

'Yes, lovely,' I say. 'So how old is she?' I ask, as he goes into the kitchen in his chic black trunks. I wonder if he got blood all over him, and my face burns. If so, he's managed to deal with it quickly.

'This is her first job. She's twenty-three,' Guy says, and I hear him pop the cork on a bottle. Thank God it'll be something white and fizzy. I'd hate another red wine now. I'm forcing myself to think about wine, but the number *twenty-three* is ricocheting through my head like a bullet.

Twenty-three years old, and he's fifty. That's a huge age gap. That's just a bit much. Too much. Much too much.

He hands me a flute glass and sees my face.

'Hey, Miss Prim, she's not a child,' he says. 'I was that age when I first started teaching you. And it was all her idea. She's just passing time until she finds someone more exciting and less set in their ways.'

He sees me staring. 'Ellie, I don't want you to worry about Kim. I promise you, she's just a friend,' he says. 'If it really upsets you, I'll stop seeing her.'

'No, don't do that,' I say, though inside I'm shrieking *Yes, yes, do exactly that.*

'I want *us* to be more than friends, Ellie. I was really envious when Jean got invited to your party – and not me!'

'I told you, I didn't know there was even going to *be* a party.' I pause. '*I'd* have invited you.'

He kisses me and I manage to respond without spilling my wine. He's been completely honest about this Kim. He says he'll stop seeing her if it makes me uncomfortable. What more do I want?

He carries on being sweet and tender all evening. He cooks me another meal, a fish pie and then raspberry mousse, both home-made. I tell him he's a much better cook than I am. He protests that they're both incredibly easy to make and chants the recipes. I nod and smile, but don't bother to take it all in properly. I wasn't looking for a cooking lesson.

There's still a lot of evening left before it's bedtime. We chat for a while about people we used to know, teachers and girls, and I tell him an edited version of Nadine and Magda's current lives.

I wonder what he does the nights that Kim stays. Perhaps they crack open a beer, share some crisps, and watch the sport on television. If I didn't have my wretched period we'd probably go back to bed and have sex again, but it's too much of a performance now, though I feel a bit achy and unsatisfied.

I wander over to look at his bookshelves, sifting through his art books. There are some old DVDs too. There's one about Frida Kahlo I've never seen before. I tell him about dressing up as Frida for my Year Eights and he loves the story.

'Your students don't know how lucky they are. *I've* never dressed up as Frida Kahlo,' he says.

'All you have to do is grow your eyebrows,' I say, which makes him chuckle.

'Have you seen the Frida film? It's got some wonderful footage of her. Do you want to watch it?'

We sit on the sofa and sip wine and watch the film. He pulls me closer, his arm wrapped round me, so my head rests comfortably on his shoulder. It's a fascinating film and I'm totally absorbed, though starting to get a little sleepy now. I nod off for a few seconds and hope he hasn't noticed.

'Let's watch the rest in the morning,' he says. 'Come on, let's cuddle up in bed.'

I change the tampon again, relieved that the bleeding is calming down a bit, but I still wear the knickers I brought for tomorrow, just in case. He's lovely, stroking my stomach and muttering sweet things, and then he strokes my breasts too, and then I'm not sleepy at all because his hand is sliding into my pants, and I come properly this time. Then we sleep in each other's arms, just as I'd hoped.

13

We watch the rest of the Frida film while we have breakfast –
Greek yoghurt, blueberries, toast and honey, and coffee. Then
he has a shower while I take another cup of coffee back to
bed with me and flip through one of his books about Titian.
Fantastic painter obviously, and I've always found his women
comforting, because they're large and beautiful.

Then I shower too and change into the V&A Alice teeshirt,
jeans and trainers that I brought with me. Inevitably Guy
went to the Alice exhibition too, and we compare notes on
other V&A shows. I yawn once or twice, worrying that our
conversation generally has just the one topic, art – but we're
art teachers, for God's sake, so it's not really surprising.

Then we go for a walk over Clapham Common and it's the
way I'd imagined, wandering around arm in arm companionably, and I start to wonder if this is really it. Could Guy be the
man I've been waiting for all these years? We must be looking good together, because some old lady walking her Bichon
smiles at us fondly.

I make a fuss of her little white dog and remember Alice's
wistful longing for a dog herself.

'Would you ever want a dog, Guy?' I ask.

'I've had one – several. Love them. I had a girlfriend once
who worked at Battersea and she fostered some of the dogs.

It was great walking them early in the morning or when I got home from school. There was one incredible lurcher I just adored. We did talk about adopting him ourselves but we weren't really at that kind of commitment stage,' he says.

'Have you ever been at that stage?' I ask.

'Maybe twice. But it didn't work out in the end. Still waiting,' he says. I can't work out if his glance is meaningful or not. I can't work out if I want it to be.

I imagine owning a dog with Guy. Living in our own place together. But *which* place? I quite like Guy's house but I don't think I could ever feel it was home. It's too neat, too organized, too masculine. Guy doesn't seem to have any clutter whatsoever. Everything is tucked away in drawers and cupboards. Perhaps he'd try to tidy me away eventually too.

I know he'd be unbelievably uncomfortable in my flat. He'd hate all the piles of books, the disorganized desk, the shoes kicked off, Stella's litter tray . . . Even if I tidied like mad, he'd still be appalled by my sagging sofa and ancient armchairs, the Indian throws covering seven shades of shabbiness. He'd fuss about my broken vintage chandelier, the fading montage of Lottie at every age, the ancient television, my crumpled bedding.

So might we both move and start again? Where? Guy would never want to live in Lambeth. I like Earlsfield but can't imagine living there. Where do oddly matched couples like us live? *If we ever got that far . . .*

What would Lottie think? I'm not sure whether she'd like him or not. He might be a bit too Mr Smooth for her. She's certainly too old to look on him as a father figure. I wonder what Dad would think of him? They could talk about art together – but they'd vie to be the most knowledgeable, like some sort of painterly pissing contest.

If I'd gone to Dad and Anna's last night, there wouldn't have been all the embarrassment of starting my period at the most inconvenient moment. Still, full marks to Guy for being so kind and understanding.

I squeeze his arm and he smiles at me.

'Happy?' he asks.

'Very,' I say.

'Me too,' he says.

We have brunch at a café overlooking the common, and then I explain that I've got to dash home to feed Stella and then rush out again to Magda's new home with Chris.

'You said she's been married before, didn't you?'

'Twice.'

'Oh, trust Magda, bless her,' says Guy.

I bristle at his tone. 'Hey, it was just bad luck before, that's all,' I say fiercely.

'OK, OK! Sorry. I didn't mean to sound judgy.' He pauses. 'Haven't you ever wanted to get married, Ellie? Just the once?'

'Absolutely not,' I say.

'What if the right guy comes along?' he asks.

I roll my eyes. He's sounding like a women's magazine now. Is he implying *he's* the right one? No, of course not. Surely.

'Oh well, never say never,' I say lightly. I finish my last mouthful of scrambled eggs. My tummy feels scrambled too. It's not just my period, it's because I feel so unsettled. I don't know what he's feeling. I don't know what *I'm* feeling. If only I could sit back and coolly analyse the situation – but I'm far too hot and flustered.

We kiss goodbye at the tube station. No one seems remotely bothered. I wonder how they'd have felt seeing us twenty-seven years ago. I think I would have been thrilled but terrified if Mr Windsor had kissed me then. Nadine too, for all she struggled to seem so cool and wanted an older boyfriend – but not *that* old. Magda wouldn't have minded, though.

She will want to know all about my two dates with Guy, every tiny detail, but luckily the children will be there. I hurry home to feed Stella and breathe a sigh of relief when there's no present waiting on the doorstep. I pick up a little pile of post from the hall floor. A letter from a charity, a bill, and a card. My name's written on the front in elaborate cursive, and it hasn't got my address or a postmark.

Stella is mewing indignantly, telling me she's hungry, and how very dare I leave her all night long. I see to Her Majesty's needs and give her a thorough stroking to say sorry. I keep staring at the envelope beside me. The spiky writing dances in front of my eyes. I can feel my throat drying. I want to shove it straight in the bin – and yet I feel I can't not find out what the card says inside.

When Stella stalks off to her cat tree I flop on the sofa and open the card. It's a rose design, big blowsy roses that seem somehow suggestive. I look inside it. More italics. It's a poem.

Roses are red
Violets are blue
Will you be my girl?
Because I love you

No signature. It's so pathetic I think it must be from a child, and yet it doesn't look like the scribbly handwriting of any of the kids I know. It's definitely not Nick Rivers' writing either. Plus, he'd make a much better stab at a poem. So who in God's name is it? And what game is he playing? I clasp my hands and rock backwards and forwards, unnerved.

'Oh Stella, what am I going to do? Who on earth is this crazy person?' I ask her.

She hunches her shoulders as if she's shrugging, and telling me it's my problem, not hers. It *is* a problem. Somehow the bunch of roses, the chocolates, the card seem slightly threatening.

I shove the card under a pile of lesson plans. I don't want to look at it any longer, but I feel the need to keep it. As what? Evidence? It's not a crime to send someone a card, chocolates, flowers. But I shiver at the thought that they've all been delivered personally. I look over at my door. This man has been hovering right outside. Could be there now . . .

I check the lock, the bolt. It seems secure – but I've seen enough TV series over the years to know how easy it is to get into anyone's flat. In fact, Jason along the balcony had his own door caved in by a rival supplier, which unnerved me terribly. I was stupid enough to tell Ben, who told Anna, who told Dad – and that made him even more determined to make me move.

I feel a twinge of guilt at the thought of him. Should I give him a quick call now? I suppose I could dash all the way back home to spend half an hour with him before charging off to Magda's? I glance at my watch. No, I'd be horribly late. I'll sort things out somehow for next weekend. Or whenever. It's almost the end of term, so I'll pop Stella in her cat basket (somehow!) and we'll stay for a few days with Dad and Anna.

Guy will be on holiday too. We'll be able to spend more time together and I'll have a chance to work out what I really feel about him. And Alice will be on vacation. I wonder if she ever goes to Brockwell Lido? That might be fun. Summer's looking up, even though I wish Lottie were coming home.

I feel such a wave of missing her that I break all my resolutions and phone her right this minute, without even texting to see if it's convenient.

She answers on the fifth ring, sounding a little breathless.

'Mum? Are you OK? Has anything happened?' she asks anxiously. Her generation seem to only phone each other directly if there's a total emergency.

186

'I'm fine, Lots. Just wanted to chat,' I say lamely.

'Oh Mum. Are you feeling a bit lonely?' she asks, sounding concerned.

'No, no, I'm ever so busy, working on a new project—' No, don't tell her yet, keep it a secret! 'This new swimming friend, Alice, is helping me with some research. Then I saw Nadine the other day and later I'm meeting up with Magda,' I gabble. 'What are you up to?'

'Oh, not much,' she says, and she giggles.

I hear a murmur in the background.

'Ah, you're with someone,' I say. 'Sorry, I'll ring back another time.'

'No, it's fine, Mum. It's just my friend Luke.'

I can hear laughter. My-friend-Luke hasn't even been mentioned before, but it sounds as if they're maybe more than friends. I'd better tread carefully now. She won't want me giving her the third degree. But I wonder what sort of guy he is, and whether he's kind and loving and understanding, worthy of my Lottie.

'Well, that's great,' I say vaguely.

'What about your hot date?' Lottie asks.

'We've had an amazing time,' I say, and add, unable to resist showing off, 'I've only just got back from his place.'

'Mum!' Lottie exclaims. 'You mean you spent the night with him!'

'Yep,' I say. 'Well, I'll let you go, darling. Lots of love.' I ring off, smiling. I'll keep her guessing. Show her the ancient mum isn't quite past it yet. It's so good to talk to her; she always grounds me. What am I doing, getting in a flap about some sad, silly fool who's sending me rose-themed presents and banal poetry?

I sigh. I'm feeling tired out now, and I'm still getting period pains. I'd like to curl up in bed with Stella and have a long

187

nap – but I promised I'd go to help Magda with Chris's kids. I'm not sure I'm going to warm to them. I certainly don't think much of Chris.

A few weeks after she met him, Magda had a special supper so that he could meet her 'two best friends in all the world'. Which we are. Perhaps that was why he didn't seem particularly keen on us. I think he was worried that Magda might have told us intimate secrets about their love life. Which she did, of course, because Magda can't resist oversharing to the nth degree.

She'd already told us that he had a strangely shaped penis, rather like a banana, but insisted he still managed to be an amazing lover. Nadine said, 'So he's Willy Wonka!' and we burst out laughing. We knew we were being mean and childish but we couldn't help it. If men only knew what women say about them behind their backs.

Perhaps Magda wishes she'd been more discreet now she's decided that Chris is her 'One'. The supper was an ordeal, though at least Chris's children were with their mother. Nadine and I did our best to pretend to be impressed by him, but we both failed to see why Magda was so keen. Chris was a bit of a banana in every way – proud of his progress with his personal trainer and forever patting his six pack complacently. And when Magda opened a second bottle of wine to try to get us all to relax a little, he raised his eyebrows, and actually said, 'Now, now, ladies!'

It was all a bit of a disaster and Magda must have known it. But she persevered. She invited us to a barbecue a couple of weeks later. Lots of Chris's business friends and their WAGs were there – and Nadine and me. It was hilarious at first, because quite a few of Chris's friends assumed Nadine and I were a couple. We couldn't resist playing up to this, until Magda told us to pack it in.

'I want to show everyone how fantastic you both are, and yet you're mucking about. You're being incredibly childish,' Magda hissed at us. 'This means a lot to me – why can't you take it seriously?'

She looked near tears and we both felt ashamed. Why *were* we being so childish? Were we feeling a little bit jealous that Magda was in love again and had found herself a halfway decent bloke by most people's standards – whereas Nadine mostly had quick flings and I had no flings at all, quick or otherwise?

So we pulled ourselves together, split up, and tried to work the party, pretending to be interested when people told us about their prestigious jobs and their exotic holidays and their £50,000 new kitchens and the posh prep schools little Ava and Oliver were attending. Chris's own Nat and Corrie weren't around, having a long weekend in North Norfolk with their mother and her new boyfriend. We'd been quite curious to meet them too, especially as Magda found them such a trial.

I'm going to be one up on Nadine to be actually meeting them this afternoon, though. I make it to the Richmond house dead on three o'clock as promised.

'Oh Ellie, thank you so much for coming,' Magda says breathlessly as she answers the door. There are screams and shouting coming from somewhere behind her.

'Ellie Poppins at your service, Madam,' I say. 'Shall I batter the kids with my parrot-headed umbrella?'

'Please do!' Magda breathes. 'They're driving me crazy. They wouldn't eat their lunch, saying it was smelly poo – why are children so disgusting? Then they devoured a whole packet of Hobnobs, and I tried to sit them down with Nat's game console but all they do is accuse each other of cheating, and when I try to intervene they scream at me instead. Nat actually called me a stupid tart. Do you think he's heard Chris talking about me like that?'

I give her a hug.

'It's OK, Magda. I'm here to quell them. Of course Chris hasn't called you a stupid tart. That's classic little prep school-boy language. They're just winding you up deliberately,' I say.

'My baby won't talk to me like that, will she?' Magda asks.

'A she? You're having a girl?' I say delightedly.

'Oh shit, I swore to Chris I'd keep it a secret. But yes, she is a little girl, and I'm so thrilled. I've started buying all sorts of lovely little-girly stuff but I've had to keep them all secret because we're not telling people the sex,' says Magda. 'Can I show you? They're adorable! But I don't want the children to see!'

I put my head round the living room door. Nat and Corrie stop shouting and stare at me curiously. I'd expected them to look like cartoon monster children, but they seem surprisingly sweet. Nat, the eight-year-old, is quite small, with an odd side parting, but I like his perky face. He twitches his snub nose at me and I twitch mine back. I expected Corrie, who's six, to have ringlets and a party frock, but she's in a Barbie teeshirt and shorts, with hair at that awkward lumpy stage. The poor kid is rather awkward and lumpy herself. She's sucking her thumb.

'Hi, you two. I'm Ellie, Magda's friend. If you two stay quiet as mice for ten minutes, no squeaking at all, I'll let you bake a cake for tea, OK?' I say.

They blink at me.

'We can't bake cakes,' Nat says uncertainly.

'Of course you can. I'll show you how. I take it you can *eat* them?' I ask.

'Mummy says they make you fat,' says Corrie indistinctly, because her thumb is in the way.

'You're not at Mummy's house now. This is Daddy and Magda's house. Magda says you can always eat cake on Sundays,' I say. 'Isn't that right, Magda?'

Magda nods.

'So, absolute quiet. Look at my ears!' I uncover them from under my curls. 'They're quite big, aren't they? I shall hear if you say anything at all. Now carry on with your game.'

They carry on, utterly silent.

We go out the room and close the door on them. 'Right, show me the baby clothes and then we've got time for a quick coffee,' I say.

'They *are* quiet!' says Magda. 'You're a genius!'

'No, I'm just good at bribing children. I'm a teacher, after all! They're a doddle at this age,' I say.

We go up the stairs. There are four bedrooms, and I peep into the main one. It's pristine, subtle Farrow & Ball blue and white, with bedding to match. Do Magda and Chris ever cavort on top of all the white satin cushions? The second bedroom is much messier, with footprints on the yellow duvet. Nat has obviously been using his bed as a trampoline. Discarded tee-shirts, socks and underwear and hundreds of Lego bricks litter the floor.

Corrie's lilac room is neater, with a huge doll's house taking up most of the space. It looks as if a thumb-sized Stacey Solomon has started a severe decluttering campaign, because most of its contents are piled up on the green flannel acting as grass.

Magda unlocks the fourth bedroom. It is pink and white and perfect, with candy-striped bedding on a little cot and a pink teddy sitting on the white fur rug. There's a small white ward-robe, which Magda opens with a flourish. There are six little outfits hanging there already, several with designer labels. They are all extremely feminine, with pink the predominant colour.

'Good luck keeping the sex of the baby a secret!' I comment.

'You're the only person I've shown it to, apart from Chris,' says Magda.

'You've done all this since your scan?' I ask incredulously.

'I took a week off work and did the painting myself. Do you like everything?'

'It's beautiful,' I say. But I look at Magda anxiously. She's been putting so much effort into the baby's room she's forgotten about herself. She's hardly wearing any make-up and she's dressed in another mumsy floral with little white plimsolls. She's worn heels since she turned thirteen. She walks like a duck in flatties.

'It's exquisite, Mags,' I say. I pat her tummy. 'You're going to have the best mum in the world, little baby.' Then I give a bunch of material a little tug. 'But what's with all the flowery dresses, Mags?'

'Well, obviously, I'm going to be a mum,' she says.

'Yes, but can't you still be yourself? Where's all the make-up, the glam blonde hair, the tight clothes showing off your figure?' I ask.

'I can't show off my figure, Ellie! I'm getting a real tum already,' she says, pressing the dress against herself and showing me.

'Well, it's smaller than mine, and I can guarantee I'm not having a baby,' I say, thanking God for my period. 'It's not really about the clothes, though, it's about *you*. You don't have to change who you are to be a mum. Think of Beyoncé, Rihanna, all the women who wore whatever they wanted when they were pregnant.'

'Yeah, I get you, but Chris is a bit conservative. I wanted to look like all the other mums in his crowd,' Magda says.

'Oh Magda! Did he ever want any of them? No! He saw you, with your sexy curves and your bright hair and scarlet lipstick and he thought *she's* the girl for me,' I say. 'He fell for you because you're *you* – so stop trying to be someone else.'

Magda stares at me, wavering. 'Really?'

'A hundred per cent. And you don't have to be all sweet and soft with those kids of his either. Boss them about a bit, and they'll learn to respect you.'

'I want them to *love* me,' Magda protests.

'Well, maybe they will, maybe they won't. Look, I've been in their position, I know exactly what it's like to have a step-mother. I absolutely hated Anna when she and Dad got together because I thought she was trying to take my mum's place. Don't try and be a mum to Nat and Corrie. Be a friend, but a grown-up one who won't take any nonsense. No grovelling. You tell them what's what.'

'Jesus, Ellie! You're turning into Philippa Perry,' Magda says.

'Yes, well, I always think I know how to sort out other people's lives. I'm pretty hopeless when it comes to my own, though,' I say, sighing.

'Your life seems pretty incredible to me. Speaking of which, this Mr Windsor thing – how's it going?' Magda asks. 'Is he great in bed?'

'He is, actually,' I tell her.

'So you've had sex with him?' Magda shrieks. 'I was joking!'

'Several times. It was amazing, truly. But then yesterday—'

'You've seen him twice already? So he's really keen?'

'I think so. But I started my period.'

'Oh no! So was he put off?'

'He said he didn't mind at all,' I say.

'Really? How sweet of him,' Magda says.

'*I* minded. But then this morning it all worked out perfectly anyway.'

'Imagine! Mr Windsor!' Magda says, hooting with laughter. 'So didn't it feel weird going to bed with him? Did you find yourself calling "Oh Mr Windsor" when you were doing it?'

'For God's sake, you make it sound like a *Carry On* film!' I protest, but I start laughing too.

'What are you two laughing at?' Nat bursts into the room and peers round, looking astonished. 'What's happened? This used to be the junk room.'

'And it was so junky I decided to sort it out,' says Magda. 'Now, didn't Ellie tell you that you had to stay downstairs absolutely silent or you wouldn't get to bake a cake?'

'Yes, but she said ten minutes, and you two have been gassing away for ages now,' says Nat.

'True enough,' I say. 'Come on, then, we'll go downstairs and start baking.'

'This is a very girly room,' says Nat. 'Is it for Corrie?' His chin juts at the imagined unfairness.

'No, it's not for anyone just yet,' Magda says. 'Now come on.' She tries to take his hand but he snatches it away.

'You can't tell me what to do,' says Nat. 'You're not my mum.'

'No, she's your stepmum, so you have to try extra hard to please her,' I say. 'What's your favourite cake, Nat?'

He wavers, distracted. 'Flapjacks?' he suggests.

'Are they technically cakes? But brilliant choice because they're easy-peasy to make,' I say. 'Do you ever have porridge for breakfast when you're here?'

Nat nods, bewildered.

'And please tell me you've got a tin of golden syrup in the cupboard,' I say.

'I think so,' Nat says.

I high five him. 'Then we'll definitely make flapjacks, pal!' I say.

'Do you know how to make them?' Magda mouths at me.

Typical Magda. Her parents run a restaurant and by the time she was twelve she could make an elaborate three course meal for a dinner party. She's the only person I know who made that Jubilee trifle from scratch – and it was delicious too. But she's never made the easiest cake in the world.

'You just mix oats and butter and sugar with golden syrup, spread it in a tin and bake it. A child of six can make it, no worries,' I say.

'Excuse me, I'm eight and a half,' Nat declares indignantly.

'I was thinking of your sister,' I say. Corrie is standing in the doorway.

'Is this going to be *my* room?' she asks, her eyes round.

'It's Magda's room,' I say.

'But she sleeps with Daddy!' says Nat, wrinkling his nose.

'Well, I expect she needs a cuddle, with you two giving her grief every weekend,' I retort. 'Now go to the bathroom, both of you, and wash your hands really well. You can't cook with dirty fingernails,' I say.

'Could you please come and stay every weekend?' Magda asks. 'You're so good with them!'

'It's just practice,' I say. 'I was pretty terrified of Lottie when she was a baby. She just cried and cried and I felt totally useless. I thought she didn't like me at all. But then she smiled at me one day and it was incredible.'

'I'm going to feed my baby on demand so that she never really has to cry,' says Magda.

'Good luck with that,' I say. I give her a hug. 'Have you thought of a name yet? Don't let Chris choose!'

'Maybe I'll call her after you, Ellie,' says Magda. 'Though I can't do that because Nadine would get upset.'

'Poor Nadine,' I say without thinking.

'Why? What's happened to her?' Magda asks.

I'm desperate to confide in her because I'm still very worried about Nadine, but I promised not to tell anyone, especially Magda.

'She just seems a bit down at the moment,' I say vaguely. There are shrieks and splashing noises from the bathroom. I deal with the two kids, Magda mops up the mess. She gets splashed herself, but she splashes Nat right back and he stops, surprised.

I take the children down to the kitchen while Magda changes her sodden floral frock. She takes a while, and we're putting the flapjacks in the oven when she comes back. We all stare at her. She's wearing a blue figure-hugging dress with a very low neck showing off her cleavage. She's applied bright red lipstick, fluffed up her hair, and exchanged the tennis shoes for white heels.

'You look fantastic!' I say.

'No she doesn't, she's showing her chest. It looks rude,' says Nat.

'I think she looks pretty,' Corrie says unexpectedly. 'Will you let me wear your lipstick, Magda?'

'Sure,' says Magda. 'But only indoors.' She fetches it and shows Corrie how to stretch her lips so that the colour goes on evenly.

'Yuck. You look stupid,' says Nat.

'Would you like some too?' says Magda.

'No! Boys don't wear lipstick!' he says.

'Some do. And clowns do too,' says Magda.

She uses her expensive Chanel lipstick to turn Nat into a very creepy-looking clown. But it's money well spent because he's much better behaved as a clown than he is as an ordinary little boy.

'I'll have to make sure they scrub their faces before Chris gets home,' says Magda. 'And maybe mine, too!'

'I bet he'll be bowled over,' I say. I can't stop myself adding, 'Your womanly curves are way more impressive than mine.'

'My what?'

'Don't laugh. Well, you *will*, but Guy said it to me when we were – you know,' I whisper.

'Who's Guy and what's you know?' Nat asks nevertheless, pushing in between us and peering up at our faces.

'Sh! I have to keep it quiet that I know Guy . . . Ritchie,' I say randomly.

'Who's he?' Nat asks, looking blank.

'He's a film-maker. Used to be married to Madonna,' I explain.

'Who's she?' Nat is clearly none the wiser.

'Oh, forget it! Just don't tell anyone, or else!' I say.

'I won't,' Nat promises, bless him.

'I'm not sure Gina Ford would approve of your childcare methods, but I think they're genius,' says Magda, smiling at me with her beautiful bright lips.

When the flapjacks come out of the oven and they've cooled down, we leave the children munching happily in the kitchen and take our coffee into the living room, where I can tell Magda an unexpurgated version of my encounter with the real Guy.

'You are so lucky, Ellie,' she says. 'If I didn't have Chris I'd be going wild with jealousy. In fact, I'll have to check myself in the mirror. I bet there's a green tinge to my face. You must be over the moon!'

'Well, I am. Sort of,' I say uncertainly.

'Surely you can see that Mr Windsor – sorry, Guy! – is the biggest catch ever. He *is* still good-looking, isn't he? Mrs Henderson promised at your party that he's still got his lovely hair.'

'No, he's really fit, with a great head of hair,' I say. 'He seriously doesn't look his age.'

'And he's great at sex and thoughtful and tender and treats you like a princess, from the sound of it,' says Magda.

'I suppose. He's a bit overly assertive, though. He's always the one who decides things, and tells me stuff I already know,' I say, sighing. I so wish he wouldn't do that.

'That's just because he's a man, you twerp. That's what

they're all like,' says Magda. 'What do you want, some kind of wet wimp who dithers about and wants you to make all the decisions?'

'I suppose not.'

'Are there any other problems with Mr . . . Guy?'

'There isn't any problem. He's fantastic. You're right. I *am* over the moon. And the stars. I'm swooping above the entire Milky Way,' I say.

I can say it over and over again. But why don't I actually feel it?

14

I think about it all the way home. I can offer wise, well-meaning advice to Magda and Nadine. Why can't I work out what's wrong with *me*? Maybe there's nothing wrong, and I just over-think everything.

I'm probably feeling flat because I'm tired out, seeing Alice, then Guy, now Magda. I didn't sleep much last night, scared I might be leaking all over his bed. I'll go home now, have some supper, curl up with Stella, read a book, watch the telly, and then have an early night. There'd better not be another doorstep gift waiting for me. I hate the thought of that rose card on my table. It's as if the mystery admirer folded himself flat and managed to slither through my letter box himself. I'll tear it into tiny pieces when I get home and stir it into Stella's litter tray.

I let myself in, say hello to Stella, and try to do exactly that, but it's made of such thick shiny paper it's too much like hard work. I'll try and find the scissors later. My bladder's clamouring so I go to the loo and check my phone. Three missed calls, all from Anna, sent when I was on the tube home.

Oh God, is Dad really down in the dumps? Maybe I should get right back on the tube and train it all the way home, after all. I ring Anna.

'Hi, Anna, sorry to have missed your calls. Look, I'm feeling really bad now about not coming over – shall I come for supper tonight?' I say before she can get a word in.

'Ellie, your dad's had a cardiac arrest,' she blurts out.

'Like, a heart attack?' I say, scarcely able to speak.

'No. His heart actually stopped,' she says, breathing fast. I think she's crying.

'He's – he's dead?' I stammer.

'No, I did CPR until the ambulance came, but he's very poorly, he's in Intensive Care at Kingtown Hospital. I'm there now, and they're not sure he'll recover,' she says, clearly sobbing now.

'Oh God, oh God,' I say, starting to cry too. 'I'm coming, Anna. I'll be there as soon as I can. I'm so sorry, so sorry, I'm coming!'

I can't think straight. I dash here and there, stuff a change of clothes, tampons, washing things in a bag, feed Stella, fill her water bowl, find a spare key and rush next door. I explain the situation to Andreea as quickly as I can and she agrees to look after Stella, then I'm off.

I run towards the tube. Everything looks blurry because I'm crying. I can't believe this is happening. Perhaps it's one of those awful guilt nightmares. I'm dreaming it because I didn't go to see Dad, and now my conscience is putting me through hell. I'll wake up in a cold sweat soon, feeling awful but relieved, because it isn't real. But it is, it is, I can hear Anna's voice in my head, her fear, her sorrow, her pain, and I feel so dreadful.

If I'd been there I could have helped, I could have taken my turn doing the CPR. I could have told Dad how much I love him and been there for him, and oh God, *why* didn't I agree to supper last night? How could I have been so selfish? I *knew* Anna would never beg me to come unless she was pretty desperate. If I'd gone there yesterday maybe Dad would have cheered up, be fine now, be watching *Countryfile* or whatever, and everything would be fine. I've killed my dad with my own selfishness.

Breathe, I tell myself. He's not dead yet. He's not going to die. He's in Intensive Care so they will be caring for him intensively, and he will recover and I will be the daughter of his dreams for evermore. I've lost Mum. I can't bear the thought of losing Dad too. I need him, I love him, I want him to be there for me always. When I'm off the tube and on the train I google cardiac arrest and immediately wish I hadn't. Most people don't survive it. Only one in ten. My eyes blur but it hovers in front of me, as though imprinted on my retinas. *One in ten!*

I look for causes. And then I see that in a relatively healthy person – and that's Dad, surely, getting a bit tubby maybe, but nothing really wrong with him – stress can be a cause. Stress because he's feeling his age and he doesn't know what to do with himself and his only daughter can't be bothered to come and have supper, even though he's tried to show her how much she means to him.

I groan out loud and a woman leans towards me and tentatively pats my shoulder.

'Are you all right?' she asks. She points at my phone. 'Is it bad news?'

I nod, unable to speak to her.

'Oh dear, I'm so sorry. Can I help in any way?'

I shake my head, wishing that there was some magic way she could sprout fairy godmother wings and make it all right. I peer at her desperately, but she's just an ordinary nice woman in White Stuff clothes, clutching a Royal Academy bag after a day out with a friend. I wish she'd just leave me alone, but she's being so kind that I sit and nod and try to smile, until I get to the station nearest the hospital. I manage to blurt out a thank you and then rush out of the train, while she calls after me, 'I hope things turn out all right!'

I run all the way to the hospital, a ten-minute sprint that leaves me so gasping I'm incoherent when I race into the entrance. It takes me another ten minutes blundering in and out of lifts and up and down corridors before I find the right Intensive Care, and then a nurse shows me to the dreaded Family Room and there's Anna, crying, with Ben on one side of her and Simon on the other.

I hug all three and keep my arms tight round Anna. I must have seen her cry occasionally, but never like this, with tears streaming, nose running, her lovely face ugly with grief.

'Oh Anna, it must have been so awful for you. What exactly happened? Did he just pass out?' I ask, gently wiping her face with a tissue.

'He said he wasn't feeling very well. Sick and dizzy, and his chest hurt. I didn't take him too seriously at first, because he's had these funny turns before, and I thought they were panic attacks because he's been getting so agitated recently,' Anna says. 'But then he told me to call an ambulance and thank God I did, because I was in the midst of telling the person on the phone when he suddenly slumped forward and fell off his chair. He didn't hit his head or anything, he just sort of slipped to the carpet, but when I knelt down beside him I realized he'd actually stopped breathing.'

'Oh God!' I say, clutching her.

'I was so scared but the woman on the phone was marvellous, so calm. She told me how to do the CPR, talking me through it on speakerphone – she even sang that old Bee Gees song "Staying Alive" so I got the right rhythm – and I think his heart started beating again but I wasn't sure so I just kept on doing it for what seemed an absolute age but I don't think it can have been very long, and then the ambulance arrived. They said I'd saved his life, and I thought that meant he was going to be fine – but now he's all hooked up to machines and they've put him in a coma and are still working on getting his heart stabilized.'

'They'll manage it, Mum. Dad will pull through this, you'll see,' Ben says, gripping her hand. 'Dad's as strong as an ox. Look how he was at Ellie's party, dancing and singing like a guy half his age.'

'He loved that party – but he was so down afterwards,' Anna weeps.

'And you begged me to come to see him and I didn't and now he's nearly died and it's all my fault!' I wail.

'Of course it's not your fault, Ellie. It's not anyone's fault,' Anna says, holding me now. 'We can't control the way your dad's brain works, we can't stop the blood vessels in his heart being faulty.'

'You're just being kind to me, the way you always are,' I say, wiping my eyes.

'It's none of our faults – or it's all our faults,' says Ben. 'Anna asked Si and me to come to dinner too and we said no, because we were seeing friends. It's actually our anniversary.'

'Oh no, I forgot all about it – I didn't even send you a card! And yet you planned that amazing party for me. I feel like the worst person in the world,' I sob.

Then the door to the Family Room opens and a nurse comes in, looking very solemn. We stare at her in sudden terror.

It's Simon who clears his throat and asks huskily, 'Is it bad news? Has – has Mr Allard died?'

'No, he's still with us, but I'm afraid he's very ill. The doctors are still trying to stabilize his heart, but we're not sure if it's going to be possible. We were wondering – are there any other immediate members of the family who would like to be here, in case you need to say goodbye to him?' she asks gently.

Goodbye. It's an everyday word, and yet it sounds so shocking.

'Lottie?' I whisper. I don't want her to have to go through this, and it will be the second time she's had to leave her job – and yet she loves Dad as if he were her own parent.

'Lottie,' says Anna, nodding.

'The doctors will be with him for a while. Perhaps you'd like to get a coffee? I can rustle up a few leftover sandwiches? Or just have a walk round the grounds for some fresh air. I'll take your phone number, Mrs Allard, and let you know when it's time to come in,' she says.

'Thank you, but I'm staying here,' Anna says.

'I'll go and get coffees for us,' Simon offers. He gives Ben a quick kiss on the top of his head and then goes off.

I ring Lottie, not stopping to text first.

'Mum? Hey, I want to know all about this new guy of yours!' she says chirpily.

'Lottie, listen to me, darling. I'm afraid Grandad's not very well.'

'What do you mean?' she asks.

I take a deep breath. 'He's actually in Intensive Care. He had a cardiac arrest.'

'But he will get better, won't he?' Lottie says, her voice suddenly very young.

'We're all hoping so, but he's really not at all well and – and he might not make it. So we were wondering if you wanted to come and be at the hospital with us? We're at Kingtown.'

'Of course I do!' she says hastily. 'I'm coming right now.'

'Have you got enough money for another train fare?' I ask. She's talking rapidly to someone else.

'Don't worry, Luke will bring me.'

'Are you sure that's OK?' I ask, meaning has Luke got a car that won't break down, is he sensible, is he totally sober, will he keep you safe?

'Mum, it's fine. See you as soon as possible. And tell Grandad to hang on in there and that I love him heaps, if you get to see him first,' she says, and then rings off.

I look around to see Ben, bereft without Simon beside him. He's always so clever and funny and capable, but now he suddenly shrinks back into being my little brother.

I give him a hug and he clings to me for a moment. Then we huddle together with Anna. She keeps her eyes shut most of the time. I wonder if she's praying, though I've never thought of her as religious. Perhaps she's simply willing Dad to recover. I'm willing it too, so hard, and yet I've done too much googling on the train. Even if Dad manages to pull through, he could have suffered brain damage. What if he's left unable to talk, to walk, to do anything at all for himself?

When Simon comes back with a tray of coffees, sandwiches in plastic packages and a handful of KitKats, I find my hands are trembling so badly that I can't drink properly. I try to take big breaths in and out, but I still manage to spill coffee all down my front. Anna barely sips hers and just shakes her head when she's offered any food. I nibble at the chocolate. Ben wolfs down several sandwiches and then a KitKat. He's halfway through another when he suddenly has to bolt to the loo.

Simon goes after him and eventually brings him back, looking horribly pale and sweaty. He gives Ben a drink from the water cooler and sits him down gently.

'What would we do without you, Si?' I say. He's just as much immediate family as we are. I wonder if Guy could ever be like this, part of us all. He's gentle and caring with me, but I'm not sure how he'd get on with the rest of us.

I think Dad led Guy's sort of life for a while, having affairs, sometimes with some of his own students in the days when that wasn't as scandalous as it is now. But he was committed to Mum. And hopefully Anna.

I used to feel so angry with Dad when I thought he might be

playing around. I thought he was a bit pathetic too, going on about his painting, when I privately thought it derivative – big canvases with distorted, anguished figures. I didn't like his attitude with his students either, forever wanting their attention, their adulation. But now that he's lying unconscious in some terrifying sterile room, with men and women in masks sticking tubes in him and monitoring every breath and heartbeat, I feel so sorry for him. He might not have always managed to be a good husband, but he's been a good dad in many ways, and has tried so hard to give me support and love all these years, even if he's gone too far sometimes, been too disapproving and interfering. He's been an even better Grandad to Lottie. She will be heartbroken if he dies.

She gets to the hospital in two and a half hours, while we're still waiting. She's with a young man in a tracksuit, with curly hair, long-lashed, brown eyes, and an eager expression, like a big puppy dog.

'Is Grandad . . .?' Lottie gasps, running to me.

'He's still hanging on. But I have to tell you this, Lots, the staff aren't sure he's going to make it,' I say.

'Yes, he is!' says Lottie. 'Grandad's stubborn, Mum, like you, like me.'

'I hope you're right, darling.' I look at Luke. 'Thank you so much for driving her here.'

'Yes, everyone, this is my friend Luke. The kids at the camp all adore him,' Lottie tells us proudly, though she's got tears streaming down her face.

Luke nods at us all politely, murmuring his sympathies, then sits down while Lottie squeezes up with Anna and hears the whole story of Dad's cardiac arrest.

Can they still really be working on him, whatever that means? I know Dad's in a coma, but can he still feel it if they need to shock his heart back into beating? Is he screaming inside his head? I hold myself back from rushing out into the corridor and barging my way to his bedside.

Then a doctor in a white coat comes into the room and we're all silent, waiting. I hold hands with Lottie, and as we listen our grip relaxes ever so slightly. Dad's alive. He's still unstable, needing help to keep his heart beating properly, but we can visit him, one or two at a time, if we'd like to.

'You go first, Anna,' I say.

She gives me a grateful nod, wipes her eyes and smooths her hair, though she knows Dad is in a coma. She walks forward bravely, rolling up her sleeves as if preparing for a battle.

'Oh God, this is so awful,' says Lottie.

'Come and have a cuddle with us, Lots,' Ben says weakly.

She squashes between Ben and Simon. Luke looks so concerned. He must really care about her. I wonder if they've only just met up at this camp, or whether he's been at university with Lottie. It's not really the time to start asking these sorts of questions.

I remember when Lottie was little and could keep nothing to herself, telling me all about her lovely 'boyfriend' when she was at nursery school, confiding startling details when she started going out properly with boys at fourteen or fifteen. But now there are so many aspects of her life that I don't know about.

I suppose it's the same for Dad and me. I was always rather a Mummy's girl, but when she got ill Dad tried really hard to help and reassure me, and after she died he'd sit me on his lap and rock me whenever I had a crying fit. I was so anxious that he'd die too, and he'd always hold me close and promise that he wouldn't ever die and leave me all alone.

It must have been so bleak for him, doing his own grieving and yet forever having to reassure his sad little daughter. We were so close that first year after Mum died – until he took up with Anna. I can see now that he was lonely and desperately needing someone. I'm sure he was hoping he was doing his best for me, providing me with another mother figure in my life. It came as a shock to him when I hated Anna from the start, sure that she was doing her best to replace my mum. I behaved like a little brat, just like Chris's kids. It must have been so upsetting for Dad.

Somehow we were never really close again, even after Anna and I started to get along. It was almost as if I blamed him for Mum dying. Oh Dad, don't die now. You promised you wouldn't when I was a little girl. I need you now even more!

I stand up and pace around, unable to keep still. I manage to trip over one of Luke's long legs and he immediately apologizes profusely, even though it was my fault.

'Sit down, Ellie,' says Ben. 'You can go in next.'

'Mum?' says Lottie in a small voice. 'Could we go together?'

'Of course,' I say.

Lottie looks at Luke. 'Is that OK?' she asks.

He nods eagerly, probably very relieved she's not asking him to go with her.

'Sure, Blotto,' he says. *Blotto?* No one's ever called her that. I dread to think how she got that nickname.

Anna comes back, tears pouring down her face again.

'It's all right,' she says quickly. 'His heart's beating. But he just looks so different. So powerless. I just love him so much.'

I don't think I've ever heard Anna say she actually loves Dad. She's usually such a restrained woman, dignified and in control. It makes me realize more than anything that this is real, my father might die, and no matter how much I forbid him to with child-like intensity, there's nothing I can do about it.

Lottie stands up.

'Let's see him, Mum,' she says.

We put on masks and gowns in an outer room and are then led into Intensive Care, towards Dad's bed. We need to be pointed in the right direction because Dad himself is unrecognizable. He's wearing a mask, with a tracheal tube down his throat, and God knows how many other tubes and wires and bags attached to him.

We stand either side of him. Lottie's more composed than I am. She takes hold of his hand naturally, leans over him, and starts talking into his ear. There's no privacy, because of the medical staff and me too, but she ignores us all.

'You've got to get better, Grandad. You have so much more living to do, OK? I can't bear to lose you. Hang on in there, do you hear me? I love you, love you, love you.'

There's no flicker from the body on the bed, but perhaps Dad is still there inside his head, and he's loving her right back.

Now it's my turn. I don't know what to say. I feel so awkward and self-conscious. I take Dad's other hand, realizing that I haven't done this since I was a child. I expect it to feel waxy and cold, but it gives off normal human warmth, which helps a lot. I bend down even closer to Dad than Lottie.

'I love you, Dad,' I mutter. 'I'm so sorry I've always been such a trial to you. No matter how I've argued and fought, I've always loved you. Please get better so I can make everything up to you. You're a dad in a million.' Maybe I'm going a bit over the top now, but I need to say it.

Dad doesn't open his eyes and sit up. The monitor carries on beeping, neither faster nor slower. He's started to go a little bit deaf. Perhaps he simply can't hear a word I'm saying.

'I love you, Dad,' I repeat, more loudly, and I straighten up. I'd like to stay there for ever, but I have to give Ben a turn – and Simon, too, because he's just like another son to Dad.

Lottie and I walk out of the unit with our arms round each other. I don't know who's supporting whom, but it doesn't really matter.

15

Dad's not one in a million – but he might just manage to be one in ten. He's kept in a coma the next day, while we camp at the hospital. He's making good progress the day after and they bring him out of the coma. We're elated – but terrified too, because no one knows what effect the whole ordeal has had on his brain. He's very sleepy at first, and irritable too. Anna says his first words were a querulous 'Are you here *again*?' She burst into tears of joy and decided to interpret it as a very feeble joke.

Lottie and I steel ourselves for a similar reaction when we're allowed in to see him. He stares at us, and then says quite distinctly, 'Fucking hell!'

We're so startled we both burst out laughing. Dad's always hated swearing, saying it's a sign of impoverished vocabulary. When I was a stroppy teenager and first dared say *fuck* in front of him, he was furious, and sent me to my room like a Victorian caricature of a father.

'Why have you two got the giggles?' he asks. His voice is weak and raspy, because he's had a tube down his throat.

'We're laughing at you swearing, Dad!' I say. 'And in front of Lottie too!'

'Lottie doesn't mind, do you, love?' says Dad. 'And I've heard you swear like a trooper, Ellie.'

Oh, the joy of seeing that he knows who we are, that he's himself again, and yet a slightly different Dad too, because he usually condemns the use of 'love', saying it's common. So perhaps he's mellowed by his near-death experience – or just simply a bit muddled still, not quite back in his own personality. But what does it matter? He's alive, if not actually kicking yet.

There are still several blips in his heart rate but he's generally doing well. I stay with Anna, and the school gives me compassionate leave as it's nearly the end of term.

'You can all bugger off home now,' Dad tells us, when he's transferred to a general cardiology ward.

Anna still spends all her time with him. Ben and Simon go back to work, promising to return at the weekend to give Anna a break, though we're pretty sure she won't take it. She's visibly lost weight and the dark circles under her eyes show she's not sleeping, even though she's going back to the house each night. But she's under control now. Her eyes glint with steely determination, not tears.

'He's going to get completely better and I'm going to make sure he starts to eat healthily, drinks less and does a lot more exercise,' she says.

'Good luck with that!' Lottie says. 'I can't quite see Grandad complying.'

She's sent the lovely Luke back to camp and when it's clear Dad's out of the woods, she has to go back too, trekking by train this time. I go with her to the station and hug her hard. She hugs me back and then looks me straight in the face.

'Mum, there's something I need to ask you,' she says, chewing at her lip, a habit she's had when she's anxious ever since she was little.

'Of course,' I say.

'It's just – look, when we saw Grandad in a coma you were crying like anything, and saying such lovely things to him,' Lottie says. 'I didn't realize just how much he means to you.'

'Well, I thought he was dying,' I say.

'It was beautiful to see how much your relationship really means to you. And it made me think . . .' Lottie hesitates.

Whatever it is, it must be big. She usually comes right out with things. I put my arm around her shoulders and give them a squeeze, trying to help her.

'It's about *my* father,' she says. 'I just keep wondering what he's really like now. I know it sounds mad, and you, Grandad, Anna, Ben and Simon are my real family and always will be – but I'd like to meet him, Mum. Would you mind terribly?'

I swallow. *Oh God! I only raised the subject because I was trying so hard to be a good mother – but I never dreamt you'd want to meet him. Of course I mind, Lottie. But for your sake, not for mine. If you go ahead, you'll realize what a piece of shit he is. He's never once tried to get in touch with you. He's never given a toss about you – or me either. It will be a disaster.*

I can't say it to her, though. It's her right to know her own father. I force a smile to my face.

'Of course I don't mind,' I say.

'There! Luke said you'd be cool with it,' Lottie says, looking immensely relieved.

I try not to feel hurt that she spoke to him about it before me.

'Mum?' she says, peering into my face. 'Do say if you don't want me to get in touch with him.'

'No, it's fine, darling,' I say quickly.

'So, what's his name?'

I take a deep breath. 'Steve. It's probably Stephen. He was at art school with me.'

'Do you have his email, or his phone number or whatever?'

'No, but there's a good chance I can track him down online. Or some of the art school crowd at my party might know where he is now. I'll do my best, and then get in touch with him. And I'll definitely come with you if you decide to meet up,' I say.

She considers for a moment. 'I think I want to get in contact with him first – and see him by myself. It could kind of complicate things if you're there too,' she says apologetically.

I keep the bland smile on my face, though I can't help feeling rejected. She's probably right. I'd be feeling so angry and hostile if I ever met up with him again, they'd both sense it and it wouldn't help their potential relationship. Although is that seriously a possibility? He was so hateful to me, making it totally clear it was my problem that I was pregnant, not his. I can't stand the thought if he makes it plain that he still feels this way, because Lottie will be so hurt. Maybe he'll even deny that he's her father . . .

I remind myself he was very young, and probably scared silly at the thought that a strange girl he didn't even care for was having his child. He might have changed out of all recognition – physically, as well. I don't have a clue what he looks like now. I'm sure we would walk right past each other if we were on the same street.

But he's her father and she has to have a chance of knowing him – even if she ends up disliking him, or he ends up letting her down.

'If I can get hold of his details, I'll send them straight to you and you can decide what you want to do. Meanwhile, look after yourself, darling. And I have to say this, I think Luke's a total sweetheart – definitely a keeper.'

Lottie beams. 'He *is*, isn't he? But he's really just a very special mate at the moment. I don't want to settle down with anyone just yet.'

'How come you're so much more sensible than me?' I say fondly.

'But what about you and your love life?' Lottie asks. 'You've got a new guy on the scene, then?'

'Well, sort of,' I say coyly. I glance at the departure board. 'You'd better get on your train now, darling.'

'I could always catch the next one! I want to hear all about him! What's his name?'

We end up having a drink together in the station bar.

'His name's Guy,' I tell Lottie, crunching crisps.

'And have you known him long?'

'About twenty-seven years,' I say as casually as I can.

'What? That means you met when you were . . . Hang on . . . thirteen! Were you girlfriend and boyfriend then, when you were teenagers?' she says, laughing.

'No, he just happened to be my teacher at school,' I say, as if it's the most ordinary thing in the world.

'*Mum!*' she shrieks, nearly falling off her bar stool. She leans forward, eyes sparkling. 'How did you meet up again?'

'We went to a gallery, that's all,' I insist, trying to hang on to a little dignity.

'And then slept together afterwards?' Lottie asks relentlessly.

Memories like little photo clips flash inside my head, and I know I'm blushing.

'You dark horse, Mum! And do you think *he's* a keeper?' Lottie asks.

I take a big sip of wine. 'I'm not sure,' I say honestly. 'I mean, he's pretty terrific in many ways, but—'

'But what?'

'Maybe I don't really want a man in my life right now, a permanent one. I've got used to being on my own,' I say.

'So when am I going to get to meet him?' Lottie asks.

'Well, when I'm brave enough. If it lasts.'

'Whatever feels right for you, Mum,' says Lottie, which is funny because it's exactly what I've always said to her when she's asked me about her relationships.

We're having such a fond mother and daughter chat that Lottie very nearly misses the next train. I go back to the hospital feeling so happy – and find Anna happier too, because Dad has been sitting up, laughing and joking and managing not to swear so much.

'The doctors are very pleased with him,' she says. 'They really think he's going to be OK now. He'll have to take lots of medication and he'll be a few days getting over his defibrillator op, but they think he could be home in a week, maybe earlier, almost as good as new.'

I spend the next couple of days between the hospital and Dad and Anna's place, texting Andreea to check it's still all right for her to look after Stella.

I message Nadine and Magda too, and they're so supportive. They both offer to come to be with me, but I assure them that Dad's getting better and I'm coping, and they send me big hugs and kisses.

Guy sends me a message too, obviously with no idea that Dad's been so ill, suggesting we have lunch on Saturday, wanting to make the most of our time together.

I'm missing you so much already, Ellie! In fact, why wait till Saturday? Shall we meet tomorrow? Today? When? G x

I reply:

I miss you too but I can't make any arrangements. My dad had a cardiac arrest on Sunday, but thank God seems to be recovering, though we're all still very worried about him. I need to stay here at the moment. I know you'll understand. Ellie x

He gets back to me almost immediately:

Oh you poor darling, how awful for you! Which hospital? I'll
come and sit with you! Stay the night, whatever. G x

I sigh without realizing. Anna and Dad look at me.

'What's up, Ellie?' Anna asks.

'It's just a message from Guy,' I murmur.

'Guy?' they ask simultaneously.

'He's a new . . .' I don't know what to call him. Boyfriend?
Lover? Neither sounds right. 'It's this guy I've started seeing.
He wants to come here to be with me.'

'Well, that's sweet of him, isn't it?' Anna asks.

'Yes, I suppose,' I say. 'It just feels a bit . . . intrusive.'

'I don't mind,' says Dad. 'I'm curious! What does he do for
a living?'

'What a ridiculously Victorian question! He's . . . a teacher,'
I say warily.

'The teacher at your party?' Anna asks, surprised.

'No, not him – someone else entirely. Anyway, he lives miles
away and I really don't want him to come,' I insist.

'Lottie brought Luke,' Anna reminds me.

'Yes, well, they're at the love's-young-dream stage,' I say.

'We still are,' Dad says, taking Anna's hand. She hangs on
to it as if she's never going to let it go.

I can't help being touched, seeing how much they truly care
for each other. I wonder if Guy and I will ever get to that stage.
He sounds a little hurt when I tell him not to come to the hospital, but pretends to understand.

Actually I almost wish I'd taken him up on his offer. The
days seem to last for ever. Dad's still having a lot of tests and
sleeping much more than usual, and when he's awake I sense
he wants to talk to Anna most of all.

I know I could go home as he's out of immediate danger, but I feel I need to stay a little longer, to try to build up a really close relationship with him now I've been reminded how much he still means to me. When Anna allows herself to go and get a proper lunch or do a bit of shopping, Dad and I chat together – going right back to when I was little, when Mum was alive. We take it in turns remembering some of our early summer holidays, and birthday parties and days at the zoo.

I still wish he wouldn't try to flirt with the young female nurses, but they deal with him in a brisk, fond way, and I hear them saying to each other that he's a total sweetie. The doctors refer to him as the Miracle Man, though it was their skilled work that stabilized him – and Anna is the real miracle worker getting his heart going again.

'What did it feel like when your heart stopped, Dad? When you were technically dead? Can you remember it at all?' I ask when he's wide awake.

He pulls at his beard thoughtfully. Eventually he just shakes his head.

'To be truthful, I can't remember a thing. I felt a bit sick, and the room seemed to be going round and round, like it does when you're really drunk, and I think I was talking to Anna, probably grumbling about something – but the next thing I was here in the hospital with those damn machines beeping. I had a pain in my chest, but I think that wasn't my heart, it was a cracked rib from all the thumping to get me going again. It still bloody hurts. I daren't laugh any more!' Dad says. 'Isn't it a waste? I literally came back from the dead, a once in a lifetime experience – ha! Yet I can't remember a bloody thing.'

'Well, thank goodness you *did* come back,' I say. I reach out and pat his hand, carefully to avoid the little tube still stuck in him, and he curls his fingers round mine and hangs on for a few seconds.

'I promised you I wouldn't die, didn't I?' he says gruffly. 'I might tell a few porky pies, but I always keep my promises.'

'That's right. So keep getting better,' I say, giving him a kiss.

'Yep. It would be too much of a waste of everyone's time and effort if I conked out right away. And life feels sweet now, to be truthful,' he says.

Life feels sweet for me, too. I go home on Friday night and am pleased to see there's no rose-themed tribute from mystery man. I make a long, apologetic fuss of Stella and give Andreea the big box of chocolates and bottle of prosecco I bought at the station.

'I look after Stella any time, Ellie,' she says. 'She's a nice little cat. Maybe I get a kitten now.'

I sit at my desk with Stella curled rather inconveniently on my lap, making elephant sketches at last, drawing Mosi from all different perspectives, and at all different ages, enjoying the feeling of blissful absorption in what I love after such a stressful time. But it does remind me just how much I don't yet know about elephants. I've got so many questions for Alice. I really want to see her, anyway. I suddenly have to get my phone out and message her.

I do hope it's still OK to meet up at swimming tomorrow? My dad's had a cardiac arrest but amazingly he's recovered. I feel I can breathe again. I need a swim now! X

She replies the very next minute.

So sorry about your dad! I'll definitely be at swimming. Can't wait to see you x

I get up early on Saturday morning and hurry to the pool. She's waiting for me in the changing room and comes rushing up to me, and we have a big hug. She's so warm and concerned and comforting I can't help having a little cry. She mops my face with her towel and we sit down on the slatted benches, and I tell her all about Dad. When I'm finished, she gives me another hug.

'I'm so sorry, Ellie. It must have been so awful for you. How are you doing now?' she asks.

'I'm fine, I promise. Dad's getting so much better. And it's been so good talking to him the last couple of days, really bonding with him,' I say with a watery smile.

'That's so great. I'm happy for you both. I can't imagine my dad and I ever bonding in similar circumstances,' she says ruefully. 'He's made it plain that I'm not welcome back home unless I see the error of my ways and beg God's forgiveness.'

'What about your mum? Do you still get to see her?' I ask.

'We meet up sometimes – in the café at John Lewis, perhaps because it's the most wholesome place she can think of.'

'And she thinks you're a sinner too?'

'Pretty much. She did come to our house once, but she seemed very uncomfortable. She looked as if she thought we might start getting physical right in front of her. She made it plain she totally disapproved of Wendy,' Alice says.

'Oh dear,' I say sympathetically, though I certainly didn't warm to Wendy myself.

As we swim, I think how lucky I am to have Anna and Dad as parents. They've never had any kind of problem about Ben being gay. Well, perhaps they were a bit fussed during his clubbing days, but as soon as he met Simon they relaxed.

Out of breath, I pause at the end of the lane and watch Alice as she glides smoothly backwards and forwards, looking stunning with her brown skin in her white costume in the turquoise water. I so want to talk more to Alice, but I very much *don't* want to go back to Wendy's after our swim and coffee.

When we're out and dried and sipping coffee and munching almond croissants, before I know it I've asked her if she wants to come back to mine instead. As soon as I say the words, I wish I could take them back. I've become the least sociable person I know over the years. I never invite anyone back. It's my private space – well, Lottie's and mine. I've been casual friends with my neighbours for years but I've never once invited them in for supper, though I do have coffee with Andreea every now and then.

I hope Alice will say she has to get back to her own house. But she's looking pleased.

'Love to!' she says.

Ten minutes later, her eyebrows shoot up when she sees I live on the Artists' Estate.

'I live in Constable. It used to be the least popular because of the name – people who live here haven't heard of the artist and think it's to do with the police,' I explain. 'The estate had a bit of a reputation once, but it's all very quiet and respectable now. Well, mostly.'

Today, the lads are busy removing the wheels from a rusty abandoned car. They yell to me happily.

'Hi, Miss! Who's that? Is she your girlfriend?'

'Hey, you lot. She's my *friend* friend,' I say, glancing apologetically at Alice.

'They call you Miss?' she mutters.

'I teach some of them,' I say.

'Wow!' says Alice. 'You're brave. I imagined you helping little kids to do finger painting.'

'Well, my lot often *act* like little kids, but they're mostly quite sweet when you get to know them,' I tell her.

I hope one of my sweet lads hasn't decided to urinate or worse in the lift, but it's relatively clean and in full working order.

'You're right at the top?' Alice asks, as we swoop upwards.

'Yep. Lottie and I used to look out of the window and pretend to be birds,' I say.

'And you lived here, just the two of you?' Alice asks. 'Lottie's father was never around?'

'Nope,' I say, as the lift door opens. 'Here we are. I hope you don't suffer from vertigo.'

'Oh, it's fantastic!' Alice says, gazing all around. 'Better than the London Eye! You can see so far!'

I positively glow. She really likes it! Magda was horrified when she first visited and couldn't even look over the railings. Nadine's always been more adventurous, and pretended she thought it was a cool place to live – but even she looked round nervously when she heard footsteps behind her and clutched her shoulder bag to her chest.

'Come in,' I say to Alice, unlocking the door.

She steps inside and peers around as if she's walked into her own Wonderland.

'I love it!' she breathes.

I survey it, trying to see it through new eyes. It's definitely not *House Beautiful*. All my furniture comes from charity shops (it was hell getting the sofa in the lift) and it's battered and worn now, but I cover most of it with cheap Indian throws so everywhere looks bright and decorative. I've sanded and polished the floorboards so I don't bother with carpet, but I'm proud of my Persian rug. My walls are plain white, but you can hardly see them. One wall is all books and the other three are covered in paintings and posters. Some are my own art, mostly portraits of Lottie and Stella, and a few framed Myrtles, and the rest are posters: one of Paula Rego's dog women, a Frida Kahlo picture of herself and a monkey, several Lucian Freuds of Kitty and Lady Caroline, a circle of little Flemish saints with pink cheeks and golden hair, a Crivelli Madonna on a throne, a Picasso of two women running along a beach, and a languid Delvaux lady lounging on a sofa.

Alice wanders around, looking at them.

'They're all women,' she says.

'Not intentionally,' I say.

'And all white women, too,' she adds. 'Apart from Frida, of course.'

'Definitely *not* intentionally!' I say, alarmed that she might think me racist.

'Only teasing,' she says. 'Though I shall look hard to find one to add to your collection.'

'Would a grey female count for now?' I suggest, pointing to my best portrait of Stella lying on a cushion like a feline princess.

'Definitely,' says Alice, spotting the cat tower in the corner. 'She's yours?'

'Yes, my Stella, love of my life. Though she's seriously pissed off with me at the moment because I keep disappearing,' I say. 'Stella? *Stella?*'

I resort to rattling her treats jar and a beautiful grey head emerges from the bedroom, where she's probably been shedding hair all over my pillow.

'She's absolutely gorgeous,' says Alice, sitting cross-legged on the floor at Stella-level. 'Here, Stella!'

She's calling her the way you would a dog. I'm about to tell her not to take it personally when Stella ignores her with disdain – but to my astonishment she pads over on her delicate paws and butts her head against Alice's thigh for a head rub. Alice isn't even the one holding the treats, *I* am, yet Stella purrs with pleasure as she's stroked.

'You're a cat whisperer! She never does that, not even to me,' I say, starting to make coffee. 'Why don't you and Wendy have a cat? It wouldn't mind if Wendy slept till the afternoon. It would just curl up with her and doze too.'

'Oh, Wendy starts sneezing if she so much as looks at a cat,' says Alice flatly.

I have to fight not to say that Wendy seems a right pain.

'How about a gerbil?' I say.

Alice looks at me, not sure whether I'm teasing. I'm not sure either. We don't laugh, don't say anything, but share a quick smile. We take a sip of our coffee and then Alice says, 'Come on, then, show me your elephant sketches.'

I was hoping she'd ask, hoping she *wouldn't* ask. No one else has seen them. She's too polite to be openly critical, but I'll know if she thinks they're hopeless. My heart is thudding as I fetch them. My throat is dry, though I've just swallowed a mug of coffee. My hand actually shakes as I pass them to her.

She sits up straight, looking at each drawing carefully.

'That's Mosi, and that's her eldest daughter Binti, and this little calf here is Amani, which means peace, though he won't be born till three-quarters of the way through,' I say shyly. 'These aren't the finished versions, they're just ideas, I'll probably change everything when I get started. If I do. Perhaps I'm just wasting my time.'

'Oh, Ellie! They're magnificent! They're stylized, obviously, but with perfect accurate detail. And real character. They're all individuals. And the poses! What do you mean "when I get started"? Start now!' she says.

16

I wish Alice and I could stay together all day, but Guy has arranged a special lunch. When he suggested going for a bite to eat, I thought he meant a gallery café or something, not somewhere as glamorous and expensive as the Wolseley. I've wanted to see what it's like ever since I read that Lucian Freud used to dine there every evening. When he told me that's where we were going, I googled it and felt a bit taken aback at how smart and stylish it looks – and so beautifully art deco. Reluctant as I am to say goodbye to Alice, I can't help feeling excited.

When midday rolls around, we have a farewell hug and I see her to the door. Then I rush round madly trying to make myself look suitably special. I have to fall back on the dark red dress which, thank the lord, is slightly more flattering now. Worry and meagre hospital rations have made me lose a couple of kilos. If you've once flirted with anorexia you can't help being thrilled about weight loss, though you know it's problematic.

I slot my feet into my best strappy shoes, brush my hair one more time and slip a few washing things and a spare pair of knickers in my tote bag – even though I've made a firm resolution not to stay over this time because I feel so bad about neglecting Stella – plus Anne Tyler's *The Beginner's Goodbye*. I took it to the hospital to read for comfort, but I was so tense and worried I couldn't concentrate on it – but now I know I don't have to say goodbye to Dad just yet, I can read it just as a lovely tender book about loss and mourning, a perfect size for train journeys.

I leave lots of food, water and treats for poor Stella yet again. She stares at me venomously, looking as if she's going to be dipping a long claw in my Liquitex Professional Ink to write a peeved letter to the Cats Protection League. I don't blame her. I think she'd go next door to live with Andreea, given half the chance.

I meet up with Guy outside Green Park tube station. He's spruced himself up a little too, wearing a smartly cut modern suit, with a yellow tie with orange polka dots to show he's got his quirky side. It feels as if I'm sending him up but he looks terrific – a nine out of ten older guy, whereas I would rate myself as a five at most for a newly middle-aged woman. Still, he looks at me as if I'm amazing and kisses me on the lips, perfectly decorously, yet I feel a sudden stirring.

As I smile up at him, I wonder at myself. What's all this hesitation been about? He's fantastic. The Wolseley is splendid too, with chandeliers and pillars and shining black and white tiles, spotless white linen, a warm welcome at the desk and attentive waiters. The menu is a huge relief too, written in plain English, and mostly the sort of simple food I like.

Guy encourages me to order oysters, the most expensive item on the menu, but I've never had them before and wouldn't have a clue how to eat them. I choose chicken instead and so Guy has it too, and then we both go for apple crumble and custard. Our drinks are slightly more exotic, though – a glass each of Pommery champagne and then a bottle of Albariño, which I'd never even heard of but tastes delicious.

I don't usually drink at lunchtime so I'm feeling very woozy by the end of the meal, but in a good way. Guy is talking about the Wallace Collection in Marylebone, telling me I'll love it. I smile and make interested noises, but it's another gallery I know well. Why doesn't it ever occur to him that I might've been to any of these places before? I'm not really in the mood for trudging through all those jam-packed rooms, being told what to look at. I'd much sooner go straight back to Guy's house, go to bed, and have joyful sex.

When we're outside the Wolseley I slip my hand through his arm and suggest this, but he looks really disappointed.

'It's a very tempting thought,' he says politely, 'but I really think you'll love the Wallace Collection. Give it a try, darling.'

And without waiting for my response, he's nodding to the doorman at the Wolseley to summon a taxi. We are off to the Wallace Collection whether I like it or not, and we're not tubing or walking, we're getting there in style. I clamber into the taxi, seething, but after a few minutes, doubt begins to trickle in. Am I being unreasonable? How would I feel if I'd made plans and all he wanted to do was fuck? If only he could ask what I actually want to do, though . . .

By the time we pull up in front of the imposing building, I've managed myself into a better mood – until we hit the exhibition. I feel as if I'm plugged into an invisible audio guide. Guy starts talking about the opulence of the grand townhouse, telling me about the State Rooms, where the most important visitors were received by Sir Richard and Lady Wallace. He's got it all weirdly off pat, as if he's learnt it by heart.

In fact, I start to suspect that he's done exactly that. It's as if he's diligently prepared this private lesson for a favourite pupil. I get more and more irritated as he lectures on the Sèvres porcelain and the Astronomical clock.

He loosens up a little in the gallery of cabinets, and we have fun lifting all the leather flaps that protect the precious trinkets from daylight. I look carefully at the beautiful little painting of The Wheel of Fortune. Surely I should feel like I'm right up at the top now, with a great-looking older boyfriend who's going to enormous lengths to charm and impress me. I should feel touched that he's prepared to go to all this effort. I'm just being ungrateful again.

'I'm really glad we came,' I tell him earnestly, and he looks pleased.

We don't hang about too long in the endless armour galleries. We're going upstairs now, past all the Boucher paintings. Guy is surprisingly enthusiastic about all the shrimp-pink, naked nymphs who could all lose a few kilos. And I've always loved the Watteau pastoral scenes. They seem part of a fairytale too, and the people are so dreamily delicate.

I tell Guy I enjoyed reading Anita Brookner's elegant novels when I was in my late teens.

'She was a Watteau expert, and that helped me appreciate his paintings. She was such a strange woman. She even acted as a spy for Anthony Blunt, though I think it was unwittingly,' I say.

'Really?' says Guy doubtfully, clearly not as enthusiastic to take on the role of pupil, even for a minute. I suddenly feel exhausted. I could do with a sit down. I definitely had too much to eat and drink at lunchtime.

Still, I'm cheered when we get to the Madame Vigée Le Brun painting – but then Guy's off again, giving me her potted biography, and my earlier irritation returns in full force. Does he really think I've never heard of her when I'm so passionate about female art? We're back in fairytale land with Fragonard's *Swing*, which is very prettily done but too lascivious for my taste, though I like all the erotic miniatures of naked women in the cabinet room. Surely Guy has seen enough womanly curves now to make him want to hurry off to bed with me – but he steers me to a trip to Venice with Canaletto and Guardi.

'Have you ever been to Venice, Ellie?' Guy asks.

'I've been to Rome and Florence but never made it to Venice. It sounds wonderful,' I say.

'Maybe I'll take you there one day,' says Guy, as we wander through the Great Gallery, and I smile at the suggestion. We're nearly finished now, just the Dutch art and then we'll be out in the sunshine again. But then I'm stopped in my tracks by a painting I'd forgotten, *A Woman Peeling Apples* by Pieter de Hooch. It's a charming domestic painting of a gentle mother offering her little girl a long strip of apple peel. I remember Mum doing that for me when she was going to make her apple crumble (just as good as the Wolseley's). Mum didn't look at all like the placid plump woman in her scarlet skirt, and I wasn't as cute as the little girl in her bonnet and long dress – but their pose takes me right back to that time when I thought Mum would be there for ever. My eyes fill, and the painting blurs.

'Ellie! What's wrong?' Guy asks anxiously.

I duck my head, and rub my eyes with the back of my hand. I don't want to tell him. Talking to Dad has brought back such lovely memories of Mum, but it's too private, too raw to tell Guy.

'Are you thinking about your dad?' he asks, putting his arm round me protectively.

I nod, because it's easiest, and partly true, at least.

'But you said he's getting better?'

'I know. I just feel a bit down, that's all, though goodness knows why. I'm sorry, you're trying so hard to be lovely to me,' I say.

'I'm being thoughtless, dragging you around galleries. You're probably exhausted because you've had such a worrying time. I'm so sorry. Come, let's go back to my house. Unless – it's such a journey – shall we go back to yours?' Guy asks.

I'm so surprised I don't know what to say. I just have the strongest feeling that I don't want to bring him back to my home. I know he will hate the estate and my little flat with all its makeshift furniture and clutter and colours. God bless Alice, who genuinely seems to love it. I suppose I invited her because I sensed she would.

Besides, I left in a rush this morning. The bed isn't properly made. In fact, I'm not even sure the sheets are particularly clean. Half my wardrobe is scattered about my bedroom. The kitchen sink has probably got coffee cups and yesterday's plates in it. Stella might well have used her litter tray. It's the sort of squalor you expect from a twenty-year-old student – not the home of a forty-year-old professional.

Guy won't criticize exactly, he's not that rude. He'll try to ignore the mess, and we'll sit on my wonky sofa sipping our wine . . . Hang on, there's no wine, just the birthday champagne, and I want to keep that for a truly special occasion.

'I'd sooner not,' I say eventually. 'It's in a bit of a mess.'

He laughs indulgently. 'You've always been untidy, Ellie, right from when you were a kid.'

I don't like his tone. It's my business how I keep my place. I definitely don't want him to come back to my place now. I frown and he gets the message.

'All right, we'll go back to Earlsfield then,' he says with reasonable grace.

It's very warm outside now, and what with the meal and the wine and the emotion I nod off on the train, and he has to wake me when we get to the right station.

I've got a headache now and am finding it hard to make lively conversation. I'm also wondering if there was a specific reason why he wanted to go back to my flat. Is Lipstick Girl in residence? Lipstick Kim, in her PE kit, bouncing her ball against the walls, her whistle bobbing up and down on her womanly chest. I rub the palm of my hand against my forehead, trying to stop thinking nonsense.

'Poor Ellie,' Guy says softly. 'You look exhausted. And so pale. I don't suppose you've been sleeping properly. Maybe you'd like a little nap?'

When we get back to his house (immaculate as always, and

229

no sign of Lipstick Girl or any others) he gently pulls off my red dress, unstraps my shoes, and then tucks me up in his bed between his crisp, clean sheets. Then he takes off his clothes and gets into bed with me.

He strokes me gently and soothingly, and I relax at last and fall asleep almost instantly. I've no idea whether he goes to sleep too. When I wake up hours later he's not beside me. I go into his bathroom, splash my face, clean my teeth, and then go to find him.

He's sitting at his kitchen island drinking coffee and reading the paper in his dressing gown.

'Hello!' he says. 'Are you feeling a bit better now? You're certainly looking fantastic.'

I'm wearing my Rosie underwear today, which is actually quite flattering. He gets up and puts his arms round me and starts a very different sort of stroking. Soon we're back in bed, underwear off, and making love. There are no thoughts at all now, just the darkness behind my eyes and the urgent need for more and more until I come.

Maybe he is The One. *Enjoy him*, I tell myself. *Seize the day and the next day and the next. Go to Venice with him some time. Go to the ends of the earth with him. Stay with him until you're both old and grey.* Well, we're getting old now, and I've already got several silvery hairs in among my curls and maybe his dark blond hair has a little help nowadays. The shade doesn't quite match anywhere else.

Much later on, I ring Anna, just to make sure Dad hasn't had a sudden relapse.

'He's absolutely fine now, Ellie. He's out of bed at the moment, sitting in his chair. Say hello!' she says.

I feel a bit weird, being stark naked in bed, but manage to sound reasonably composed.

'Hi, Dad, how are you doing?'

'I'm fine, thank you, sweetheart,' he says.

He tells me about the talk he's had with the doctors and they're hoping to do the defibrillator operation next week, and then he'll be able to go home.

'As right as rain,' he says. 'Why is rain considered right, I wonder? I was thinking about painting rain actually. Not a downpour, just that damp glistening look, like Atkinson Grimshaw. Did you know he was actually a policeman?'

Oh God, not one but two men telling me stuff I already know! And I think it was Atkinson Grimshaw's father who was a policeman, not the artist himself. But I humour Dad too, have another little chat with Anna, and then say goodbye. Guy has been lying beside me all this time, leaning up on one elbow, looking at me fondly. I wriggle nearer and kiss him.

He cooks crêpes for supper, very light and fluffy. We have a glass of cider to wash them down, and then curl up on the sofa and choose something to watch on television. I want to see the first series of *Heartstopper* to see how to turn a graphic novel into film – though I'm not mad enough to think that will ever be a possibility for me, as a large cast of wild elephants and an African location would be impossibly expensive to film.

'Not schoolkids!' Guy groans. 'Don't we have enough of them at work?'

But it's a lovely adaptation and the cast are adorable and he's soon enjoying it as much as I am. I'm far too comfortable to think about going home now. Andreea's still got my spare key so I message her to ask if she'd be kind enough to check on Stella. Then Guy and I go to bed. I rather hope we'll have sex again but he just cuddles up to me. I suppose several times a day might be a bit much to ask for a man his age. That's one advantage women have over men.

I sleep soundly all night, in spite of the long afternoon nap. We do have sex when we wake up, in a warm, sleepy, sensual way. Guy dozes off again afterwards, and I sit up and look at him, wondering what I really feel about him. He looks younger and more vulnerable fast asleep, his hair ruffled, frowning slightly as if something's on his mind. Maybe he's wondering what he really feels about me too.

I slide out of bed and pad to the bathroom. His dressing gown pockets are empty, the Tampax packet is still nearly full. Has Kim stopped coming round, or is he carefully tidying up afterwards? I go to the kitchen and put the kettle on. I imagine myself making meals here, running a mop over those shiny tiles, stocking that gleaming Smeg. If I moved in with him I'm not sure I'd ever feel properly at home.

I wouldn't feel me without my coloured walls, my pictures, my books, my throws – and yet I know they wouldn't ever fit in here. *And what about me?* Stella mews inside my head. Guy might not mind cats, but he would mind her shabby tower, her smelly food, her litter tray.

Even more importantly, what about Lottie? She'd have lost her *home* home. She'd probably try to get along with Guy for my sake but it would be impossibly awkward, all of us in dressing gowns at breakfast. Plus, the two bedrooms are next door to each other. I'd always be uncomfortably aware that she could hear whatever we were up to – and it would be the same for her if she ever brought anyone back. She'd probably have to ask Guy if it was all right. It would always be his house, his rules, his way of doing things.

I sigh and take the coffee in to him.

'Hey, sleepyhead,' I say, putting the coffee down and giving him a kiss.

He wakes up with a jerk. 'Oh God, sorry! I should be making *you* coffee.' He takes a sip. He doesn't say anything, but it's clear he doesn't think I've made it properly – though I've made it just the way *I* like it. I remember the way he used to feel free to paint over little parts of my artwork at school, showing me the right way to do something. His contribution probably looked better, but I'd always wished he'd leave it alone.

He sits up and starts chatting about plans for the morning. He thinks it will be a good idea to go to Richmond Park, have a stroll to Pen Ponds, do some deer watching, and have lunch in a good pub nearby.

As he's talking, though, I realize that I want some space, and cast around for an excuse. 'Perhaps next week?' I suggest. 'I can't really walk far in my strappy shoes. And I've got to get home to feed Stella too.'

He sighs, looking disappointed.

'That's such a shame. But OK, next time,' he says, taking another sip of coffee and wincing slightly.

I feel a bit guilty and do my best to be sweet to Guy before I leave. I ask him about the art lessons he's giving the boys at his school, and he spends a happy half hour telling me in too much detail. He asks me about my own lessons, but I sense he's stopped listening after two minutes. I ask him instead what *he* was like as a boy, and whether he'd always been keen on painting. Little boy Guy had loved colouring in those intricate geometric design books, starting a new picture if he inadvertently went over the lines. I always hated that sort of colouring book – any sort, really. I liked doing my own pictures.

Guy makes breakfast for us, coffee his way, this time, and avocados on sourdough toast with a special home-made vinaigrette sauce.

'I expect you made the sourdough bread yourself too,' I say.

'I did, actually.' He gives me a quizzical look. 'Are you teasing me?'

'No! I think it's brilliant you can make sourdough,' I say, but my lips twitch a bit.

'I wonder if you get together with Magda and Nadine and all have a giggle about me, the way you did when you were schoolgirls,' he says.

'No, we don't,' I insist, which is absolutely true because life has been so hectic recently that the three of us haven't met together since my party. 'And you probably *liked* us giggling, because you knew we all had a crush on you.' I pause. Then I dare ask it. 'Which one of us did you like best then?'

It's his turn to tease me. 'Well, Magda was the most glamorous, and she made it plain she liked me a lot. But Nadine was so cool with her long black hair and her long black nails to match. It's hard to choose between the two.'

I wait. 'I liked *you* best, Ellie, and you know it,' he says. 'But in a very appropriate way.'

'Have you told Mrs Henderson – Jean – that we're spending time together?' I ask.

'No, I haven't! I'm not at all sure she'd approve. I said we'd met up and been to an art gallery together, that's all. I haven't said that *we've* got together too.'

'Have you told Kim about me?' I ask as casually as I can, not quite looking at him.

'I've told her I've met up with someone I used to know,' he says cagily.

'And she doesn't mind?'

'Why should she? I don't mind if she sees other men.'

'Would you mind if *I* saw someone else?'

'That's different,' he says.

Unbelievable! But I don't want to start a row now.

I tell Guy I'd better be going, because I have a lot to do. I give him what's meant to be a quick goodbye kiss, but he hangs on to me, pulling me close. I don't think he's overcome with passion – he just doesn't want me to go. We end up in a rather clumsy embrace on his sofa, which gradually becomes much more intense and means that eventually I have to go and shower all over again.

I might as well have agreed to stay at the beginning because by the time I get to the Artists' Estate I'll only have ten minutes to get changed and fuss over Stella before setting out again for the hospital. All this travelling is getting expensive.

I freeze when I get to my door. There's an envelope poking through the letter box.

Please let it just be ordinary post! An advert, a charity letter, a bank statement, a bill.

I pull it out and feel that there's something small and hard inside, wrapped in tissue paper. And oh no, oh no – another envelope with just my name in those distinctive italics. There's a card, patterned with more red roses. And a message.

I hope you like the present! See you very soon xxx

I unwrap the tissue paper clumsily, my hands shaking. It's a small silver-gilt brooch in the shape of a rose. I look up and down the balcony, wondering if he's still lurking, watching me. I scrabble to get the key in the door and run into the flat, feeling sick. I rush towards the bathroom, my hand over my mouth – and then stop abruptly.

Someone's in there! They're running a tap, murmuring indistinctly. Has the mad stalker broken into my flat? I wind the handles of my tote bag round my fingers, ready to use as a clumsy cosh, and charge in there.

There's a shriek – and a screech from Stella. It isn't a crazy guy, it's only dear Andreea, washing her hands after dealing with the cat tray.

'Oh my lord, you gave me a fright, Ellie! I nearly peed on myself!' Her English is brilliant, but just occasionally she gets it slightly wrong.

'I'm so sorry! I thought you were this crazy fool who keeps leaving me cryptic messages,' I gasp.

'You had another one in your letter box! I thought I'd leave it there just as it is, in case you want to go to police,' she says.

'Do you think I should?' I say. 'He's just leaving me cards and creepy little presents. Is that a crime?'

She sees the cheap brooch in my hand.

'Ah, you opened it. That's quite a nice brooch. I'll have it if you don't want it,' she says.

'Of course you can have it,' I say, thrusting it into her hands.

'And I liked those chocolates too,' says Andreea, a glint in her eye. 'Maybe hang on a week or two before going to police.'

'Do you think he could be really dangerous?' I ask her, though how on earth could she know. 'Or just pathetic?'

'Lovesick?' she says, pondering. 'Well, no man ever pursued me romantically. Perhaps wait till you get a peep at him. He might be hunk.'

'I very much doubt that,' I say, calming down a little.

'I think you have found hunk already?' she says. 'Specially for Saturday nights?'

I blush ridiculously. 'Maybe,' I mutter.

'Well, good for you. You deserve some fun,' she says. Stella is winding herself round Andreea's ankles rather than mine, purring hopefully. Andreea is probably much more generous with treats than I am. Or maybe Stella just wants to pay me out for leaving her again.

When Andreea goes, the brooch pinned onto her cardigan, I sit down and brush Stella, crooning my way back into her affections, and when we're friends again I change into a tee-shirt, jeans and Docs, grab a Jane Austen off the shelf, and charge back to the tube station. I peer all round me as I jog along, looking out for a weird man crouching behind a wall or lurking in an alleyway.

See you soon, see you soon, see you soon! Maybe I *should* go to the police. I could go to see Dad at the hospital and then pop into the local station on the way back home. I try to distract myself by reading *Persuasion* on the train, alarmed that at the age of twenty-seven Anne Elliot is considered a faded flower, destined for a lonely life of spinsterhood.

I should have bought a little present for Dad. He's not a fan of flowers, and though I know he'd love a bumper bag of Mars bars, he's supposed to be sticking to a healthy eating regime. One square of dark chocolate per week is probably his limit. He doesn't even like grapes much and spits the pips out contemptuously. All I've got is my book and I'm pretty sure Jane Austen isn't his cup of tea. I rush into a newsagent and buy the *Observer* and a *New Statesman* for him, which is a pretty pathetic gesture. But there's not much I can do about it now.

Ben and Simon live up to expectations, giving Dad a glossy illustrated biography of Francis Bacon. Anna's bought Dad a big punnet of giant strawberries and we all tuck in happily – but then there are lumbering footsteps up the ward and when we see who it is, we stare at each other, horrified. It's Aunty Freda, with sad Nigel holding her arm and helping her along. For some reason, he's grinning all over his face.

While Aunty Freda is busy telling poor Dad his cardiac arrest is all his own fault, and he should calm down and stop all his silly antics, dancing like a fool at Ellie's birthday and drinking like a fish, blah blah blah, Nigel is looking at me expectantly.

I give him a polite nod. He edges up close beside me and bends down.

'You're not wearing your new brooch!' he whispers into my ear.

17

I gape up at him, appalled. *Nigel* is my secret admirer? Weird cousin Nigel, who I've long feared is one of those incel guys who's never had a relationship and secretly blames women? Surely he doesn't want a relationship with *me*!

He's winking at me in a bizarre way that he must think is attractive. Dear God, please don't let Ben and Simon see, they'd collapse in hysterics. I can't say anything in front of them, or Anna, or poor old Dad, who is still being held hostage by Aunty Freda.

'Nigel, I think we all could do with a cup of coffee. Would you come with me to the café and help me carry them?' I ask sweetly.

'Certainly, Ellie,' he says, with a wolfish grin that makes me shiver – and not in a good way.

Ben and Simon raise their eyebrows at each other, and even Anna looks surprised, but I manage to keep a dignified calm until we're out of the ward and on our way towards the Costa on the ground floor.

I swallow hard, praying I don't make a mess of this. 'So you're my secret admirer, Nigel?' I ask, trying to sound matter of fact.

'Surely you must have guessed right from the start?' he says. He's edging closer, in an awful nudge nudge, wink wink kind of way, and I shuffle away.

'Nigel, I honestly didn't have a clue,' I say. 'Is this all a prank?' Please let him have the wherewithal to say yes and save face . . .

But no, he simply looks astonished, twisting his face sideways in a grimace that shows too much teeth. 'Of course not!' he protests. 'I've been wooing you.'

My stomach lurches. 'But whatever made you suddenly start . . . wooing me?' I can hardly say the awful word.

'Well, you made it obvious you were up for it,' he says, leaning close and giving me a poke. 'And I thought you'd appreciate a little romance.'

This is so terrible I'm wondering if I'm going to faint right away, like the Regency heroine he seems to think I am. I should be reading *Pride and Prejudice* rather than *Persuasion*. He's the very spit of Mr Collins.

'What do you mean, you thought I was . . . keen?' I ask.

'In your message!' he says.

'Nigel, I think someone might be playing a trick on you – on us. I promise you I've never sent you a message in my life,' I insist.

'The old-fashioned card with the girl just like you, with lots of curly hair, in the rose garden,' Nigel says.

Oh! I used an old pack of Pre-Raphaelite cards when I was writing thank-you letters after my party. That Rossetti girl wasn't remotely like me, though. How could he have possibly taken that card and my brief message as active encouragement?

'That was a card for your mother, Nigel, thanking her for my birthday present,' I say, trying to keep my voice even. I'm not sure whether I'm going to laugh or cry.

'Yes, I know it was for Mum too, but you added *Love to Nigel*. You know you did,' he says. 'You were making it plain how you felt about me.'

'But that was just . . . it's the sort of thing I always put on cards. I wasn't going to put *Yours faithfully* or *Sincere regards*! It was just a way of signing off! Oh, I'm so sorry, you've got it all wrong.'

'Come off it, Ellie! You made it plain enough at your party. You kissed me!' he says.

I *kissed* him? I think back. Wait, didn't I give him a quick peck on the cheek when he was trying to protect me? I remember the slightly damp feel of his skin. This is beyond dreadful. How could poor old Nigel ever in a million years think I fancied him? He's blinking at me now, looking bewildered.

'I thought you'd like all the little gifts with the special rose theme,' he says. 'We're not like all these people who jump into bed at the drop of a hat. I know you like art and books and all that sort of stuff. So I left you flowers from the garden – roses, because they were on your card – and then the chocolates and—'

'But why didn't you simply knock on the door and *give* them to me?' I ask. My legs are shaking so much I have to lean against the corridor wall.

'I did knock the first time, but you were out. I just left the roses on your doormat so you could have a lovely surprise when you came home. Then I got to thinking it could be our secret game. I'd leave you a present every now and then and you'd get a little thrill and wonder when we'd actually meet face to face,' he says. 'And now we are, ready for a relationship!'

This is getting worse and worse! I take a deep breath.

'Nigel, we're cousins! We can't have a relationship,' I say in my best firm-teacher voice.

'Don't worry, I've looked it up. It's perfectly legal, I promise you,' he says. He stands so close to me I have to inch away again.

'But we've known each other all our lives. We never *liked* each other!' I insist. 'We didn't know how to play together.

You just wanted to stick stamps in your album and make those Airfix aeroplanes, and I wanted to draw and paint. We barely talked!'

'We were children then. We're both adults now, and life hasn't really worked out for us, has it?'

'Well, I don't know about that,' I say. 'I – I quite like my life.'

'Yes, but you ended up with a baby and no wedding ring on your finger and you're not a proper artist, you just do those cartoony things,' he says.

I feel myself going red with fury.

'It's all right, I don't mind,' he says, misunderstanding. 'I'm nothing to write home about either. I've got a good job in the building society but I've never had much luck with the ladies. We're both on our own – and this is our chance of finding true love.'

He lunges forward, squashing me against the wall again, and puts his lips on mine in a slobbery parody of a kiss.

'Get off me!' I gasp, as soon as I can break free. 'This is all a terrible mistake! I don't fancy you! I don't want anything to do with you, don't you see that?' I push him away, and he stares at me. Then his face crumples. He puts his hands over his face.

He looks so lonely and pathetic, and I feel a pang of remorse.

'Oh God, Nigel, you're not crying, are you?' I ask anxiously.

'I've been so happy these last few weeks,' he mumbles. 'But it turns out I've just been kidding myself. Even *you* don't want me.'

Even me? I want to tell him exactly what I think of him – but I don't want to be a complete bitch. How on earth can I help him keep his pride? Then I have an idea – a foolproof brilliant idea!

'It's not just *you* I don't want, Nigel,' I say, wiping my mouth again with a shudder. 'It's any man. I'm gay.'

241

He twitches, and rears back a little.

'You mean you're a *lesbian?*' he says incredulously.

'Yep. Definitely. I like women,' I say stoutly.

A plump nurse bustles past us towards the Costa. 'Good for you, girl!' she says.

Nigel breathes out slowly. 'So, you and Ben, you're *both* queer?'

'If that's the way you want to put it, yes,' I say.

'So obviously I've been wasting my time,' he says.

'I'm sorry. But maybe you'll find the right woman one day who'll love a few romantic gestures. Though I'd be a bit more direct, actually, just so she doesn't get the wrong idea and think you're a weird stalker,' I say.

He snorts at the idea. We go and get coffees in the Costa without further conversation – and are silent all the way back to the ward. It's like being children again. It's a huge relief to be back with Dad and Anna and Ben and Simon. Even Aunty Freda. I wonder if she's had any inkling what her son's been up to? Probably not. She's always disapproved of me because I'm a single mother.

I think everyone can tell that Nigel and I have had some sort of contretemps because we stay far apart and studiedly don't look at each other. Luckily, Aunty Freda is starting to get fidgety already. She complains about the coffee and the hardness of the chair and tells Nigel that she wants to go home now.

She gives Dad an abrupt pat on his hand and shuffles off, hanging on to her strange son. When they're out of earshot Ben says, 'Come on then, Ellie, what happened? Did he try to kiss you?'

They all laugh uproariously at the thought.

'He did, actually,' I say, enjoying their horrified expressions.

'Well, you could do worse,' says Dad.

I stare at him, wondering if his brain could be affected after all – but then he cracks up laughing again.

'Dad! Stop it!' I say, pretending to swot at him.

I'm as good a sport as the next person, but it all gets a bit tiresome when they carry on teasing me, so I get away as soon as possible.

When I'm home (no parcel at the front door, no roses, no cards, oh glory) I WhatsApp Nadine and Magda to suggest we meet up for a drink or three at the Hare and Moon in Bloomsbury this week or next.

Then I take a deep breath and force myself to google Steve Fedden. My hands are suddenly so clammy my fingers slip on the keyboard. There are several of them, on Facebook, Instagram and LinkedIn. It's easy to work out the right one. There's even a photo. I don't actually recognize him, but there's only one the right sort of age and working in a design office. I have his work email.

I'm tempted to email him myself first and beg him to be nice to Lottie for a couple of hours, even if he wants no further contact. Or if he doesn't even want that, to let her down as gently as possible. Don't say she's nothing to you. She's your daughter, whether you like it or not.

But I can't because Lottie's asked me not to. I have to let her handle this herself. I send her the email address and write *Good luck, Lots. And lots and lots of love, Mum xxx*

She doesn't reply, though I can see she's read it. Maybe she's thinking things over. And she can't leave her camp job just like that – she's already pushed her luck to the limit. Perhaps she's discussing it with Luke.

I don't hear back from Nadine. I hope she's OK and hasn't gone out with another sadist. I don't hear back from Magda. Perhaps the kids have pushed her down the stairs. I hear from Guy instead.

Darling Ellie – I want you back in my bed right this minute!

How many darlings is that? Three? Maybe four or five in the midst of sex? I remember exactly when and in spite of myself I tingle all over again. What's the matter with me? I've had more sex in the past weeks than I have in the past years.

I know it's crazy to expect you to trail out to Earlsfield all over again. Maybe we could meet up in London somewhere if you don't want me to come to your flat? I've got something to tell you! G xx

I message back:

When?

Now!

Can't it wait till Saturday?

No! Please! You'll be thrilled, I promise.

Can't you tell me now? Phone?

I want to hold you in my arms when I tell you.

I can't help but roll my eyes. What could it possibly be? Has he said farewell to Lipstick Kim? Although I don't really care so much about her now, somehow.

I consider saying no, but decide it'll cause too much fuss. *Where?* I message, and when he tells me the name of a pub near Waterloo station I start to get ready. No red dress this time. Black shirt over silver sleeveless teeshirt, short black skirt, black tights and little black ballet-type shoes. I give Stella her supper. She eats slowly and delicately, pausing every now and then to peer at me disapprovingly.

'I'm sorry, I know I'm being a terrible mum to you,' I say softly, crouching down beside her and rubbing the back of her head.

She purrs a little, agreeing with me. Then she gives me several slow blinks. It's a sign of acceptance and affection, which is lovely – but when I straighten up again she looks affronted. I know exactly what she's thinking.

What are you playing at, rushing off to see this man? You're not even sure you really like him.

Oh come on, Stella. Give me a break. I've lived like a nun for years.

Stella gives a disgusted mew that sounds very much like *ew*. She stops eating and stalks off, tail in the air. And I rush out of the flat to meet Guy.

He's waiting outside the pub, in jeans, a casual shirt and a denim jacket. He used to wear something similar at school. He suddenly blurs into long-ago Mr Windsor, with fairer hair and slimmer build. I blink hard and he's back being Guy, thank God.

He looks delighted to see me. There are people drinking outside the pub, mostly younger, girls drinking summer cocktails, guys sticking to beer, all laughing, chatting, enjoying the warm evening. Guy pulls me close and kisses me, and I melt instantly. When poor mad Nigel kissed me it felt awful, and I had to push him away. When Guy kisses me it feels so good I have to fight not to pull him even closer.

'I'm not sure about this place,' he says. 'I looked it up online because it seemed the most convenient for both of us, but it's very crowded.'

'Never mind. We'll crowd it a bit more.'

We go inside and fight our way to the bar. It's not really the sort of place for fine wine. Guy orders a beer and I have a half of cider and we look at the menu because neither of us has eaten.

'It's all a bit too basic and touristy,' Guy says, his nose wrinkling. 'Shall we find somewhere else?'

'Sometimes I like basic touristy stuff,' I say. 'I quite fancy the Best of British crispy battered fish and golden chunky chips.'

'OK, then I'll have the Best of British Big Bangers with creamy mash,' he says, grinning.

'So what have you got to tell me?' I say, when we've found a booth right at the back and settled in.

He pulls out his phone, taps a few times, then shows me the screen. I peer at it. It's hard to make it out. It's some sort of confirmation email. I glance at Guy, who's looking at me expectantly.

'What is it?' I ask.

'Can't you read it?'

I squint carefully. 'Flight tickets?'

'For two. To Venice,' he says. He swipes again. 'And a little hotel on the outskirts, hopefully romantic.'

I stare at him, too stunned to say anything.

'Don't worry, it's not for the summer – Venice is awful then, so hot and muggy. It's for late October, when it's hopefully still reasonably warm – and it's half term!'

'Oh my God!'

'The Biennale is on then too. It's this huge exhibition of all the arts that takes place every two years,' he says. 'And we'll go to the Accademia of course, and the Peggy Guggenheim and all the churches – wait till you see the beautiful Bellinis, and if you don't mind touristy things then we'll actually drink Bellinis at Harry's Bar. We can even take a trip on a gondola, if you really want to!'

I'm so taken aback I don't know what to say, so I kiss him – and we're still kissing when the waiter brings us one of those little baskets full of cutlery and condiments. He coughs and gives Guy a conspiratorial grin. I wriggle away from him and try to look composed.

'There, I just had to tell you in person,' Guy says triumphantly. 'I knew you'd be thrilled.'

I *am* thrilled. Well, thrilled that he's made such a flamboyantly romantic gesture. It will be wonderful to go to Venice. OK, he gives me ponderous lectures the minute we set foot in a gallery, but does that really matter? He's clearly making out an itinerary already, but that simply means I don't have to go through all the guidebooks and pore over maps. It isn't just going to be art and culture. Bellinis in Harry's Bar sounds great fun. And the gondola too, though I've heard they're ludicrously expensive. In fact, the whole trip is going to cost a fortune.

'You must let me pay half,' I say eventually, though God knows how I'm going to manage it.

'I wouldn't dream of it,' he says firmly. 'It's my treat.'

It's all so spur of the moment, without checking I haven't got plans for the half term holiday. I was hoping Lottie and I might manage a day or two together. Perhaps Nadine and I could have had a short beach holiday somewhere warm. Or I could have gone baby shopping with Magda, and helped her with her breathing exercises or whatever. The point is, I want a say in how I'm spending my time.

But doesn't a sexy week with a romantic man beat everything? I imagine us walking along moonlit canals to our hotel, going upstairs to our room, closing the Venetian lace curtains, lying down together and having the most blissful sex, night after night . . .

I just wish he'd asked me first.

Then our meals come, providing a welcome distraction. They

must have been waiting for a while in the kitchen because they're lukewarm, and if the fish and sausages are the Best of British then who knows what the Worst are like. But we eat with gusto all the same, with more beer and cider, and then leave.

'For God's sake, Ellie, can't we possibly go back to your place now?' Guy begs.

I cast around for more excuses, but when my eyes meet his, I know he won't take no for an answer this time. Even as I'm saying yes, I know it's going to be a mistake. He phones for an Uber, which suddenly diverts to another call and we have to start all over again, and I sigh about the whole performance when it's so easy to tube it. We could probably walk it in half an hour. We end up bickering pointlessly, which is madness when this was supposed to be his big romantic gesture.

We barely speak in the car, looking out of the windows, not at each other. Guy gives a sharp intake of breath when we get to the estate. We get out and he looks round dubiously in the dusk.

'This is really where you live?' he asks incredulously.

'Yes! For God's sake, there's no need to act like you're going to be knifed any minute,' I say irritably. 'It's perfectly safe. Ordinary, decent people live here. Don't be such a snob.'

'I just don't get why you'd want to live here all on your own,' he says.

'You sound just like my dad!' I say, then flinch and look at him, gauging his reaction. It's not good.

'Is that how you see me – as a *Dad* figure?' he says, his voice clipped.

'Well, you seem to think I'm still a schoolgirl, the way you keep telling me what to do,' I bluster.

We're on dangerous territory now. It would be so easy to go a little further and start saying things that can't ever be forgotten. I think it frightens both of us.

'I'm sorry if you think that,' he says, not very sincerely.

'I'm just a bit touchy about people criticizing my home,' I say. 'It was the best I could do for Lottie and me. My dad kept wanting to help me out, but I was determined to be independent.'

'I think that's admirable,' he says, putting his arm around me warily. 'You've been fantastic, bringing up your daughter by yourself. Didn't her father have the decency to contribute at all?'

I wince. He's touched a nerve, though he doesn't realize why. Has Lottie emailed Steve already? Has he replied? Are they really going to meet up?

Guy sees my face. 'I'm sorry,' he says, genuinely now. 'It's none of my business anyway.'

'It's OK. I don't have anything to do with him now,' I say. 'Come on, then. I'm on the top floor.'

'The top floor?' he says, craning his neck. Then he takes a deep breath. 'You must have a great view,' he adds valiantly.

I pray that the lift is working and that it's clean and thank goodness it is. We go along the walkway, Guy holding tight to the peeling rail. As I'm fishing for my key Andreea's door opens, and she comes out with a bag of rubbish to chuck down the chute. She blinks at us.

'Ah!' she says. 'So is this your secret admirer, Ellie?'

'No! This is . . . someone else entirely,' I say.

'Oh my! Lucky you. Some of us have to make do with no man, and yet you've got two!' she jokes.

'Andreea, honestly!' I roll my eyes as I open my own door. 'Catch you later, eh?'

'I hope this one's brought you chocolates,' she calls, as I pull Guy inside.

'Here we are,' I say, snapping the hall light on. 'Come in.'

There's a pause as he takes it all in, blinking.

'Oh, it's great,' he says quickly, though I can tell he thinks it anything but. 'Very . . . colourful!'

Stella slinks out of the kitchen and meows imperiously, demanding to know who this stranger is.

'This is Stella, the love of my life, next to Lottie,' I say. I pick her up and she struggles for a second or two, playing hard to get, but then she relaxes and rubs her head against my neck.

Guy comes close. 'Hello, Stella,' he says.

I feel her sleek body tensing, her ears and whiskers forward. Guy has the sense not to try and stroke her.

'Maybe we'll make friends in a little while,' he says.

'Good idea.' I nod approvingly. 'You've passed the first test. Coffee?' I put the kettle on and open the fridge to see if I've got enough milk. The birthday bottle is still there. 'Or even better, champagne?' I say, trying hard. A holiday in Venice is surely a special enough occasion.

'You're the girl who fusses about the expense of Ubers and yet you've got a bottle of Bollinger in your fridge!' he teases.

But it's OK, the mood's changed. We're smiling at each other as I bring out the champagne, and he takes hold of the bottle.

Irritation bubbles back up, but I'm not going to spoil the changed mood by protesting that I can pop the cork perfectly well by myself. As if it really matters. We go into my living room with the bottle and two tumblers, because I haven't got any flutes. He sounds genuinely enthusiastic about my wall of female artists, and does his best to ignore the unwashed coffee cups, kicked-off shoes, the clutter of old letters and magazines, and books in an unsteady tower.

He tries to peer at my desk, wanting to see what I'm working on, but I cover everything quickly.

'It's not really secret, it's just I'm trying out something and it's not ready to show anyone yet,' I say.

'I'm the same when I'm working on anything,' he says. 'Don't worry.'

We sit on the sofa, clink the clumsy tumblers and drink to each other. 'And to Venice,' he adds, and I give him a weak smile.

'Did you know it's made up of a hundred and eighteen islands separated by a hundred and fifty canals?' Guy starts.

'Shh, Mr Google Man!' I dare say. I wonder if I've gone too far, but he just smiles in acknowledgement.

'It also happens to be the most romantic city in the world,' he says, and kisses me. We sip and kiss again and then take the bottle and glasses to bed with us. My bed is as unmade as I'd feared, but he doesn't comment. We have passionate sex and unmake it even more. I think Stella peers in at one point. I sense her narrowing her eyes at us, wondering why my head is here and his is there, then stalks off in disgust.

We lie back together at last, drinking more champagne, both of us glowing.

'I hope you don't bring your secret admirer back to your bed too,' says Guy.

I'd hoped he was elegantly ignoring Andreea's remarks. I wrinkle my nose.

'She was just teasing me,' I say.

'Well, I gathered that. But *have* you got a secret admirer?' he asks, leaning up on one elbow and peering closely at me.

'I did have. But they've stopped admiring me now, thank goodness,' I say, nestling against him. I don't want to talk about Nigel – just thinking about him makes my skin crawl.

'Is he a complete stranger?' Guy sounds alarmed.

'No, he's a relative, actually. A cousin. He thought I'm now a sad, lonely, middle-aged woman who'd jump at the chance of going out with him.'

'You – sad, lonely and middle-aged?' says Guy, dipping his

finger in his glass of champagne and trailing it from my breasts downwards. 'You're the most beautiful girl in the world.'

This is utter nonsense of course, but I like him saying it, and I like it even more when he starts licking the trail of champagne.

He stays in bed with me until the morning, when we have breakfast together. I've only got a loaf of rather stale bread, but we eat buttered toast companionably, and then kiss goodbye.

I go back to bed and lie thinking about him. He's tender, kind, romantic, great at sex. He's amazingly generous. He didn't criticize my flat. He let Stella set her own terms. He let me tease him.

What more could I want in a man?

18

Lottie doesn't acknowledge my message. Perhaps she's decided not to contact her father, after all. Or if she has, he hasn't bothered to reply. I long to phone to see if she's all right but I have to respect that she wants to do this by herself.

Then I start to worry that something might have happened to her. It gnaws at my stomach. I still don't phone her – but I do message.

> Hi darling Lots, How are you doing? Hope the kids aren't too unruly. All love xxx

She answers almost at once.

> Hey Mum, yep, fine. Kids fun actually. Luke and I taking them to beach today. Love you xxx

Which is a relief – but I'm still none the wiser. I wonder about asking outright, but don't want her to think me a prying old bag. I'm not having much luck arranging a date with Nadine and Magda either, who have at last messaged back. There's a flurry of suggestions back and forth. Any weekday is good for me, now school's broken up for the summer, but they're both at the office or tied up with Zoom calls at home. I don't really want to meet them at the weekend because I see Alice on Saturday mornings and then Guy the rest of the day, and maybe most of Sunday too, plus I need to see more of Dad. Magda can rarely manage a Sunday, though, because of Chris and his kids. Evenings aren't easy either, because Nadine says she's got herself a temporary evening job in this new glamorous wine bar helping out her landlord friend Harry who's stuck for staff, and she only has Mondays off. Plus Magda wants to make the most of having Chris to herself in the evenings.

This is crazy. We're best friends for ever, as we solemnly vowed when we were schoolgirls. We have to meet up!

I send a terse voice note: 'For God's sake, let's strike while the iron's hot, or whatever that stupid saying is. How about tonight! You're off, Nadine, and Chris can surely do without you one little night, Magda?'

So we agree to meet at the Hare and Moon at seven. It's all settled – and then Guy phones to say he's booked tickets for us to go to a documentary about Maggi Hambling at some art cinema – *tonight!*

'That's so sweet of you, darling,' – I seem to have caught the habit now – 'but I'm afraid I've arranged to meet up with Nadine and Magda.'

'Well, can't you make it the next evening, any old evening? The Hambling film is only getting one showing – and I know you'll love it,' he says.

'I would,' I say. For once I haven't already seen it, and he's right, I'm sure I'd love it. 'But I can't let them down,' I add.

'So your girlfriends are more important than me?' He says it lightly, but he sounds hurt.

'No!' I insist, trying to reassure him. 'But you know how close we are. We need to catch up. It's all arranged, seven o'clock at the Hare and Moon. It's our special place. Nadine discovered it. The building is wonderfully Victorian Gothic, with original fittings and great period paintings and posters. Lots of alternative arty people hang out there.' I pause. Guy maybe thinks himself an alternative arty man. What if he tries to muscle in on things? This is *our* evening. I think quickly. 'It's mostly women. It's not a blokey kind of pub at all,' I add. 'You'd loathe it.'

'Fine. But there are three hundred and sixty-five evenings in a year. Surely you girls can pick another night so that you can come to the film with me?' he says. 'You'll really be missing out if you don't see the Hambling documentary.'

When I reply, my voice is firmer. 'I told you, it's all arranged. You should have asked me before you booked the tickets. You can't keep arranging things without discussing them with me first.'

'I wanted to surprise you. You were ecstatic when I told you about Venice,' he says.

I *was* – but I still wish he'd checked with me before booking it. I'm going to have to be more direct with him. Why on earth have I dug myself into this pit of meek compliance? So I stick to my guns and refuse to change the date with the girls. It's time I stopped being grateful to him for making decisions for me. We ring off barely saying goodbye.

I can't stop worrying about it, wondering why we seem to be stuck in such a volatile relationship. We bicker over the slightest thing and then have amazing sex and then quarrel all over again. I need to discuss it all with Nadine and Magda tonight.

There's a ring at my doorbell shortly after lunch. Is it Guy, come to argue and persuade me? Please God, no. Or Nigel, come to remonstrate, so much worse! But it's Alice – *Alice!*

'Do say if you're busy, Ellie,' she says anxiously.

'I'm not in the slightest bit busy!' I cry. 'Come in. It's great to see you.'

'Sorry I didn't message first – my phone's out of charge. It's just I've found some files I've been searching for. There's some fantastic photos of the birth of a baby elephant, you just have to see them!'

I make coffees and then we sit down together and I exclaim over the photos, which really are marvellous. I try doing a few quick sketches of the mother elephant straining, the head appearing, the afterbirth dropping to the ground, the calf flapping its ear experimentally as it struggles out.

Alice watches. 'I love the way you get the exact image with just a few lines. I'll try and dig out some more files,' she says. 'If you'd find it helpful?'

'That would be brilliant! Perhaps we can spend more time together now we've both broken up for the summer,' I say shyly. Then I feel embarrassed. 'Though of course, I expect you and Wendy are going on holiday together?'

Alice pulls a face. 'She's tied to her job – there are always crowds at Catz in July and August. Wendy is a bit of a vampire anyway. She shudders at the thought of a sunny beach.'

'That's a bit hard on you, isn't it?' I ask, as I make her another coffee. Alice doesn't look down her nose at the instant sort, unlike Guy.

She shrugs. 'I suppose I knew what kind of girl Wendy is right from the start. I was just dazzled, like I said.'

'Oh,' I say inadequately. 'That's wonderful.'

'Well, it was. Once. Not really any more,' says Alice.

'Is there something wrong between you?' I ask.

Alice shakes her head. 'No more so than usual,' she says, sighing. 'Anyway, borrow these photos, keep them as long as you like. I took them, so you don't have to worry about copyright.'

'Thanks so much. But . . . are you sure you don't want to talk about it?' I ask, not wanting to pry exactly, but I'm worried about her. She seems sad, though she's making an effort to be bright.

'It's just not the way it used to be,' Alice says.

I feel a little thrill, which is dreadful, because I like Alice so much and want her to be happy. What's the matter with me?

'Maybe you're just going through a sticky patch,' I suggest.

'Maybe,' says Alice, but she doesn't sound convinced. 'Oh well. Tell me about this new guy you're seeing. Is it going well?'

Shall I tell her? I don't want her to think everything's going wonderfully with Guy and me, when her relationship is floundering. 'Well, it seems to be. He's taking me to Venice in October,' I say.

'He's obviously very keen,' Alice says. She's trying hard, but she still looks very down.

'It's a very romantic gesture,' I say. 'But he didn't even ask me if I wanted to go.'

'A little controlling?' she ventures.

'Yes, he is. More than anyone else I've ever been involved with. It really annoys me – unless we're having sex, and then I don't mind a bit,' I say, then my face burns. Why did I say that? I'm so used to blurting out the first thing in my head when I'm with Nadine and Magda.

'Well, I should make the most of it, if he really turns you on,' Alice says.

'He's so up for it. And so am I. But it's almost as if we don't know what to do when we're not having sex.'

'If that's working for you, though, there's nothing wrong with it,' says Alice. 'Oh dear, I sound like a sex therapist. Though perhaps I need one myself, seeing as I'm not having any sex at all.'

There's a little silence.

'So, you and Wendy don't . . .?'

'Not for quite a while,' she says. 'Well, *we* don't have sex.

257

I rather think Wendy does with other people she meets at the club.'

I stare at her. 'Don't you mind?'

'I minded like hell once,' says Alice. She sighs again. 'But I suppose I've got used to it now.'

'Well, I think she's mad,' I say. 'If I were gay, you're exactly the sort of girl I'd want.'

I find I'm blushing again, but I truly mean it.

'I wish you were,' says Alice. She means it as a joke but her words hang in the air, resonating. My heart starts thudding. Does she really mean it? She certainly looks embarrassed enough.

'Well, I'm so glad I met you,' I say at last.

After that, she stays for another hour or so, but the mood is different now. We're both awkward and self-conscious, dancing around that strange conversation. We leave at the same time, her to go home and me to meet Nadine and Magda. She tries to go without giving me a hug but I pull her to me and after a second or two she relaxes against me. We smile shyly at one another, and part ways.

I get to the Hare and Moon first, and buy a bottle of Albariño for us. Then I remember that Magda can't drink – but oh well, more for me and Nadine. I sip by myself for ten minutes or so, feeling slightly self-conscious. I felt like dressing up a little so I'm wearing new black and white pinstripe trousers with a white silk shirt. I haven't gone as far as an actual tie, though, using a narrow black velvet ribbon instead.

Nadine and Magda certainly are taking their time arriving. I've finished one glass of wine and started on another when they swan in together, arm in arm. They make a flamboyant couple. Nadine's hair is way past her shoulders now, almost to her waist, straight and shining blue-black. Her face is chalk white, but she's wearing scarlet lipstick. She looks like a goth

Snow White, in a long tight black dress with jet buttons down the front, and she seems even taller than she is in black high heels. Magda has dyed her hair back to blonde, with little pink highlights, and she's wearing a new pink dress, very low cut and clinging to her curves. Her baby-belly is proudly on show, looking splendid.

'I'll get another bottle of wine in for later,' says Nadine. 'And what about you, Magda? Orange juice?'

'A Virgin Mary – I'll have to pretend it's got vodka,' she says, sighing.

'You're looking wonderful, Magda,' I say. 'And you, Nadine.'

'You're looking great too, Ellie,' says Nadine. 'Sexy, in a crisp sort of way.'

'Well, no wonder, now she's got a lover,' purrs Magda. 'Come on, tell us all about your latest date, Ellie. In full detail!'

'Don't get started until I'm back from the bar,' calls Nadine.

Magda gives a dainty burp and fishes in her tote bag for a packet of Rennies.

'Oh dear,' I say sympathetically. 'I remember I had chronic indigestion too when I was carrying Lottie.'

'I don't know how you went through all this when you were so young,' Magda says. 'I've started childbirth classes, but there's so much to remember. And I can't get the hang of the breathing through the contractions. I sound like a dog panting!'

'You'll be fine when you're actually in labour.'

'Does it really hurt terribly?' Magda asks.

'Yes, it hurts,' I say, deciding not to add *'unbelievably, and for far too long'*. 'But I promise you just want to explode with happiness when you hold your baby for the first time.'

'After you've exploded with effort giving birth,' says Nadine, coming back with the drinks.

'Shut up, Nadine, you haven't even had a baby,' I say firmly.

'I never intend to either,' says Nadine.

'Remember when we vowed to make sure we all had baby girls in the same year so they could grow up best friends just like us?' I say.

'Well, you jumped the gun, and Magda's a late starter and I'm a total refuser,' says Nadine, handing round crisps.

'Not for me. I'm watching my salt intake,' says Magda, but after Nadine and I have chomped away for a few seconds she can't resist joining in too.

'So, are you going to keep helping out at the wine bar, Nadine?' Magda asks. 'And you're still at Gem radio during the day? Isn't it exhausting? Look at you! You're obviously working too hard, you're skin and bone,' says Magda. She rubs her new round tummy. She looks marvellous, like a full-blown rose. Oh God, I'll start saying she's got gorgeous womanly curves next.

'I like working there. It gives me something to do in the evenings. I'm giving the dating scene a miss for a little while,' Nadine says, looking at me meaningfully. 'Besides, Harry's place is really stylish. Well, he is too, in a flash kind of way. He's bought himself a vintage Rolex and he's like a kid with a new toy. He keeps pushing up his shirt cuffs and checking the time ostentatiously.' Nadine's laughing at him, but fondly.

'Are you two sort of . . . together now?' I ask delicately.

'Well, "sort of" really describes it. We had a little benefit time after we closed the bar last night, but it's not necessarily going to be a regular thing. He's very preoccupied with making The Other One a big success,' says Nadine.

'The Other One?' Magda asks.

'You know, as opposed to the famous Harry's Bar in Venice,' says Nadine.

'Oh, the Bellini one,' says Magda.

'I'm going there in October,' I say.

They turn and stare at me.

'You lucky cow!' says Magda. 'Chris and I were hoping to go there too this autumn, but I don't really want to risk flying, with the baby due late November.'

'Are you going with Lottie? Or Ben and Simon?' Nadine asks, sipping her wine.

I shake my head, smiling at them brightly.

'Nope. Who do you *think* I'm going with?' I ask.

'Not Mr Windsor!' they chorus, leaning forward eagerly.

'Do stop calling him that! Yes, Guy's taking me. He's booked the flight and the hotel already. I can't wait!' I claim. Perhaps the more I say it, the more I'll feel it.

'Oh wow, Ellie! Double wow!' says Magda.

'He's really serious then,' says Nadine.

I shrug. 'I suppose he must be,' I admit.

'So did you whisper wistfully about the Bridge of Sighs in the middle of a passionate embrace?' Magda asks.

'No. He just booked it out of the blue, without even asking me,' I say.

'How romantic!' Magda says.

'I guess so,' I say, fiddling with my hair. 'Or . . . controlling?' I say tentatively.

'Are you mad? I absolutely love being surprised by Chris. He didn't breathe a word to me about Paris, bless him. He just told me to pack an overnight bag and wear a pretty dress,' says Magda, smiling reminiscently. 'We had the most blissful time. And I'm more or less certain it was when we conceived.' She pats her tummy happily.

'Ellie, for God's sake don't get pregnant again!' Nadine says urgently.

'I've no intention of getting pregnant,' I insist. 'In fact, I'm not really sure I even want to go.'

'Why on earth not?' Magda asks, astonished. 'I thought it

would be exactly your kind of place, with all those paintings and ancient churches.'

'Yes, but I'm not sure I want to go with Guy,' I say. The words come out of my mouth before I can stop them.

They're both staring at me dumbfounded.

'Have you had a row?' Nadine asks.

'Not a row, as such. But we can't stop bickering. He keeps telling me what to do.'

'In a mean way?' Nadine asks.

'No, he's gentle, he's sweet, but he always wants to be the one who makes all the decisions,' I say.

'In bed?' Nadine asks.

'No, that's the one thing that's still incredible,' I say, lowering my voice. 'He's a truly unselfish lover and yet really passionate too – it's the best sex I've ever had.' They bend their heads towards me eagerly, and I start describing in detail.

'What are you three girls whispering about?' My head whips around and there's Guy himself, standing beside us.

I jump violently and nearly knock the bottle of wine over. Nadine scatters crisps across the table. Magda chokes over her tomato juice.

How long has he been standing there? Could he possibly have heard? He looks incredibly cocky and complacent.

'What are you doing here, Guy? I thought you were going to the film?' I say.

'I've actually seen it before,' he says smoothly. 'So I thought it might be more fun to catch up with you three girls. Hi, Nadine. Hi, Magda. Wow, you both look amazingly grown up!'

'Hello, Mr Windsor!' says Nadine, flicking her hair over her shoulders.

'Hi – Guy!' says Magda, dabbing her mouth and smiling.

Oh my God, they're both flirting with him. I scowl at him.

How dare he turn up here uninvited! I made it absolutely plain that this was a girls' night out. He's looking great, though, I think grudgingly. His hair is casually ruffled, his thin blue sweater tight across his chest, showing off his taut stomach, and his good jeans are just the right sort of tightness too.

'What can I get you to drink?' he says.

'We've already got wine,' I say, though it sounds surly.

'You could get me a fruit juice, please,' Magda asks, dimpling at him. 'I can't drink, for obvious reasons.'

'So I see. You look absolutely blooming, Magda,' Guy says. 'And Nadine? More crisps? Have you girls eaten? I'll get a menu.'

We don't usually eat proper meals when we get together. We snack instead – crisps, nuts, olives, and a big sharing bowl of chips – but when Guy brings the menu they pore over it eagerly. Magda is enthusiastic about her pomegranate juice, saying it's a brilliant choice. They all seem to be having a lovely time, while I'm still glowering.

Guy sits down beside me and puts his arm round my shoulders. I sit stiffly, refusing to nestle up.

'Hey, darling,' he says, and kisses my cheek. Nadine and Magda blink at the darling, at the kiss.

'So girls, tell me all about yourselves,' Guy says. 'I expect Ellie has been telling you all about me?'

'You're right about that,' says Nadine, her scarlet mouth smirking.

'Should I be blushing?' he asks.

I tut and fold my arms. This is all such nonsense. And it doesn't stop. Guy tells them stories about his teaching now and his teaching then, with us. He reminds us of all the silly things we once did.

'You three were always my favourites,' he says. 'Especially you, Magda.'

She brushes her hair back and smiles uncertainly. She's struggling to look unconcerned, but I can see a little nerve twitching on her smooth face. It's the look she gets when she's uncomfortable. I look at Guy. He's leaning forward, smiling back at her.

'You brought a bit of excitement to my day,' he says.

I turn to stare at him, and Nadine splutters.

'I could never guess what colour hair you were going to have,' he carries on smoothly. 'Blonde, pink, bright red – and you carried them all off with style.'

Magda laughs, relieved.

'Mind you, the joke's on me,' says Guy. 'I'm no stranger myself nowadays to Garnier Nutrisse.'

So he *does* need to touch up his own hair! And how clever to tease himself too. I feel myself softening.

'I'll take a shrewd bet you don't need to help your own gorgeous jet-black hair, Nadine,' he says. 'You were also my favourite, especially at the end of the school day. I'd peer out of the staff room to see which sultry bad boy was waiting for you outside the playground.'

'I haven't grown out of bad boys,' says Nadine ruefully. 'Well, until recently. Maybe I've decided to stop partying. But wasn't Ellie always your favourite?'

'Little Ellie?' says Guy, wrinkling his nose. Then he grins. 'Of course! *She's* wonderful. I can't believe she wants to hang out with an old guy like me.' He kisses my cheek again in a proprietorial fashion.

I smile stiffly but Magda and Nadine are lapping it all up.

They choose what they want to eat. Magda wants chicken and vegetables, nourishing food for the baby. Nadine asks for asparagus risotto, with a bowl of chips. She never puts on an ounce, which has always been infuriating for Magda and me. I have a salad – though we all know I'll snaffle some of Nadine's chips. Guy has spaghetti and manages not to splash sauce down his blue sweater. He also insists on paying, though we protest.

He's taken over the entire evening, and I can't deny I'm finding it hard going. I keep glancing at Nadine and Magda, wondering what they're really thinking. They seem to be having a marvellous time, but they could well be as adept as me at pretending. When he excuses himself to go to the Gents we all look at each other.

'Oh my God!' says Magda. 'He's fantastic, Ellie! If I wasn't having my baby I'd make a play for him myself. But he's clearly so crazy about you I'd be wasting my time.'

'I'll go to Venice with him if you don't want to!' says Nadine. 'It's so unfair! I've put so much effort into meeting men and never managed to find one like Guy.'

'But don't you think he's a bit . . .?' I flounder.

'A bit what?' Magda asks.

'Pushy. Full of himself. Overconfident?'

'You mean *male*?' says Nadine.

'What?'

'Ellie, that's what men are like, isn't it?' says Nadine.

'No, of course it isn't. Not all men. They can be considerate and sensitive and ask you how you're feeling, and also be so funny and scandalous you crack up laughing!' I say indignantly.

'I've only ever met gay men like that,' Magda says gently.

'Straight men too,' I insist.

'You're so sweet, Ellie. Stop fighting it. It's clear from that job description that you don't want a man at all. You want a woman,' says Nadine.

Nadine's hardly an expert on men, judging by her latest encounter. I take a big slurp of wine and try to look superior.

'Could you just give up on this theory, Nadine? I wouldn't mind in the slightest being gay, in fact it would have defin- ite advantages.' Alice's face pops into my mind, but I push it away. 'However, I know for a fact that I'm a hundred per cent straight. You should see me and Guy in bed,' I declare – and then shut up abruptly because Guy is coming back from the loo.

'OK, that's me told,' mutters Nadine.

That's the last bit of straight talking – in all senses of the phrase. The rest is flirting and flannel and endless trips down Memory Lane, which are starting to get tedious. At last Magda gives a great yawn like a kitten, somehow managing to look cute.

'I'm so sorry,' she says. 'It's the baby. I'm usually a total owl, happy to stay up past midnight, but now I've gone all dozy and it's not even ten o'clock. My Cinderella days are over. I'll have to start making tracks now.'

'I'll walk with you to the tube, Mags,' says Nadine.

'And I'll come back with you, Ellie,' says Guy.

'No, I'm absolutely fine!' I say. 'I can get home myself.'

'I won't hear of it. Did Ellie tell you about her crazy stalker?' Guy says. 'He keeps leaving her tacky presents and weirdo cards. I think she should tell the police, don't you? Or come and stay at my place till we find out who we're dealing with.'

'I told you, it's finished now,' I snap. I think of poor Nigel, carefully choosing presents and racking his brains to write something romantic. 'They weren't really tacky and weird. He meant well, bless him.'

'Well, he'd better not start harassing you again,' Guy insists. 'I'm not having him scaring my girl.'

I glower at him. I hate him in this mood. He's so possessive. *My girl* indeed! I want to shout that it's none of his business, but perhaps I'm being unreasonable. Nadine and Magda are looking at me anxiously, mouthing *Who?*

'It's OK. It was just my cousin – Nigel, you know. A total misunderstanding,' I say. 'He's just a bit socially awkward.

And he managed to get the wrong idea about me. He thought I was encouraging him.'

'For God's sake, *Nigel* thought you fancied him?' says Nadine.

'That pale creepy guy at your party?' Magda asks.

'He's not creepy. He's just lonely, that's all. Anyway, I've put him right. He's not going to be wooing me any more, Guy, so you really don't need to come home with me. And even if he *were* lurking, I could flatten him one-handed,' I insist.

It's no use, though. Magda and Nadine go off arm in arm, glancing back at us every few steps, and Guy calls yet another Uber to take me all the way back to the estate.

'Just how much do you earn, Guy?' I ask, so exasperated I can't be bothered to be tactful. 'Because you don't seem to mind wasting a hell of a lot of money.'

'If you must know, I inherited quite a bit when my old aunt died. Anyway, now that's out of the way, will you please allow me to give you a few treats without you getting so snappy and snarly with me?' he says, and he actually taps me on the nose!

I feel like punching him on *his* nose, but we're in the Uber now and I hate the thought of making a scene. A drunken scene, because I've had far too much wine as a way of coping with a very difficult evening. I shut up until we get to the estate, and then I suggest Guy keeps the car and goes back to Earlsfield in it, seeing as he's now made of money.

'I'm taking you right home and putting you to bed, Ellie. You may not realize it, but you're a little the worse for wear,' he says, as if I'm an over-tired toddler.

'No, I'm not! How dare you!' I hiss at him, though I know I'm proving his point.

He helps me out of the car and then steers me towards Constable, gripping me firmly. Is this the sort of behaviour that most women *want*? But then I think of glowering Mr

Rochester, feral Heathcliff, lordly Mr Darcy, know-it-all Mr Knightley, Rhett Butler striding up the staircase with Scarlett in his arms . . . all so-called romantic heroes.

The lift's not working. Is Guy going to flex his muscles and channel his own Rhett?

'How can it not be working?' he says, perplexed. 'Have you got the number for the engineers?'

'Do you seriously think they'll come out at this time?' I ask incredulously.

'So how are we going to get up to your fucking flat?' Not quite so gentlemanly now, then. He's glaring at me. I glare back.

'How do you think? Walk up the fucking steps! Call another Uber and go home, Guy,' I say, and start towards the stairwell.

He still insists on coming with me, even trying to help me up, pushing the small of my back, though he starts getting out of breath before I do.

'For Christ's sake, Ellie, how can you bear to live in this dump?' he puffs. 'It's sheer obstinacy. I'm sure your parents would help you get a decent flat,' he says.

'I'm sure they would too, but how many more times do I have to say it – I'd sooner be independent, thanks very much. And stop giving me faux-fatherly talks. I've already got a dad, thank you very much.' I suddenly think of Dad lying in hospital with all those tubes, looking so frail and helpless, and I give a maudlin sob, even though I know he's fine now, almost recovered.

'Oh Ellie!' Guy says, softer now. 'Don't cry. I didn't mean to come over all heavy with you. I just worry about you, that's all.'

'Why on earth should you worry about me?' I say, wiping my eyes with the back of my hand.

'Because—'

Oh no. He's going to say it.

'Because you're my girlfriend,' he says.

It's what I wanted, isn't it? Longed for. But how could he have just decided that without asking me if I even *wanted* to be his girlfriend? Is that normal? How can it be?

I carry on up the stairs, quicker now, as if I'm trying to leave him behind. I hope he'll give up and stomp back down again, but he struggles on determinedly. My head's swimming, and I think of all the times I've dragged myself up these stairs. It was a real challenge when Lottie was very young and I had to carry her, but she was a determined little thing and she'd walk up independently as soon as she could. We'd count the stairs or sing songs or play guessing games or sing *uppity uppity uppity* and make it somehow.

And just as I'm thinking this my mobile starts ringing. I stop and sit on the stairs – where am I now, the ninth floor, the tenth? – and see that it's Lottie herself, as if I've conjured her up. I panic the moment I see her name. What's happened to make her phone so late?

'Lots?' I say urgently. 'Are you all right?'

'Oh Mum!' she says, and I breathe out, because she sounds bubbling over with happiness.

'What's happened, darling?' I ask, trying to sober up.

'Oh Mum,' she repeats. 'We've been in touch, Dad and me.'

Dad? I sit up straight, rigid with fury. How dare he call himself Dad when he didn't want anything to do with her, did nothing to support her her whole life!

'Mum, are you still there?'

I make an extreme effort. 'Yes, of course. Well, that's – that's lovely,' I say. I take a deep breath. 'So, are you going to meet him?'

'We did meet, today! We've been emailing each other, and he's been so keen to see me. He wanted to come imediately, but we had this big Gala disco to organize for the kids. Anyway, he came today and took me out to lunch, and then we just strolled about and sat in a park, and we ended up having supper together too, though he's got a long drive back. He's only just gone and I'm kind of missing him already! Oh Mum, it's so weird, we've got so much in common – we even really look alike!'

No, no, no, Lottie, you can't have anything in common with that selfish creep! He's nothing to do with you!

'It's really good that you got on well together,' I say, trying to keep calm. 'But don't get too excited, Lottie. I'm sure he's thrilled to discover he's got a daughter like you but try not to mind too much if he doesn't want to get too involved.'

'But he does, he does! He's coming back next week, it's all arranged – and he wants me to come to London to meet his family,' she says.

'His family?' I repeat weakly.

'Yes, he got married about ten years ago, his wife Shena sounds lovely, I actually talked to her a little bit on the phone – and guess what!'

'What?' I say, swallowing. Tears are running down my cheeks, but I'm scrunching my face up tight to stop myself sobbing. I can't let her hear.

'I've got two brothers! Isn't that the coolest thing ever? One's nine, the other's only four. Dad showed me all these photos on his phone, and they're so cute, especially the little one. He goes round clutching a teddy all the time, just like I did!'

Nearly all little kids have a teddy! They're not proper brothers, they're only half siblings, nothing to do with you after all these years. And you're coming to London to meet this new family at the drop of a hat when you only come to see me on my wretched birthday and when Grandad nearly died!

I swallow down all this bitter rant and stammer, 'That's – that's great, Lottie.'

'Oh Mum, I haven't hurt your feelings, have I? I mean, obviously you'll always be my number one parent, I hope that goes without saying. But it just seems so good to find I've got a proper father too, and he's so sweet and funny. No wonder you fell for him way back,' she says.

Oh, that's too much, way too much!

'I didn't exactly fall for him, darling. We weren't a proper couple,' I say.

'Yes, he told me. Do you know, he never even knew you were going to have a baby – me! I mean, he remembers you, of course he does, and he said he was sorry you'd both drifted apart, but he wishes like anything you'd told him,' she burbles innocently.

The bastard! The lying cowardly bastard! I told him face to face and he turned away and said it was nothing to do with him. He can't have forgotten! And now he's filling Lottie with all these wicked lies and she'll end up finding out and she'll be so hurt. Tell her now. Tell her what he's really like!

But I can't. She'll find out soon enough. Or maybe she won't. Maybe he's changed. Maybe he truly wants to be a father to her now, even though he's got no right whatsoever.

'That's great,' I repeat, hardly able to talk for tears.

'Mum? Are you all right? You're not crying, are you?' Lottie asks anxiously.

'No, I'm fine, really. Just a bit tired – and I've maybe had one glass of wine too many,' I say.

'With the hot man?' says Lottie.

'Something like that,' I mumble.

'Dad really wants to meet up with you too, Mum. How do you feel about that?'

'Perhaps – perhaps I need to have a little think about it,' I say. 'And Lottie – don't get too carried away, darling. Take things one step at a time.'

'OK, Mum. Don't worry! But I'm so happy. Try to be happy for me!'

'I am happy, truly,' I say. 'Bye now. Take care.'

I switch off my phone and start howling.

19

I'd completely forgotten Guy crouching several steps below me. He gets up and gathers me into his arms. I hang on to him helplessly and we trudge up to the fourteenth floor. I fumble for the key and then stumble indoors, Guy with me.

Stella sees I'm sobbing and lets me cradle her for comfort. I sit on the sofa with her while Guy puts the kettle on, looks for clean mugs, shakes his head as he has to wash up the only mugs in my possession, then makes us coffee. He sniffs once at the instant jar, but knows it's not the time to drone on about percolators.

I've reached the hiccuping snorty stage now. I fumble for a tissue, conscious that my nose is running. He looks in a cupboard or two for the tissues and ends up going to the bathroom to thrust some Andrex at me. Then he sits with his arm round me and waits until I've recovered.

'I'm sorry,' I mumble. 'I'm not usually such a dribbling fool. It's just, that was Lottie on the phone, and – and—'

'I couldn't help overhearing most of it,' Guy says. 'So Lottie's met her father?'

'Yes. She's never shown any interest before, she's been so happy being just us two, but then Dad was so ill and Lottie realized how much I love him even though he drives me mad sometimes,' I say.

'So she wanted to see whether she might have a relationship with her own father?'

'He's been lying his head off and making out I didn't tell him about her, when of course I did,' I say shakily. 'And now, apparently, he wants to be Father of the Year.'

'Oh, my poor Ellie.'

'I sound so mean and jealous, and I don't want to stop Lottie being happy, but I'm absolutely certain he'll let her down horribly and I don't want her to be hurt,' I sniff. 'Oh, sod it, I admit it: I'm scared they'll have a wonderful relationship and Lottie will hardly give me a second thought. Feel free to despise me.'

'As if!' says Guy, pulling me closer and rocking me gently. 'I feel desperately sorry for you. But I know Lottie thinks the absolute world of you. You're obviously her first concern.'

'How can you be sure? You've never even met her,' I say.

'I'd like to, though. Very much. I just didn't make it clear before because I didn't want to seem pushy,' he says.

'You didn't mind seeming pushy barging in on Nadine and Magda and me at the pub,' I retort.

'Oh, come on. I know them already. I couldn't help longing to see the three of you in your girl gang all over again. They haven't changed a bit. Well, they *have*, obviously, but they were both instantly recognizable. And both fantastic.'

I give a grunt.

'But not remotely as fantastic as you, sweetheart,' he says. He gives me little kisses on my tear-stained cheek, on my neck, tender rather than sexy. I hate being the needy little girl again but even so I cuddle up against him and close my eyes.

'Hey, let's go to bed,' he says. 'You're exhausted. Come on, let me help you.'

He leads me into the bedroom and undresses me, taking care, unbuttoning and unzipping, until I'm in my underwear, and then undoes my bra, much more cleverly than most men, and eases me out of my knickers, kissing my stomach as he does so.

I make an involuntary little moan, which he misinterprets.

'Don't worry, I'm not going to be crass enough to try to make love to you just now when you're so unhappy. I'm just going to strip off and get in bed with you and cuddle up so you drift off to sleep,' he says.

'You're being so kind to me – when I've been moody with you all evening,' I say.

'Don't you worry, darling. You've got a lot on your mind. Here, in you get. That's right, snuggle down,' he says.

It feels so good when he wraps himself round me. I can't help wriggling against him, and almost immediately I feel his erection against my back.

'Sorry, sorry,' he says. 'I just can't help it when you move like that.'

I can't help moving more, and then he touches me tentatively, and I turn, and soon we're making love, and it's the best way to stop thinking about Lottie, stop thinking about anything at all except the urgent wanting and the moving and his voice in my ear. I'm still no further forward knowing whether I love him or hate him, but in this moment, I don't care. I just want to go on being touched like this, and then I want to sleep and forget everything else.

I don't wake up till nine in the morning. My head hurts, I feel vaguely sick with a hangover, and my eyes are sore with crying – but I don't feel so despairing. What on earth was the matter with me last night? It was silly to get so upset. Lottie is a strong, clever girl who's always been ultra resilient. Why shouldn't she get to know her father? If she establishes a proper relationship with him then surely that's good. And if it doesn't work out that's good too, because she'll have found out for herself that he's a rubbish guy incapable of taking any kind of responsibility. Though he's married now, with these little boys, and why on earth is it anything but good for Lottie to discover she's got these brand new relations?

And what about my own relationship? Why did I make such a fuss about Guy coming to join us at the pub? Of course he wants to see Nadine and Magda grown up. He was so kind afterwards, taking me home and looking after me. My girls are right. He's fantastic. Perhaps I just don't want to get close to any man in my life because I feel let down by that stupid prick who fathered my daughter? And all the other men I've been close to, come to that. Is it that simple?

I roll out of bed and have a good stretch. Guy murmurs but turns over and goes back to sleep. I make myself a coffee and then pore over my elephants. I flick through all my sketches, my storylines, my potential layouts. I get a wonderful tingling rush of excitement and have a little dance around the room, startling Stella. I'm ready to begin!

I'll start when Guy goes home. I've got my paper, my special pens, I've got my watercolours for the cover. I'll finish the first ten pages and then send them to Nicola. If she thinks it's working, I'll carry on. Sod it, I'll finish it even if she hates it. I'll send it to Jude and if she doesn't like it, I'll send it to publishers myself. I'm not going to give up.

I feed Stella and she jumps into my lap when she's finished, pinioning me into my swivel chair. She's had enough of my gallivanting. She wants me to stay home and work, keeping her company. I stroke her rhythmically while she preens and purrs. Then suddenly there are hands on my shoulders and I'm twirled round to find Guy's face inches from mine.

Stella sinks her claws in me as if it's my fault, then leaps off my lap into a corner, where she hisses furiously.

'For God's sake, Guy, you really scared us!' I cry, examining the scratches on my arm. One is starting to bleed dramatically.

'Oh darling, I'm so sorry. Where do you keep your antiseptic and plasters?' he asks.

'Don't be silly, it's only a scratch,' I say, dabbing at it. 'It'll stop bleeding in a minute.'

'You mean you haven't got any?' He gives an exaggerated sigh.

'It's not a crime. I haven't got around to replenishing my supplies. I expect *you* have a special well-stocked first aid box,' I say grudgingly.

'Of course I do, like any sensible adult,' he retorts. 'And as you choose to live with a manic cat, I would think it's a necessity. For Christ's sake, stop dabbing at that scratch with crumpled Andrex. You need to hold your arm under the cold tap.'

'Stella isn't manic,' I insist, as he marches me to the sink and soaks my dressing gown sleeve.

'She just attacks you out of affection?' Guy says. He picks up the tea towel hanging on a hook, and then discards it with a look of disgust. 'Have you at least got a clean tea towel?'

'She was frightened. *You* frightened her! And stop fussing, my arm's fine,' I insist.

'You *haven't* got a clean tea towel?' he says.

'Just leave it. Do stop fussing like a nineteen-fifties housewife.'

'Grow up, Ellie. It's time you stopped living in such mucky chaos. That scratch could get seriously infected if you don't look after it. It's still bleeding! Hold your arm in the air, it'll stop the blood flowing.'

He forces it up. I feel ridiculous. Like a schoolgirl.

'Please, Sir, may I be excused?' I say.

The joke falls flat and we both look away from each other uncomfortably. It's a relief when the doorbell rings.

'Who's that? You're not expecting anyone, are you?' says Guy. He's only wearing his pants, so I suppose he has a right to be concerned.

'It's probably Andreea, giving me back my spare key. Just stay here,' I say.

It's not Andreea, though. It's Alice. She's wearing green studs in her ears that match the green mermaid design on her black sweatshirt. She looks great, though she's got dark circles under her eyes and looks a bit wan. I must, too – in fact, I'm sure I look a terrible mess, my face a wreck, my hair all over the place, and I'm just wearing my old blue dressing gown that's definitely seen better days.

'Hey, Alice. Sorry I look such a sight. I'm not properly up yet,' I say.

'Oh Ellie, I'm so sorry, I should have messaged you. I've come round much too early,' she says, aghast. 'I'll go away and come back another time.'

'No, please, come in!' I say, because she's looking sad and disappointed. 'Come and have a coffee.'

I take hold of her arm and steer her into the kitchen so she can avoid Guy in his pants. I sit her down at the kitchen table.

'Won't be a moment,' I say, and scurry into the living room. Guy is standing by my desk, peering at my elephant artwork. He's looking at one of my experimental double spreads showing Mosi getting to know her newborn calf throughout the day. I want it to be one of the most emotional tender scenes and yet I haven't got it quite working yet.

'Hey! I told you, that's *private*!' I say, appalled. How dare he invade my secret imaginary world! I try to snatch it away from him.

The paper rips.

'Now look!' I hiss furiously. I snatch the two pieces and shove them back in my folder. 'What are you doing, snooping through my private work?'

'So you're working on a graphic novel? Actually, it's really good,' Guy says, in the encouraging tone he used when I was in his art class.

'I'm not looking for your approval. Anyway, Alice is here – do you want her to see you lolling around in your pants? Have a quick shower and then throw some clothes on while we have coffee in the kitchen.'

He frowns at me. 'Who the hell is Alice, and why did you invite her in?'

'Just go and sort yourself out, *please*, and then I'll introduce you,' I snap, and rush back to the kitchen.

Alice is looking at me anxiously. 'I really think I'd better go now. I'm only here because I've found some more of my elephant stuff that I thought might be helpful. I'll leave them with you, OK?' She hands over the canvas bag she's been carrying.

'That's great. But please stay! The advantage of instant coffee is that it really is instant. And would you like some toast? Do you like Nutella?'

'Ah. I can't say no to Nutella,' says Alice. 'So how's your project going?'

'I want to check all sorts of details with you, is that OK?'

'Consider me your very own Elephant Woman,' she says, smiling now.

I put bread in the toaster, just for the two of us. I'm hoping that Guy will spend ages in the shower – which is of course nonsensical. I can't parcel him out of the flat unseen. I'll have to introduce them and I really don't want to, though I don't quite know why. I keep licking my lips, preparing to announce his presence, but can't seem to manage it.

As we spread our toast, happily ladling on Nutella, Alice gives me a funny look.

'Is that your shower?' she asks.

'Mm, yes.'

'And you're here.'

'Maybe I left it running?' I suggest ridiculously.

Alice narrows her eyes. 'Who's in it?'

I have to come out with it. 'It's Guy. My . . . friend.'

'Oh God! I'm so sorry! Why didn't you *say*? I'll leave you in peace,' Alice says, jumping up.

'Please don't go! You haven't had your toast yet! *He'll* be going in a minute or two,' I say. 'Well, definitely after breakfast.'

We hear Guy singing 'Somebody to Love' slightly out of tune, and both struggle not to giggle. Alice raises her eyebrows.

'Sounds as if he's serious about you,' she says.

'You wait. He'll be singing "Fat-bottomed Girls" next.'

Alice looks at me sternly. 'There's absolutely nothing wrong with your bottom. So, are you serious about him?' she asks.

I hesitate.

'Sorry, it's none of my business. Look, I'm going to get out of here before he comes in.'

'No, please don't! Stay, Alice! I want to know what you think of him. So I can work out what *I* think of him. Because the truth is, I have no idea. Please?'

She pulls a face but stays where she is. We talk elephants for a few minutes until Guy comes into the room. He's got a false smile on his face but I can tell he's irritated when he sees Alice sitting down eating toast. He gives me a quick sideways look, clearly saying *Why have you invited her for breakfast?*

'Hi, I'm Guy. I expect Ellie's told you all about me,' he says, as if he's sure I've been boasting about him.

Alice nods uncertainly.

'And you're . . . Alice?' he says, making it clear he knows nothing about her.

'Ellie and I are swimming buddies,' she says. 'And I know a bit about elephants, so I'm advising her on her new book.'

'She lets you see it, then?' Guy asks.

'No, no – I just advise, like I said,' Alice says.

'So, do you work in a zoo or something?'

I scowl at him. Why is he being downright belligerent?

'Yes, I clear out the animal shit in the morning and feed them throughout the day,' Alice says straight-faced.

'At London Zoo?' Guy asks, wrong-footed.

'They don't actually keep elephants at London Zoo any more,' I say. 'And Alice is *joking*. She's a lecturer in animal behaviour.'

That shuts him up. Any kind of lecturer aces all teachers.

'Anyway, I'd better be going. Keep the files as long as you like, Ellie. It's mostly just research stuff, but I found the diary I kept when I was in Amboseli – it might be useful.' She crunches her last piece of toast and stands up.

'OK, well, good to have met you,' Guy says with transparent insincerity.

I go with her to the door.

'I'm so sorry about that,' I whisper. 'God knows why he's acting like such an idiot. He can sometimes be Mr Charm, honestly.'

'I'll take your word for it,' Alice says dryly, her arms folded.

She has a smear of Nutella in the corner of her mouth. She looks so sweet, as if she's a little girl experimenting with lipstick. I reach out and brush her lip with my finger without quite realizing what I'm doing. She looks startled. I'm startled too. That was way too intimate.

'You had a bit of Nutella there,' I explain hurriedly.

'Oh. Right. Messy me,' she says, looking embarrassed. She gives me a lovely smile, turns on her heel, and goes.

'Do come round any time,' I call after her. 'And see you at swimming?'

She nods without turning round. I go back inside the flat. I'm so irritated by Guy's behaviour that I can't face him yet. I go to the bathroom and wipe the mirror, misted from the heat of Guy's shower. I look terrible. I think of Wendy, incredibly gorgeous straight out of bed, damn her.

'Ellie?' Guy puts his head round the door.

'Guy, I'm in the bathroom!'

'But you're not on the loo or anything. I'm cooking French toast. Want some?' he says, unabashed.

'I've already had breakfast, with Alice,' I say.

'Yes, just that horrible chocolate spready stuff. Honestly!' He shakes his head at my childish taste. But it's my flat, my kitchen, my childish tastebuds. I should feel free to have a packet of Haribo and a mug of Ribena if I fancy it.

'Why do you have to be so domineering all the time?' I ask, unable to hold it in any longer.

'In bed?' he says, puzzled.

'No, you're absolutely fine in bed, very tender and generous – but out of it you're a control freak,' I say.

'No, I'm not,' he says, taking hold of me, lifting my hair and kissing my neck, just at the place which makes me shiver.

'Stop it,' I say, pushing him away. 'I'm cross with you, Guy. You were horrible to Alice, making it plain that you didn't want her around.'

He shrugs. 'Well, I didn't. No one else would hang about and have bloody breakfast when it's plain we want to spend a lazy morning having sex.'

'You might want to do that, but I've got work to do,' I say briskly. 'And you're not getting round me that easily. I'm worried about Alice. She didn't look very well.'

'She was just put out because she obviously fancies you and didn't like to think of you and me together,' says Guy.

'That's utterly ridiculous!' I spit at him, blushing crimson.

'You do know she's a lesbian, don't you?' Guy asks. 'It couldn't be more obvious.'

'Yes, I do know, but just because we're friends it doesn't

mean she wants to go to bed with me. She's got an absolutely stunning girlfriend anyway,' I insist.

A small voice in the back of my head, though, is wondering *why* he thinks Alice fancies me. It's nonsense, of course, but I'm still curious – though I won't give Guy the satisfaction of quizzing him.

He's still kissing my neck and now my shoulder.

'I've got an absolutely stunning girlfriend too,' he murmurs.

'Oh please! Look at the state of me!' I say, weakening slightly.

'Yes, look at the state of you,' he says, easing my dressing gown off, and starting to kiss my breasts.

'Are you on Viagra or something? I thought older men found it difficult to get going more than once a week,' I say, so furious that I want to hurt him. My whole body is melting, though, and I can't help pushing against him, encouraging him.

'This is going to be all about you, Ellie,' he says, and he leans me against the damp bathroom wall, splays my legs and kneels down.

It ends up being about him too, and bathrooms are all hard surfaces, but we are both too carried away to shuffle to the bedroom. Even so, my fury gets in the way and I can't let go entirely – until I start fantasizing about a girl with green earrings . . .

She wasn't necessarily Alice of course, I tell myself afterwards. And fantasies are often bizarre and unlikely. I remember Nadine once telling me when we were kids that one of her favourite fantasies was imagining a great lion with a magnificent mane licking her all over. I had been horrified, because I'd read the Narnia books and it seemed like sacrilege to imagine Aslan indulging in foreplay.

'There! You can't be *that* cross with me,' Guy says triumphantly. 'That was good, wasn't it?'

I let him think that it was all because of him – after all, he's the one who put in most of the work. I give him a cuddle, feeling fonder of him now, and we share a shower and then get dressed.

Guy's clearly hoping that we're going to spend the whole day together. I nibble at my lip, wondering how I can deal with this. We can't carry on like this all summer. I need to be free. I want to work on my elephant book every day and have those first pages polished and ready as soon as I can. I take several deep breaths, as if I'm about to jump off a diving board.

'I'd absolutely love us to hang out together, Guy, but I really *have* to work,' I say as sweetly as I can. 'I can't concentrate when you're around.'

'But there's no urgency. You've got all the summer holidays. You need to relax, darling. That's why you keep getting so worked up about things.'

Don't start patronizing me! I want to shout. But I don't want to spoil everything with a big row. He was so understanding about Lottie. How can I convince him? I give him a bright smile and adopt the I'm-in-control-here stance I use for unruly kids, chin up, hands on hips.

'I haven't told you my latest news. I've already contacted a publisher and they're very interested. I have to submit ten pages and a detailed synopsis by the end of August before they can take things further, though.' I look him straight in the eye, too. I'm startled by my ability to lie spontaneously.

'Oh, that's great news,' he says heartily, but he looks disconcerted. 'Maybe I'd better have a go at this graphic novel lark too.'

He's joking surely – or is he? *Anything you can do, I can do better?*

'I'm sure you could do a brilliant one,' I say generously. Anything to get him out of here.

But he hangs around a while, wanting to watch me get started.

'After all, you're sharing all this stuff with that Alice,' he says.

'Why call her *that* Alice?' I say. 'Anyway, she's different. She's working in a professional capacity, advising me about elephants.'

'Well, I can advise you artistically,' he says.

'I haven't asked you to do that. I don't need you peering over my shoulder, altering this and that, the way you used to at school.'

'Even if I can help you?' he asks.

'I don't need your help, Guy,' I say, and at last he gives up and goes. I know I've hurt his feelings but I don't care. I feel triumphant.

I sit at my desk and get going, only stopping to feed Stella, grab a sandwich or do a few exercises to get the blood flowing, working all day long. Then I crack open a beer, munch crisps and check my messages.

One from Guy.

How's it going? I'm not sure elephants are really graphic novel material, but it's great that a publisher's interested. If you feel like a little diversion get in touch. I'm missing you. G xxx

I laugh at his sheer audacity, and move on to the new message from Nadine.

Looks like I'm going to be the sad spinster at two weddings this year! He's gorgeous though, even more handsome now he's a bit rugged. Very assertive, but you say he's generous in bed. And he's certainly generous with his money! Lucky you, not needing to binge on Hinge. xxx

And a new one from Magda:

You have to marry him! And he hasn't got any children! He is just heaven. I love my Chris to bits, you know I do, and he's definitely my third time lucky, and I'm thrilled beyond words that I'm having his baby – but OMG what wouldn't I give for a night with Mr W!!! Love & xxx

And finally, one from Lottie:

Hi Mum, So sorry I went over the top last night, going on about the brand new Dad, but you're my dear beloved Mum, OK? Still number one parent and always will be. Lots and lots and lots of love from your own Lots xxxxxx

I read it over and over, stroking the screen as if it's Lottie's lovely face. I reply straight away, telling her that she'll always be my number one daughter even if the hot man gives me female triplets. Though that's never going to happen! I reply to Magda and Nadine, telling them that I'll loan Guy out whenever it's a blue moon. I text Guy, telling him that I'm making brilliant progress with my elephants (true) and that I'm missing him too (not actually true at all).

I pause for a moment, thinking about it. I *don't* miss him. So why am I seeing him? I find I'm doodling question marks all over one of the torn pages.

There's no message from Alice, though I rather hoped there would be. So I message her.

So sorry about Guy. He won't be around this week (well, I hope not) so do feel free to call round whenever – coffee and Nutella toast always available. xx

She doesn't reply, though I keep looking. I spend the evening curled up on the sofa, Stella asleep on my feet, while I leaf through the new elephant file. There are more fantastic photographs, a lot of detailed reportage of elephant habits – and best of all, her diary.

It's not a dry scientific account. It's much more personal, and so involving I feel I'm crouched in her tent with her, listening to the male elephants vying with each other at roaring the loudest. I'm with her agonizing over a weakly baby elephant unlikely to survive. I triumph with her when it does against all the odds. I panic with her when the tribe isn't wary enough at their watering place where lions are lurking. I share her doubts when she wonders if her research is ever going to make a meaningful contribution to knowledge of elephant behaviour.

I wish she'd reply to my message. But she doesn't. Not the next day or the next. So I try once more.

Hey Alice, thanks so much for the latest file – and the amazing diary. You're a great writer. Maybe you should be writing this elephant book instead of me. Then I'll illustrate it for you – though perhaps you're a great artist too? Hope to see you soon. xxx

I get the briefest of replies.

Glad it's useful. See you at swimming. A x

20

I get up very early on Saturday morning. I take my time in the communal changing room at the pool, and then sit on a wooden bench reading an old Alan Hollinghurst novel for nearly half an hour before I resign myself to the fact that Alice isn't coming.

Maybe Guy put her off. Or maybe I did? I looked a perfect fright and so *old*. I replay the whole breakfast scene, the three of us together, and when I get to the moment where I wiped Nutella off her lip I find I'm clenching my fists, cringing. I need to clear my head.

I shower, walk dripping to the pool and dive in, threshing up and down for six lengths – and then I see a white swimming costume, a sleek black head, a slim brown body and it's her! I wait when I get to the end of the pool and she stops too, smiling at me a little hesitantly.

'Thank goodness! I thought you weren't coming!' I say.

'Sorry, I just got a bit held up. But here I am!' she says.

The acoustics are dreadful, so we can't have a proper conversation and neither of us can see properly in our goggles, but we're both grinning now. Then we start swimming in the same lane. I make her go in front because she's faster than me and I skim along after her, determined to keep up. But the eight years between us counts, and I'm pretty sure Alice works out at a gym too, so by the time she's done her fifty lengths she's lapped me twice over. She sits on the edge and waits for me, until I puff along my last length and catch hold of her by the ankle.

'Good swim?' I say.

'I really needed that,' she says.

'Me too.'

We take off our goggles and smile at each other, dazzled by the dancing water, like a Hockney painting.

I expect the weather to be Californian hot when we're dry and dressed and walking to the café but it's overcast, drizzling slightly. Somehow it doesn't matter in the slightest. Rosa greets us warmly, and we sit at our table, with our good coffee and fresh almond croissants. I feel hyper-alive and happy.

'You're Ms Smiley this morning,' says Alice. She puts her head on one side. 'Has Guy been staying?'

'No – the opposite, in fact. I've been keeping him at bay, getting on with a lot of work. If he's around he just puts me off,' I say quickly. 'Alice, I'm sorry he was so rude when you came over.'

'He was a bit. It's clear he just wants to keep you all to himself,' she says.

'I suppose. But I can't stand that about him. To be totally truthful, I'm getting a bit sick of him,' I admit.

'Oh, come on. I sensed a real connection between the two of you,' says Alice.

'Well, the sex bit is fine. Great, actually,' I say.

Alice winces, though she tries to hide it.

'Sorry, too much information. But I'm starting to think that's the only thing we've got going for us. We just argue the rest of the time. Long ago he was my art teacher at school—'

'*What?*' says Alice.

'I know, it sounds mega-weird, and maybe it *is*. He still acts

289

like my teacher, telling me what to do all the time, and it drives me crazy. Did you ever have a crush on a teacher when you were at school?'

'Oh, yes. The PE teacher.'

'Really? I just met up with my old PE teacher at my party and I can't imagine ever having a crush on her!'

'Yes, but you're not gay, are you?' says Alice.

'Even if I were a thousand per cent gay, I could never have fancied Mrs Henderson. I actually like her now, though she seemed my worst enemy when I was thirteen or fourteen. But I promise you, she's no gay icon.'

'Ah well,' says Alice, and there's a short silence.

'Did you always know you were gay, right from when you were little?' I dare ask. Do all gay people know they want same sex relationships right from puberty? Is it possible you might find you could be gay halfway through your life, even though you've never thought about it before? I find I really want to know.

'Yep, right from when I was very little. Though I did fool around with several boys, just to see what it was like. I wanted to please my dad, be the sort of daughter he hoped for. But it didn't work,' she says.

'I suppose I'm lucky with my own dad. He's always been totally cool about my brother being gay. I'm starting to realize just how much he means to me. And Lottie got carried away and now she's met *her* dad. She seems to think he's wonderful, but he's starting to twist things, telling her lies,' I say, my voice suddenly shaky.

Alice puts her hand over mine and squeezes it.

'It must be hard for you,' she says.

'I guess I'm just a pathetic possessive mum,' I admit.

'I think you sound a great mum.'

I turn my hand round and hold hers properly.

'Thanks, Alice,' I say. 'Sorry to go on about it. It's just that I feel I can tell you anything.'

Rosa comes up with more pastries and we disentangle quickly and thank her. She smiles at us fondly, obviously coming to the wrong conclusion. It feels a bit odd, but I'm pleased she thinks I could have someone as great as Alice as a girlfriend.

We walk along together afterwards, dawdling a little, like we're both spinning out time. I'm seeing Guy later but we've still got an hour or so, maybe longer.

'Do you think I could pop back to yours for a while so I could have another look at the elephant photos on your wall?' I ask.

She looks agonized.

'Or do you think it might disturb Wendy again?' I add.

'It's maybe not a good idea,' she says reluctantly.

'No problem. Well, do you want to come back to *my* place and have a proper look how I'm getting on with my elephants? I've made quite a bit of progress.'

She's clearly wavering. 'I'd love to – but perhaps not,' she says, without explaining why.

'OK, sure,' I say quickly, trying hard to make out I don't mind in the slightest. Though *why* doesn't she want to?

When we part at the tube station, we attempt a casual kiss on the cheek, and make a mess of it, dodging about like sparring boxers. We laugh to try to ease the situation but don't make another attempt. I do wish we could have spent that extra hour together. Why did it all go suddenly wrong?

I trudge back to the flat, hang up my wet swimming things, feed Stella, then work on another close-up picture of Mosi before it's time to dress up in a short skirt to meet Guy. Another gallery trip. I love art, but am not sure I can take another one so soon.

We were supposed to be going to Tate Britain to lunch in

their posh restaurant with the Rex Whistler murals, but when we get there we discover you can't eat there any more because some of the murals are problematic in today's climate.

'We could go to Tate Modern instead,' Guy suggests, as we have a quick lunch in a nearby pub.

'We could,' I say, and then add, emboldened by two glasses of wine, 'or we could do something else instead. Something . . . fun?'

Guy gives me a sideways glance, and then looks at his phone. 'I'll see what I can find,' he says.

I'd have been happy strolling along the riverbank and through St James's Park to peer at the pelicans. I start suggesting it, but Guy interrupts with his own idea.

'Let's go to this comedy club near Soho,' he says, smiling triumphantly. 'Doors open at two thirty, matinee at three. That suit you?'

I'm not actually that keen on stand up, but I don't want to be a killjoy. I'm not up to an afternoon of bickering today.

'Sounds good,' I say, and try to mean it.

You can't book seats so we get there early. I see from the posters that it's some kind of ventriloquist act, which doesn't sound promising. When the doors open I take Guy's hand and rush him forwards. I'm smaller than most people and I don't see that well even with my glasses on, so I need to be at the front to see what's going on.

This turns out to be a massive mistake. The show's star is a woman with puppets, but it's not a bit like a twee kids' show, it's a highly complex adult routine, with all sorts of banter and magic tricks and illusions, mostly depending on audience participation. And there we are, Guy and me, sitting ducks right in the front row.

The audience roars with laughter when she picks people from either end, encourages them on stage and has her puppets tease them and then perform baffling tricks which make them look stupid. Guy laughs uproariously, but I'm so scared she'll pick me that I can't laugh to save my life. I think Guy's nervous too, because his laughter is very high-pitched – and of course, the comedian picks up on this like a lion scenting a gazelle.

Sure enough she starts flirting with Guy, pulling him up on stage and having her old lady puppet go all coy, pretending she fancies him. She makes a thing about his fair hair and wants to tousle it with her little rubbery fingers. Everyone laughs and Guy manages to laugh too, but he's starting to sweat. There's more banter, a little trick, but perhaps because he's trying his best to be a good sport, she lets him off lightly. He rejoins me, smiling with relief. He gives my hand a squeeze. His is very damp.

Then she looks at me. Oh God, no!

'Are you with him?' the old lady puppet asks.

I nod dumbly.

'Bit cringy, wasn't it, watching him?' she says.

'Yep!' I say.

'He did well, didn't he? Mr Smooth. But he got a bit moist, didn't he?' the puppet says, and cackles.

The audience creases up at the word moist. I see the sudden panic on Guy's face as he wonders what's coming next.

'I think he's a bit frightened of you,' I say. 'I am too!'

'A little old woman like me! Still, I'm not to be trusted. I'd have him off you at the drop of a hat,' she says, and she knocks her bonnet off so it falls to the stage.

'Granny!' the comedian scolds. 'Behave now. We mustn't embarrass this lovely couple. Have you known each other long?'

She's looking at me, her eyes glinting in the spotlight. What do I say? I swallow hard.

'Quite a while,' I hedge.

'Ah! So he's definitely the man for you, is he?' she asks.

What do I say now? The audience is waiting eagerly. I don't know! Is he? No, I don't think he is, not for ever anyway. But I can't say it, not in front of everyone. It will make Guy look such a fool.

'Yes, definitely,' I lie – and Guy puts his arm round me and kisses my cheek.

The audience laughs again, especially when the old lady curses and shakes her fist in mock anger.

The comedian takes mercy on me now and moves on, picking on someone else.

'I think we both got off lightly!' Guy whispers. He sounds thrilled. And my heart sinks.

Everyone claps heartily at the end of the show. Guy actually stands up and cheers, and he gets a clap too. I have to smile in front of everyone as if I'm just as delighted.

People stop us on the way out and chat as if they know us, and Guy basks in the attention, making quips as if he's a comedian too. I feel myself shrivelling inside. What am I *doing* with this silly show-off?

'Shall we go back to yours now?' I murmur in his ear.

I see by the look on his face he's misinterpreted the message and thinks I can't wait to shag him. I've properly got the ick now, though – the idea of sleeping with him is suddenly repellent. It would be funny if it wasn't so awful.

We go near Waterloo in the Uber and I fantasize about stopping the car and rushing to get the tube home and spending the evening with Stella – but it would seem such a kneejerk hysterical reaction. I message Andreea instead, promising her more fancy chocolates if she can feed Stella, and grit my teeth, resigning myself to a final night in Earlsfield.

Guy pulls a bottle out of the fridge as soon as we're indoors.

'Champagne?' I say weakly.

'Well, I got a bottle in as we had the fabulous Bollinger

at yours. And it's perfect timing – we have to celebrate our public declaration!' he says happily, pouring champagne into two shining flutes. He puts one in my hand and raises his own glass in a toast. 'You told everyone I'm definitely the man for you – and I'm telling you now you're definitely the woman for me,' he says with true sincerity, which only makes me feel even worse.

Tell him now that you only said it so he wouldn't look a fool in the comedy club! But I can't spoil it all when he's smiling at me and being so loving.

I take a long drink from my glass, needing it badly.

Coward! the little voice says.

I'm not a coward, I'm simply being kind, I argue. *We'll have one more night and then I'll try to find some way of stopping all this pretending and pleasing.*

I find I'm alarmingly good at it, though, as we sit together on his sofa, drinking and talking about the show. Guy kisses my neck, slides his hand up my short skirt and along my satiny black tights.

'You look so sexy in little skirts,' he says. 'Come on, I can't wait any more. I need to get those tights off right away.'

I take another long gulp of champagne and then he holds my hand and we take the ten second walk to the bedroom and the designer bed and the crisp sheets. And I can smile and act all sweet and sexy, but I can't *make* myself want him, no matter how much I will it. I just keep thinking of that moment blinking in the spotlight, realizing that he isn't the man for me.

When I can no longer bear it, I push him away as gently as possible. 'I'm so sorry, darling, I'm just not in the right mood now,' I whisper. 'Can we just cuddle up for a while?'

'Of course, of course,' he says, but after a few minutes of chaste snuggling, he picks up again, seemingly determined to prove himself. He does his best to turn me on, but I stay dry and unresponsive at first. He won't give up, though, pours us another glass of champagne, and sets to it again. He's trying so hard, and I shut my eyes and fantasize that I'm not with Guy at all; someone else is holding me close and whispering beautiful words in my ear, and I start responding. Then it gets wilder, and better, and I stop thinking and worrying and come and come and come until I'm gasping for breath.

Then I slowly slip back into myself and Guy kisses my face, and I hope he mistakes the tears on my cheeks for sweat.

'Definitely, definitely, definitely,' he murmurs. And then '*Indefinitely!*'

I stiffen. Does he mean it? Is he saying it because the sex has been great for both of us? Or is he reliving his brief moment being the star of the show? He doesn't seriously mean he wants us to be a couple indefinitely? But what if he does? A few weeks ago, I'd have been thrilled at the thought, but now I'm not so sure. It's so horribly ironic – I was worried about his lack of commitment, and now I'm not at all sure of *mine*.

But I'm tired and satisfied and I don't want to start a horribly uncomfortable discussion right now, so I keep quiet and eat pasta in bed with him and drink wine now and drift into sleep the moment we lie down together.

I can have hardly moved all night long, because I wake up in his arms. He has them tightly wound round me, and suddenly they feel like ropes binding me, and I'm struggling to breathe. It takes me a while to wriggle free so I can slip to his bathroom. I sit on the loo and breathe deeply, trying to work things out, though I'm still muzzy with sleep and a hangover.

I hero-worshipped Guy when I was a schoolgirl. I admired him because he knew so much about art and introduced me to various women painters who have stayed my special people ever since. Then when I saw him again as an adult, I was flattered he was interested in me when he could have anyone. He's a good man, a kind man, a great teacher – but I'm not that little fucked-up uncertain girl any more. I'm me, a middle-aged woman, and maybe it's time I acted like it.

I go back to his bed. He's fast asleep, on his back, gently snoring. It's not the prettiest sight, but I feel a tender pity for him. He's tried so hard to be right for me. Well, he's succeeded in one way – but the sex isn't enough. I was crazy about the way he makes me feel physically, but I'm not crazy about *him*. I don't want to see him every day. I don't even want to go to Venice with him on this romantic holiday. I know for certain now. I don't want to see him any more.

I get back into bed, and he curls round me in his sleep and holds me close again. I doze and don't wake up properly until gone nine. I should tell him now. Gently but firmly. I rehearse the words in my head.

But he gets up, showers, brings us breakfast, and then settles back into bed with me, looking at me so fondly that the words stick in my throat.

'I can't believe how random life is, Ellie,' he says. 'Imagine, if Jean hadn't been invited to your party we'd never have met again! If someone had told me that the funny little schoolgirl I once taught would now mean so much to me I'd have been astonished.'

I give him a brittle smile, not trusting myself to speak.

'It's just so amazing that we've found each other now,' he says.

'Well – yes, but—' *Say it! Say it NOW!*

'I don't know about you, Ellie, but somehow long-term relationships for me have always been problematic. Once or twice I've thought things were really going to work out – but they didn't. Maybe it was my fault, who knows.'

He starts elaborating, reminding me about this girl and that, and it sounds a bit like showing off, though he looks plaintive enough, even shaking his head and sighing as he drinks his coffee.

'But I was never one hundred per cent sure enough – or they weren't – so I was certain that I'd never find the right girl for me. Yet here you are!' he says, looking into my eyes.

There's a little needy part of me that still thrills at this, that I'm the one who's changed his mind, that he's implying he wants to settle down with me – but it's his dream, not mine. I have to make this clear, but I don't seem to have the guts to do so right now.

We cuddle down in bed and do the sweet talk, and the silly games, and invent new nicknames, but I don't really feel anything deep inside. I kiss him and act kittenish and he seems so sure I'm feeling exactly the way he does – while I'm veering off his yellow brick road and rushing back to Kansas as fast as I can.

I pretend I have to leave because Anna is fixing a special lunch for all of us, celebrating Dad's recovery. Guy wants to come to this invented feast with me, but I say it's family only, because Dad still needs to keep very quiet and relaxed. I'm turning into an inveterate liar, but it can't be helped.

I rush home and spend the afternoon and evening alone. I work hard on my elephants. I need to know which animals are the biggest threat to elephant calves and try emailing Alice. She doesn't reply and I feel stupid and let down, though I know it's ridiculous to feel that way. She's not ignoring me on purpose, she's probably made it up with Wendy and now they're both at Catz. Somewhere I wouldn't belong in a million years.

The days go by with no further contact from her. There's way too many messages from Guy, but I keep putting him off, telling him I'm working day and night on my graphic novel. I promise to see him on Saturday. It looks like Alice is a Saturday-only friend too. I tell myself that this is fine. I have two best friends already. I have a daughter. I have a lover – for the moment, anyway. So why do I feel so bereft?

I'm wide awake on Saturday morning, ready to go swimming. I force myself to calm down, take my time over breakfast, read more of Alice's diary, make another sketch, and in the end I have to leave in a rush. I practically run to the leisure centre, but she's not in the changing room. I wait again. It's even later than last time, now. I check the pool, wondering if she's gone in already. No brown girl in a white costume anywhere. I even call her name, going up and down the curtained cubicles, but she's not there either.

So she's not coming, even though she said she'd see me at swimming. I get in the pool and it seems chillier than usual. I don't warm up, even after a couple of lengths. I carry on determinedly, though it seems pointless now. And then when I've done fourteen or sixteen or eighteen lengths (too much in a turmoil to count accurately) I see her standing on the edge, peering up and down the lanes.

I stop, tread water and wave. She waves back and jumps in. I swim over to her, so eager I swallow a mouthful of water and I'm coughing so much I can't even say hello. She pats me on the back until I recover.

'Are you OK now?' she asks. 'Sorry I'm so late. I – I got held up.'

'I'm fine,' I gasp. And I *am* fine, even though I'm still spluttering.

'You need to warm up,' says Alice, rubbing the goosepimples on my arms. 'Come on. Race you!'

I burst out laughing, because she's a much faster swimmer than me. But I accept the challenge, and she swims deliberately slowly so I can flash past her in triumph. Then we settle into our usual speed and because I've had a head start I finish my fifty lengths long before her.

I stand on the edge of the pool, waiting for her, my towel wrapped round me. The general swim is starting. There's a queue for the steps so I hold out my hand to Alice, and she uses it to haul herself out the water. Two young girls suddenly point at me.

'Hey, it's Miss Allard!'

'Hi, Miss, fancy seeing you here!'

It's Amy and Becky, who've just finished Year Eight. They're naughty girls, but great fun.'

'Didn't have you down as the athletic type, Miss!'

'Oh, that's me,' I say, lifting my arms and tensing my muscles, and they giggle.

Alice watches, smiling.

'Who's that, Miss?' Amy asks.

'Is she your girlfriend, Miss?' Becky says.

'Cheeky,' I say, my voice full of warning.

'Go on, give her a kiss, Miss,' Amy suggests.

'*Too* cheeky,' I say. 'Scram!'

Thank God the communal dressing room is for adults only. I'd die if those two could watch me struggle out of my swimming costume.

'I'm so glad the kids I teach are pretty much grown up,' says Alice. 'You're so good with them, Ellie. And they're clearly very fond of you, in spite of the lip.'

'You should have seen me the first time I did teaching practice. I was so scared I thought I'd throw up in front of them. I could hardly get my words out. When I got home I cried, thinking I'd have to pack my teaching career in before I even got started. But hey, now I enjoy teaching – well, most of the time,' I say.

'What will you do if your elephant book is a huge success? Might you pack it all in then?' Alice asks, when we go for our coffee and croissants.

'I don't think that's very likely,' I say. 'I'm not sure where my agent will try it – or which market I'm really aiming at. Maybe Mosi will never see the light of day. But it's wonderful drawing her and her tribe.' I hold out my arms. Myrtle is waving at me on the left. 'Shall I get a tattoo of Mosi on my right arm? Though that might look a bit unbalanced, a tiny mouse one side and a big elephant on the other.'

'If you have a number one bestseller you could have the whole tribe going up one leg and down the other,' Alice suggests.

'With an African orange sun on one buttock and a milk white moon on the other,' I quip. 'I love those sky descriptions in your diary. You're a great writer, Alice. You should keep a diary all the time.'

'I do,' she mutters.

'Seriously? Every day? I'm very impressed. I've been trying to keep a diary since I was a little kid. This year I managed two and a half weeks of January precisely. Which is a shame, because a lot seems to have happened lately.' I'm burbling away, but I'm not sure she's listening. She's looking anxious.

'Alice? What's the matter?' I ask her.

'Nothing!' she says, too quickly. 'Here, do you fancy going halves on another croissant?'

I agree, but Alice only toys with her half and I end up eating it all. There *is* something wrong. Is it to do with me? Doesn't she want to keep seeing me any more? Is she fed up with all my elephant questions? Yet she seems keen to talk elephants herself, and we have an interesting discussion about matriarchs and how they age.

'There's a close-up photo of one on your wall,' I say. 'I took a photo of it when I came round to your house, but it's pretty blurred. I don't want to barge in on you again, but maybe you could photograph it and then send it to me? I'd love to get on with a close-up portrait of Mosi this weekend.'

She hesitates.

'I mean, you don't have to,' I say quickly. Perhaps she doesn't want me barging in again. Maybe Wendy has objected? Or perhaps she thinks I've got a cheek wanting to use her beautiful photograph . . . 'I know the photo is your copyright and I shouldn't really be copying it,' I add.

'It's not that. It's just all my photos are packed up at the moment,' she says.

'Why? Are they going to be exhibited somewhere?'

'No, no, it's just – I'm moving,' Alice says in a rush, and then bursts into tears.

I look at her, horrified. 'Oh Alice!' I slip out of the booth and sit beside her, putting my arm round her shoulders. 'I'm so sorry. What's happened? Are you moving with Wendy?'

Alice sobs incoherently. Rosa is looking over at us, concerned. She holds a coffee cup up with her head on one side in query, but I shake my head.

'Talk to me, Alice,' I urge.

She tries to say something, but can't manage it. Tears slide down her cheeks, and her nose runs a little, but her mouth doesn't take on that awful letter-box shape that generally accompanies howling. I hold her tight.

'You don't have to tell me if you don't want to,' I say.

She's sitting rigidly, her eyes shut, as if she doesn't want to see me, and as soon as seems polite she wriggles away from me.

Rosa brings a glass of water and then scurries off again. I hand it to Alice. She has to open her eyes to avoid spilling it. She takes a gulp of water and then hiccups.

'Oh God,' she says and then hiccups again. 'Oh God, oh God, oh God.'

Alice takes another sip of water, more cautiously this time. 'Oh God. My father would be going mad if he could hear me. "Thou must not take the Lord's name in vain."'

'Has something happened to do with your father?' I ask.

'No. And I'd sooner sleep on a park bench than go and live with my parents again,' she mutters, more to herself than me.

'Alice. Look at me. What are you talking about?'

'It's Wendy and me,' she mumbles. 'We've split up.'

'Oh Alice, I'm so sorry,' I say, not entirely truthfully. I hate seeing her so sad, but I feel a little leap inside me. Oh no, that's dreadful. She's so unhappy. I feel drenched in shame.

'Has Wendy got someone else now? I thought you had a kind of laissez-faire policy about other girlfriends?'

'It's not her. It's – it's me,' Alice says. She bends her head and says quietly, almost to herself, 'I think I'm in love with someone else.'

I feel like she's poured the glass of cold water over my head. I hope I haven't flinched.

'I see,' I say, as calmly as I can. Why didn't I have an inkling? Alice is so funny, so clever, so attractive – totally wasted on a selfish show-off like Wendy. Of course she was bound to have someone else making a play for her. 'Well, it didn't sound as if things were that great with you and Wendy recently. So now you and this new girl can be together. Isn't that what you want?'

'It's not that simple,' Alice murmurs. 'It's never going to work out. But Wendy read my diary, where I'd written about my feelings for the other woman, and chucked me out. Literally. And I've spent days going round and round renting agencies and looking up flat-sharing ads and I can't find anywhere yet. I'm camping in my office at work for now. I can't use any of the students' rooms because we've got foreign students doing a course and they've taken over all the accommodation. I can't even have a proper shower. I'm scared one of the porters or cleaners will report me – it's so horribly embarrassing. I suppose I can afford £60 a night at a Travelodge for a bit, or sofa-surf

303

with different friends – though they're mostly Wendy's friends too, and it'll be so awkward. Plus I've got so much luggage, a backpack and two big cases and boxes full of stuff and—'

'For God's sake, Alice, don't be daft,' I say, interrupting her spiral. 'It *is* simple. I have a spare bedroom. Come to me.'

'I can't do that!' she says, distraught. 'I promise I wasn't hinting or anything.'

'I know you weren't. But it's the obvious answer. Lottie's not going to be needing it – and if she pops home for a weekend or whatever, she can always come in with me,' I say. 'I know she won't mind.'

I feel a moment's doubt, hoping that's true. Of course if she and Luke become an item it might be awkward, but we'll get round it somehow.

'I can't possibly, Ellie. I mean, it's so kind of you, but it wouldn't be fair. What would Guy say?' she asks.

I'd actually forgotten Guy. What's the matter with me? My brain's gone to mush.

'Never mind Guy,' I say quickly. It doesn't seem the right moment to mention I'm probably going to break up with him. 'And obviously, if things work out with this girl of yours, I'll make myself scarce,' I offer, though the thought of Alice and some stranger having sex in the next room is unsettling. I'm not sure why exactly. It just makes me feel very uncomfortable. It almost feels like . . . jealousy?

Alice gives a strange, bitter little laugh. 'That won't happen, I'm one hundred per cent sure.' She wipes her eyes. 'Ellie, are you really serious?'

'Absolutely.'

'It won't be for long. I'll keep on trying hard to get somewhere. But it would be marvellous if I could camp at yours for a couple of weeks, if you really don't mind. And of course I'll pay rent and expenses and all the rest of it,' she says earnestly.

'Rubbish! Look, this is what friends are for. You said you'd try to sofa-surf. Well, I've got a well-sprung bed with a lovely patchwork quilt that's much comfier than any old sofa – and Stella already likes you, so you've got a purring hot water bottle thrown in free,' I say.

'Oh Ellie,' she says, and this time she gives me a hug, though she pulls away quickly.

'So, it's settled, right?' I say, holding out my hand.

She shakes it. 'You're one in a million,' she says.

'Where's your stuff now then?'

'At work. That's why I've been late for swimming. It's two bus rides away, and it takes for ever.'

'You should have said! We'll go together, and we'll take a cab back to mine and get you settled in,' I say.

'But it's Saturday. Aren't you seeing Guy?' she asks.

'Yes, but not till this afternoon. We're meant to be meeting at a gallery to see this new exhibition but I can't say I'm really that keen. I'll message him to say something's cropped up. And then . . .'

And then? I could suggest I go over to Guy's and spend the night with him – but how could I let Alice spend the first night in my flat all on her own? Especially as she's so miserable. And why am I thinking of seeing Guy anyway? I've got to sort things out properly with him. Tell him how I feel. But I don't want to think about that now. There's far more important things on my mind.

Who is this mystery girl? Why is it complicated? Why isn't Alice telling me all about her?

I look at her, longing to know, but she's looking so pale and tense I don't feel I can ask.

And when *exactly* am I going to tell Guy? In the middle of Tate Modern? Shall I simply text to say I can't make it, that I'm not sure I want to see him any more? No, I can't break it off by text, that's awful. And he might still want to come over to my flat to talk it over. We'd sit there like lemons, the three of us. It would be terrible. What am I going to do?

I put off messaging him just yet, though. Maybe I'll wait till lunchtime. He might be having a lie-in, after all.

When we leave the café Rosa looks anxiously at both of us.

'Everything OK now?' she says.

Alice nods a little sheepishly.

'That's good. No more squabbles! You two are made for each other!' she says, beaming.

'Oh no, it's not like that,' Alice says quickly.

'It's a bit complicated,' I add. I shrug awkwardly.

Alice and I giggle a little when we're outside, both of us embarrassed.

'I'm sorry,' she says.

'Don't be so daft,' I say. I'm rather proud to be thought her girlfriend. I wonder about saying that out loud, but decide it would be a bit odd, especially with her in such a vulnerable place at the moment.

We take the two buses to the university, and it really does take for ever. Alice keeps apologizing, and I shake my head at her.

'Stop it! I'm dying to see what it's like. I wish Lottie had gone there and lived just two bus rides away,' I say.

The place is teeming with excitable young Italians setting off to see the sights of London. They seem much more interested in each other than any towers or palaces or galleries though, fooling about, the girls giggling, the boys shouting.

'I'm so glad I'm not a teenager any more,' I say.

'Me too,' says Alice. 'Did you have a best friend?'

'I had two, Nadine and Magda. We're still great friends now.'

'Which did you like the best?' Alice asks.

'I'm not sure,' I say, wondering. 'They're so different.

Sometimes I'd fall out with one, then the next term I'd fall out with the other. One time both of them weren't speaking to me and that was awful – and yet I can't even remember what that was all about now. You know what girls are like.'

'Yeah,' says Alice. 'I had two best friends too, until we were fourteen or so. Then they started getting interested in boys. I mean, I *liked* boys, but not romantically.'

'Did you have an actual girlfriend at school?' I wonder.

'Well, I had secret crushes, but I was still a bit conflicted. By Year Eleven I did have this thing with another girl, kisses behind the bike sheds, that sort of thing, but I never felt I could be open about it. I was terrified of my mum and dad finding out. I didn't dare tell them I was gay until I was a student living away from home, and then they were horrified. Dad wanted me to pray to Jesus for forgiveness,' says Alice. 'And Mum cried because she said I was choosing a life of unhappiness. Ha! Maybe she was right.'

'You don't mean that, do you?' I ask, shocked.

'No, of course not,' says Alice. 'In fact, I'm really happy right this moment because you're being so lovely to me.' She reaches out and pats my arm lightly.

'I'm just acting like a friend, that's all,' I say.

Alice smiles wanly.

We go through a side door, up a couple of flights of stairs, to Alice's office. It's small but lovely, with more fantastic elephant photographs on the wall, and three shelves of her books. Her desk is cluttered with academic papers and documents and several ebony elephants acting as paperweights. There's hardly any room for the two of us because of her luggage, which takes up the whole floor.

'Where on earth have you been sleeping?' I ask.

'I piled the cases on top of each other and had my sleeping bag on the floor – though I was scared they might topple and crush me to death,' she says. 'It will be fantastic to have a proper bed to sleep in tonight, if you're absolutely certain your daughter won't mind.'

'Look, I'll ring her right now, so you can hear for yourself,' I say, and I dial Lottie's number, putting her on speakerphone.

'Hi, Mum,' she says. 'Listen, I'm on the train, don't worry if we get cut off by a tunnel, OK? I'm going to see Dad.'

I can't stop myself pulling a face. I hate her calling him Dad so naturally. I thought she might start off calling him by his name until she got to know him properly.

'Mum? Look, I could come and see you too. Or you could come to Dad's place – he says there's an open invitation for you.'

I'd sooner visit Nigel in the cupboard under his stairs, but I simply murmur a 'thanks but no thanks' response.

'Well, I hope you have a lovely time,' I say, trying harder.

Lottie bursts out laughing. 'Oh Mum, you're hopeless! You don't hope that in the slightest! And I do understand, truly. Luke says this will all be very hard for you and I should try to be as tactful and reassuring as possible.'

'Luke's very sweet and sensitive,' I say, though I burn to think of them discussing me in such kindly but patronizing terms. 'Anyway, darling, I'm phoning because I've got a friend who's suddenly homeless and I've offered her your room for a week or two until she finds somewhere else. Is that OK?'

'Which friend?' Lottie asks, all agog.

'It's Alice.'

'Who?'

It seems astonishing that Lottie doesn't even remember who she is, when Alice has become so much a part of my life.

'She's the special friend I met at swimming. She's been so helpful over my new project,' I say.

'Well, of course I don't mind her having my room for a bit.

Tell her she can even take Nellie to bed with her! Bye then, Mum. Love you.'

'Love you lots, Lots,' I say, smiling.

'She sounds lovely,' says Alice. 'So, who's Nellie?'

'It's an old toy elephant. My Mum knitted one for me when I was little, so I made one just like it for Lottie. Nellie's very much the worse for wear now, but she's still very special,' I say.

'You'll find I've got an old monkey with only half a tail tucked at the bottom of my suitcase,' says Alice.

'Can interspecies ever make friends?' I ask.

'I once saw a baboon clamber right up an elephant and sit on its back,' says Alice. 'The elephant didn't seem to mind at all.'

'Well, there you are then,' I say. 'Right, let's get all this lot back to mine.'

'You're sure, Ellie?' Alice says seriously.

'I'm positive,' I say. It's a relief to *feel* positive about something, when I've been in such a dither over Guy.

21

We manage to haul Alice's luggage down the two flights of stairs between us, though it's a struggle and we have to make three trips. The cab driver isn't that thrilled about all the luggage either.

'I'm not a bleeding furniture van, ladies,' he says. 'And I've got a bad back so I can't help with any lifting.'

We manage to stuff the suitcases in his boot ourselves and sit with the boxes and bags on our laps. Alice insists on paying when we get to Constable and gives him a big tip, so he leaves happy. Then we drag the suitcases and everything else through the entrance.

'Oh God, please let the lift be OK!' I pray urgently.

God has other matters on his mind, though. Someone has scrawled *This shitty lift is broken for the fifth fucking time this year* on the door. They are telling the truth.

'Oh no,' says Alice, screwing up her eyes.

'I'm so so so sorry,' I say. 'But don't worry. We'll get your luggage up somehow.'

As I'm saying it, though, I have no idea how. Even if we managed to grab either end of one suitcase and stagger up fourteen flights of stairs with it, we'll never manage the other one and all the rest of the stuff – and someone might nick it anyway.

'What you got there, Miss?' a voice says, and I wheel around. It's the cheeky lads, gathering round us.

'What does it look like?' I say, sighing heavily.

'Is that your girlfriend's stuff?' the biggest one asks.

I can't be bothered to quibble about his terminology.

'Yes, it is,' I say wearily.

'You moving in together, eh?'

'And your flat's right up at the top, innit?'

'Yep.'

'The lift's broken, Miss,' another points out.

'I've gathered that,' I say.

'Want a hand, then?' says the big lad.

I goggle at him, hardly daring to hope that he's serious. But it seems he is.

He jerks his head to one of his mates and they start pulling the first suitcase to the stairwell. Two others take the second. A little tag-on kid of about nine picks up a box. Alice and I look at each other and grab the rest. Then we start the long trek upwards. The boys are magnificent. The older ones have bulked up a bit at the gym at the Estate Youth Club and prove amazingly strong. They push and pull and heave and make tremendous progress. Halfway up they all sit down for a vape, even the little one, but I'm hardly in a position to tell them off.

They start chatting up Alice and she jokes with them and I feel really impressed by her. They can be quite intimidating if you're not used to them, and I know she's despairing inside, but she's putting on a great act.

When we get everything up to my flat at last there's a great cheer. Alice gives the boys money for more vapes and a six pack of beer, and they all cheer.

'And Haribo and cola for the little kid,' she adds.

Andreea pops her head round her door to see what's going on. She blinks at the boys and gives Alice a double take.

'Is *she* your secret admirer, Ellie?' she says, grinning hopefully.

'What?' says Alice.

'Never mind,' I say quickly. 'Come on, let's get in and settled.'

Stella stands up in her cat tower, stretching, eyeing Alice up and down.

'Hello, Stella!' says Alice. 'Remember me?'

Stella blinks impassively, but when I show Alice Lottie's bedroom Stella comes too, and rubs herself against Alice's ankles.

'That's right, we're friends, aren't we?' Alice says, and bends to stroke her.

Alice breathes in deeply in Lottie's room. She looks round at the teal walls covered in posters and the shelves of books and the patchwork quilt on the ancient coral chaise longue and clasps her hands.

'It's a fantastic room,' she says.

Thankfully there are clean sheets already on the bed, waiting for Lottie's return, and half her clothes are still at uni so there's space in the wardrobe for Alice's clothes.

I make us fail-safe cheese on toast for lunch. It's golden and bubbly and delicious, requiring no faffing about. We sit together at the kitchen table munching companionably, and drinking tea. Alice likes the herby stuff, but so does Lottie, so I have packets of raspberry, peppermint and camomile on tap.

'I sometimes drink camomile too. I don't like the taste much, but Mum made me a little cup of it so I could see what it was like when she read me *Peter Rabbit*,' I say. 'It still seems special simply because it was in a book.'

'Did you do the same for Lottie?' Alice asks.

'Of course I did. I read her the *Flopsy Bunnies* as well to encourage her to eat lettuce, but that didn't work,' I say.

'My mum read me stories about Jesus providing loaves and fishes for the multitude and turning water into wine at the wedding in Cana, but fish and chips for supper was a rare treat and our household was strictly teetotal,' says Alice. 'My upbringing wasn't a bundle of laughs.'

There's a pause, and I pluck up all my courage.

'Alice, about this new girl in your life?' I start tentatively. I intend to make it clear she can bring her here whenever she wants, but she's shaking her head firmly.

'I don't want to talk about her,' she mutters.

I can't really press her. There's an awkward silence. I get my mobile out of my pocket.

'I'm going to phone Guy,' I say.

'Oh – well, I'll leave you in peace,' says Alice.

'No, it's fine, I'm just going to try to rearrange things. It's maybe better if I simply tell him I can't make it today.'

'No, you mustn't put him off just because of me!' Alice insists.

I run my hands through my hair. 'I don't really want to see him, to be honest. We're meeting at Tate Modern this time – our dating is like one of those Cultural Tours of the Capital. He's got tickets for the Expressionist exhibition, and I just *know* he's going to tell me all about Marianne von Werefkin when actually I probably know far more about her than he does. And then after a couple of glasses of wine I'll be so irritated at having to act like his little pupil that I'll start getting tetchy and we'll start bickering and it will turn into a row and we'll both get worked up and then he'll want to go back to his place to have sex and it's all getting so predictable,' I say, realizing this is a totally accurate summing up of our relationship.

'Well, at least you're having sex,' says Alice.

So does this mean she and this new girl on the scene haven't got together yet? And why does this make me feel so pleased?

'I'm going to call it off,' I say.

'No. I couldn't bear it if I mucked up your relationship, Ellie.'

She looks so distressed that I relent. 'OK, I'll keep the date with Guy. He's the sort who'll kick off if I want to change all the arrangements, anyway. He's probably deep in a book about the Expressionists right this minute just so he can show off on his private guided tour,' I grumble.

'Give the poor guy a break,' says Alice. 'He clearly just wants to impress you.'

'I know. I don't know why I get so ratty about him. Nadine and Magda think I'm a fool. They think he's incredible. Sensitive. Kind. Romantic. Did I tell you he's taking me to Venice in October?' I say.

'Well, there you are then. He sounds a total gem,' says Alice, but her face is twitching. I can't tell whether she wants to laugh or cry.

'You go out with him then, and I'll stay here and work on my elephants,' I say. I pause. Take a deep breath. 'Do you want to see how it's developing? I've done a lot of new work, nearly the finished version.'

'I'd really love to see it. But don't show me if you're not ready yet,' she says.

'You so understand me. It's uncanny. But I really want to see what you think of it,' I say.

I take her to my desk and show her the cover first.

'Oh Ellie! It's incredible. Exactly right! Are you sure you haven't been there?'

'No, but I've read the diary of someone who has,' I say.

'Well, sometimes reading someone's diary is a good thing,' says Alice. 'So is this one Mosi?'

'I start off with her just being born. It's going to be her whole life cycle, until she dies when she's seventy. She'll have some big crisis when she's forty and she thinks her life is over – but then great things happen to her,' I say.

'What great things? Does she spurn the roars of the biggest bull elephant?' Alice asks.

'I think that's a huge possibility,' I say, and sigh. 'Right, I'd better tart myself up a bit if I'm going to see Guy.'

I go to my bedroom and reappear ten minutes later in my white shirt and black and white striped trousers, ribbon tied, lipstick on.

'Wow,' says Alice. 'Lucky Guy. You'll definitely be dragged back to his place tonight.'

'That's not going to happen. And I'm not bringing him back here, either,' I say. I'm going to stop this shilly-shallying once and for all.

'Ellie. Stay over at his. I'll unpack slowly and sort everything out, and then I'll catch up with some work and maybe watch something on your television, have an early night, whatever. Do you have a spare key so I can nip out to the shops if I need to?'

Or nip out to see the girlfriend? Well, she's got a perfect right to see anyone she wants, I tell myself.

'Of course,' I say, smiling determinedly, and hand her Andreea's spare.

'And I'll be back tonight,' I say.

'No! Come back tomorrow, any time that works. I'll be fine, I promise. Promise, promise, promise,' says Alice.

I go, though I don't want to. I tube to Waterloo, walk to Tate Modern along the embankment, watching all the couples wandering hand in hand. Am I going to miss not being a couple with Guy?

Guy isn't waiting outside the Tate. I stand there, reading *The Swimming-Pool Library*. I look at my watch every now and then. Ten minutes late. Fifteen. *Twenty?* For God's sake, he's stood me up! I could have stayed back at the flat with Alice, helping her unpack and settle in. We could have worked companionably and shared that pizza and bottle of wine for supper and to hell with the mystery girlfriend and to hell with Guy too. But then I realize that if he's stood me up, that means I don't have to see him any more. He's done the breaking up for me. I stuff my book into my bag and turn to walk back to the tube. But then—

'Ellie, I'm so sorry!' It's Guy, out of breath, red in the face, his hair blowing in the wind, not his usual cool self at all. 'The train was held up at Vauxhall, and it was in that bit where there's no fucking signal, and then I got to Waterloo and ran for it, and I texted but I couldn't make the phone send it either, maybe there's something wrong with it, I don't know, but I'm so sorry to keep you waiting like this,' he blurts.

'It's fine, don't worry,' I say, touched by this new anxious, flustered side of him, even as my heart sinks at having to spend the afternoon together after all. I reach up to give him a chaste kiss but he gets carried away, trying to whirl me round as if we're in a rom-com, although I'm sturdy and he's not as strong as he thinks, so we very nearly topple over.

We go into the Tate and see the Expressionist exhibition – and I find I'm loving the paintings, especially those by Marianne von Werefkin. I smile politely while he compares her *Twins* painting with *The Cholmondeley Ladies* in the other Tate. He's saying it quite loudly as if he's at the front of a classroom.

Two twenty-somethings saunter by, hear his tone and roll their eyes. I feel sick at their expressions. Amusement? Pity? Contempt?

'Actually, Guy, I figured that out for myself,' I say as calmly as I can, though I'm trembling.

'Did you, darling?' he says. He seems on the verge of saying, 'Well done!'

'I'm really interested in Von Werefkin. She was from a noble Russian family, highly acclaimed as a painter, but she had this younger philandering husband who—'

'Yes, Ellie, but it's the art that really matters, isn't it, not the salacious details of the artist's love life,' Guy says.

It's such a patronizing put-down that I blush like a schoolgirl.

I don't trust myself to speak. I march off to the other end of the gallery and pretend to be looking at other paintings, though my eyes are blurred. He's right of course, it *is* the art that matters, though knowing about the artists as people makes their work much more interesting.

I take deep breaths, trying hard to calm down. I am not going to have a shouting match in the middle of Tate Modern. When Guy eventually works his way round to me he murmurs tentatively, 'Are you OK? Sorry if I upset you just then.'

'I'm fine,' I say, in a clipped voice.

Then we carry on, trailing around the permanent exhibits and watching parents doing their best to interest their kids, though most would sooner simply run riot in the Turbine Hall.

'It's great that it's such a family place,' says Guy. He's watching a curly-haired small boy piping enthusiastically about mini-beasts.

'Listen to that little kid,' he says. 'That's one of the worst things about getting older – realizing you're not likely to have any kids yourself.'

'It's much harder for women your age,' I say tartly.

'But you can still have babies though, can't you, Ellie?' he says.

'Theoretically, I can. But it's never going to happen. One's enough for me,' I say firmly.

'It must have been hard having your daughter so young,' he says. 'You were very brave. But if you were settled down and secure with the right partner, you might find it a lot easier,' he says.

'But I don't *want* another baby,' I insist.

'You never know. You might change your mind,' he says infuriatingly.

'I might. But I won't,' I say. 'I don't want to lumber around

317

like a bloated whale for months and then be torn apart for twenty-four hours giving birth.' This is true, but also not true. My pregnancy and childbirth were no picnic, but it was all wondrously worth it to have Lottie.

'I think you'll find childbirth has become much more civilized,' Guy says. 'They say water births are brilliant, so much more relaxing for the mother than lying back with their feet in stirrups.'

Is he really trying to mansplain childbirth to me?

'Try having a great grapefruit bursting out of you and see if you find it relaxing,' I suggest.

'Ellie! You could always plump for an epidural if you found the pain too much to bear.'

I peer at him. He's clearly been learning up about the whole process, which is seriously unnerving.

'Guy, I really really don't want to have another child,' I say. 'Please trust me that I know my own mind.'

'OK, OK, I hear you,' he says, but with an irritating smile as if he's sure he could change it.

We leave the Tate and wander towards Waterloo.

'Are you thinking we're going back to your place?' I ask.

'Of course I am,' he says. 'And I've got a surprise for you back at mine.'

'What is it?'

'Well, it wouldn't be a surprise then, would it, darling?'

I wish he wouldn't call me darling. Wouldn't stop and marvel at some sand artists down by the river, making a sculpture of two nudes lying together. Wouldn't buy me an elaborate cocktail at a pub and link arms with me as we toast each other. Wouldn't kiss me ostentatiously right in front of everyone. Wouldn't try to find a dark corner where we can fondle each other and get carried away.

It's not working. It's not Guy's fault, because he's trying his hardest to be gentle and romantic and tender. I suppose it's my fault that my head is full of poor Alice sitting cross-legged in the middle of my flat with only Stella for company.

We go back to Earlsfield on the train and Guy is so horny that the moment we're indoors he starts kissing my lips, my neck, my breasts – and there's a remote flicker of response in me that I give in to. We go to the grey bed, as clinically clean as ever, and lie down together, and he dutifully does his best to make me aroused, and I go along with it because I don't want to disappoint him and perform in exactly the way I've done before, faking enthusiasm, and then when he's laboured for a reasonable length of time I take pity on him and pretend to come. He's so happy then, rushing to a climax himself, and then lying back in triumph, holding me close.

'That was wonderful, wasn't it, darling?' he says.

I murmur a response.

'You make me feel a young man again,' he says.

'I'm glad,' I respond stiffly.

He cuddles me close and then slowly breathes out, in and out, and I realize he's fallen asleep. I lie there and I see into the future how many other times I might lie beside him, and I realize I simply can't do it any more. It's not his fault, he's a kind, lovely man, probably no more patronizing than most men his age, but I don't want to go along with it now. I don't love him. I don't want to stay here. I want to go home.

I try to ease myself out of his arms but he wakes up.

'Where are you going, angel?' he asks, smiling at me sleepily.

'Well, I thought I might go home,' I say.

'What?' He sits up. 'But we haven't even had dinner yet!' He says it slowly, as if I'm a thick child who doesn't understand the rules.

'I'm actually not very hungry,' I say. 'I've got a bit of a stomach ache.'

'Oh, poor darling.' His voice softens again. 'Come back to bed and I'll rub it for you.'

'No, I feel sick, that wouldn't help,' I say. 'I have to go to the bathroom.'

I hurry out the bedroom and then hide in there, giving myself time to gather courage. I really do feel sick. I've got to tell him, but I'm such a coward. I shouldn't ever have come back here. I peer at myself in his mirror. I look awful. Maybe he'll be glad to be rid of me.

'Ellie?' He's knocking at the door. 'Have you been sick?'

'Just a little bit,' I lie. I glance at the door nervously, praying he doesn't come barging in. 'I'm just going to have a shower.'

I give myself a wash with his lemon verbena body gel under his excellent hot shower (that's one thing I'll miss – my own shower dribbles and splutters and suddenly runs cold if you so much as brush against the thermostat) and dry myself on his fluffy white towel. I go back to the bedroom to dress, and use his hairdryer on my curls. They look much more tamed afterwards. If I lived with Guy, would I become as sleekly well groomed as he is? Would I research every exhibition I go to? Would I learn to love the muted shades of Farrow & Ball? Or would *I* become so muted I'd lose all trace of my real self?

I find him in the kitchen, where he's made me a cup of camomile tea and arranged Bath Olivers in a pretty pale ring on a green plate.

'They might help the queasiness, darling,' he says. The endearments are two a penny now.

'That's so kind of you,' I say. Not wanting to sit down with him quite yet, I wander over to his bookshelves and get distracted by his collection of old Penguins. There are several recent purchases crammed into the neat orange row. One's *The L-Shaped Room* by Lynne Reid Banks. An unlikely choice for him. I find Margaret Drabble's *The Millstone* too. Is he researching what it's like to be a single mother? I flick through both novels and then deliberately put them on top of the white paperbacks. Guy says nothing, but I glance back as I return to the kitchen, and see him slotting them back into the right place.

I sit down at the kitchen island and nibble on a Bath Oliver. I bought a packet once because they often crop up in Edwardian children's books and they sounded splendid, but I discovered I vastly prefer an ordinary cream cracker.

Guy comes and kisses the top of my damp head.

'Your hair looks very pretty,' he says.

'Thank you,' I say wanly.

'Not sure about this new look, though,' says Guy, playfully pulling my ribbon tie. 'I mean, you look great but I'm not sure about the trousers.'

'Guy. It's the twenty-first century. Women wear trousers nowadays,' I say.

'Granted – but I'm an old-fashioned guy who loves you looking all curvy in that tight red dress of yours,' he says. 'Or that little short skirt.'

I wrinkle my nose in distaste.

'I didn't mean to hurt your feelings, darling. You wear anything you want,' he says quickly. 'Hey, let me show you your surprise.'

He goes to the cupboard in the hall and brings back a big carrier bag.

'What is it?' I ask. He'd better not have bought me clothes . . .

'Take a look!'

It's not clothes, but almost as bad. He's bought a duvet cover with matching sheets and pillowcases. Egyptian cotton, which means they'll be sods to iron. They're bright white (meaning washing them once a week) but there's a little red pattern on them. I look closer and see they're stylized tiny red lips.

'It's a Salvador Dalí design. There's one of his red lip sofas in Brighton Art Gallery,' he says eagerly. 'I thought we could go on a trip to the seaside next weekend and take a look at it.'

'Guy, it's very kind of you,' I say after a long silence, 'but why on earth are you buying me bedclothes?'

'Well, honestly, darling, yours are a bit of a disgrace,' he says. 'Don't you like them? I thought you'd be thrilled. I suppose I could change them, though.'

'I want to buy my *own* bedding, if and when I choose,' I say.

He frowns at me. 'No need to get shirty. You're so determined to be independent, aren't you – when you're just a little girl inside needing to be looked after,' he says, putting his arm round me.

'I am not a fucking little girl!' I explode.

'OK, OK,' he says, backing away, arms raised defensively. 'I didn't mean that in a sleazy way. What do you think I am?'

'I think you're totally hung up on this teacher/pupil thing,' I say, so furious now I don't care about hurting his feelings.

'For God's sake, Ellie, what a thing to suggest!' he says, getting angry himself. He takes a deep breath. 'Look, let's both calm down. I know you're not feeling very well. When your stomach's settled we'll take an Uber over to your place and try the sheets and cover and I think you'll be thrilled with the way they look. I was thinking, maybe we could get you a little red plush sofa against one wall, to bring the whole thing together – or do you feel that would be too much?'

'And I could add a melting alarm clock to finish the design?' I say.

For a second he thinks I'm serious. Then he sighs at me impatiently. I remember that sigh from way back. But I don't have to put up with it now.

'I'm going home. You keep the bedding. I don't want a sofa. And I don't want to feel guilty about it, because I didn't bloody well ask you to buy me anything,' I say. I get up and accidentally spill the tea.

'Now you really are being childish!' he says angrily, mopping the puddle. 'OK, we'll leave the stuff here and I'll take you home and—'

'And if you do you'll find you've got company,' I say.

'What do you mean?' he asks. 'For Christ's sake, are you seeing someone else?'

'This is rich, coming from someone who's quite open about his friend with benefits,' I say. 'But I'm not seeing anyone, I'm helping out a friend who's in a bit of a sticky situation.'

'Oh, that's OK then. Which one is it: Nadine or Magda?' he asks, calming down.

'It's neither, as a matter of fact. It's my friend Alice.'

'The lesbian?' he asks incredulously.

'Oh, for God's sake, why do you have to go on about her sexuality? It's probably the least pertinent thing about her,' I say. 'She's an academic and has got all kinds of interests and knows just as much about art as we do, and she's an incredibly good swimmer and she can be really dry and witty at times and—'

'And you sound as if you're in love with her,' Guy says bitterly.

'Of course I'm not,' I say, feeling my cheeks glow. 'Alice is just a friend.' I feel like St Peter denying Christ as the cock crows, though. If I ever get to meet Alice's terrifying father he might at least admire my biblical knowledge.

'Well, is she staying the night?' Guy demands.

'Yes, of course.'

'Jesus, she's staying the whole weekend?'

'*Yes!*'

'So she's going on Monday?' he continues.

'I don't know when she's going,' I say.

'You mean she's staying *indefinitely*?' He's standing with his arms akimbo, his face very red.

'No, of course not. She's just broken up with her girlfriend. She's just staying until she's found another place to live.'

'Until she's found another mug who will take her in, you mean. I can't believe you could be so naive, Ellie. You've got to get rid of her before she's entrenched,' he says.

'You mean I should go home now and kick her out my door, with all her luggage?' I say. 'Should I expect her to wander the streets all night with two huge suitcases and God knows what else?'

'She's brought all her stuff? And you've let her? Then you're even more stupid than I thought. Come on. We're going over there right away and I'll deal with this,' he says.

'No, you're not!' I insist, outraged.

'I can see you're simply too sweet and gullible for your own good. She's not going to go anywhere if you're not careful. She'll worm her way into your life, maybe even worm her way into your bed,' he says.

'Maybe I'd like her to,' I say hotly. I'm saying it just to infuriate him further, of course. Or am I? Is this why I like her so much? Why I need to see her so often? Why I feel so close to her? Why I watch her so often? Why I'm guiltily thrilled that she's split up with Wendy? Why I'm burning with curiosity about this new great love of hers? Why I've even started fantasizing about her?

Guy and I both breathe heavily in the sudden silence.

'That's not funny,' he says at last.

'It's not meant to be funny,' I reply. 'I'm sorry, Guy. I know you've been lovely to me in so many ways, but we can't go on like this. This is it. It's over.'

'But we're going to Venice together!' he says.

'I know we were. But now you'll have to go with someone else. I'm sure there will be lots of takers,' I say.

'You can't transfer tickets just like that!' he says.

'OK, send me the fucking bill for my ticket then,' I say. 'And I'll pay for the duvet too. I'll pay for every glass of wine and plate of food you've given me, and all the tickets for art galleries. The thing is, Guy, you've never stopped to ask what *I'd* like to do – you're always too busy *telling* me.'

'So this is the thanks I get for trying to sweep you off your feet?' he says. He's actually shaking he's so angry. 'And you're walking out on me for a lesbian you've known for ten minutes? You can't kid me, Ellie. You're completely heterosexual. I've never had a woman more up for it than you. You're practically gagging for it every time we meet.'

I'm the one shaking now. 'Goodbye,' I say, and I walk out.

I'm out in the street and halfway down the road before he runs after me, a dressing gown over his pants. Oh Christ, this is bloody Bridget Jones in reverse.

'Ellie, wait! *Wait!* I'm sorry, that was truly offensive. I didn't mean it, darling. Let's go back indoors and start all over again. Look, have your friend stay over, you've got a perfect right. I'm just jealous, that's all. Come here.' He catches me up, puts his arms round me, and kisses me on the lips.

This is when I'm supposed to melt and we'll kiss more and go back to his bed and have sex. But it's not going to happen. It's really truly over.

I put my hands on his chest and push him back, gentle but firm. 'I'm sorry too, Guy. You've been great to me. The teenage me adored you. But I'm a grown-up now. Goodbye.' I kiss him on the cheek and then walk on quickly. I hope to God he doesn't follow me again. I don't dare look round till I get to the end of the street. He must have retreated indoors because there's no sign of him. I feel sorry for him now – but one hundred per cent relieved that it's over at last.

I get the train to Waterloo, and then the tube. I'm so hyped up I can't even concentrate on my book. I send Alice a text to say I'm on my way. I'll take her out to supper somewhere rather than making do with a scratch meal at home.

Several of the cheeky lads have constructed a dangerous-looking slide to hurtle down on their skateboards, and give me a wave as I get near them.

'Come and have a go, Miss?' they chorus.

'No fear!' I say. 'Thanks again for all your help this morning, guys.'

'Feel free to give us a tip too, Miss. You don't want your girlfriend to outdo you,' the oldest says.

'I can live with that,' I say. 'But thanks again, all of you.' I blow them exaggerated kisses, which make them writhe and groan – but they look pleased.

It's too much to hope that the engineers will have materialized late on Saturday afternoon – and I'm right. I climb all the way up the stairs, but I'm feeling full of adrenaline-fuelled anticipation so arrive barely out of breath. Andreea for once doesn't peer round her door. I hear her laughing inside her flat, and another deeper voice joining in. I smile at the thought that she might have an admirer now.

I open my own door with my key and call, 'Surprise!' But the surprise is on me. The flat is empty apart from Stella, who greets me lazily, barely bothering to raise her head.

'Alice?' No reply. I check Lottie's room quickly, and at least all her luggage is still there, half unpacked. She's not thought better of it and cleared off.

She must have gone to see the new woman in her life. The idea gnaws at me, almost physically painful. And now I'm the one to sit here by myself. I trudge over to my desk, sit down and stare at my elephants. They stare back at me with their tiny eyes. I stroke their broad heads all the way down their long trunks. It's as if we're holding hands, and I'm not alone, after all. Who cares if no one publishes my graphic novel? Well, I *will* care, obviously, but it's been such a pleasure to create them without thinking of an audience and popularity and contracts and deadlines. But perhaps it's time to gauge a professional response. I'm not ready to send them to Jude, though I know she'll be encouraging and supportive. It's time to send them to Nicola Sharp, my childhood mentor.

I haven't completed ten finished pages. I haven't started on a summary. But to hell with it. I photograph each page, write a quick email to Nicola, and then press send before I lose courage. Then I sit back, heart thudding. That's it, done. Maybe Nicola will think them rubbish. Probably, in fact. She'll try to be kind and tactful, but it will still be devastating. I need to know, though. There's too much uncertainty in my life right now . . .

My head spins. So much has happened in just one day. I go over the fight with Guy, trying to remember exactly what sparked it. I see him telling me all about the Expressionist movement as if he's giving me a private tutorial. I see him showing me the bedding he's bought for me because he despises my own. I see his face, red with anger, saying such ugly things. I see him contrite and ridiculous, in his pants and dressing gown. It's hard to remember how I felt the first time I met him again as an adult, that overwhelming attraction, wanting him desperately.

I don't want him now. I haven't made a mistake. I know Alice will be as good as her word and only stay a few days. I know her new complicated relationship will absorb her. I know I will be so lonely again with Lottie gone. But it can't be helped. I can't go out with Guy just to have someone to see. I don't want to settle down with him in his house and holiday with him and trek round a hundred and one galleries to be told what to admire. I don't want another baby. And I don't want to become the friend with benefits either.

I'm starting to know what I *do* want, but it doesn't seem remotely possible. This isn't a romantic comedy; this is real life. The cheery little motto on my birthday cards isn't going to come true. *Life begins at forty?* Rubbish. I'm on the downward slope now.

I reach for my phone again. Alice hasn't texted me back. She's obviously with the new girl. She's not even looking at her phone. She might even have gone back to Wendy's to beg her to take her back.

I wrap my arms round myself, feeling so lonely. I notice several Stella hairs on my trousers and pick them off. Why the fuck did Guy object to them, anyway? Maybe I simply look ridiculous, a parody of a middle-aged woman trying to look young. Is it time for the sensible aqua jumpers and beige Mum-trousers? It's certainly time to stop obsessing about my looks, because what the hell does it really matter?

I hear a key in the lock, and then the front door opening, and my heart leaps.

'Alice?' I say, rushing into the hall.

'Oh Ellie, you've beaten me back!' She's got a full shopping bag, which she puts down in the kitchen. I hear a promising clank.

'What's that?' I ask.

'Supper. I got your text. I wasn't sure if you were a white wine or red wine person so I've bought both. And don't get too excited about the food, I just bought eggs and cheese and tomatoes and thought I'd make omelettes, and plums and chocolate for pudding. Is that OK?' she says.

'It sounds fantastic!' I say, breathing out slowly.

Alice puts the white wine in the fridge.

'But let's have a glass of red now. You look as if you need a drink,' she says. 'Have you had a row with Guy, seeing as you're here and not there?'

'I've actually broken up with him,' I say, fetching two tumblers. 'I haven't got proper wine glasses, though I keep meaning to get them. I'm not intending to get totally drunk.'

'Maybe I am,' says Alice. 'I feel absolutely dreadful. Did you two have a row about my being here?'

'No. Well, a bit. But it was much more than that. I just realized I didn't want to see him any more. I know everyone will think I'm completely crazy, but I can't help it,' I say, opening the wine.

'Who's everyone?' Alice asks.

'My friends. Magda and Nadine.'

'Well, I'm your friend too and I don't think you're crazy,' says Alice. 'I thought he was . . .'

'Go on, say it?'

'A bit of a prat,' she says, her voice full of apology. 'He bosses you about too much.'

'Yes. He does. Did. I'm really glad it's over,' I say, realizing just how much I mean it.

'And I'm glad it's over with Wendy,' she says.

'Truly?'

'Absolutely. It hasn't been working for ages. But it was still a horrible break-up – and I don't know what I'd have done if you hadn't been so wonderfully kind.'

'I'm not being kind. It's going to be fun having you here,' I say. We clink tumblers. I want to say 'Here's to us' but it sounds way too presumptuous.

We sip wine and talk about all the relationships we've had in the past, and how none have really worked out the way we'd hoped.

'In spite of everything, men and women can be so different,' I sigh. 'Gay men are lovely, you can be really friendly and open and confide anything – I totally adore Simon, my brother's husband – but straight men sometimes seem a different species altogether. You're lucky being gay, Alice. Women are so much easier to get on with.'

'Not if you keep picking the wrong ones. I mean, I was crazy about Wendy at first, but we're totally mismatched. I ended up turning into her dreary little dogsbody, which was horrible,' Alice says ruefully.

'You're way too gorgeous to be anybody's dogsbody,' I say indignantly, and then worry in case that sounds inappropriate. I'd say the same to Magda or Nadine, but somehow that's different.

'Would that that were true,' says Alice, finishing off her glass of wine and averting her gaze from mine. 'I'd better get cooking before I get too drunk.'

'I'll cook – though I warn you, I'm pretty hopeless at it,' I say.

'No, let me do it. I want to. Though I'm certainly not a Nigella,' she says.

'Have another drink. They're only *little* tumblers,' I say, pouring the wine again. We've practically finished the bottle. It's loosened my tongue enough to say, 'I hope this new girl in your life thinks you're gorgeous too.'

She tenses up, and I know it was a mistake to say anything.

'Sorry, sorry. It's none of my business,' I say hurriedly.

'It's OK,' she says. 'I just don't want to talk about the whole situation.'

'Of course,' I say. 'I understand.' Though I so want to know who it is.

She starts whisking eggs and grating cheese and shaking a few dried herbs about that she finds at the back of my food cupboard while I prattle on about nothing at all. We both sip more wine and by the time she serves the supper she's relaxed again, though the omelettes aren't a perfect triumph. Guy's had been light and fluffy and beautifully seasoned. Alice's omelettes are rather limp and flat and chewy, truth be told. I tell her that mine is heavenly and she bursts out laughing, telling me I'm a dreadful liar.

I'm not lying, though. It tastes good simply because she's made it and she's here with me and she seems to belong in my flat. After we've eaten our first course and gorged on plums and chocolate, we open the chilled white wine and have just a little splash each as we watch *Beaches*, one of my all-time favourite movies, about the lasting friendship between two women. The ending always makes me cry, even when I'm not half drunk.

'If you were dying when Lottie was still a little girl, who would you have wanted to bring her up – Nadine or Magda?' Alice asks.

'Oh, impossible question,' I say. 'If I chose one, the other one would be mortally wounded. No, I know – I'd have asked Ben and Simon to bring her up. They'd have spoiled her dreadfully, though they'd be sensible too, and she adored them already.'

'I feel I know Lottie already, just from being in her bedroom,' Alice says. 'It's such a warm, fun space. I love her photos and posters and all those books. Is it OK to borrow one to read tonight?'

'Of course! I should close your door when you go to sleep, though, just in case Stella wanders in and jumps up on your bed,' I say.

'I would think that an honour,' says Alice. 'Do you mind if I go to bed now, Ellie? I'm feeling pretty exhausted.'

'Of course. Me too,' I say, yawning.

There's a little awkwardness again about who uses the bathroom first, and I have a quick glimpse of Alice in cute shorts and a camisole. She looks fantastic. I press my lips firmly together to stop myself telling her this. I'm a little bit drunk now. More than a little. I have to watch I don't embarrass her, embarrass myself.

331

'Night night,' I say quickly and dart into the bathroom myself.

I wish I had the right sort of nightclothes – I've just got my comfy stripy pyjamas. I once did a cartoon of Myrtle pondering her bedwear choices. I find myself kissing the image of Myrtle on my wrist. She's been a dear friend to me. I still miss drawing her terribly.

Still, I have my elephants now. I count the elephants in my tribe instead of sheep and fall asleep almost instantly because I've had too much wine. I wake up a few hours later, with a dry mouth and a thudding heart.

I creep to the bathroom, drink a tumbler of water, have a pee, and then tiptoe back to bed. I'm wide awake now. I lie flat on my back, thinking about Alice in the next room, just a few paces away. After several minutes I hear her moving about, creeping to the bathroom herself. I hold my breath, wondering if she might put her head around my door because she must know I'm awake. But she slips back to the next bedroom and settles down again.

I try to sleep myself, but it's hopeless. I think about Nicola Sharp and what she'll say about my elephants. I'm wishing I hadn't sent her those first few pages now. I've put her in a terrible position. She probably wasn't serious when she asked me to send them to her. Maybe she's lying awake right this minute, trying to think of a tactful way to tell me I'm wasting my time.

I wonder if Guy's awake too, and what he's feeling. Does he love me or hate me now? Maybe he's phoned Lipstick Kim and she's having sex with him right this minute, thrilled that she's going on a trip to Venice. And I really don't care. It's such a relief. In fact, I truly hope they have a good time.

I think of Magda nestled against her Chris, her hands cradling her tummy. I hope with all my heart that it really is third time lucky for her. I don't get what she sees in Chris but it's what *she* sees in him that matters. She'll be a lovely mum to that little girl of hers. I really hope Nadine and I get to be joint godmothers.

I think of Nadine now and hope she's curled up in Harry's arms. Maybe they'll realize that it's time to get together properly. Or maybe Nadine's such a free spirit she doesn't want a permanent partner. I just need her to be *safe*, that's all. If we were living in a romantic comedy then I'd have her fall in love with the best man at Natasha's winter wedding and live happily ever after – but it doesn't seem likely.

I think of Simon and Ben spooning in sweet marital fashion, setting all of us an example of a true and lasting loving partnership. I think of Dad lying awake glad that he's alive, and Anna beside him, feeling his heart beating. I think of Lottie maybe cuddled up with Luke, or any of her other friends, or lying peacefully on her side, perhaps sucking the tip of her thumb as she sometimes does in her sleep. And I think of Alice, I think of Alice, I think of Alice.

My phone pings. I pick it up, press the little email envelope. A reply from Nicola!

I'm sorry it's so late but I simply have to tell you – I think your graphic novel is SUPERB! I don't know if you've approached anyone yet. I would love to send it to the publishers of my own graphic novel adaptation. I think they'll bite your hand off to give you a contract. However, I don't want to interfere – just let me know. You're brilliant, Ellie! I'm thrilled that I singled you out when you were a schoolgirl.
Warmest wishes,
Nicola

My heart thuds violently. I rock backwards and forwards, reading the message again and again. My eyes keep blurring as if they can't take it in properly. It's so wonderful! Oh Nicola, thank you so much! You like it. No, you *love* it!

I tap back immediately.

Dearest Nicola
You've made me so happy! PLEASE send my elephants to your publisher! I'm so excited I'm not going to sleep a wink tonight. Enormous thanks and much love,
Ellie xxx

I'm far too fizzing even to try to sleep. I get up again, step softly to my door, planning to creep to the kitchen. There's some wine left over in the fridge. I'll toast Nicola with it! But when I quietly open the door I see the gleam of light under Lottie's door. I stand still, hesitating. Alice isn't asleep yet. Shall I see if she wants more wine too? I can't. She'd think I'm using my wonderful news as a ploy. I can't just go barging in. Can I? My feet are tiptoeing across the floor. I stand outside and then reach out and knock gingerly.

'Alice? Can I come in?' I whisper.

She murmurs something. I hope it's yes. I go in and find her sitting up in bed, writing furiously.

'Oh, I'm sorry!' I say, blinking in the sudden light. I look at the notebook, the page covered with her small, neat handwriting. 'Is that your diary?'

'Yes,' she says, snapping it shut, looking at me warily.

My throat dries. I shouldn't have intruded. But it's too late now.

'I'm so sorry to disturb you – but I've had the most incredible news! I sent the first few pages of my elephant book to Nicola Sharp, the children's novelist. I know her – she was actually at my party, and oh Alice, she likes it, she says it's *superb*, she's going to send it to her own publishers, oh God, I'm so happy!' I say in a mad rush, hopping from one foot to the other.

'That's wonderful, Ellie!' Alice says, and she leaps out of bed and we have a real hug, we're dancing round together, stumbling a little and then collapsing on the bed, laughing.

'I'm sorry,' I say, trying hard to sober up. 'I know it's tactless when you're going through a terrible break-up and you don't think it's working out with this other girl and all the rest of it, but I just can't help it. I'm so relieved and happy.'

'It's fine, really. I'm happy too – so happy for you!' Alice says.

Something's digging into my back. I wriggle round and find I'm lying on Alice's diary.

'Oh, give me that,' she says anxiously, reaching for it.

I hand it over, apologizing.

'Is this the one that Wendy read?'

Alice nods.

'The one where you write about your new girl?'

She nods again, not looking at me.

'Do you . . . really care about her?' I ask, sitting up properly.

She nods a third time and then shakes her head. 'I'm turning into Noddy,' she says, giving a little snort, half laugh, half sob. 'I think you know who she is, don't you?'

'No,' I say, but my heart is pounding now. Perhaps I do.

'For God's sake, Ellie,' she says. 'It's you!' She looks down at her lap, not meeting my eyes. 'I think I fell for you the first time we met. We just got on so well together. Obviously I had to hide the way I feel because I know you're not gay, and I know you'll never be able to feel the same way. I've tried so hard to keep my feelings to myself, just letting it all out in my diary. I never dreamt that Wendy would go snooping and find out. I'm so sorry, Ellie. I'll leave tomorrow. This must be so awkward for you.'

'Alice,' I say softly. 'Look at me. Who says I don't feel the same way?'

We look into each other's eyes for a long moment. Then I lean towards her slowly, so slowly, an inch at a time, and she stares at me, lips parted, scarcely breathing. I kiss her lightly, barely touching her soft, sweet lips. She kisses me back, gently, tentatively. I put my hand behind her neck, pressing her closer.

And now we are kissing properly, deep and urgent, and the feel of her smooth, supple body makes me dizzy with desire.

'Come here,' she says, and she leans up on one elbow, smiles at my pyjamas and tenderly unbuttons them. She pulls them off me and wriggles quickly out of hers.

We gaze at each other again, both of us trembling. It feels so beautiful, so new and strange and perfect.

'Oh Ellie, I can't believe this is happening,' Alice says huskily, and then kisses me again.

'Neither can I,' I murmur, and the feel of her, smell of her, touch of her is so overwhelming I can hardly speak.

How many paintings depict Cupid as blind? But for the first time in my life, I feel I am finally seeing in glorious technicolour. I am seeing Alice, and she is seeing me.

This is it, at long last. My birthday wish. My own happy ending. And it's only just beginning . . .

Acknowledgements

When I've been up for an award, I always have a scribbled list of names tucked in my pocket as I'm terrified of forgetting to thank someone important and dear to me (it's always a bit humiliating when I next wear my fancy jacket and discover the totally uncalled-for crumpled piece of paper). I've given the following acknowledgements a great deal of thought – but please forgive me if I've left anyone vitally important off the list!

First of all, I want to thank Professor Emma Wilson (best daughter ever), who first wondered what might have happened to Ellie, Magda and Nadine, featured in my long-ago teenage *Girls in Love* series. Then Amy Kwolek, who played Nadine in the stylish TV adaptation, got in touch hoping I'd write about the Girls when they grew up. Over the years I've had various requests from special fans for an adult sequel – and a group of young women had fun on Twitter predicting what might happen to the Girls, with inventive and hilarious suggestions.

I discussed the possibility with my children's book editor, Kelly Hurst – and then the dynamic Frankie Gray, then at Transworld, now Managing Director and Publisher at HarperFiction, asked if I'd be interested in writing an adult book about my Girls, and I jumped at the chance!

Lovely Thorne Ryan has now taken over from Frankie, and I'm immensely grateful to her for her guidance and thoughtful suggestions and enormous hard work and encouragement. The entire delightful and enthusiastic team at Transworld have been wonderful: Becky Short – brilliant publicist; Tamsin Shelton – eagle-eyed copy-editor; Anna Carvanova – ultra-helpful editorial assistant; Hannah Winter – shrewd marketer; Beci Kelly – stylish cover designer; Hannah Cawse – sharp-eared audiobook manager; Helena Sheffield – adept marketer and publicist for audiobook; and Deirdre O'Connell, Phoebe Llanwarne, Rhian Steer and the rest of the fantastic sales team.

Huge thanks also to the trio of women who have worked with such enthusiasm and encouragement over the years: my great long-time agents Caroline Walsh and Georgina Ruffhead, and of course Naomi Cooper, marvellous freelance publicist and very dear friend. Plus heartfelt thanks to Nick Sharratt, who illustrated my books so beautifully for thirty years and did the original iconic illustrations for the Girls books, including Ellie's cartoon of Myrtle Mouse.

I was overwhelmed by the response when *Think Again* was first announced – from complete strangers, from sister writers like Holly Bourne, from special corresponding friends like Clare Rea and Liz Sharma who have been in touch with me since they were schoolgirls, and my dear daily-email buddy, the theatre producer Mark Bentley. Long-term special friends like Christine Wiltshire, Anne Brichto and Nancy Landsiedel have been warmly enthusiastic, and my almost-family Nick White and Will Emmett have been extremely kind and curious, even though they've teased me unmercifully. Professor Karen McComb has put up with my endless questions about elephants – and sweetly spoilt me with Bear Yoyos, health remedies and crystals.

My partner Trish has the entire book dedicated to her (I hope to God she likes it. She might well disapprove). But I shall acknowledge her, too – for everything, for ever.

Jacqueline Wilson wrote her first novel when she was nine years old, and she has been writing ever since. She is now one of Britain's bestselling and most beloved children's authors, with total sales of over 40 million copies. She has written over one hundred books, including the iconic Girls series, with sales of over 1.3 million copies across the four novels.

As well as winning many awards, including the Children's Book of the Year, Jacqueline is a former Children's Laureate, and in 2008 she was appointed a Dame.

Jacqueline is also a great reader, and has amassed over twenty thousand books, along with her famous collection of silver rings.

Find out more about Jacqueline and her books at:
www.jacquelinewilson.co.uk